THE KOMMISSAR'S CASEBOOK

(Three pre-war cases for Kommissar Saxon)
JJ TONER

Published by JJ Toner Publishing 2025

I0652695

THE KOMMISSAR'S CASEBOOK
(Three pre-war cases for Kommissar Saxon)
JJ TONER

###

Cover: Anya Kelleye
Published June 2019
Smashwords Edition
eBook ISBN: 9781908519689
Paperback ISBN: 9781908519955

Table of Contents

Three stories set in Munich in the 1930s. Kriminal Kommissar Saxon is a talented police detective facing the new realities of a hostile Nazi regime and an uncertain future.

CASE 1 – ZUGZWANG

(a short story)
First published April 2015
Copyright 2015 – 2019 © JJ Toner Publishing

Chapter 1

On March 3, 1933, four days after the burning of the Reichstag in Berlin, Kriminalkommissar Saxon of the Munich police arrived at work late. He'd had little sleep. His wife, Ruth, had spent half the night nursing a colicky baby in their one bedroomed apartment in Piperstrasse.

His telephone was ringing as he approached his desk. He picked it up and barked, "What is it?"

"You will be aware of this morning's murder in Schwabing." It was Saxon's boss, Kriminaldirektor Mydas.

"Of course, sir, a most unfortunate murder." Saxon signalled wildly to his assistant who had just entered the room balancing a couple of cups of coffee on a tray. Kriminaloberassistent Glasser put down the tray, grabbed the incident log from the front desk, and dropped it in front of Saxon. Saxon ran a finger down the overnight entries and found the incident in question.

Mydas grunted. "That's not how I would have described it. But I've decided it would be best if you take over the case. We need to find this maniac and put him away quickly. It won't take the newspapers long to make the connection between the two killings. And when that happens every woman in Munich will be too terrified to venture into the streets, and we will all come under extreme pressure from our political masters. Bernd Hessel has the two files. Drop into my office when you've read them."

Mydas terminated the call. Saxon groped for his coffee, his eyes glued to the incident log. "Why was I not told about this?"

Glasser used a bony finger to slide Saxon's coffee under his searching hand. "The report came in at 2:00 am, sir. The duty sergeant called Kommissar Hessel. I expect he thought you probably needed your sleep – you and your good lady, both."

One look at the preliminary notes from the crime scene told Saxon what connection the newspapers would make. A prostitute had been the subject of a gruesome murder in Hofgraben in the red light district a couple of weeks earlier. The mutilations sounded remarkably similar. "He should have called me. Do we have the victim's name?"

"Frau Henrietta Happeck, aged 59. She was a housekeeper for a Jewish banker."

More than any man Saxon had ever met, Glasser resembled the grim reaper. A tall man, he was nothing but skin and bone, all he needed was a hooded cape and a scythe. His voice had a hollow, echoing tone, too, the words 'Jewish banker' sounding like a death knell from his mouth.

#

Bernd Hessel was surprisingly cooperative.

"I've been asked to take over the red light case now that it looks like a double murder," said Saxon.

"I heard. Kriminaldirektor Mydas informed me this morning. I have assembled everything from both cases in these files."

Saxon took the files. The first one was unexpectedly bulky for such a recent case.

"I'm sorry for stepping on your toes, my friend..."

"Don't give it a second thought. And please let me know if there's anything I can do to help. Just be sure to catch this monster before he kills any more women." Hessel's pale, round face always appeared cherubic, his smile cold; today's angelic beam was warm and genuine, but strangely unsettling.

Saxon opened the first file. The photographs turned his stomach. Maria Kazinski, aged 24, had been disembowelled and decapitated 9 days earlier. She was naked. Whoever had done this had meant to obliterate her. Leaving her remains in a public place the killer had removed every vestige of humanity from the poor girl. It was a crime of pure evil, an act of undiluted hatred.

"She was Polish?" said Saxon.

"Originally, yes."

"A street walker?"

"No. She worked in a brothel. It's all there in the file."

Saxon turned a few pages and found the written record of the interview with Maria's roommate, Tania. Both girls worked in a registered brothel called Angel Wings located within 200 metres of the murder site.

He opened the second file. It contained very little more than the name and address of the victim: Frau Henrietta Happeck, housekeeper, Mozartstrasse 20. The photographs showed a remarkably similar crime. The age of the second victim made the pictures even more nauseating. It was like looking at the mutilated remains of your own mother.

#

Kriminaldirektor Mydas peered into his silver cigarette case and picked one out with the care of a man selecting a delicacy from a box of chocolates. "Take a seat, Kommissar. I take it you've read both files?"

Kommissar Saxon remained standing. "Why give these murders to me? You know I'm under pressure at home. Ruth has her hands full with a young baby."

Overweight and with a fondness for his beer, Mydas was not so much a policeman these days as a burnt out local government official, his chair moulded to the form of his fat behind, his eyes firmly fixed on his retirement. He flipped open his gold lighter, lit his cigarette and snapped the lighter shut. "What can I say, Saxon? The SS have been on the telephone already, demanding results. And you are my best investigator, after all."

"I was hoping for some leave..." Saxon crossed his arms.

"All leave is cancelled. For God's sake, sit down, man." He waved his cigarette like a smouldering dagger. "You know I have to give you this case. Who else do I have?"

"Bernd Hessel."

Mydas snorted smoke through his nostrils. "Kommissar Hessel is a fine policeman, but he's too slow. If you're asking me would I trust him with a case this important, the answer is no. No, it's your case now."

"Who do I report to, SS-Standartenführer Kratschik or you?"

"You report to me, as usual. I will keep the SS informed."

#

The sandstone terraces in Mozartstrasse appeared like a monumental golden ingot in the evening sunlight.

Glasser laughed mirthlessly. "It seems not everyone suffered in the financial crash, boss." He switched off the engine. "People like that have brought this country to its knees..."

Saxon laid a heavy hand on Glasser's arm. "Wait in the car." He squeezed Glasser's arm.

"You're serious?"

"Wait here. I won't be long."

Isaac Goldfarb opened the door dressed in an elaborate green frogged smoking jacket. For a banker he seemed ill at ease, as if unused to having strangers in the house. He led Saxon into the front parlour and stood at an awkward distance, leaving his visitor standing.

Saxon removed his hat. "I'm sorry for your loss, Herr Goldfarb." He ran his eyes over the furniture. Carved fruit was much in evidence in light cherry, maple and walnut pieces. A Jewish menorah with nine fresh candles held pride of place over the mantel. Saxon parked his behind on a chaise longue.

Goldfarb took a chair, his hands resting in his lap. "Yes. Thank you, Kommissar. It was a terrible shock, the way... the way she..."

They remained an uncomfortable distance apart. Saxon felt he had to raise his voice to be heard. "How long was Frau Happeck in service with you?"

"A year and a half. She was an excellent housekeeper. I don't know how I'm going to replace her..."

"She lived here, in this house?" Saxon touched the side of his head; Goldfarb mirrored the movement. Saxon put the banker in his mid forties, tall, erect, with a full head of hair.

"Yes."

"Do you have other servants?"

"None. Frau Happeck is – or was – the only one."

"What was she doing out of the house at such an early hour?"

"She liked to buy fresh vegetables from the market in Haydnplatz. She visited the market two days each week."

"Which days?"

"Wednesdays and Saturdays."

"Did she have family?"

"Her husband died in the War. They had no children."

Saxon said, "I don't suppose you have any idea who might have killed her." Not exactly an open question, but he was suffering from lack of sleep.

"None. I assumed it must have been the madman who murdered that girl two weeks ago. Unless..." He stood up. "Can I get you anything, Kommissar? Tea? Coffee?"

"Unless what, Herr Goldfarb?"

"Unless maybe someone was sending me a message..."

It took a couple of moments for Saxon to wrap that suggestion in any sort of logic. The rise of the Brownshirts had cast a shadow over Germany, and since Hitler's accession to power certain groups were under the spotlight. The Jews were top of the Nazis' list of *undesirables.* "You're suggesting the killing might have been political?"

Goldfarb shrugged. "Henrietta came to me direct from Prinzregentenplatz 16."

The address rang a loud bell in Saxon's head, but he failed to make the connection. Rather than show his ignorance, he nodded. Goldfarb nodded back.

"Has anything else out of the ordinary happened recently?"

"Who can say these days? Everything seems out of the ordinary."

"What do you mean?"

Goldfarb's shoulders drooped. He looked older than his years. "Everything has changed. We've lost a lot of friends in the past year. This was our town. We used to throw parties." He gave a small laugh, shaking his head. "It's not safe for us in the streets. There are Brownshirt thugs everywhere, and they all seem to know who we are."

"You think the Brownshirts could have killed your housekeeper?"

Goldfarb ignored the question. "My wife... She's taken it very badly. I fear for her mental health."

Saxon gave the banker a moment to gather himself. Then he said, "I'd like to see Frau Happeck's room."

Goldfarb led Saxon to a room at the back of the house, opened the door and ushered him in.

"Thank you, Herr Goldfarb." Saxon waited by the open door, making it plain that he wished to be left alone.

Goldfarb left, and the Kommissar conducted a thorough search of the room. Henrietta Happeck was a tidy soul, with a neatly made bed, and everything in its proper place. The absence of photographs or letters spoke volumes. This woman was alone, isolated, probably lonely. Her housekeeping duties were her life.

Glasser had filled the car with cigarette smoke. "How was Herr Goldfarb?"

"Worried. Frightened."

Glasser suppressed a smile. "His sort always fall on their feet. But for his sake I hope he has his bags packed."

When Saxon mentioned Prinzregentenplatz 16, Glasser said, "That's where our Führer lives."

Of course! Frau Happeck used to be Hitler's housekeeper. Now that was a potential lead.

\#

"Where to next?" Glasser edged the car into the traffic.

"The brothel. What was it called again?"

"Angel Wings." Glasser swung the car around, crossing the tram tracks and heading north.

They drove in silence for a few moments. Then Glasser said, "Why do you think you were given the case, Boss?"

"I'm sure the Kriminaldirektor had his reasons."

"You think it was his decision? The whole thing stinks to high heaven if you ask me."

"All right, spit it out before it chokes you." They were entering familiar territory. Glasser was a political animal, an early recruit to the Nazi Party, fully versed in the shenanigans of the Nazis.

"I'd say it was Standartenführer Kratschik's decision. This case is a classic poison chalice. Hessel has been earmarked for promotion. Nothing must be allowed to interfere with that. If you catch the killer, Kratschik will take the credit. If you fail you'll find yourself all alone watching your career disappear into the toilet."

Saxon grunted. He couldn't argue with Glasser's analysis, which was pinpoint accurate, as usual. As a member of the SS, Hessel was destined for greatness. His meteoric career spoke of favouritism and the eager greasing of palms. The undercurrent in Glasser's voice spoke volumes, too. He had been refused entry to the SS at least twice, probably because he lacked a gymnasium education.

They flashed their police badges at the door of the brothel and were shown into the Madam's private office.

An aura of cheap perfume announced Frau Bruckmann's arrival and accompanied her wherever she went. It was like an invisible shield, and every bit as effective. She nodded to Glasser, with whom she was obviously acquainted. Glasser introduced the Kommissar.

Saxon asked about Maria Kazinski. How long had she worked at the brothel? Did she have any special customers?

Frau Bruckmann inserted a black Russian cigarette into a ridiculously long cigarette holder. Glasser lit it for her; her arms weren't long enough to light it herself. "I've answered these questions already. Don't you policemen talk to one another?"

"Was she working on the night that she was killed?"

"Yes. She was here most nights."

"Who was she with that night?"

"That I can't tell you, Kommissar."

"Can't or won't?" said Glasser.

She turned on Glasser at that. "We don't keep records, and even if we did, our customers all use pseudonyms – as you well know."

"Did she have any difficult customers?" said Saxon.

"None, Herr Kommissar. All my customers pay in advance. And if you're asking me about violent customers..." she cut off Glasser's objection with an imperious wave of her cigarette holder, "...I really couldn't say. As long as my girls have no visible bruises, the clients can be as heavy-handed as they wish, and I never discuss the clients with the girls. Our customers are guaranteed absolute confidentiality." She turned her head, allowing her cigarette holder to point at Glasser for a second. "Idle talk is forbidden. The business wouldn't last a day if the girls gossiped about their clients."

Tania was a delight: tall and painfully thin, with long blonde hair tied in pigtails, and wearing a short skirt and tight blouse that left little to the imagination. Her only blemish was her fingernails which were chewed to the bone. Glasser invited her to sit. She did so, crossing her legs slowly. Saxon smiled at her and asked if she had any idea who could have killed her roommate.

Tania was tongue-tied. Eyes brimming with tears, she shook her head. Her chin trembled. The way her pigtails bounced on her bare shoulders with the movement of her head sent a primitive shimmer through Saxon's bones. He gave her a minute to regain a measure of composure.

"Do you know who she was with that night?" said Glasser.

She shook her head again, emphatically.

"Did she ever speak of any violent customers?" said Saxon.

"We never talked about the men."

"Never?" This seemed unlikely, in spite of what Frau Bruckmann had said.

"Look, we had better things to talk about than our work. We put all that behind us when we left here each morning. She was a good roommate – the best. I miss her so much."

Saxon said, "Who was her last customer that night?"

Her eyes opened wide in terror. Saxon was unsure if she had been touched by the horror of what her friend had endured or if there was something else troubling her.

"H... Heinrich. He calls himself Heinrich."

#

The next day was Saturday. Saxon spent the day with his wife and child. He tried pushing all thoughts of the investigation to the back of his mind, but the name 'Heinrich' rattled around like a marble in his skull.

In the early evening, Glasser parked outside the apartment and knocked on the door.

Saxon opened the door and said in a loud voice, "Yes, Glasser, I understand. Wait here while I get my coat."

Ruth glared at her husband. "You're not leaving me again? It's Saturday night! Surely you're entitled to some sort of home life."

"I'm sorry, dear. Something's come up. I have to go out for a few hours." He planted a kiss on her cheek and made a quick exit.

"You did warn Ruth that we were going on watch tonight?" said Glasser.

"Get in the car."

They stopped off at police headquarters where Glasser went in search of a camera.

"How are Ruth and the boy?" said Glasser when they were both back in the car.

'The boy.' Even Ruth called him 'the baby'. It was high time they settled on a name.

"They are well, thank you."

Glasser parked the car opposite the entrance to Angel Wings and they settled down to keep watch.

They had agreed with Frau Bruckmann that she would signal them if and when 'Heinrich' made an appearance.

Glasser said, "What age would you say she was?"

"Frau Bruckmann? Anywhere between late forties and mid fifties, I'd say."

"I think she's a lot older. I meant Tania, the one with the peroxide hair." Glasser leered at the Kommissar.

It was a busy night in Angel Wings.

They watched the entrance, waiting for a signal from Frau Bruckmann. Glasser took pictures. They discussed the Hitler connection. Glasser felt there was nothing in it, nothing more than a coincidence. Unless the Kommissar was suggesting some connection between the Führer and a common prostitute! Saxon was happy to let Glasser win that argument for the moment. Tucking the lead away in his head like a precious jewel to be savoured later, he closed his weary eyes for a moment.

Glasser woke him with a shout in the dead of night. "Wake up! Boss, wake up."

Saxon grasped at the fleeting memory of a dream, but it was gone, leaving nothing behind but an image of peroxide pigtails and a sensation of anxiety. His body was cold. He wiped his eyes and peered out through the misted windows. He saw no one.

"Did we get a signal from the Madam?"

"No, but you'll never guess who just arrived!"

"Tell me. And tell me you have his photograph."

"Only the highest ranking SS officer in the south of Germany, SS-Standartenführer Karl Kratschik." He grinned like a skull. "And yes, I have his picture."

Chapter 2

Saxon was surprised that Glasser knew Kratschik by sight. Saxon himself had never met him – Kratschik was based in the SS headquarters in Schellingstrasse, on the other side of the city – but he had a strong mental image of the man: tall, silver-haired, wearing the black SS uniform and carrying a riding crop. He'd spoken to him on the telephone. Karl Kratschik's voice was always smooth as a baby's bottom. He spoke a brand of perfect German that came only from a privileged background and an expensive education in a private gymnasium. Saxon fancied he might sport a duelling scar on his left cheek.

Saxon wiped his eyes, stretched his limbs and offered to buy some food.

"Nothing for me, thank you," said Glasser.

Saxon bought Brötchen and Bratwurst for two from a street cart. "You've got to eat," he said to Glasser.

Glasser accepted the food. Saxon devoured his own, and watched his assistant pick at the bread. He never touched the sausage. The man was clearly an automaton. He needed no food – and no sleep.

#

As dawn broke, a suffocating fog descended on the city, making further photography impossible. Glasser drove Saxon home.

Saxon opened the front door of his apartment quietly. Ruth was in bed, the baby in the crook of her arm. Both were sleeping like angels. He leant down and kissed the infant's forehead. The child woke with a start, arms flailing, took one look at his father, opened his mouth, filled his lungs with air and screamed. And then all three were awake, Ruth chastising her husband for his stupidity while offering a breast to the infant.

With the baby guzzling milk, peace returned to the Saxon household. The boy was a picture of health. Saxon imagined he'd put on weight in the past 24 hours. Ruth, on the other hand, looked exhausted, eyes red-rimmed and bloodshot.

"Tell me why you couldn't have come home last night. What was so important that you had to leave me to cope on my own?"

"You've heard about the woman murdered in Schwabing? I've been given the case."

"Couldn't they give it to somebody else?"

"It's a high profile case, Ruth. I could be famous if I solve it."

"And what if you can't solve it? Not every case gets solved."

He made her breakfast, feeling guilty because he was neither hungry nor tired as he'd eaten and slept in the car. For Ruth's sake he would eat something and feign sleep.

Ruth put the sleeping infant back in his cot. Keeping her voice low, she said, "That man scares me."

"Who? Glasser? Because he's a Nazi?"

"Because he's so thin!"

Saxon nodded. "He eats like a bird. Sometimes I wonder what keeps him upright."

He dressed for bed and lay down beside Ruth. She rolled toward him, wrapping an arm across his chest. "I really needed you last night."

"I know. I'm sorry I left you alone with the baby."

She snuggled closer. He wrapped an arm around her and closed his eyes. Within minutes, Ruth was snoring on his chest. He remained wide awake.

#

The telephone rang early on Monday morning. Saxon leapt out of bed to answer it, afraid that it would wake the baby.

It was Glasser. "Good morning, Kommissar. I'm sending a car around to collect you. There's been another killing."

A small crowd had gathered at the junction of Moralstrasse and Glötzleweg, held back by two uniformed policemen.

"This one's a teacher," said Glasser. "Her name's Maxine Limburg."

"The method?"

"The same."

The body lay under a mature fir tree in Glötzleweg, covered in a sheet. At a signal from Saxon, Professor Valachek, the Medical Examiner, pulled the sheet back to reveal the headless corpse of a young woman, naked, the stomach ripped open. Saxon's Sunday night meal made a dash for freedom. He clamped his teeth shut and covered his mouth with a hand.

"The head's over there." Valachek nodded to his left where a blood-stained towel covered something. He took a step toward it. "Do you want to see it?"

Saxon swallowed his food for a second time. "No thank you. How do we know who she is?"

Glasser answered. "She was discovered by her husband, Erik. They lived just around the corner."

Saxon tried to imagine the shock of discovering Ruth like this. He shivered.

Professor Valachek gave an approximate time of death – no more than 2 hours earlier, between 5 and 6 am. "I may be able to tie it down more precisely when I get the body to the morgue."

Saxon and Glasser found the Limburgs' house in Hofbrunnstrasse. Erik Limburg sat in the kitchen surrounded by concerned friends and neighbours. They'd made him tea.

"I'm terribly sorry, Herr Limburg," said Saxon. "Do you feel up to answering a few questions?"

Limburg's hands shook so much he couldn't pick up his teacup without help. He nodded to Saxon.

"Do you have any idea who might have done this?"

Limburg shook his head.

"How long were you married?" asked Glasser.

One of the neighbours answered. "Six months."

Barely past their honeymoon, thought Saxon. "When did you last see your wife?"

Limburg found his voice. "Early this morning. There was a telephone call... She went out..."

"Do you know who the call was from?"

"She didn't say."

"What did she say?"

"She said she had to leave early – before breakfast. She usually makes – made – breakfast before she left for work..."

"What time was this?"

"Five thirty."

"Your wife was a teacher, I believe. Where did she work?"

One of the neighbours answered again. "Altenadler School for Boys."

They found Altenadler School for Boys on Lochhamer Strasse, a brooding redbrick building, its entrance hall dominated by a massive portrait of Martin Luther hanging on a wall. They showed their police badges to the caretaker who led them to the headmaster's office.

Glasser did the introductions.

Bart Freudl, the headmaster, a short man with a strong head of hair, dressed in coarse Bavarian tweed, looked at his watch pointedly. "I don't have much time to spare. The morning is the busiest time of the day for me. What's this about, anyway? I hope my seniors haven't been causing mischief again."

"It's nothing like that, sir," said Glasser. He glanced at Saxon.

Saxon said, "I'm afraid we have bad news, Herr Freudl. One of your teachers, Frau Limburg, has been found dead."

The headmaster's hand shot to his mouth. "Maxine? Oh, no! What happened? Was it a car accident?"

"Frau Limburg has been murdered," said Saxon.

The headmaster blanched. "That can't be. She was perfectly well yesterday."

"As I said, sir, she was murdered – early this morning."

"You mean someone killed her?"

"I'm afraid so, yes."

"But who would want to kill her? Maxine was well liked by everyone in the school – boys and teachers. I can't believe anyone would want to kill her."

True to type, the headmaster's first instinct was to question everything he was told.

Glasser said, "When did you see her last?"

"Yesterday evening, when she left the school at closing time."

"How did she seem?" asked Saxon. "Was she upset, anxious, in a hurry, anything like that?"

"No, she was her normal happy self."

"Did you call her on the telephone this morning for any reason?"

"No, although she is overdue. I would have called her number in the next half-hour if... if she hadn't... if you hadn't..."

"How long has she worked here in the school?"

"Eighteen months. Since October, 1931."

"Since before she was married."

"Yes. She was Maxine Weiss then."

"Where did she come from?"

"I'm not sure. She had a private teaching position somewhere."

"You never asked where?" said Glasser, a little harshly.

"I had no reason to."

Saxon asked for a photograph of Frau Limburg. Herr Freudl rummaged in his desk and found a picture of the senior class from 1932, taken in bright sunshine. He pointed out the smiling figure of Frau Limburg standing by his side to the left of the class. It seemed impossible that the bloody headless ruin Saxon had seen in Glötzleweg could be all that remained of this smiling woman.

"Thank you. I'll hold onto this," he said.

#

Back at the office, Saxon found a stranger dressed in an expensive Italian suit waiting for him. His first thought was that this was a banking friend of Goldfarb's, but when he saw the stranger's full length leather coat draped across the back of a chair, he stiffened. What business could the Schutzstaffel have with him?

"Kriminalkommissar Saxon?"

Saxon recognized the honey voice immediately. The SS man was older and shorter than Saxon expected. His broad face and distinctive square chin looked nothing like Saxon's mental picture, and there was no sign of a riding crop or a duelling scar on either cheek. "Herr Kratschik, good to meet you in person at last." He offered a smile and a hand.

Kratschik ignored the hand. "I was disappointed to hear that your killer has struck again so soon. And unfortunately the newspapers have connected the three deaths." He dropped a rolled up newspaper on Saxon's desk. It sprang open and Saxon read the headline:

KILLER STALKS THE STREETS OF MUNICH
3 WOMEN BRUTALLY MURDERED

"I have decided to take personal charge of the investigation. Now that the story has broken, it is all the more imperative that we find the killer before he strikes again."

"Kriminaldirektor Mydas—"

"— has been informed of my decision. For the remainder of the investigation, until the case has been resolved, you will report to me. Is that clear?"

"Perfectly, Herr Standartenführer."

Kratschik sat down. "You will start by briefing me on your progress so far."

Saxon sat at his desk, aware of an annoying tremor in his hands, its cause mostly anger, but there was a spoonful of fear mixed in there as well.

"We have spoken to the owner of the brothel where Maria Kazinski worked and also with her roommate, Tania. We have also interviewed Frau Happeck's employer, the banker Goldfarb."

"What of this latest victim?"

"She was a young schoolteacher, I have spoken with her husband and her headmaster."

"How many suspects do we have?"

"We have no obvious suspects, yet, sir, and nothing that might be called a positive lead."

"Have you spoken to the Medical Examiner?"

"I met him at the crime scene this morning."

"Did you discuss the three cases?"

"No, sir. There wasn't time."

"I'm disappointed, Saxon. Should you not be there right now? I would have thought the Medical Examiner's office would be at the very top of your list."

"Yes, sir."

"I want your very best work on this case, Saxon, do you hear me? And if you need more resources, please ask.

"Thank you, sir, but I have as much as I need for the moment."

#

Kratschik left, and Glasser took his place.

"What did he want?" said Glasser.

"We are now reporting to him until the case is solved. We must work harder."

"How does Herr Mydas feel about that?"

"The Kriminaldirektor has been informed. Is there anything in last night's photographs?"

"Nothing obvious, but I have a good clear picture of Standartenführer Kratschik."

"Keep that safe. It might be useful," said Saxon. "Give me the school photograph that Freudl gave us."

Glasser handed the picture over, and Saxon examined it under a magnifying glass. He pointed to one of the boys in the middle row. "Who does this remind you of?"

Glasser took the picture. "Kratschik! That chin is unmistakable. I'd bet a week's wages that this is Kratschik junior."

"Check it with the headmaster. I have to visit the Medical Examiner's office."

Glasser stopped at the office door. "You do realize if the boy in the picture is Kratschik's son, that will give us links between Kratschik and two of the three victims."

#

Professor Valachek had both hands inside Frau Limburg's headless cadaver. The blood smears reached his elbows. Kommissar Saxon asked him if he could shed any light on the case.

"What did you have in mind?" said Valachek.

"Anything that would help us to identify the killer. His motive, perhaps."

"Sorry, Saxon. I can tell you what killed each of the three women, but I'm a medical man. I have no skills in reading entrails. Hire a spiritualist or buy yourself a Ouija board."

Saxon asked to see the other two victims, and Professor Valachek peeled back two sheets without ceremony, revealing two decapitated corpses on adjacent tables. Saxon looked them over. He was not unfamiliar with the sight of death, but each of these bloodless cadavers had been the subject of a frenzied attack, and the separation of the heads was not easy to look at. He thanked the professor, and asked, "What of the sequence of events?"

"Frau Happeck was killed by a single blow to the back of the head. The mutilations were all post mortem. Fräulein Kazinski, on the other hand, was alive until the end."

"You mean the decapitation killed her?"

"Most likely, yes. The initial blow to her head would have rendered her unconscious, but it didn't kill her."

"What about our latest victim, Frau Limburg?"

"She was lucky. The mutilations were all inflicted post mortem."

The professor gave Saxon a copy of the first autopsy report and promised to send on the second and third as soon as they were complete. As he was leaving, Professor Valachek said, "I hope there won't be too many more like this."

The professor's tone suggested that he held Saxon to blame personally for the three killings.

#

A thin vestige of the early morning fog lingered in Munich's low-lying streets as Saxon drove toward the office the next morning, deep in thought. If Freudl confirmed that Kratschik's son was a student at the school last year, then that would link Kratschik to two of the victims, making him a suspect, not that he could report the fact to his new supervisor! Any link between Kratschik and Frau Happeck, no matter how tenuous, would almost certainly close the case.

Kriminaloberassistent Glasser had shown himself to be a customer of the Angel Wings brothel. If there was anything connecting him to either of the other two victims he too would have to be placed on the list of suspects and removed from the investigation.

The murder of Frau Happeck was the most puzzling. The other two victims were young women while Frau Happeck was beyond middle age. If the killer was a crazed sex maniac, as seemed likely, then the murder of Frau Happeck made little sense. That killing was surely the key to the whole case.

He turned the car around and headed back toward Prinzregentenplatz.

#

Saxon parked across the road from Prinzregentenplatz 16 and watched the comings and goings for a while. Two food vans and one from a flower shop made deliveries, and one Reichswehr dispatch motorcyclist delivered a parcel to the apartment building, but he thought that Adolf Hitler was not in residence. His personal SS guards were nowhere to be seen. Surely, the Führer was in the opera house in Berlin, where the Reichstag would be in session.

Hitler's armour-plated Mercedes Benz drove up and parked outside the apartment building. The driver got out and went inside. When he re-emerged carrying a bucket of water, Saxon got out of his car and walked across to talk to him.

He showed his police badge to the driver. "You are the Führer's driver?"

"His chauffeur. What of it?" He ran a finger across his moustache, indistinguishable from his master's. This was not a gesture of a nervous man, rather a signal of supreme assurance, as if the square on his upper lip possessed the spirit of the Führer himself.

Saxon snapped his fingers. "Your papers."

The driver handed over his identity card. It bore the name Julius Schreck.

Saxon said, "I am engaged in an active murder investigation. One of the victims, a Frau Happeck used to work here, I believe."

"I can't help you," said Schreck. He dropped a sponge into the bucket, splashing Saxon's trousers.

"Can you confirm that Frau Happeck worked as a housekeeper to the Führer until about 18 months ago?"

"I haven't been driving for the Führer that long. You need to speak with his previous driver, Emil Maurice."

"Where can I find Herr Maurice?"

The driver shrugged. He turned his back to Saxon and began applying soapy water to the car.

#

A quick check of the archives at headquarters produced police files for both Emil Maurice and Julius Schreck. A former watchmaker, Maurice had a long criminal record dating back to the Munich Beer Hall Putsch of 1923, when Maurice, Schreck and Adolf Hitler, were all jailed in Landsberg Prison. Maurice's SS number was 2.

Schreck was SS number 5. He had been a close friend of Hitler's since the foundation of the Nazi Party, and commanded his personal bodyguard for two years from 1925 to 1926.

Maurice's present whereabouts were unknown. Saxon put Glasser to the task of finding him, saying, "I'm going back to the brothel to speak with Tania again."

At Angel Wings, Tania quickly confirmed that Glasser was an occasional visitor to the brothel. There was nothing kinky about his sexual preferences and nothing unusually violent about his behaviour. Saxon showed her the school picture and asked her if any of the boys were patrons of the business. She pointed out several of the boys.

"This is Heinrich," she said, pointing to Kratschik junior.

"Is he ever violent?"

"It's more than my life's worth to answer that question." Tania flushed, casting her gaze down to her shoes.

"In confidence, Tania. I swear no one will ever know that you told me."

It took a few more minutes to persuade her to give him the information, but finally, she said, "The boy is a tiger. He has sharp claws and can be heavy-handed at times."

"How heavy-handed?"

"Very, and that's all I'm going to say on that subject."

As Saxon adjusted his hat to leave, Tania picked up the school photograph and pointed to it again.

"This man is a regular customer," she said.

Chapter 3

Glasser was open-mouthed. "Freudl, the headmaster of Altenadler School for Boys? I don't believe it."

"Tania picked him out of the school picture. That makes him a live suspect, since we can link him to two of the victims."

"But not the third."

Saxon listed his suspects on his fingers. "Kratschik senior, Kratschik junior, alias Heinrich the heavy-handed, and Freudl. We can link them all to the two young women."

"But none of them links to Frau Happeck," said Glasser, thoughtfully. "What about your fourth suspect?"

"What fourth suspect?"

"That miserable reprobate Glasser. You know he's a regular visitor to the brothel."

Saxon laughed at Glasser's solemn, straight-faced delivery. "If we included all the clients of Angel Wings, half the male population of Munich would be suspects."

"I assume you asked Tania about me."

"I did. She confirmed that you are always well behaved. You're not a suspect, not until I can link you to at least one of the other two victims."

Glasser gave his toothy grin. "I located Emil Maurice, Hitler's ex-driver. He's living in Innsbruck. Hitler fired him and he moved there immediately after Geli Raubal's suicide."

Saxon recalled the case of Geli Raubal. Hitler's niece and lover had committed suicide in Hitler's apartment in September, 1931. At the time, there were rumours, spread by his political opponents, that Hitler had murdered the girl, but murder was ruled out.

#

SS-Standartenführer Kratschik dropped in after lunch. Saxon told him that Freudl was now a suspect. He made no mention of his other two suspects.

Kratschik gripped his hands together as if in prayer. "Progress at last! But Herr Freudl? I know him, Kommissar. He's a most unlikely killer, headmaster of my son's old school, a pillar of the community."

"A pillar of the community who attends a brothel?"

"Good point, good point, and you must follow up on every possible suspect, leave no stone unturned until the madman has been apprehended. I'll arrange a search warrant for his home for this afternoon."

#

While they waited for the search warrant, Glasser fetched the Geli Raubal case file from the archives and gave it to Saxon to read.

The file consisted of a couple of pictures of the dead girl, and half-a-dozen sheets of paper: The Medical Examiner's report concluded that Geli had died at Prinzregentenplatz 16 on Friday, September 18, 1931 as a result of a single gunshot wound to the chest. The Examining Magistrate's determination was that the young woman had used Hitler's gun to take her own life. A statement from Hitler's chauffeur, Emil Maurice, was the basis for Hitler's alibi: he had driven Hitler to Nuremburg that day. They spent the night in a small hotel and had picked up a speeding ticket as they dashed back to Munich the following morning on receiving news of the tragedy. The file contained a copy of the speeding ticket. The housekeeper, Frau Happeck, had given a statement as she had discovered the body. Apparently no one had heard the shot.

A quick mental calculation told Saxon that Hitler's alibi was as watertight as a sieve with a large hole in it. He could easily have shot Geli Raubal on Friday and sped away north to spent the night at the Nuremburg hotel. Nuremburg was only two hours away.

Frau Happeck had left Prinzregentenplatz and joined the Goldfarb's household a month after Geli's 'suicide', in October, 1931.

#

Armed with a search warrant, and accompanied by four uniformed Orpo municipal policemen in a meat wagon, they arrived at Herr Freudl's home at dusk. Located in Feldafingerplatz, within easy walking distance of the school to the north, the 3-storey house had the look of something from the film *Nosferatu* with leaded windows, overhanging gables and encircling giant fir trees.

An elderly woman met them at the door and tried to bar their way. Glasser waved the warrant at her and pushed past into the hallway, followed by the uniforms.

Saxon asked the old lady to announce their arrival to the headmaster. She shuffled off to do his bidding while Glasser organised the search party.

When Freudl arrived he steered Saxon into a cavernous study, three of the walls lined with bookcases, floor to ceiling. They sat face to face by a cold fireplace.

Saxon presented the warrant. Freudl put on his glasses and read it slowly.

"And the reason for the search? You suspect me of some crime?"

"Tell me, Herr Freudl," Saxon replied. "Are you acquainted with a Frau Henrietta Happeck, a woman of middle years, a housekeeper?"

Freudl shook his head. "No, but I've seen the name in the newspaper. Wasn't she of one of the three murder victims?"

"Did you know her? Had you ever met her?"

"Never."

A stray thought scampered across Saxon's mind. Freudl had the look of a petty thief – the classic slack jawed stare and hollow smile of a life of crime. His eyes were too close together. His receding hairline suggested receding morals. The man could not be trusted.

"Who does your housekeeping?"

"Mother looks after the house."

"That was your mother who opened the door? It's a big house for one woman on her own."

Freudl laughed, "She may be old, but she's fiercely proud. She would never allow another woman into this house."

Saxon felt a twinge of pity for the man. "You're not married, Herr Freudl?"

"I've never had a wife."

"You have been seen at a brothel in Hofgraben."

Freudl coloured quickly. "I have to... I need... I'm sure you understand. But Angel Wings is fully registered. I have broken no law."

"Even so..."

"Even so, I know the school board would frown on the practice."

"Your feet wouldn't touch the ground," said Saxon with a blank face.

"They don't have to know, do they? I have broken no laws, after all." Freudl's eyes were pleading.

"They won't hear it from me," said Saxon, thinking he couldn't guarantee Glasser's silence. "Now tell me where you were on Thursday night."

"I was here, marking papers."

"Can anyone confirm that?"

"My mother. What are you accusing me of, Kommissar?"

"I am accusing you of nothing, Herr Freudl, but we must eliminate your name from our enquiries. Where were you on the night of Saturday the eighteenth of February?"

Freudl hesitated before answering. "That Saturday night I spent some time at... that place."

"Angel Wings?"

"Yes, but I wasn't there for more than a couple of hours. I was home and tucked up in bed by eleven."

"Your mother will confirm that?"

"Yes."

"Who were you with in the brothel? Were you with Maria Kazinski?"

"I don't recall, but it wasn't her."

"You're certain?"

"Positive. I was definitely not with Maria that night."

"But you've spent time with Maria on other nights?"

"Not often, but yes."

"And where were you last night?"

"I was here all night."

"Your mother will confirm that?"

"Yes, of course."

#

Saxon and Glasser sat at a quiet table in a tavern some distance from headquarters. The search of Freudl's house had revealed nothing but an unusual collection of exotic magazines hidden in a box in an attic.

Saxon paid for two steins of beer. "I won't be in the office tomorrow. I want you to keep things ticking over while I'm away."

"Where will you be, Boss?" said Glasser.

"I'm travelling to Austria tonight. I hope to talk to Emil Maurice in Innsbruck in the morning. I don't want the Standartenführer to know where I'm going, so I'll be relying on you to cover for me."

"Right, Boss."

The train journey from Munich to Innsbruck took four hours. Saxon was weary, and if it hadn't been for the spectacular scenery – the Austrian Alps, the precipitous viaducts spanning fast-flowing rivers – the clack-clack of the wagon wheels on the rails would have lulled him to sleep.

He had left an angry wife at home with a baby on one hip, a book of baby names on the other. She would finally have to choose a name by the weekend when they had an appointment with the pastor at his christening font. Ruth had been hoping for a girl. She was caught unprepared when her baby arrived with that unexpected extra appendage.

Saxon turned his mind to the case. Of his three suspects, the SS man seemed the most likely, especially given the way that he had inserted himself into the investigation, presumably intending to interfere with the outcome. Of course, he might have done the same in order to protect his son. Freudl seemed the least likely candidate. There was no evidence against him and while living a life of enforced celibacy in a cavernous old house with an infirm mother was probably not good for his nerves, and dipping his quill in a house of ill repute was doing little to advance his career, nothing had suggested that he was a frenzied killer of women.

Surrounded on all sides by towering snow-capped mountains, Innsbruck was shrouded in perpetual mist. Saxon took to the streets on foot. Emil Maurice's address was not far from the railway station.

The city had an altogether Austrian feel, with brightly painted houses sandwiched together in narrow thoroughfares that owed much to the German style of urban planning. Hitler's grim portrait adorned every shop window. The women wore colourful flared dirndl skirts and aprons; some of the men wore lederhosen. And while Bavaria was no stranger to felt alpine hats, here every man seemed to wear one. Saxon felt conspicuous in his plain suit, police boots and Homburg.

Maurice was not at home. His landlady hadn't seen him for several days. Saxon explained that he was a distant cousin of Emil's on a walking tour. He had hoped to meet Emil before he continuing his journey. She suggested that Maurice might be found in Elferhaus, a popular beer cellar.

The beer cellar was full of happy drinkers. Saxon asked a young serving wench with a prominent mole on her upper lip where he might find his distant cousin.

"He's not in tonight, but it's early," she said. "What can I get you?"

He ordered a half glass of the local brew.

As the night wore on the place filled to capacity. Saxon kept his glass topped up. He checked with his serving wench from time to time, but Maurice never appeared. At 11 pm, with drooping eyes, he picked two cards from the bar advertising a local hotel and handed one to her. They'd spoken so many times during the evening that Saxon thought of her as an old friend.

"I can't wait any longer. If you see Maurice, ask him to contact me here."

Returning to Maurice's lodgings, he gave the landlady the second card and the same message.

In order to avoid awkward questions about his lack of luggage, Saxon paid the hotel owner in advance for a room for a single night. He hadn't eaten for hours, but he was too tired to care. He called his wife on the telephone and listened to the account of her day. After the call he barely had enough energy to take off his clothes and climb into bed.

A knock at the door woke him in total darkness. He switched on a light and checked his watch: 4 am.

He went to the door and called out, "Who's there?"

When no one answered, he opened the door cautiously. The corridor was deserted, but someone had pushed an envelope under the door. Inside the envelope he found a single sheet of paper bearing the words: 'Valluga midday'. It was signed with the initials E.M.

#

Maurice couldn't have chosen a safer place for a meeting. Valluga: the highest peak overlooking Innsbruck, reachable only by cable car. The gondola could carry no more than a handful of people at a time, and anyone in there would be clearly visible long before they arrived.

The journey to the peak took 2 hours in a succession of funiculars, each gondola smaller than the last, all swinging in the breeze at mind-numbing distances from the ground.

Saxon was accompanied to the top by three excited skiers, finally stepping from the gondola at the mountaintop in bright sunlight, gasping in the thin, icy air. The skiers dispersed, leaving the detective alone with the 360 degree panorama of the Alps and Innsbruck laid out below like a model village.

He climbed the last few metres to the rest station and stumbled inside, took a table by a window and ordered coffee. The clock on the wall read 12:10. Casting his gaze around, he checked out the 10 people sitting at the tables. Maurice was not among them.

At 12:45 he ordered a second cup of coffee. As the waiter moved away, a man approached wearing a ski suit and heavy boots. He sat at Saxon's table and removed his gloves. Saxon recognised Emil Maurice, older, more wrinkled and more tanned than the photograph on his Munich police file, but definitely him.

"My name is Saxon. Thank you for meeting me, Herr Maurice."

"Police?"

"Yes. I'm investigating the recent spate of murders in Munich, and I'm hoping you can help me."

Maurice shrugged. "I left Munich nearly two years ago. I haven't been near the place since then."

"I need to ask you some questions about 1931."

Maurice picked up his gloves and got to his feet. "I have nothing to say about that. The Geli case is closed. Why dredge all that up again? Why do you think we're meeting on the top of an Austrian Alp?"

"I'm not interested in the old case. I'm just looking for some background information. I can pay."

Maurice sat down again. Saxon placed 100 Reichsmark on the table. Maurice swept up the notes and tucked them inside one of his gloves.

"One of my murder victims is called Frau Henrietta Happeck. Can you confirm that she worked at Prinzregentenplatz 16 in September 1931?"

"She was the housekeeper at the time, yes."

"Who else was present when Geli died?"

"The boss and I were in Nuremburg. Hoffmann, the photographer was with us, so I can't be sure who was there, but Geli had a close companion, a young woman who tutored her from the age of about 15, when the boss took her – under his wing. She may have been in the apartment when Geli died. Her name was Maxine."

"Maxine Weiss?"

"That's right."

Saxon's heart did a somersault. "Was there anybody else present at the time? What about Maria Kazinski?"

"Never heard of her."

"Did the Führer ever use the services of a prostitute?"

"Not that I know of, but you should ask Georg Bell about that." He got to his feet and put on his gloves. "I have to go."

"Where can I find this Georg Bell?"

"Speak to Michael Gerlich." And Maurice swept out the door. Saxon watched him clip on his skis and head off down the mountain.

The return journey down in the cable cars was a blur of happy skiers and stunning vertiginous views. Saxon now had a positive link between victims 2 and 3 and a possible motive for their deaths. He knew Michael Gerlich, editor of the anti-Nazi newspaper *The*

Straight Path, one of a handful of journalists who consistently questioned the Party's anti-Semitism and dubious tactics. If Gerlich could supply the missing link to tie Maria Kazinski to the Geli case he might be able to solve the case.

He took the train back to Munich, arriving at the apartment well after dark.

He kissed Ruth. "How's the baby?" he whispered, peering at the infant asleep in his cot.

"Little Samuel's been well, but he refuses to sleep more than four hours between feeds. I'm exhausted. I'm going to put him on a bottle."

Samuel. Good name, he thought. "Remember what the doctor said, Ruth. Breast milk is best for young babies."

"What would he know? He's never had to undergo torture like this. I've got to get a night's unbroken sleep."

#

The early morning fog was there to welcome Saxon back to the city.

"Where were you?" roared Kriminaldirektor Mydas. "I've had Kratschik in my ear for the past 24 hours demanding to talk to you."

"I took a short trip to Austria."

Mydas clenched his sausage fingers into fists. "This is no time for holidays, Saxon, what were you thinking?"

"I was following a line of enquiry, sir."

"What line of enquiry? No," he held up a podgy palm. "Don't tell me. I don't want to know. Just get in touch with the Standartenführer and get him off my back."

Saxon called Glasser into his office and filled him in on the results of his trip. Glasser ran to the archives and returned carrying a thin file with the name Georg Bell on it.

They went through the file together. After the War, Bell found work in Munich as an electrical engineer. In 1931 he was appointed personal secretary to Ernst Röhm, Chief of Staff of the Brownshirts. The latest entry in the file was dated June 1931. An unsubstantiated report from a police informant stated that Bell was now head of the intelligence service of that organisation.

"He's some sort of spy!" said Glasser.

Saxon grunted. "So it would seem, but there's no mention of any direct contact with the Führer. Look into it. See what more you can find out about the man, and get me his current address."

The telephone rang. Saxon picked it up without thinking.

"Where the hell have you been?" Kratschik's voice had lost its oiliness. It was sharp enough to cut through steel.

"I was chasing a lead, sir," Saxon replied.

"Tell me about that later. I have a warrant for you to search Freudl's home."

"We conducted that search already. We found nothing."

"I want you to do it again. Be more careful this time."

#

The old lady was incredulous when Saxon, Glasser and six uniformed Orpo policemen knocked on her door. Saxon showed her the warrant.

"Not again! I'm still cleaning up after your last search." She held a mop in her hand.

Glasser said, "Stand aside, mother."

"I'm not your mother." She brandished her mop like a weapon.

Saxon asked to speak with Freudl, but the headmaster was at the school.

The uniforms dispersed around the upper floors; Glasser and Saxon took the ground floor. Within minutes Glasser discovered a pane of glass missing from a French window in a back parlour.

"Someone broke in last night," said Frau Freudl.

"Did you report it to the police?"

"No. Nothing was taken."

Five minutes after that one of the uniforms called for Glasser to come to a bedroom on the third floor. Glasser bounded up the stairs. Saxon followed at a more leisurely pace.

Saxon entered the bedroom to find Glasser and the Orpo man peering into a leather trunk full of clothing dating from the previous century. Three items of clothing were modern – two shirts and a woman's undergarment – and they were covered in blood.

"These weren't here three days ago," said Glasser to Saxon.

"You're certain?"

"Yes, I'm certain. I searched this room myself."

Saxon took the three bloodied items downstairs and showed them to Frau Freudl. "Whose are these, Frau Freudl?"

"I've never seen them before. Where did you find them?"

"We found them in a trunk in the front bedroom on the left on the third floor. Whose room is that?"

"No one's. It's a big house. We don't use the upper floors."

Saxon took the bloodied clothing to the morgue. Medical Examiner Valachek passed the garments to his assistant with instructions to test the blood type on the garments to see if it matched that of any of the victims.

"It would be helpful if the tests took a couple of days," said Saxon.

"Understood," Valachek replied, handing over a copy of the second and third autopsy reports. Saxon found an empty desk and sat down to read them. They made depressing reading.

#

Glasser said, "That clothing was planted by someone."

"Someone like Kratschik?"

Glasser chewed the inside of his cheek. "I don't like the way this is going, Boss. He's leading us by the nose, forcing us into a corner."

Saxon gave his assistant a cigarette. "Let's wait and see what Valachek comes up with. Maybe the blood on the clothing won't match any of the victims." He put his hat on and strode to the door. "In the meantime, concentrate on Georg Bell. Get me an address."

"Where are you going, Boss?"

"To talk to an old friend."

#

The office of the newspaper, *The Straight Path*, was deserted, the door swinging crazily from one hinge, the contents of the file cabinets strewn around the floor, the drawers of all the desks smashed and emptied. Saxon picked up a few pieces of paper, but found nothing of interest. He was on nodding terms with Herr Hoffmann, a tailor whose workshop was in the next office. He asked an office boy there what had happened.

"Brownshirts," said the boy. "They came yesterday and took most of the staff away."

"Where can I find someone who worked here?"

"Fräulein Vassan lives somewhere in Betzenweg."

There were only two apartment blocks on Betzenweg, and it didn't take him long to find Fräulein Vassan. He remembered her as a bright, cheerful girl, but now she appeared pale as a ghost with wild, terrified eyes.

Her hands shook as she closed the door.

She remembered Saxon from his occasional visits to the office. Under gentle prompting from Saxon she took him through the events of the day before. The Brownshirts had stormed the office. They had beaten Herr Gerlich and two other journalists and ransacked the office. Gerlich and the others were arrested and taken away.

"Do you know where they were taken?"

She shook her head. "No."

"Did they give a reason for the arrests?"

"No, but Herr Gerlich had been worried for several weeks that something like this might happen. He was working on a big story..."

"The Geli Raubal story?"

"You know about that? The Brownshirts removed boxes and boxes of papers. I'm sure they took everything he had on the case."

She buried her head in her hands and wept. Her shoulders shook. Saxon handed her a handkerchief. She took it, wiped her face, and blew her nose. He fetched a glass of water from the kitchen.

She handed back the handkerchief. "Forgive me."

He gave her the water. "You've had a severe shock. My questions are not helping. I'll leave you."

She looked up. "What will happen to Herr Gerlich and the others?"

The Brownshirts operated outside the law, and with Hitler in power there was little prospect of anything being done to rein them in, but he said, "They should be released fairly quickly. They have committed no crime."

He put his hat on. She accompanied him to the door. "One last thing I need to ask you before I go, Fräulein: Do you know where I could contact Georg Bell? I believe Herr Gerlich spoke to him about the case."

The wide-eyed look of terror returned. "I know nothing about him, sorry, Kommissar."

She closed the door sharply, leaving Saxon with the overwhelming feeling of a job only half done, like a half-eaten meal.

Chapter 4

"Georg Bell has gone to ground," said Glasser. "If he's half the spy I think he is, we'll never find him."

"Put out the word that we want to talk to him about something that happened in 1931. If he gets a hint that we're looking at the Geli Raubal case again we won't need to find him. He'll find us."

"I don't see that, Boss."

"Trust me. He's a spy, and spies are endlessly curious. He won't be able to resist."

Kratschik called on the telephone. "I trust you have Bart Freudl in custody."

"No, sir, we have no evidence against the headmaster."

"Your search uncovered blood-stained garments belonging to the three victims, I believe. What more evidence do you need?"

"We found some blood-stained garments, that's true, sir. But we won't know if they relate to the murders until the Medical Examiner has completed his tests."

Kratschik slammed the telephone down. Saxon went home for the weekend, wondering where Kratschik was getting his information from.

#

On Monday morning Saxon found the results of the laboratory tests on his desk. As expected, the blood taken from the three garments matched the blood groups of the three victims. This evidence was not conclusive, but, given the links between Freudl and two of the victims, it couldn't be ignored.

Saxon looked at his telephone, which remained like a silent brooding hen on his desk, ready to lay an egg at any moment.

"Nothing from Kratschik this morning?" said Glasser.

"Thank the gods. Better bring Freudl in. We can't delay any longer."

Glasser left and returned with the headmaster in tow. Saxon heard the tirade of abuse as they entered the stationhouse and gave him a few moments to settle before starting the interview.

He went through Freudl's alibis again for the nights of the three murders. His mother was his only corroboration for all three nights. Saxon presented the headmaster with the new evidence of the blood-stained clothing.

"That's preposterous. You found no such evidence during your first search."

"We must have missed it."

"You can't really believe that! We had a burglary the night before your second search. You saw the broken windowpane. Nothing was taken. It's obvious that someone broke in to the house and planted that new evidence. Someone is trying to frame me for crimes that I did not commit."

Saxon couldn't disagree with Freudl's analysis, but without solid alibis he would stand little chance in the courts of the Third Reich. Things were changing fast. Already, the police were no longer the sole guardians of the law as they were subordinate to the Schutzstaffel. And, under pressure from the Party, the courts could no longer be relied on for the impartial administration of justice.

He pressed Freudl to reveal any knowledge of Frau Happeck, the second victim. Freudl insisted that he had never met the woman. Saxon put Freudl in a holding cell and called Glasser into his office.

"Our friend is in a bind. With the evidence we have the courts will surely send him to the scaffold." Saxon shuddered. The scaffold was no more than a figure of speech, and they both knew it. Since Hitler had come to power the Munich courts had sentenced several people to death by guillotine.

"What if we keep him here until the killer strikes again, Boss? That would strengthen his hand."

"I think we need to take more direct action than that."

"Like what?"

"You do realise whoever planted those three garments must be the killer, and whoever he is, he's a worried man."

"Kratschik."

"Yes, Kratschik may be the killer or it may be his son. Find out where the Standartenführer lives, but do nothing until I give the word."

Ruth called on the telephone at midday. "Samuel's not well, *Schatzl*. I need you here." Saxon could hear the infant crying in the background.

"Take him to the doctor if he's ill. What can I do for him?"

"You're his father. I need you with me. Frau Snydacker next door has been no help at all."

"I'm not sure I can—" She cut the line.

Frau Snydacker? He racked his brain. Frau Snydacker was the neighbour who died last year! And Ruth never called him *Schatzl*. The hairs stood up on the back of his neck. Ruth was sending him a message. She was not alone. Someone had invaded their home. He called Glasser.

"I think there's somebody with my wife."

"Where is she?"

"She's in the apartment at home, but I received a strange telephone call from her." He opened his desk, pulled out his holster and strapped it on. He loaded his handgun with ammunition and put it in the holster. Glasser did the same, and they left the office together.

"I'll go in alone," said Saxon as they drew up outside his apartment building. "You wait here. If I need you I'll blow my whistle."

Ruth and baby Samuel were sleeping. He shook her awake.

"You had someone with you. What happened?"

"A stranger. A big man with a long jaw. He told me to call you on the telephone, to ask you to come home. I mentioned poor Frau Snydacker. I tried to warn you..."

"That worked well, but where is the stranger now?"

"He said he'd meet you in Marienplatz in time for the chimes at 11 o'clock. He said you should come alone."

#

Marienplatz was teeming with tourists and locals. At exactly 11 o'clock the clock rang and all eyes turned to the Rathaus clock tower as the glockenspiel display began. Saxon cast his eyes over the people around him, but failed to identify anyone even remotely sinister-looking.

Then a hand gripped his arm. "You were looking for me, Kommissar."

He spun around and found himself face to face with a smiling face with a long jaw. He was older than the picture on his file and his hairline had receded like an ocean before a tsunami, but Saxon recognised Georg Bell. "Herr Bell, I should arrest you for breaking into my home and frightening my wife."

"Forgive me," said Bell. "I didn't mean to frighten her."

"I need to ask you a few questions about 1931 in Prinzregentenplatz."

"Anything I can do to help, Kommissar."

"You are aware that both Frau Happeck and Maxine Weiss were killed in the last seven days?"

"Yes. I was greatly saddened by their deaths."

"They were the last two of three identical murders. The first was a prostitute called Maria Kazinski. She worked in a brothel..."

"What is your question?"

"Is there any connection between the Geli suicide and Maria Kazinski?"

"None that I know of, and it wasn't suicide."

"You gave information about the Geli… affair to Michael Gerlich. You must know that Gerlich has been arrested, his records removed? I assume Gerlich spoke with Frau Happeck and Maxine Weiss?"

Bell nodded. "Yes."

"So that's why they died?"

"Very probably. Gerlich was about to blow the top off the whole case."

"What can you tell me about his findings?"

"I can tell you that Geli was murdered and he had the evidence to prove it."

"Gerlich could name the murderer?"

"Why do you think the Brownshirts arrested him and killed the only two people present in the apartment?"

"Were you involved in the killing?"

"Not directly."

"You weren't in the apartment when Geli Raubal died?"

"No, but I supplied the key that allowed the SS to gain access."

"Give me a name. Give me something – anything."

"I can't. I wouldn't last a week." He looked around nervously. The chimes were nearing the end. "Goodbye, Kommissar. I wish you good fortune with your investigation. Just remember that not everything is as it appears."

And Georg Bell disappeared into the crowd.

#

Saxon returned to the office with Georg Bell's words ringing in his head. He invited his assistant into his office, closed the door, and ran through his meeting with Georg Bell.

When he'd finished, Glasser said, "He confirmed that Frau Happeck and Maxine were witnesses to the killing of Geli Raubal?"

"Perhaps not witnesses, but they were present in the apartment at the time. The only ones, he said."

"And the assassin was SS?"

"Yes. We must assume the killing was ordered by the Führer himself."

"That's dynamite, Boss. It could bring the Nazi government down."

"Undoubtedly. But without Gerlich and his records we have nothing."

"What did he mean, 'not everything is as it appears'?" said Glasser.

"I don't know, but I want to take another look at the Medical Examiner's reports." He opened the three reports and spread them out on his desk.

"What are we looking for, Boss?"

"Professor Valachek mentioned that all three victims had been struck on the head. Frau Happeck and the teacher, Maxine, had been killed by the initial blow, but Maria Kazinski was alive but unconscious until the end of the mutilations." He read Professor Valachek's breakdown of the gruesome mutilations and could find no differences.

Glasser said, "Listen to this, Boss." He read from the first report: "The blade used to kill Maria Kazinski was short and narrow, like a dagger, 15 cm long." He picked up a page from the second autopsy report: "The weapon that killed Frau Happeck was at least 30 cm long and had a broad blade, like a rapier."

Saxon leafed through the third report and found the description of the weapon used. "This one was long and broad. The last two were identical, the first was a different weapon!"

In his excitement, Saxon patted his jacket pockets looking for a cigarette. Glasser opened a packet and they lit up together in a cloud of smoke.

"We're looking for two killers," said Glasser. "The second and third murders were political, the first killing was something else."

"You're right," said Saxon, "but still, the three killings are connected. The last two were copies of the first. The SS intended us to lay the blame for all three murders on the killer of Maria Kazinski."

"And the three blood-stained garments pointed the fingers squarely at the headmaster," said Glasser. "I wonder why they chose him?"

"I identified him as a possible suspect, remember. The SS probably want to remove him from his post and put one of their own in there. But the discovery of those garments also proves that whoever the two killers are, they are closely connected."

"Like father and son?" said Glasser.

Saxon stubbed out his cigarette. "If we bring Kratschik junior in for questioning, the consequences don't bear thinking about."

Glasser said, "We could do nothing, Boss."

"And let a brutal murderer go free? I don't think so. And anyway, Kratschik is insisting that we solve the case. If we fail we'll be back in uniform by morning, arresting carthorses for fouling the streets."

"What if we charge Freudl?"

"He would face the guillotine. An innocent man. Could you live with that?"

"No."

"This is Zugzwang," said Saxon, gloomily.

"Zugzwang, Boss?"

"It's a chess term. It means we are obliged to move, but whatever move we make will lose us the game.

#

Saxon shivered as he entered SS headquarters clutching a briefcase. Entry to the building was through a courtyard at the rear of Schellingstrasse 50. Up until 1931 this had been the Nazi Party's national headquarters, and all the signs were there – the eagle over the lintel, the shrine in the vestibule where the bloodflag used to hang, and swastikas everywhere you looked.

He was made to wait the customary 20 minutes before being shown into the office of SS-Standartenführer Karl Kratschik.

"Take a seat, Kommissar." It was an order, not an invitation.

The office was spacious enough to accommodate a small table and four chairs. Saxon took one of those.

Kratschik joined him at the table. "Why has Bart Freudl not been charged?" said the SS man as he settled into a chair.

"I believe Herr Freudl is innocent, Herr Standartenführer. We now have compelling evidence against another man." Saxon opened his briefcase, took out the school photograph and placed it on the table in front of the SS man. "This individual, here. He calls himself 'Heinrich.'"

Kratschik took one look at the face in the picture and blanched.

Saxon continued, "We have yet to identify the young man, but anyone present at the school when this photograph was taken should be able to name him."

Kratschik picked up the photograph and took it to his desk. "Join me here." An invitation, not an order this time. Saxon took the chair facing the desk.

Kratschik opened a silver cigarette box and offered it to Saxon. "What evidence do you have against this man?"

Saxon took a cigarette, but the lighter was out of reach on Kratschik's desk.

"He was Maria Kazinski's last customer on the night she was killed, and he has a reputation for violence. It shouldn't be difficult to break him down once we have him under lock and key."

"You can connect him to the other two victims?"

"The teacher, Frau Limburg, is there in the photograph."

"Ah, but can you link him to the third victim?"

"As I said, Herr Standartenführer, once we have him under interrogation..."

"What of the blood-stained clothing you found? That clearly linked the schoolmaster to the three killings."

"That evidence was false. The killer broke in to Herr Freudl's home and placed it there."

Kratschik sat forward in his chair and put his hands together, his fingertips to his lips.

"You are married, Kommissar?"

"Yes, sir."

"Children?"

"Just one child, a boy, three weeks old."

"I have one son. He leaves today to join the Reichswehr, his grandfather's regiment, based in the north."

"Congratulations, Herr Standartenfuhrer."

Kratschik stood. He slid the school photograph into a desk drawer. "You have done a remarkable job, Saxon, and I thank you. But you need do nothing more. Send me the entire file. The Schutzstaffel will take over the investigation from here."

Saxon placed his unlit cigarette in his breast pocket. He closed the clasp on his briefcase and got to his feet. "I have never abandoned an investigation before completing it, Herr Standartenführer."

"You wife's name is Ruth?"

An icy finger touched the back of Saxon's neck.

"Yes, sir."

"Isn't that a Jewish name?"

THE END – ZUGZWANG

CASE 2 – QUEEN SACRIFICE

(a short story)
First published December 2016
Copyright 2016 – 2019 © JJ Toner Publishing

Chapter 1

Munich, Friday June 29, 1934

KriminalKommissar Saxon peered at the boy's photograph once
more. Johann Grau, the missing youth, had a boyish face with
mousey brown hair and traces of acne about the forehead. The first
fluffy bloom of a moustache appeared like a shadow on his upper lip.
A typical boy of 16 with an impudent half-smile, and yet... There was
definitely something about the eyes.

He passed the picture across the desk to his new assistant. "Look
closely, Keller. Tell me what you see."

"What am I looking for, Boss?"

"Whatever occurs to you."

Oberassistent Werner Keller looked barely older than the
missing boy. His experience to date – messing about in boats with
the Water Police – hardly equipped him for the rough and tumble of
a city police force, but Saxon was glad to have him. Since the Gestapo
takeover of the Munich police force, 9 months earlier, many of their
best men had been scattered to the four corners of the country. Good
men were hard to come by.

Keller puckered his brow in concentration. "He looks
constipated."

"Constipated."

"Either that or there's a turn in his eye."

Keller handed the picture back. Saxon looked at it again. Keller
was right. Grau did have a slight astigmatism in his left eye, but even
allowing for that, there was still something... "Well spotted, Keller. Is
that all you can see?"

"His smile is a bit creepy, Boss. It's a wide-eyed look of false innocence. The *who-me* look. You see it when someone farts in the wheelhouse. I've met smugglers on the Rhine with more genuine smiles on their faces."

Saxon laughed. "You think Johann Grau might be a constipated smuggler?"

"Maybe not, Boss, but I think he has something to hide."

Saxon flipped through the file. "We should start with his father, to get a list of his friends. Find us a car."

Before Keller could reach the door, it burst open. Kriminalrat Glasser, the walking skeleton, strode in.

"Leave us, Keller." Glasser waved a bony hand, as if swatting a fly, and Keller scurried out, closing the door behind him.

Glasser sat in the vacant seat. "What are you working on, Saxon?"

Saxon ground his teeth. Barely 6 months earlier Glasser was a lowly Kriminaloberassistent, calling Saxon "Boss", but, since his promotion, their roles were reversed.

Saxon handed the photograph across his desk. The superfluous question put him on his guard. They had discussed the case 12 hours earlier, when Glasser had stressed its importance, not just to the boy's parents, but to the SS and by extension to the Third Reich.

"Ah yes, the missing schoolboy. You haven't found him yet, I suppose?"

"I've only been on the case for a couple of hours. I had to clear my desk."

"You need to be less defensive, Saxon. No one's questioning your abilities or your dedication to your work. What else are you working on?"

Saxon's file cabinet was full to bursting. Painted gunmetal grey, it had the lopsided look of a sinking battleship. He rattled off the litany of his caseload: 5 possible suicides, 17 probable murders, 33 burglaries and countless reports of assault in the streets.

New cases poured in every day. Everyone was working crazy hours, but there was little that the Munich police could do to stem the flow. The list of unsolved crimes kept mounting. The dogs in the streets knew that Ernst Röhm's Brownshirts were responsible for most of these crimes, but they had effective immunity from the law.

Saxon steeled himself for the next onslaught, some new case to add to the ever-growing pile, no doubt. Since the Gestapo takeover of the Munich police, and the appointment of *SA-Obergruppenführer* August Schneidhuber as the new Chief of Police, everything had changed. Priorities changed daily, driven by political imperatives that were as unpredictable as they were imponderable.

Glasser leaned forward, baring his teeth in a ghastly rictus. "Tell me, when did you last take time off?"

Saxon took a moment to recover from the shock before responding with a short snort of derision. "When was the last time any of us had time off?" If this was the opening gambit in some twisted game, he couldn't guess its purpose.

"I'd like you to take a day's leave. I'm acutely aware that you have had no time for your wife and your young son – how old is he now? When was the last time you had a break?"

Saxon sat bolt upright, his mind racing, seeking out the hidden threat behind the unprecedented offer. "It was over a year ago, when the boy was born. He's 17 months old."

"Seventeen months! How time flies! What was the boy's name again? And how is your wife?"

"The boy's name is Samuel. My wife is well. They are both well, thank you."

"Take the rest of day. I don't want to see you back here before Monday."

#

Saxon headed home on foot in the midday sun. Confronted by a phalanx of marching Brownshirts, he stood to attention and gave the odious Hitler salute. To do otherwise would have invited a beating.

When he got home, he found Ruth rocking Baby Samuel on her shoulder. "What do you mean? Don't you have any cases to work on?"

"I've never been busier."

"So why are you here?" Samuel was whimpering. "Hush, little one."

"I told you, Glasser gave me the day. What's the matter with Samuel?"

"And you let that pipsqueak order you around? He has new teeth coming through. We need to give him something to chew."

"He may be a pipsqueak, my love, but he's a senior pipsqueak."

Saxon went to the closet and removed the transverse belt from his old uniform. He handed it to Ruth, and she gave it to Samuel. The baby sank his gums into the belt and peace was restored.

"Glasser's my boss now, Ruth. When he tells me to take a day, I take a day."

"Well, I don't like it. I don't trust Glasser, or Chief Schneidhuber, or any Gestapo. They're scheming something, mark my words."

#

Baby Samuel was quiet most of that night, but Saxon got little sleep. The sounds of Brownshirts rampaging in the streets outside kept him awake. He sat by an open window, smoking, and watched the glow from fires in the city centre.

The next day was Saturday, June 30. Saxon, Ruth and baby Samuel took a tram to the Munich zoo in Hellabrunn Tierpark.

The sun shone on streets littered with broken glass and teams of municipal workers with handcarts, clearing up.

The zoo was crowded – one of the few remaining places in the city where people could take their children in relative safety. Samuel laughed at the monkeys and clapped his hands at the rock-hopper penguins, but the old elephant frightened him. He cried, and Saxon bought him a toy giraffe made out of rubber.

By 4:00 pm they were on the return journey, Samuel fast asleep in his father's arms on the tram. He'd had an exhausting day. Approaching their stop on Franz-Nissl-Strasse near the Piperstrasse junction, the tram driver braked suddenly to avoid a convoy of Kubelwagens heading toward the centre of town at speed.

Saxon shifted the child from one shoulder to the other. "The Brownshirts are out in force again this evening."

Ruth shook her head. "They didn't look like Brownshirts to me, dear."

A second glance told Saxon that she was right. The Kubelwagens were full of Gestapo in uniform, all heavily armed. A prickling sensation of anxiety swept over his scalp at the sight. The nocturnal activities of the Brownshirts were bad enough. Armed Gestapo squads would add a toxic element that would make the streets even more hazardous for the ordinary residents of Munich.

The streets were strangely quiet that night. Ruth slept well. Samuel woke twice, and each time Saxon got up to change his diaper and give him a bottle he thought about smoking a cigarette. He had none. There were places where he might buy a packet at such a late hour, but he rejected the idea of leaving the apartment. The streets were not safe at night, not even for an armed police officer, and Ruth objected to his smoking in the apartment, in any case. For some reason, she thought the smoke was bad for Samuel's health.

Saxon fell into a deep sleep in the early hours. The telephone woke him at 7:00 am. Ruth picked it up quickly and handed it to him.

It was Werner Keller. "Sorry to call so early on a Sunday, Boss, but there's been trouble overnight. I thought you would wish to be informed."

#

Saxon walked the two kilometres to the police station in bright sunlight. He marvelled at the city's transformation. There were few people about and the streets, littered with debris 12 hours earlier, were spotless. The scene should have lightened his heart, but there was something sinister about it, some brooding evil lying hidden. Perhaps Keller's words had put him on edge.

A restless, raucous crowd crammed the public area of the police station. Saxon waded past to his office, collecting Keller on the way.

"So, tell me." Saxon opened his desk, found a packet of desiccated cigarettes and took one out. "What have the Brownshirts been up to this time?" He offered a cigarette to his assistant.

Keller declined. "The Führer flew into Munich yesterday morning. He drove straight to the Hotel Hanselbauer where the SS and Gestapo arrested most of the leaders of the Brownshirts. Many have been taken to Stadelheim Prison, some have been shot already."

Saxon froze in the act of lighting his cigarette. "Did I hear you right? The Führer is here in Munich in person, and the Gestapo are carrying out a purge of the Brownshirts?"

"Yes, Boss. He called them all to Munich on some pretext…"

"How many were taken?"

"At least twelve. Some were arrested at the station as they got off their trains and were taken straight to the prison."

"Ernst Röhm?"

"He was the first."

"Do we have a list of names?"

"The desk sergeant has some of the names. Herr Kriminalrat Glasser has the complete list, Boss."

The burning match reached Saxon's fingers. He swore and dropped it into his ashtray. "And where is Glasser now?"

Keller shrugged. "At the prison, I suppose."

#

The desk sergeant wrote out a list of 14 names, adding a note on each one: 'suicide' or 'evading arrest.' One was marked 'heart failure.' Saxon recognized the names of eight senior members of the Brownshirts.

Keller and Saxon slipped out of the police station through the back door, took a car, and headed south to the city morgue.

They found Professor Valachek, the Medical Examiner, hard at work in the inner sanctum, his eyes bloodshot and red-rimmed. He waved a hand at the bodies laid out in the examination room, two to a table. "If you have to slaughter half the population, I wish you'd do it at a civilized hour and stagger the body count a bit. I need my sleep, and I don't have room here for so many."

"Nothing to do with me, Professor." Saxon splayed his palms. "This is the work of the Gestapo."

"Orpo, Schupo, Kripo, Gestapo, it's all the same. All you ever do is create work for me."

Saxon counted 10 bodies. "I thought there were fourteen."

"I've passed four to Hartmann, the undertaker. Some of these will follow in the next couple of hours. I've been told to make room for a lot more."

"What can you tell me about them?"

"They nearly all died by gunshot. Three almost certainly took their own lives. Four were executed – a single bullet to the back of the head from close range. Three were shot in the back."

Keller said, "Attempting to escape?"

"So I'm told."

"The desk sergeant said there was one case of heart failure," said Saxon.

The professor removed the sheet from one of the bodies, a tall, heavy-set middle-aged man. "Wilhelm Berger, an Evangelist pastor. I expect he had a heart attack. I'll know better when I open him up. I'm surprised there was only one. It must have been like a war zone out there last night."

They did the rounds, Valachek peeling back the sheets one by one, while Saxon checked off the names on his list. He paused at one of the faces – a blond-haired boy wearing the uniform of the Hitler Youth.

"What happened to this youngster?"

"Shot in the back of the head." Valachek handed Saxon an identity card. Saxon read the name Stephan Weiss, born 1917.

Chapter 2

They drove to the undertaker's in silence. Hartmann's funeral home was locked and shuttered. Keller hammered on the door until Hartmann opened it. The undertaker was wearing an apron, peeling off a pair of gloves. "Sorry for the delay, Kommissar, I was working on a body in the basement."

Saxon introduced his new assistant. Hartmann shook Keller's hand. "I heard Glasser was promoted. Come through."

He led them to a low temperature room with a high ceiling. Saxon shuddered, not just from the cold. There was something forbidding and final about Hartmann's establishment – even more forbidding and final than Valachek's morgue.

The undertaker switched on a few dim lights and took them on a tour of the four open coffins. Saxon checked off the bodies from his list. Three were of the over-muscular type identified with the Brownshirts. The fourth was a local authority worker from Ulm, called Walter Müller, the year of birth on his identity card, 1883.

In the car on the way back to the police station, Keller clung to the steering wheel like a man on a rollercoaster. "Fourteen bodies, boss! The most I've ever seen in one day was three, when we rammed a smuggler's motorboat in the North Sea."

#

The police station was even more packed with people than before, all clamouring for attention.

Glasser beckoned to Saxon over the heads of the crowd. Saxon slipped through the rabble into Glasser's office and closed the door.

The Kriminalrat's colour was up. "What are you doing back at work?"

"I got a call. I thought I might be needed."

"Didn't I say I didn't want to see you until tomorrow?"

"There are ten dead bodies in the morgue and four more in Hartmann's funeral parlour."

"None of those are your concern, Saxon. What happened this morning was an operation to quell an attempted political coup. The security of the Fatherland was under direct threat from Ernst Röhm and his men. Our orders came direct from the Führer himself."

"So those fourteen murders—"

"—Were all sanctioned by the government. They were all legal killings."

Saxon consulted his list of names. "Walter Müller, a municipal officer from Ulm, Wilhelm Berger, a pastor, and Stephan Weiss, a teenager, certainly too young to be a threat to the government."

"None of your concern. This morning's killings were all political. You heard what happened to August Schneidhuber?"

"No."

"The Führer personally stripped him of his rank and then had him shot by firing squad."

Saxon's legs turned to rubber. He sat down. "Dead?"

"Yes, dead. Of course, dead. Concentrate on the missing schoolboy. That should be your only concern. Now get out of my office."

#

Keller joined the morning traffic, heading west. "Did you get the complete list from him?"

"Schneidhuber has been executed." Saxon's voice was a flat monotone.

Keller looked at him, wide-eyed. "Not our Schneidhuber, our Chief of Police?"

Saxon nodded. "Keep your eyes on the road, Keller."

"God in heaven, what's happening to us, Boss?"

"Apparently, this morning's killings are none of our concern. They were all... political. We must find the missing schoolboy."

The rest of the journey was conducted in silence, an unspoken question hanging in the air. What exactly were 'political' killings, and why couldn't they investigate them? Saxon had never turned his back on a killing before.

The missing schoolboy's father, Tristan Grau, showed them into the front parlour of his house. "You have news of Johann?"

"Nothing yet," said Saxon.

The room was darkened by heavy lace curtains and smelled slightly of damp. A heavy display cabinet occupied one wall. Piles of books, magazines and old newspapers covered the furniture. Grau drew a curtain, throwing a shaft of strong sunlight across the floor. He invited them to sit, sweeping two armchairs clear of magazines and dropping them on the floor. The sunbeam filled with a dancing cloud of dust particles.

Keller lowered his behind onto one of the chairs.

Saxon remained standing. "Have you heard from Johann since you filed the missing person's report, Herr Grau?"

Grau shook his head. "No, nothing." The pain he was feeling was clearly visible in his eyes. "He's never run away from home before. Where do you think he might be?"

"That's what we're attempting to find out. What can you tell us about his friends?"

"He doesn't have many real friends, just boys in his Hitler Youth troop."

"What school does he attend?"

Grau clasped his hands together. "He was in the Luitpold-Gymnasium, but he lost interest in school and left."

Keller said, "You didn't object?"

Saxon directed a frown at his assistant. "When did he leave school, Herr Grau?"

"On the day that Adolf Hitler became Chancellor. The last day of January last year."

"And was that when he joined the Hitler Youth?"

"No. He joined a couple of years earlier, in 1931."

The door crashed open. Keller jumped like a man bitten by a snake.

Frau Grau stumbled into the room, her eyes red from crying, holding a handkerchief to her nose. She sank onto the armchair vacated by Keller. "Shouldn't you be out searching for my son?"

Saxon said, "We need more information to help us find him, Frau Grau. May I ask you, does he have a girlfriend?"

Frau Grau blew her nose noisily on the handkerchief. "Johann's too young for girlfriends."

Saxon and Keller exchanged a quick glance.

Saxon said, "We don't have his identity card. You're sure it's not hidden in his room somewhere?"

"Certain."

"We'd like to check for ourselves."

Herr Grau led them upstairs to his son's bedroom at the back of the house. Keller followed him in.

Saxon held the door open until Grau took the hint and left the room. "Put together a list of Johann's friends and acquaintances, Herr Grau, all right? We'll be down in a few minutes."

Grau hurried down the stairs.

The room was typical of a teenager on the cusp of adulthood. A mahogany wardrobe, a chair, a single bed covered with a child's counterpane. Swastikas and pictures of famous figures from Germany's past covered the walls. The Führer's portrait held pride of place over the door.

Keller pointed to a picture of a Junkers W33 and a balsa wood model of a JU52-3m hanging from the ceiling on a thread. "A budding pilot, I think, Boss."

"Yes, but too young for girls?"

The wardrobe contained the boy's Hitler Youth uniform, newly laundered and pressed. Saxon lifted the mattress and discovered two magazines of the health and fitness variety, their covers featuring muscular young men. Under the magazines, he found a matchbook from a nightclub called 'The Black Flamingo'. He slipped it into his pocket.

Keller stood on the chair to search the wardrobe. He found a pair of boxing gloves and, hidden at the back, a tin box with a hinged lid. It was empty. He showed it to Saxon.

They went back down to the parlour.

Herr Grau handed Saxon a list of names. "I've included every name we could think of. They're all Hitler Youth."

"Thank you."

"If you have any news – any news at all – you can contact me at work. I'm a maintenance worker at the town hall."

"You look after the Rathaus-Glockenspiel?" said Keller.

"Amongst other things – yes."

Frau Grau joined them at the front door. "Please find our son, Kommissar. He's a good boy. He's never been away from the house for more than a day."

"He never goes camping?" said Keller.

"Yes, of course, he goes camping with his troop, but he never goes away on his own. Tell me you'll find him, Kommissar."

She held a hand out toward Saxon. He grasped it in both of his and met her gaze steadily. "We will find him, Frau Grau."

In the car, Keller started the engine. "You're certain we will find him?"

"Certain, but we may not find him alive. Tell me what you thought of Herr Grau and his wife."

"They looked worried, her more than him."

"Don't you think her level of distress was disproportionate? The boy's been missing less than three days."

Keller made no reply, and Saxon interpreted his silence as an admission that the mind of a woman was beyond his comprehension.

Saxon examined the list of names that Grau had given them. He recognized one name straight away. He pulled the list of the 14 bodies from his pocket and confirmed it. "A boy from Grau's troop – Stephan Weiss – is one of the bodies in the morgue."

Keller gave a low whistle.

#

On the way back to the centre of town, they pulled over at a delicatessen and bought a quick lunch. Saxon watched Keller devour enough bratwurst for a family of five. "You were hungry, I think."

Keller wiped his mouth and grinned.

Saxon rang the police station from a telephone box and asked the desk sergeant if there were any messages for him. The sergeant said, "No messages, Kommissar, but hold on, Herr Kriminalrat Glasser would like to speak—"

Saxon disconnected the call.

"Where to next?" said Keller.

"It's late. Drop me back to the station."

#

Glasser was red in the face, fists clenched on his desk. "Did you cut me off on the telephone?"

"I don't think so." Saxon should have inserted a 'sir' here, but he choked on the word.

"Tell me where you've been."

"We went to see young Grau's parents. We have established a positive link between the missing boy and one that died last night."

"What did I say about the names on the Hummingbird list?"

"Hummingbird?"

"The list of legal killings. You are not to trouble yourself about those. Concentrate on the burglaries and find the missing schoolboy."

"Yes, I understand, but Stephan Weiss was a member of Johann Grau's Hitler Youth troop. He was seventeen, far too young to be a Brownshirt."

"You're complicating the case, Kommissar. Organize a search party, find the missing boy."

"And where should we search?"

Glasser's eyes flashed at Saxon. "It's your job to work that out. Get on with it, man."

#

Saxon opened the door to a silent apartment, the strange, unmistakable, glorious smell of infant everywhere. Checking the bedroom, he found Ruth and Samuel both asleep like angels, the boy clutching his toy giraffe. He put a kettle on and prepared a bottle for Samuel. Then he made a cup of coffee and settled into his favourite armchair with Hans Fallada's latest book.

He awoke with a start two hours later, bathed in sweat, the book on the floor, his coffee cold and untouched in the cup.

Chapter 3

They spent the next couple of days visiting the youths on Grau's list, while carefully avoiding the home of Stephan Weiss. As they travelled around the city, they noticed a black car with two occupants watching them. When Keller moved to challenge them, they drove away.

"Gestapo?" said Keller.

"Probably."

On Wednesday, they visited the home of the Hitler Youth troop leader, an old man with a moustache left behind from the time of the Kaiser. He gave them a complete list of youths in the troop – 51 names.

By Friday morning, they had visited 50 of the 51 names.

Keller came into Saxon's office carrying two cups of coffee. He was in high spirits. "I checked Stephan Weiss's address. He lived in the Maisach district."

Saxon sipped his coffee, burning his tongue. "I've told you we've been forbidden from working that case."

"But he was Hitler Youth, nothing to do with the Brownshirts."

Saxon made no response. The expression on his face was enough to signal his disapproval.

"What about the pastor and the municipal officer?"

"All three were legal killings. We can't go near any of them."

"So they expect us to do our job with our hands tied behind us? We have nothing else."

"We have this." Saxon dropped the matchbook on the desk.

Keller picked it up. "The Black Flamingo, in Blumenau. I'm not familiar with it."

"We'll drop in there tomorrow night. Better dress for the occasion."

"What do you suggest, Boss?"

"It's a nightclub. Use your imagination.

#

They met at the top of the staircase leading down to the nightclub. A light mist clung to the ground as the temperature dropped and the heat of the day seeped from the pavements. Saxon had put on an ancient ill-fitting navy twill suit and a striped tie in the national colours. He barely recognized his Oberassistent. Keller had greased his hair, and he was wearing a silk shirt in lurid colours, open to his navel. A medallion hung on a chain around his neck.

"What have you come as?" said Saxon, suppressing a smile.

Keller chuckled. "I was going to ask you the same question, Boss."

"We'll go in separately. Meet me back here in an hour." Saxon checked his watch. Keller did the same.

Keller went in first. Saxon waited five minutes before descending the staircase.

The entrance was guarded by a doorman in a trilby, who placed a light fingertip on Saxon's chest. "This is a private club. Guests must be accompanied by a member."

He looked like a retired boxer, complete with broken nose and foul breath. Saxon smiled at him. "But I am a member. Don't you remember me?" He put a cigarette between his lips and lit it with a match from the matchbook.

The doorman's eyes registered the matchbook. He tipped his hat and opened the door for Saxon. "Have a good evening, sir."

The club reverberated with music with a heavy drumbeat. A bar occupied the centre of the room. Saxon looked around but couldn't see Keller anywhere in the subdued lighting. He took a seat at a vacant table. As his eyes adjusted to the gloom, he found he was overlooking a wooden dance floor the size of a postcard crammed with bodies gyrating in the flickering light of a glitter ball.

He had barely sat down when a waitress approached and offered to get him a drink from the bar. Saxon showed her Johann Grau's photograph. He shouted above the music, "He's a friend. His name's Johann Grau."

She looked at the picture and shook her head. "I can't help you. What can I get you?"

"Nothing, thank you."

"If you take a table, you are obliged to buy a drink."

Saxon ordered a bottle of beer and paid a week's wages for it.

Before the beer had arrived, he was joined at the table by a young man in a sleeveless shirt. "You're new," he shouted.

"Yes, I'm looking for a friend." He showed the picture to the stranger who shook his head and wandered off across the dance floor.

Most of the bodies on the dance floor were male. The few females that Saxon saw had long blond hair and were wearing high heels and pencil skirts. He spotted Keller's oily hair glistening in the light from the spinning glitter ball. Keller gave him a cheesy grin.

The music died, leaving Saxon's ears ringing. Keller headed for the toilets. Saxon followed him as the music started up again. It sounded to Saxon like the same beat, the same song. Mercifully, the sound was muted in the toilets.

Keller was at a basin, stripped to the waist, washing the sweat from his body. "Any luck, Boss?"

Saxon shook his head. "No. You?"

"Yes, I met this girl. She's agreed to meet me when the club closes."

"I'm not interested in your private conquests, Keller. Have you found anyone that knew the boy?"

Keller looked hurt. "This girl. She may have something for us. Leave it with me, sir. You might as well go home to your family."

"We can cover more ground working together."

"Look at yourself, Boss." Keller pointed to Saxon's reflection in the mirror. "They all know what you are."

The figure in the mirror looked older than his years. Every stitch of the suit spelled police. Only the word 'Kripo' stamped on his forehead would have made it more obvious.

Saxon left the club and went looking for a taxi. He couldn't remember the last time the streets of the city were so calm and peaceful.

#

Saxon arrived home after midnight. Samuel was screaming, Ruth rushing about looking for ways to calm him.

"What's the matter with him?" he said, hanging his jacket on a hook behind the main door.

"Don't leave that there. Put in the wardrobe where it belongs."

Saxon took the jacket into the bedroom. He removed the pants with a sigh of relief and hung the suit in the wardrobe. When he was dressed in his most comfortable clothes he returned to the kitchenette. Ruth was juggling with a screaming infant and preparing a bottle on the stove at the same time.

Saxon took the child from her. "What's he screaming about?" For one moment he thought that the peace in the city was what was upsetting his son. Perhaps Samuel had become accustomed to the sounds of tumult in the streets outside.

"It's his teeth. I gave him your leather belt, but he spat it out."

Saxon bounced the child on his shoulder and the screaming subsided.

Ruth shook her head in amazement. "That child is like two people in one body. You see to the bottle. Give him back to me." She took Samuel from Saxon and placed him on her shoulder. When the screaming resumed, Saxon knew he was in trouble.

#

On Monday morning, Saxon rose early and walked to the police station in bright sunshine. One week after the purge of the Brownshirts, the transformation was remarkable. Sunday night had been blissfully peaceful, and the streets were clear of debris. No doubt the Führer would take the credit for restoring order. Another great triumph for the Nazi Party. Never mind that they had created the problem in the first place.

The police station was quieter than the morgue, the front desk unmanned. Saxon rang the bell and the duty sergeant emerged from the back room carrying a steaming cup. "Good morning, sir."

Saxon was of a mind to reprimand the man for abandoning his post, but his smile was infectious. "Good morning, sergeant. Anything to report over the weekend?"

"Nothing, sir. That was the quietest weekend I've ever experienced."

Saxon examined the incident log. There were just four entries, all of a trivial nature. A pair of prostitutes brought in for solicitation, two drunken brawls, and a missing cat.

"No burglaries?"

"No, sir."

This was remarkable. The norm had been two or three per night. Surely this was evidence confirming his theory that the Brownshirts were responsible for the burglaries.

Ever eager, Werner Keller was waiting by Saxon's desk.

"Good morning, Keller. By the look of you, I'd guess you have something for me."

"Remember the girl that I met in the club, Boss? Her name's Lottie. She agreed to meet me outside. I waited an hour, but she never came."

"You obviously made an impression there."

"I gave her the station telephone number. She may call me."

"If she does, tell her to meet you at the police station. If she knows anything, she must be interviewed properly."

"Yes, Boss. I'll let you know if she makes contact."

Saxon wasn't optimistic. If the investigation was relying on Keller's magnetic personality, they were in serious trouble.

Keller was still hovering, shifting his weight from one foot to the other.

"Was there something else, Keller?"

"Yes, Boss. I've been thinking about that empty tin box in Johann Grau's bedroom."

"What about it?"

"What do you think it was used for?"

"It looked like a money box to me. But it was empty."

Keller said nothing. Saxon scratched his chin. "Hmm. We'll need to ask his parents about that. In the meantime, get us two coffees. You can help me go through all our burglary cases again. We need a complete list of stolen goods."

Two hours of painstaking police work later, Keller had completed the list of stolen goods. He came bounding into Saxon's office in a state of excitement.

"Boss, Boss, guess what I found."

"Tell me what you found, Keller."

"One of the burglaries on our list was in Maisach, the Weiss household."

"The home of the dead youth, Stephan Weiss?"

"Yes, Boss. That gives us a reason to visit the family."

"But not a reason to investigate the killing."

#

Glasser made an appearance at 10:00 am with a cheesy grin on his gaunt face. "Have you seen what we have in the cells?"

Saxon stiffened. This was a side of Glasser rarely seen these days. It was probably some sort of trap. "The two prostitutes picked up last night?"

"Not them, the other one, Lottie Kleiner." He whistled. "What a beauty!"

Keller jumped from his seat, "Did you say Lottie?"

"Yes, the stunning blonde. Pity about the black eye. Do we know why she was picked up?"

Saxon said, "Keller, check the incident log."

Keller dashed out to the front desk. He returned ten minutes later in a state of barely suppressed excitement. "She didn't have her identity card on her, but it's definitely Lottie, the girl I spoke to at the nightclub on Saturday. She's been beaten. She came in last night of her own volition, looking for protection."

"Take her to interview room one. We'll interrogate her there," said Saxon.

Lottie was dressed in the same tight-fitting party gown she'd been wearing at the club, now creased and twisted about her torso. Her blond hair and heavy tan made an intoxicating mix. Her makeup was in need of attention, and there was a bruise under her left eye. Overall, she had a delicious look of dishevelled vulnerability that seemed to increase her charm.

Saxon sat directly opposite her, Keller to his left. Glasser sat beside her, their elbows touching. Saxon offered her his cigarette packet. She removed one and Keller leant across the table to light it for her.

"You were not carrying your identity card with you last night. You do realize this is an offence?" said Saxon.

"I'm sorry, Herr Kommissar, it's difficult to keep up with all the new laws."

Glasser frowned at Saxon. "My name is Glasser, Kriminalrat Glasser, Fräulein Kleiner. These are my men, Saxon and Keller. The identity card is a minor matter. You're free to leave, but we'd like to ask you a few questions before you go."

She nodded. Saxon asked if she'd like a glass of water. She nodded again, and Keller left the room to fetch it.

Glasser began the interview. "Tell us what happened to you last night, Fräulein. How did you get that injury?"

"I was attacked by a man in the street on my way home."

"The brute." Glasser looked horrified. "He struck you on the face?"

"Yes, but I fought him off."

"Give us his name and we'll arrest him immediately, Fräulein."

"I don't know his name. Please call me Lottie."

"He didn't... molest you, Lottie?" Glasser broke eye contact.

"No. It was nothing, really. As I said, I fought him off. I can look after myself."

Saxon lit a cigarette. "What can you tell us about Johann Grau? You know him?"

"Yes, we are good friends."

"When did you see him last?"

"About a week ago, on the Speichersee. We enjoy boating in the fine weather."

Keller came back. He placed a glass tumbler of water on the table and she took a sip.

"Are you lovers?" said Saxon.

She looked horrified. "No, Kommissar, Johann's only fifteen."

Glasser frowned at Saxon again. "So Lottie, how did you come to spend the night here, in the cells?"

"I had a feeling that my attacker was not alone." She took a deep drag on the cigarette and crossed her legs. "I came in for protection."

"Do you wish to file an assault report?"

"No, no. I'd like to leave now. I have some sleep to catch up on."

"Very well," said Glasser. "If you have any further trouble you know where to find us."

"Keller will escort Fräulein Kleiner to her home," said Saxon.

"Yes, of course," said Glasser.

"You are too kind, gentlemen." She smiled at Glasser, while dropping her cigarette on the floor and grinding it with her high-heeled shoe.

Keller left with Lottie.

Saxon went to the front desk to examine the incident log. The shift had changed. The new desk sergeant said, "Looks like last night was a quiet one, Kommissar."

The incident log contained Lottie Kleiner's name, address and date of birth. She had been admitted to the cells following a drunken fight in the street and an altercation with the desk sergeant.

"Looks like it," said Saxon.

The sergeant laughed. "Even the missing cat turned out to be a false alarm."

#

When Keller arrived back in the station, he was breathless with excitement. "She knows the dead boy, Stephan Weiss."

"Did she have any suggestions as to who might have killed him, or why Grau might have run away from home?"

Keller shook his head. "No, she was shocked to hear about Weiss, and she seemed just as surprised as Grau's parents that Johann was missing. But I gathered there was more to last night's attack than she told us. She was on edge the whole way, and the closer we got to her apartment building the more fidgety she became. And she asked me to walk her to her door."

"She thinks someone is watching her apartment?"

"She wouldn't admit it, but I think so, yes. She knew Pastor Berger too. She was a regular visitor to his church."

"What about the municipal officer, Müller?"

"She didn't know him."

"Is she a member of the Bund?"

"I didn't ask her that, Boss."

"Check their records. And ask the technical people if they can take a set of Lottie's fingerprints from this." Saxon handed Keller a paper bag containing the glass tumbler.

#

Keller quickly established that Lottie Kleiner had never been a member of the *Bund Deutscher Mädel*.

They took a car from the pool and drove back to the Grau house. Herr Grau raised an enquiring eyebrow as he opened the door. Saxon shook his head. "Nothing yet, Herr Grau. We have a couple more questions."

Grau stood back, and they stepped inside. Keller asked permission to visit the boy's room again. Grau waved a hand. "Go ahead."

He took Saxon into the front parlour and offered him a seat.

Saxon remained standing. "Do you know Lottie Kleiner?" he asked.

"The name means nothing to me."

"She's a blonde. She says she's a friend of Johann's. You're sure you don't know her?"

"Certain. As his mother told you, he has no girlfriends. How old is she?"

"Twenty-one."

"A little old for Johann, wouldn't you agree, Kommissar? Has she given you any clues as to where Johann might have gone?"

"No, but she has been helpful. She and Johann were in a boat together on Speichersee on the day he disappeared. Did you know that Johann liked to row on the lake?"

"No, but I taught him to swim in that lake. He loves the place. We took him there often when he was growing up."

Keller came in with the tin box. He placed it on the table and stood back.

Saxon stared at it with furrowed brow. "What can you tell me about this money box, Herr Grau?"

Grau shrugged. "It's Johann's."

"How much did you find in it?"

Grau's hands were clasped like terrified children clinging together. "I don't know what you mean."

"You searched his room when he went missing."

"Yes, of course."

"You found money in this tin box."

"No, no, Kommissar, it was empty, I swear."

Saxon pursed his lips. He glared at Grau. "Why are you lying to us, Herr Grau? Don't you think I can tell a lie when I hear one? Don't you want us to find your son?"

"I'm not lying!" Grau's voice shook.

Keller said, "Should I call Frau Grau, Boss?"

Grau's chin trembled. He slumped onto a chair. "Fifty. There was fifty Marks in the box."

"Fifty."

"Yes, I swear."

"Keller..."

"No, wait, don't call my wife. I'll show you what I found." He opened the display cabinet, took out a porcelain vase and shook the contents onto the table.

Keller counted the money quickly. "3,015 Marks, Boss."

Saxon said, "Is this all you found?"

"Yes. I would never have spent any of it. Whatever he did to earn it, I know it must have been something... something disgusting."

"Like what, Herr Grau?"

"I don't know." Tears streamed down Herr Grau's face.

Chapter 4

Kriminalrat Glasser called Saxon into his office. He had something important to discuss.

"Sit," said Glasser. "Where's Keller?"

Saxon sat down. "He's working on the burglaries. I sent him out with a list of the stolen property."

"What do you think of him? Will he make the grade?"

"I believe so. He has the makings of a good detective."

"Good, good. And how have you been? How's your wife and that boy of yours? Samuel, wasn't it?"

"He's getting his first teeth, but he's well."

Glasser splayed his fingers over a document in front of him on the desk. "I've received this directive from headquarters. The *SS-Hauptamt* in Berlin has ordered the establishment of a number of training centres for SS officers. One of these Junker schools will be set up in the Munich area, and my name has been placed on the list of first intake of students."

"That's excellent news." Saxon meant it. If Glasser were fully occupied in a training camp, Saxon wouldn't have to deal with him.

Glasser showed no signs of pleasure at the prospect. "Yes, well, there are conditions attached to the enrolment. First, I have to complete a written test."

"That should be no problem."

"Second, I have to pass a test of physical fitness."

"Ah."

Glasser raised an eyebrow. "I think that won't be an obstacle."

"Of course not."

"And third, I have to meet a quota."

"A quota?"

"A list of names of undesirables, people who can be deported or sent to the labour camps."

The blood drained from Saxon's face.

"I need ten names. I want you to help me with that."

Saxon took a deep breath. "You want me to give you names..."

"I thought you might know some communists that haven't been rooted out yet, maybe some Jews in hiding. Your wife is Jewish, I'm sure she must have some names."

A hundred ants crawled over Saxon's scalp. The implication was clear: come up with ten names or Ruth and Samuel would be placed on Glasser's list.

#

Keller returned, bubbling with good news. He had found a significant number of stolen items in the possession of a fence called Dieter Peters. "Should we pick him up, Boss?"

"I'm sorry, what did you say?"

"I thought we should pick him up."

"Who?"

"The fence."

"What fence?"

"Are you feeling all right, Boss?"

"Yes, yes. Tell me again."

"Dieter Peters is holding some of the stolen property. I thought we should bring him in for questioning."

Saxon knew the name. Peters was a known criminal, a born thief and low life. He waved an arm. "Pick him up. You really don't need my permission to arrest criminals or bring people in for questioning."

Keller reacted as if he'd been slapped across the face. He stopped at the door. "I drove by the Weiss house in Maisach."

"Didn't I tell you to stay away from the Weiss's?"

"Yes, Boss. I didn't go near them. But Herr Weiss has a new Horch V8 parked outside his house. I wondered what he did for a living, so I asked the neighbours."

"And?"

"He's a common labourer. He works for the railways. That car would have cost him three year's wages."

#

Peters was a miserable individual. Saxon allowed Keller to conduct the interrogation. Keller did a creditable job. He did everything he could, short of actual physical assault, to intimidate and badger the man into naming those who sold him the stolen property. Peters refused to squeal. His smug smile never left his face. By the end of the session, Keller was sweating; Peters looked cool as an iceberg.

In his mind, Saxon placed Peters at the top of his list of undesirables. If he had to come up with ten names, perhaps they could all be petty criminals like him.

#

Peace reigned at home. Baby Samuel was sleeping. Ruth was sipping a glass of Hock. She filled a second glass and thrust it at him.

"*Leibling*, I need to talk to you about something," he said.

She shook her head. Her hair was down. "Later. Drink your wine."

"Have you considered visiting your cousin in Austria?"

"No, *Schatzl*, why? Do you want to get rid of me?" She smiled seductively.

Saxon couldn't recall the last time she'd said or done anything remotely seductive. Unfortunately, he found it impossible to respond. His mind was frozen by the word 'quota'. Ruth and the baby were living under a dire threat that she had no knowledge of.

He needed to take action to remove them from the threat without alarming her.

"I think you should spend some time in Austria. Take Samuel with you."

"What's this all about, lover? I haven't seen Benjamin in two years."

"Don't you think it's time you did?"

"Drink your wine." She stepped into the bedroom, kicking off her shoes.

"Ruth, I'm serious. I want you to pack a bag tomorrow and take Samuel to Austria. I'm sure your cousin will be delighted to see you."

She appeared in the bedroom doorway, dressed in her slip. "I'll do no such thing. Now come to bed."

#

On Friday July 13, Glasser called Saxon into his office again. "We've had new orders from Berlin. The Führer made a speech this morning in the Reichstag. He named seventy-seven people who lost their lives on the Night of the Long Knives."

Saxon raised his eyebrows. "The long knives?"

"July first. That's what they're calling it in Prinz-Albrecht Strasse. Of the seventy-seven, he has declared sixty-three legal killings. Eleven have been declared illegal. Of those eleven, just one falls within our bailiwick: the pastor, Wilhelm Berger."

"He died of a heart attack. What about Weiss the youngster, and the municipal office worker from Ulm, Walter Müller?"

"Müller's death has been classified as an accident. The boy is off limits."

Saxon snorted. "Müller was shot in the back of the neck."

"That was unfortunate. He was struck by a stray bullet."

#

Stephan Weiss's home was in Maisach, a working-class area in the northwest of the city. Approaching the house, Keller pointed out Herr Weiss's new Horch V8 luxury motorcar.

Saxon knocked on the door. "Follow my lead, Keller."

Weiss's father was a slight, mousey individual, with hooded eyes and a Hitler moustache. He invited them inside.

"Frau Weiss is not home?" said Saxon.

"She's gone to Switzerland."

"She has family in Switzerland?"

"Twin sisters in Zurich. She left a couple of days after... On July fourth. I'm not sure she'll ever come back, to be honest."

"Tell me about Stephan. What was he like? What did he like to do?"

"He enjoyed swimming and boxing. He was a good athlete. He had ambitions to qualify for the Olympic boxing team." The weight of Herr Weiss's double loss hit him and dulled the light in his eyes. His head dropped.

"Do you have any idea who might have killed him, or why?"

"No."

"You reported a burglary a week before you lost Stephan. We are here to investigate that."

"You are not looking for Stephan's killer?"

"Not officially," said Saxon.

Herr Weiss exploded. "I don't care about the break in. How can you waste time investigating that while the killers of my son are roaming the streets?"

"You have an idea who killed him?"

"The degenerate sodomites at the club. Corrupting him wasn't enough for them."

"You must understand, Herr Weiss, your son's death has been classified as legal."

"How can the death of my son be 'legal'? He was seventeen."

"He must have got mixed up in the Brownshirts' attempted coup."

"Stephan was never a Brownshirt." Weiss drove a fist down on a tabletop. "He was a member of the Hitler Youth, for God's sake. He idolized the Führer."

"I'm sure you are right, sir. As I said, we are here officially to investigate the burglary, but let me assure you that we will do everything we can to discover why he was killed. Perhaps we could start by taking a look at his room."

The similarities between Stephan's room and Johann Grau's were striking. The same pictures of public figures covered the walls, and whereas Johann preferred model aircraft, Stephan had photographs of Zeppelins. Keller checked under the mattress and found the expected health and fitness magazines. There was no tin box, empty or full. One photograph on the wall showed two youngsters posing toe-to-toe in a boxing ring, dressed in trunks, head guards, and boxing gloves. Saxon took it downstairs and showed it to Weiss.

"One of these is Stephan, I assume? Who's the other boy?"

"Yes, that's Stephan and his friend Johann Grau at the boxing club."

The name of the club, The Graf Spee, was displayed on the wall behind the ring.

#

The Graf Spee boxing academy was located in a better part of the city, not far from the Black Flamingo nightclub.

The first person they met was a janitor with a bucket and mop. Saxon asked to speak to the owner.

"Wait here," said the janitor. He scurried to a room at the back and emerged accompanied by a tall individual with a bald head.

"If you want to join the club, you'll need to talk with the boxing coach, Fritz Franck. He's not in today, but he'll be here tomorrow."

The name Fritz Franck rang serious bells in Saxon's head. Flashing his Kripo identity disk, he ran his eyes over the photographs on the wall and picked out a likely one. "Is this Herr Franck?"

"That's Fritz. That picture was taken on the day the club opened. He's a little chubbier these days."

Franck was a short, stocky type, standing beside an overweight man in clerical garb. "Who's the priest?"

"That's Pastor Berger. He died on the Night of the Long Knives." He shook his head. "They say he died of heart failure."

"You name?"

"I'm Emil Richter."

"Are you the owner of this club?"

"I'm the senior partner. How may I help you, gentlemen?"

"We're looking for this boy." Saxon pulled Grau's photograph from his pocket and showed it to Richter.

"That's young Johann Grau. He's a member of the club. What has he done?"

"Nothing that we are aware of." Saxon put the picture back in his pocket. "When did you last see him?"

"A couple of weeks ago. He was here with his good friend, Stephan Weiss."

"They were close?"

"Yes, they were the best of friends. I haven't seen Stephan for at least a week."

"Is that unusual?"

"Stephan usually comes in every day."

"Stephan's been murdered," said Keller bluntly.

Richter's hand shot to his mouth. He sat heavily on an exercise bench. "God in heaven! That's terrible. Who could have killed Stephan? He was too young to be mixed up in ... anything that would get him killed."

Streaming through the high windows, the early afternoon
sunshine fell across a huge picture of Adolf Hitler, and two smaller
pictures of the pocket battleship, the Admiral Graf Spee on its
launch day – June 30 – the day before the Night of the Long Knives.

Keller examined the pictures. "Who took the photographs?"

"Fritz did. He wangled an invitation to the launch. He has
admired the battleship since it first emerged from the drawing board.
He even named the club after it." He shook his head. "I still can't
believe it. We had hopes that Stephan might qualify for the
Olympics."

#

"So, our dead pastor was mixed up with the boxing club," said Keller,
as they climbed into the car. "And Franck has an alibi for the night of
June 30. What did you think of Emil Richter, Boss?"

"You mean you don't know who he is?"

"No, Boss."

Saxon shook his head in disbelief. "Richter is a major public
figure and philanthrope. He contributes to many youth and sports
clubs all over Germany."

"A wealthy man, so?"

"Oh yes. He's also a senior member of the SS and a personal
friend of the Führer's."

By the time they arrived back at the office, the name of the
boxing coach had emerged from the recesses of Saxon's memory.
Franck was a petty thief. He'd served time in Landsberg Prison for
burglary. He had a brother called Bernhard, also a thief. Saxon told
Keller to check the register of SS members for the two brothers.

The search took five minutes. "Fritz Franck is on the register,
Boss, but not his brother."

Saxon wasn't surprised. Times had changed. The SS were prepared to enrol all sorts of riff-raff now, to swell their ranks. They'd even taken on Glasser!

"Pull their records. I'd like to see pictures of both brothers. And ask the SS registrar for sight of the fingerprint records for Emil Richter and Fritz Franck."

"Right, Boss."

"Be polite, Keller, and be patient. You know how protective the SS can be of their records."

Keller tried every trick in the book, but he had to admit failure.

"The peacock in charge of registrations in Prinz-Albrecht Strasse wouldn't give me a glass of water if I was dying of thirst."

"Didn't I tell you to be polite and patient?"

"I was, Boss. I was polite. I was patient. But nothing worked."

"You didn't lose your temper?"

"I did, but only after all hope was gone."

#

Saxon briefed Glasser about the boxing club.

"What led you there?"

"Young Grau was an active member. The club coach is an old acquaintance of mine called Fritz Franck."

"I remember Fritz. He had a brother, too. What was he called?"

"Bernhard."

"Before the boxing club, where did you go?"

"We followed a lead that came to nothing."

"At the home of Stephan Weiss."

Finally, Saxon had confirmation that the Gestapo had been watching him.

"That house is on our list of burglaries—"

Glasser's colour deepened. "You disobeyed a direct order."

"As I said, it was on our list of burglaries."

"All right, so you visited a boxing club."

"Yes. We interviewed Emil Richter, the main sponsor."

Glasser snorted. "I never liked that Richter. He throws his money around like confetti. He's from Blumenau, you know, the same as me, but talks like a sainted aristocrat. It's a mystery to me how he ever got into the SS."

"He does a lot of good works."

"He's a slimy turd. He must have bought his way in. You can carry on, Saxon. But I want your word that you won't go near Herr Weiss again."

#

Saxon and Ruth strolled through the Nymphenburg palace park enjoying the July sunshine, along with half the population of Munich. It was Sunday afternoon. Baby Samuel was asleep in his pram, his giraffe beside him.

Saxon took charge of the pram. "Have you thought about spending time with your cousin in Austria?"

"Yes, I've thought about it, but it's not a good idea. Samuel needs his father. You've seen how much he loves you."

"He hardly ever sees me."

Ruth linked arms with Saxon. "And yet he's like an angel in your arms."

"You could go for a short time."

"How short?"

"A month. Two, maybe."

"Tell me why you want me to go."

"You've seen the brutality of the Brownshirts."

"The Führer has put a stop to that. He's removed Ernst Röhm and the other Brownshirt leaders."

Saxon placed his hand over hers on his arm. "Who do you think carried out the purge on the Brownshirts?"

"I don't know. The Führer's personal guard?"

"The Schutzstaffel, the dreaded SS."

"Why dreaded?"

"You won't see the SS causing havoc in the streets, Ruth, but they are far more dangerous than the Brownshirts. No one is safe now that they have taken over."

She looked at him sharply. "Are you telling me I'm in danger?"

"Not yet, but I don't know how much longer I can protect you."

"And Samuel?"

"There is a great Nazi storm coming and I don't want you and Samuel to be swept away."

"Now you're scaring me."

"Chancellor Dollfuss has banned the Nazis in Austria. You'll be safe there."

When they got home, they found Keller waiting at the apartment door. "Sorry to disturb your Sunday evening, Boss, but the Schupo have found Johann Grau."

"Alive?"

Keller shook his head. "He washed up on the shore of the Speichersee."

Chapter 5

Johann Grau's body was badly bloated and decomposed.

"Hardly surprising," said Saxon. "The poor guy's been in the water for two weeks."

"More like twenty days," said Keller.

Saxon looked at him. "How can you be so precise?"

"When I was with the Water Police, we pulled lots of bodies from the Rhine."

Professor Valachek ordered the uniformed Schupo to load the body into his ambulance and took it back to the morgue. Saxon and Keller followed in their police car.

"What can you tell us, Professor?" said Saxon.

Valachek tied his apron around his extended belly. "First impressions, a blow to the back of the head rendered him unconscious. He was pushed or fell into the lake. If I find water in his lungs, then he drowned. If not, the blow killed him. I'd say he's been in the water about twenty days."

Saxon glanced at Keller, who kept a straight face. "Since June 27, then. Could it have been an accident?"

"Possibly, if he drowned, but not very likely. He could have fallen and hit his head on a rock, I suppose. The head wound should tell us a lot about what hit him. We need to establish his identity before I open him up. Can you get his people in this evening? I'd like to get started as soon as possible."

Saxon asked for fingerprints from the body. The professor took a full set of prints and handed the card to Keller.

#

Saxon marvelled at how the Medical Examiner had reduced the bloating to the boy's face for Herr and Frau Grau, but the skin was flabby and a ghastly grey. Frau Grau gave one cry and collapsed. Tristan Grau caught her before she hit the floor, and Professor Valachek waved smelling salts under her nose to revive her.

Tristan Grau agreed that the body was that of his son. His calm demeanour suggested that he was in control of his feelings, but a reddening of his ears told Saxon otherwise. He took the grief-stricken father into an empty room, leaving Frau Grau in the tender care of the Medical Examiner.

"I'm sorry for your loss, Herr Grau."

As soon as Keller closed the door, Grau exploded. "Those bastards killed my boy."

"Who are you talking about, Herr Grau? Who did this to your son?"

"He fell into bad company. They turned him to abomination, and then they killed him."

"Can you give me names?"

"I don't know their names."

Keller said quietly, "You knew your son was meeting with these people, but you did nothing?"

Saxon frowned at Keller and shook his head.

Grau wailed like a soul in hell. "I spoke to him. He laughed in my face. I beat him. He laughed even louder. I locked him in his room. He climbed out the window. He risked a broken neck climbing down a drainpipe. What more could I do? I couldn't stop him."

#

On Monday morning, Saxon examined the photographs of Fritz and Bernhard Franck. Fritz was a typical slack-jawed low-life. The picture of Bernhard was 10 years old. At that time, Bernhard was a fresh-faced youngster.

When Keller arrived, Saxon sent him to find Lottie and bring her in. Keller drove to Lottie's apartment and knocked on the door.

"Who's there?"

"It's Oberassistent Keller from the Kripo. We have some questions."

"Can't it wait? I'm not dressed."

"We need you down at the station, Lottie. I'll wait while you get dressed."

It took a while, but it was worth the wait. Lottie looked even better in summer sunshine than she had in the gloom of the nightclub or the artificial light of the police station. Keller gasped when he saw her. He followed her from the apartment to the car and opened the car door for her. At the station, he ushered her into interview room one. Saxon and Glasser joined them.

"Good morning, Lottie," said Glasser. "I have to tell you that we have found the body of your friend, Johann Grau."

She covered her mouth with a hand. "His body? You mean he's dead?"

"I'm sorry to say, so, yes. I need to ask you where you last saw him."

"I told the Kommissar, the last time I saw him was on the Speichersee."

"When was that?" said Saxon.

Her brow furrowed while she thought about that. "It was a Wednesday, about two weeks ago."

"In June? The last Wednesday in June, perhaps?"

"Yes."

"June 27," said Keller.

"Where was he when you last saw him?" said Glasser.

"I left him tying up the boat in the boathouse, at about six in the evening. We had agreed to meet again, but he never turned up."

Saxon handed her a cigarette. "Where?"

"At the Black Flamingo."

Glasser said, "Wasn't he a little young for nightclubs?"

She shrugged. "He liked to dance. Where did you find him?"

"At Speichersee. He washed up on the shore," Keller said. "It looks likely that he was murdered."

"My God! You think I killed him! Is that why I'm here?"

"No, no, Fräulein." Glasser leant across the desk and patted her hand. "I'm sure you didn't kill him, but you may have seen something, someone acting suspiciously, near the lake, perhaps."

She shook her head. "I'm sorry, I saw no one."

#

While Keller drove Lottie back to her apartment, Saxon followed Glasser into his office. "Why are you letting her go? She must be our main suspect for the killing."

"Don't be ridiculous, Saxon. How could a beautiful young thing like that have committed a murder?"

"She admitted she was with Johann Grau on the lake the day he died."

"Find some real evidence." And Glasser dismissed Saxon with a wave of his fingers.

Saxon went back to his office. He called the city morgue on the telephone. "Do you have anything for us, yet, Professor?"

"Indeed I have," the professor replied. "Drop in the next time you're passing."

When Keller returned from dropping Lottie home, he and Saxon drove to the city morgue again. They found Professor Valachek in his office, enjoying a cup of coffee and an apple pastry.

Saxon smiled. "Good day, Professor."

Professor Valachek replied through a mouthful of pastry. "Sit, gentlemen."

He licked his fingers, opened a file on his desk and read from it. "As I suspected, the Grau boy died as a result of a blow to the back of his head. There was no water in his lungs. The shape of the wound suggested a metal implement of some kind – a wrench, perhaps."

"It was definitely murder, then?" said Keller.

"No question about it. It was a crushing blow, delivered with considerable force. Death would have been instantaneous. I found post-mortem rope burn marks on the body, too. I'd say whoever killed him weighed the body down with rocks. The action of the tides and the decomposition process probably worked the body loose."

"Tides? On a reservoir?"

"Why not? The moon's gravity acts on all large bodies of water."

Saxon took a moment to absorb that information. "And what about the pastor, Wilhelm Berger? Was that a heart attack as you suspected?"

"Ah, now that was an interesting case." The professor flipped through the files on his desk. "Here it is. The immediate cause of death was a sudden catastrophic cardiac arrest. There's no question that the pastor had a weak heart, but he might reasonably have expected to live several more years. Unfortunately, the poor man was the victim of a physical assault that hastened his impending heart failure."

"What kind of physical assault?"

"Somebody tried to throttle him. I found bruising around the neck and throat."

The Medical Examiner gave Saxon copies of his autopsy report on the boy and the pastor and they left the morgue.

#

The next stop was the pastor's dwelling, a modest house in a quiet suburb within walking distance of the boxing club. The journey took five minutes.

As they stepped up to the pastor's door, Keller said, "I left the pictures of the Franck brothers on your desk. Did you see them?"

"Yes, thank you, Keller."

"Did you recognize the younger one?"

"Bernhard? Yes, I know the face. Try the knocker, Keller."

"You didn't make the connection?"

"Is this one of your guessing games?"

Keller used the door knocker. "He looks a bit different now that his nose is broken, but Bernhard Franck is now the doorman at the Black Flamingo."

The door was opened by a woman in her middle years. She had been crying.

Keller flashed his badge. "Police, investigating the death of Pastor Berger."

She invited them inside. "I was beginning to wonder if anyone would ever care to find out what happened to Pastor Wilhelm. I've read in the newspaper that the killings on that night were all legally sanctioned, to put down a revolt against the government."

"I assure you Frau—"

"Frau Teeling. Pastor Wilhelm would never have been involved in anything like that. He dedicated his life to helping others. He had no interest in politics." She sniffed loudly and reached for a handkerchief in her sleeve. "He was a wonderful man. He worked tirelessly with young men who had fallen from grace, to steer them onto the path of righteousness."

"I assure you, Frau Teeling, there is no suggestion that the pastor was involved in the attempted coup."

She brightened, attempting a smile. "You mean he died of natural causes? His heart was not strong, you know."

"You said he worked with young men. Was that in the Graf Spee boxing club?"

"Yes, there and in other clubs around the city. I warned him that he was working too hard. I told him he was risking his health."

"The pastor was murdered," said Keller bluntly.

Saxon frowned at him. Frau Teeling burst into tears.

They had to wait several minutes before she was calm enough to answer more questions.

Keller asked her, "Do you live here, Frau Teeling?"

"No, my own lodgings are a few streets away."

"So the pastor was alone in this house the night he died?"

"Yes. I found his body the next morning. He was lying in the hallway."

Saxon said, "Have you any idea who might have wanted him dead? Did he have any enemies?"

She wailed again. "No. He had no enemies. Pastor Wilhelm was a walking saint. Everybody loved the man."

#

Back at the station, Saxon placed the professor's report on the dead boy into his file. The second report he put into a new manila file and marked it 'Pastor Wilhelm Berger.'

A quick glance at Bernhard Franck's picture confirmed what Keller had said. Bernhard Franck, showing the effects of a hard life, was now the doorman at the nightclub. He had been a good-looking man in his youth.

Two hours of diligent work by Keller on the station records confirmed what Saxon had suspected: Fingerprints collected from the burglaries matched those of Stephan Weiss, Johann Grau and Lottie Kleiner – taken from the glass tumbler.

"It makes sense, Boss," said Keller. "They were all small people, ideal for squeezing through small spaces. But who were they working for? They can't have been working on their own."

It was eight o'clock by that time. Saxon sent a uniformed officer out to a delicatessen to get them a quick meal.

Glasser slithered into Saxon's office. "You've made some progress, I hear."

"The professor says that Grau was murdered. And we've established that he and Stephan Weiss were involved in a number of our burglary cases, along with Lottie Kleiner."

Glasser shook his head. "I can't believe that delightful creature could be mixed up in anything so sordid as burglary."

"We'll know soon enough," said Saxon. "We are just about to pick her up again. With any luck she'll tell us who killed the two boys."

Keller went to the car pool to get a car. Glasser returned to his office. Saxon loaded his handgun and slipped it into his holster.

Glasser reappeared with his tunic buttoned. He spotted the new file on Saxon's desk. "Why the new file? I thought we agreed the pastor died of natural causes?"

"The Medical Examiner tells us the good pastor's heart failed when someone attempted to strangle him."

"So he was murdered? Do you have any suspects?"

"None."

Keller arrived rattling a set of car keys, and Glasser followed Saxon through the door. Keller took the wheel. Glasser sat in the front passenger seat and Saxon sat in the back, feeling like a minor character in his own investigation.

#

The apartment block was guarded by a stern-looking janitor. Once again, Glasser used his Kripo disk to gain entry. They knocked on Lottie's apartment door. No one answered.

"Open it," said Glasser.

The janitor searched his bundle of keys for the right one. After two unsuccessful tries, Glasser said, "Break it down, Keller."

Keller took a step back, but before he could put his boot through the door, Saxon tried the handle. The door swung open. They stepped inside.

Saxon had seen what burglars had done to dozens of homes, but he'd never seen anything like this. The whole place had been ransacked. There was debris everywhere. Steeling himself for what they might find, he drew his gun.

They searched the apartment, but the intruder was gone, and they found no sign of the girl, alive or dead.

"Thank God." Glasser shuddered. "I was sure we were going to find her in the bedroom or the bathroom."

Saxon asked the janitor how such a thing could have happened. Had he let any strangers into the building in the last few days?

"No, no one."

Hadn't he heard anything? Whoever did this must have made a lot of noise.

The janitor gave an indifferent shrug. "I'm not on guard 24 hours of every day. I have to eat. I have to buy food. A determined criminal could easily get inside."

Saxon examined the apartment door. It had been broken open.

Keller looked around in disgust. "Another burglary for our files, Boss."

"This was no burglary," said Saxon. "Whoever did this was searching for something."

"Who were they, Boss, and what were they searching for?"

"And what have they done with the lovely Lottie?" said Glasser.

#

They crammed into the car again.

This time, Glasser took the back seat. "Is it far?" he said.

"The north side of the city, sir. We should be there in thirty minutes."

"Use your, bell, man. Get us there in fifteen."

Keller put the bell on and they raced across the city.

At the door to the nightclub, Glasser flashed his Kripo disk. Bernhard the doorman stood aside to let them in. They stood near the bar while their eyes adjusted to the gloom. The same waitress as before appeared and asked what they would like to drink.

"Nothing," said Glasser. "We're here to speak with Lottie Kleiner."

The waitress smiled at Glasser. "If you stand at the bar you must order a drink, sir."

Glasser flashed his Kripo disk at her. "Is Lottie Kleiner here?"

"I don't think she's in tonight, sir. I'll check." She scuttled away.

Glasser ran his eyes over the men at the bar and the dancers. "What kind of club is this?"

The man behind the bar responded, "It's a men's club. Can I get you something to drink?"

"We're looking for Lottie Kleiner. Is she in the club?" said Saxon.

"Lottie's not here tonight. You should talk to her boyfriend, Hermann. He's over there." He nodded toward a table occupied by two young men.

Glasser led the way to the table.

"Which one of you is Hermann?" he said.

One of the young men got up and disappeared into the crowd. The second man peered at them. "I'm Hermann."

All three policemen sat at the table with Hermann.

"We're looking for Lottie Kleiner," said Glasser. "You are her boyfriend?"

Hermann smiled and a strange sense of déjà vu ran down Saxon's spine. "You could say that. Why do you ask?"

Glasser flashed his Kripo disk again. "We have some questions for her. Where can we find her?"

"She's at home. I can give you the address."

"We've been there," said Keller. "Where else could she be?"

Hermann shrugged.

#

Back at base, Glasser said, "Degenerates will do just as well as Jews for quota purposes. We will raid that club and arrest everyone. But do nothing until I've spoken to my contact in the newspapers. *Beobachter* will certainly take it and *Der Stürmer* may be interested."

Saxon was horrified by the prospect of a raid on the club. Everyone arrested would be sent to the labour camps. He pointed out that Glasser had been seen entering the club.

Glasser fixed Saxon with his pin eyes. "What's your point?"

"It might be suggested that you are one of them. You know how mud sticks."

Glasser grunted. "Speaking to undesirables is part of my job."

"Indeed," said Saxon.

"You never married, did you, sir?" said Keller.

"That's insubordination. What are you implying?"

"I'm implying nothing, sir. But you know what the newspapers are like. It's all a matter of appearances."

Chapter 6

Early Tuesday morning, Lottie called Keller on the telephone. She was in tears. "My apartment has been destroyed."

"We saw that last night. We were looking for you. Where were you?"

"I was with friends. What can I do, Kommissar?"

Keller said nothing to correct her mistake. 'Kommissar Keller' had a certain ring to it. "Do you have somewhere to stay?"

"One of my friends will make room for me. But I don't feel safe. I'm sure this has something to do with the deaths of Johann and Stephan. What if I'm next?"

"Come into the station after nine this morning. We'll see what needs to be done."

When Lottie arrived at the station, Keller took her straight into Saxon's office. She was wearing a white shirt and dark pants that gave her a slightly dominant look that Saxon found appealing. He gave her a cigarette. Keller lit it for her. She crossed her legs.

She had been crying. Her eye makeup was smudged, her eyes red-rimmed, and Saxon noticed a tremor in her hands.

He said, "You told Keller that you thought there might be a connection between the destruction to your apartment and the deaths of the two boys, Johann Grau and Stephan Weiss. Can you tell me why?"

She shrugged. "We three were close. We did everything together."

"Including burglaries?" She opened her mouth to object, but he held up a hand to stop her. "No point in denying it, Fräulein, we have found all three sets of fingerprints at the scenes of several burglaries. Would you like to tell us who you were working for?"

Her lips closed in a tight line. She leaned forward to tap ash from her cigarette into Saxon's ashtray.

Keller said, "Was it your boyfriend, Hermann?"

"No, no, Hermann had nothing to do with it."

"Who, then?" said Saxon.

She took a moment before stubbing her cigarette out in the ashtray. "I don't deny it, Kommissar. We were led astray by an older man that we all admired."

"The name of this older man?"

She gave no answer.

"We know it was Fritz Franck, the boxing coach," said Saxon.

She blushed. "You must understand we only did it to please him."

"Not for the money?" said Keller.

Saxon spoke quietly. "Tell me how that worked."

"He told us which houses were empty. We would get in wherever we could. We stole jewellery and small ornaments. Anything that might be valuable."

Saxon offered her another cigarette. She took one, and Keller lit it again. "He gave us very little money. Enough for cigarettes and an occasional glass of wine."

Saxon said, "Tell me why you think the murders of the two boys might be connected to these burglaries."

"I didn't say that, Kommissar. Johann, Stephan and I were very close. They were both murdered. When my apartment was searched, I thought—"

"Searched? Your apartment was searched? What do you think they were searching for?"

"I'm sorry, I have no idea."

Keller said, "Did they take anything?"

"It's impossible to say. You saw the place. Everything was destroyed."

Saxon said, "You will be charged with breaking into people's houses and theft. You will be held here until we have apprehended Franck."

Keller called a uniformed patrolman who escorted Lottie to the cells.

#

They drove to the boxing club. The old janitor barred their way, but they pushed past him without ceremony.

"There he goes!" Keller shouted.

Saxon caught a glimpse of a stocky figure sprinting through a door at the back of the gym. Keller gave chase. Saxon left through the front door, circled around toward the back, and came face to face with Fritz Franck in a narrow passage at the side of the building.

Kommissar Saxon held up a palm. "Give yourself up, Franck. There's nowhere you can go, nowhere you can hide."

Franck's eyes narrowed. He pulled out a knife and waved it at Saxon. "Stand aside!"

"Drop the knife, man. I'm a police officer. Use that on me and they'll string you up from the nearest tree."

Franck took a step closer. "I said stand aside, *Bulle*."

Saxon reached inside his jacket for his gun, but before he could draw it, Franck was on him. They crashed to the ground together. Saxon was no match for the stocky boxer. It was all he could do to hold Franck's knife hand at bay.

"Drop the weapon and stand up." The command was accompanied by a loud click.

Keller stood over the boxing coach, the barrel of his gun pressing against the back of his head. Everything froze. The one thought in Saxon's head was that if Keller fired, the bullet would probably pass right through Franck's head and kill both of them.

Franck dropped the knife. Saxon scrambled out from under him, and Keller put Franck in handcuffs.

#

They took the boxing coach back to the police station and put him in interview room one. Saxon began the interrogation by accusing him of organizing the burglaries and selling the stolen goods. Franck stubbornly refused to answer. Saxon told him that Dieter Peters had been found in possession of a significant amount of the stolen property and had named Franck as his supplier. Franck said nothing.

Saxon told him that he had a confession from one of the people who carried out the burglaries. They had named him as the organizer. Franck snorted.

"Nothing to say?"

Franck crossed his arms high on his chest.

"In that case, Fritz Franck, I am charging you with the double murder of two of your accomplices, Stephan Weiss and Johann Grau."

Franck jumped to his feet. "God in heaven! I never killed anybody."

"I think you did."

"Why would I kill my team?"

"So you admit the boys carried out the burglaries for you?"

"Yes, yes, the boys helped with the jobs, but you can't put their killings on my shoulders."

"You paid them for what they stole?"

"I paid them to do the jobs."

"How much?"

"A few Marks."

Keller said, "We found 3,000 Marks in Johann Grau's house."

Franck's wide-eyed amazement looked genuine. "I never paid him anything like that."

"Then who did? And who do think might have killed them?" said Saxon.

"And why?" said Keller.

\#

It was dark by the time they'd finished interrogating the boxing coach. They charged him with multiple counts of burglary and locked him in a cell. They charged Lottie with the minor offence of aiding in the execution of the burglaries.

"I'm letting you go, under license," said Saxon. "Do you have somewhere safe to spend the night?"

"I think so."

"We'd like to see you again in the morning. Can I rely on you to come back in?"

She batted her eyelashes. "Yes, of course, Kommissar."

He put on his stern face. "I want to see you here at nine o'clock. If you make us come and find you, the charges will be more severe."

"I understand."

When she'd gone, Keller fetched two cups of coffee and a couple of apple pastries. Saxon and Keller settled down in Saxon's office to discuss the case.

Saxon lit a cigarette. "We must assume that the money in Grau's possession and the cash that paid for Herr Weiss's automobile didn't come from the boys' burgling activities. They must have had another source of funds."

"Blackmail, perhaps?" said Keller.

"My thought exactly," said Saxon. "The boys shared many activities. The burglaries, the boxing, and probably the nightclub, as well. That place is a den of iniquity. Herr Weiss blamed the people there for corrupting his boy."

"He could be right, Boss."

"That seems likely. Let us assume that the boys were engaged in unnatural practices with some pervert from the nightclub..."

"And they decided to blackmail whoever that was."

"Yes. I think Lottie was involved somehow. Whatever proof the boys had – photographs, probably – we must assume the pervert was searching for that in Lottie's apartment."

"The three of them were close, Boss. Lottie said that. And we know they were all involved in Franck's burglaries. Do you think Lottie's boyfriend was involved too?"

"More than likely. He was certainly small and slim enough for the work." Saxon stood and began prowling around the office. "Whoever killed Stephan Weiss must be a member of the SS. He had prior knowledge of what was going to happen on the night of June 30, and he hoped the killing would be lost among the general carnage."

"Fritz Franck is a member of the SS, Boss."

"Yes, and so is the rich philanthrope, Emil Richter."

"How does the pastor's death fit into all this, Boss?"

"Heaven knows, Keller. It's difficult to see a connection."

They called it a night, and Saxon made his way home.

#

Once again, Ruth was juggling a crying baby with one arm while preparing a bottle for him with the other. Saxon took the baby from her.

She smiled at him. "Samuel said his first big word. He said 'giraffe.'"

Saxon held the infant in front of him. "Did you, little man? Did you say a big word like that?"

Samuel gurgled.

Ruth picked up the toy giraffe and handed it to Samuel. "What is this? Samuel? What do you call this?"

Samuel blew bubbles.

"Giraffe. Say it for your papa, Samuel. Say giraffe. Gi-raffe."

Samuel smiled and broke wind.

"He really did say it. I know you don't believe me."

"I believe you, Ruth. Give him time, I'm sure he'll say it again."

Ruth took the baby back and he burst into tears. She shook her head. "He really loves his papa." She put the bottle in his mouth, and Samuel stopped screaming.

Lying in bed that night, Saxon listened to Ruth's rhythmical breathing beside him. He recalled what Ruth had said about Samuel. He was like two people in one body, screaming in his mother's arms, but quiet in his father's.

Saxon sat bolt upright in the bed.

That was why Lottie had never been in the BDM, and why they had never seen Hermann and Lottie in the same place together. Lottie and Hermann were one and the same person! Whatever unnatural practices the boys had been up to, Hermann must have been involved as well. Hermann could be in mortal danger.

He slipped from the bed and put his clothes on. He left the apartment as quietly as he could and found a taxi to take him to the Black Flamingo nightclub.

The doorman made no attempt to prevent him from entering. He went straight to the bar and asked the bartender if Hermann or Lottie were in the club.

"I haven't seen either of them," said the barman.

Saxon ran back up the stairs to the street and hailed a passing taxi. "Take me to the Graf Spee boxing club."

"It's not far," said the driver. "You could walk there in ten minutes."

Saxon flashed his Kripo badge. "Take me there."

The boxing club was locked up for the night. Saxon ran his eyes over the building from the opposite side of the road and caught a fleeting glimpse of a light upstairs in a third-floor window.

He ran to the back of the building, used the butt of his gun to smash a small pane of glass, reached in and opened the door. Moonlight flooding through the windows helped him to find a staircase at the rear of the gym. Gun in hand, he ran up the stairs.

He reached the third floor and took a moment to get his bearings. Then he heard a sound and moved toward it. He was in a dark corridor with doors leading to rooms left and right. He carried on down the corridor, ears tuned to pick up the slightest sounds.

When the sound came, it was not what he expected, a scream of pain and anguish, the like of which he had never heard before, coming from one of the rooms he'd already passed. He drew his gun, moved back to the door, turned the handle and flung it open.

Chapter 7

Weak moonlight from the window lit the figure of Hermann, strapped to a chair in the middle of a room. He was nearly naked, blood trailing from his nose and the corner of his eyes.

Emil Richter stood over him, wearing a single boxing glove.

Saxon levelled his handgun at the big man. "Leave him, Richter. Drop the glove."

Richter stepped back. The glove hit the bare floorboards with a clunk. It was weighted. "This is not what it seems, Kommissar."

"Face the wall. Put your hands behind your back." Saxon reached for his handcuffs. "I'm arresting you for serious assault."

Richter stood facing the wall. "This is nothing but a piece of theatrical foreplay. You've heard of the Marquis de Sade?"

Saxon secured his prisoner with the handcuffs. "Explain it to the judge."

He bent down to free Hermann from his restraints. "Are you all right?"

Hermann spoke in a strangled voice. "Thank God you found me. He killed Stephan and Johann. He would have killed me, too. Behind you, Kommissar!"

Saxon straightened his back, drawing his gun.

Too late.

The point of a knife broke the skin under Saxon's chin. "Drop the gun, *Bulle*, or I'll slit your throat where you stand."

Saxon recognized the voice and foul breath of Bernhard Franck, the doorman from the nightclub, the boxing coach's brother. He dropped his gun. It clattered onto the floorboards.

Bernhard placed a hand on Saxon's back and pushed him forward. "Now you face the wall."

Saxon stood beside Richter, facing the wall. "You're only making matters worse for both of you, Bernhard. Put the knife down and let me do my job."

Bernhard picked up the gun. He searched Saxon's pockets, removed the keys to the handcuffs and freed Richter.

Richter secured Saxon's hands with his own handcuffs. "Good boy, Bernhard," he said.

"This is madness, Richter," said Saxon. "Assaulting the boy is bad enough but interfering with a police officer is much more serious."

Richter turned to his companion in crime. "Shoot him. Shoot the *Bulle*, Bernhard."

The doorman made no move to comply. Wearing his trilby, he stood with his arms by his sides, the gun in one hand, the knife in the other. His broken nose looked grotesque in the shadowy moonlight.

"What's on your mind, now? Shoot him. He has seen too much. We have to get rid of him."

Bernhard's face contorted, as if wrestling with conflicting thoughts. "I – I don't think..."

"What? Haven't I told you before? Leave the thinking to me. Now do what I ask. Then you can help me get what I need from pretty boy, here."

The doorman stepped toward Saxon. "I'm sorry," he said, pointing the gun at Saxon's chest.

Facing the barrel of his own gun, Saxon's mouth dried. "Don't do this, Bernhard. You're not a murderer."

Bernhard cocked the gun. Then he swivelled on his heel and fired.

Richter gave a strangled cry and crumpled to the floor, blood pouring from a hole in his chest. Bernhard dropped the gun and fell to his knees, cradling Richter's head in his lap.

Tears flowed down Bernhard's face. "I'm sorry, Emil. Please forgive me. You know I love you. I've always loved you."

Richter gurgled once, and the light of life left his eyes.

"Take off these handcuffs," said Saxon.

He got no response.

"Can you hear me, Franck? Set me free."

Hermann said, "Remove the handcuffs, Bernhard. It's over."

#

Hermann went to a bathroom to tidy up his face. When he returned, he was transformed into the voluptuous Lottie, dressed in a shiny, tight-fitting blue dress, the blond wig flowing across her shoulders, stunning as ever, despite the facial bruising.

Saxon used the telephone in the club office to call Keller. Keller arrived in a car within 30 minutes. As they emerged from the boxing club, blood-red skies over Munich welcomed them with a glorious summer sunrise.

Back at the station, they interviewed Bernhard Franck first, but got nothing from him. His mind was gone. All he would say was, "I used to be his pretty boy," over and over.

Lottie told them the whole sordid story. Richter was a sexual deviant with a preference for young men and teenage boys. He liked to dress up, and he encouraged the boys to do the same.

Three of his victims, Johann, Stephan and Hermann had got together and used a hidden camera to take incriminating photographs of the perverted philanthrope. They demanded money for their silence, and Richter had paid them in exchange for the pictures and the negatives.

The boys held back some of the pictures, but when they tried to visit the well a second time, Richter turned on them, resorting to burglary in search of the photographs, and eventually, to murder.

Keller filled in the rest. "He killed Johann Grau first, threw him in the lake, weighed down with rocks. The boy should never have resurfaced from his watery grave. Then he shot Stephan Weiss. As a member of the SS, Richter would have had advance knowledge of the Führer's plans for the Night of the Long Knives. He chose that night in to make it easier to cover up his crime."

"I assume that Richter never found the rest of the incriminating pictures," said Saxon. "Is that why he was beating you?"

Lottie sniffed, her fingers playing with a strand of her hair. "Yes, but I don't have the pictures. I'm sure he would have killed me if you hadn't come to the rescue and Bernhard hadn't turned on Richter the way he did."

"So where are the photographs?" said Keller.

"Stephan had them. I thought Richter must have recovered them when Stephan died."

Word of Lottie's rescue had reached Glasser, and he joined Saxon and Keller in the interview room. He gushed at Lottie, grabbing her hand. "I'm so pleased you weren't seriously injured, my dear. It pains me to think of the way that brute, Richter, beat you. How are you feeling now?"

"Show him, Lottie," said Saxon, to spare Glasser any more embarrassment.

Lottie removed her wig. She pulled down the front of her dress, exposing a pair of rubber breasts.

"Meet Hermann," said Saxon.

The blood drained from Glasser's face.

Keller stood facing the wall with a hand clamped over his mouth. Glasser left the room without a word. Once he was outside, Keller and Saxon burst into raucous laughter. Hermann joined in.

Saxon asked Hermann about the pastor. "Was he involved in these deviant activities?

"Oh no," said Hermann. "Pastor Berger was a saint. He did what he could for us boys."

#

"So who killed the pastor?" said Keller, after Lottie/Hermann had gone.

Saxon lit a cigarette and took a long drag. "Whoever it was hated him enough to try and strangle him to death in his own house."

"I think Richter killed the pastor, Boss."

"Why would he? The pastor brought a patina of respectability to the boxing club."

"Suppose the pastor stumbled across the perversions and had to be silenced."

Saxon shook his head. "Weiss would be my guess. Remember what he said. He said the degenerate sodomites from the club corrupted his son. What if he was talking about the boxing club, not the nightclub?"

"That sounds like he knew what was going on, Boss, but why kill the pastor? The pastor had nothing to do with any of the perversions."

"Those missing photographs are the key to everything, Keller. We need to locate them. Get us a car."

While Keller ran to the car pool, Saxon slipped out and bought a copy of the *Völkischer Beobachter* newspaper. Richter's picture dominated the front page. The inside pages had pictures of the boxing club and the story of the philanthrope's deviant practices with the boys. Saxon guessed the boxing club janitor must have spilled the beans.

#

The Herr Weiss who opened the door was a pale shadow of the man they'd met before. They followed him into the parlour, where the morning edition of *Völkischer Beobachter* lay scattered on the floor.

"Have you seen what they're saying about my son?"

Keller said, "Are you denying it?"

Weiss shook his head. "How can I deny it? I know what Stephan did. He was young and impressionable."

Saxon said, "You knew what Stephan and his friends were doing with Emil Richter?"

"I worked it out."

Saxon nodded. "And you knew the boys were extorting money from Richter."

"What? No. Who told you that?"

Saxon held out a hand. "Give me the photographs."

"I don't have any photographs."

Keller said, "Is that your Horch V8 outside?"

"Yes, it's mine."

Saxon said, "Where did you get the money to buy that, Herr Weiss?"

"I earned it."

"Working as a labourer on the railways?"

"I saved the money over several years. What are you suggesting, Kommissar?"

Saxon lit a cigarette. "I'm suggesting that you extorted a lot of money from Richter and used it to buy that car."

Weiss's rising panic was visible on his mousey face. "I knew nothing about it until... afterwards."

Keller said, "Since the Enabling Act, blackmail is a capital offense, Herr Weiss. Give us the pictures or we'll have to charge you."

"I don't have them, I swear."

Saxon said, "We can get a warrant to search the house if we have to. Empty your pockets."

"All right, all right." Weiss opened his jacket, pulled out an envelope, and handed it to Saxon.

Saxon emptied the envelope onto the table. There were three photographs. One showed Richter engaged in a lewd act with Johann Grau, dressed as a nurse. The other two showed Richter with Stephan Weiss. Richter was wearing a clerical gown. Stephan was dressed as a fireman, complete with brass helmet. In all of the pictures, Richter's face was obscured.

Keller said, "Richter's face is not clear in these pictures, Boss."

Saxon tossed his cigarette into the fireplace. "So tell us why you murdered Pastor Wilhelm Berger, Herr Weiss."

"I killed no one, I swear, Kommissar."

"You found these photographs, saw a large man in clerical garb, and you thought the pastor was corrupting your son. Is that why you killed him?"

"I swear it wasn't me."

"Who, then?" said Saxon.

"I showed the photographs to Tristan Grau."

They put Weiss in handcuffs and placed him in the car. Then they drove to the Grau home.

Keller hammered on the door. Frau Grau opened it. She had been crying again. She told Keller that her husband had gone to work in the town hall.

The 12 noon Glockenspiel display was just starting when they arrived in Marienplatz. The square was crowded with tourists, all craning their necks and pointing upward.

Saxon assumed they were watching the musical display until he looked up and saw Tristan Grau sitting on a third-floor window ledge.

Saxon and Keller ran up the stairs to the third floor, and quickly located the right room. Saxon approached Grau, now standing on the window ledge.

"Don't do this, Tristan. Think of your poor wife. She's lost a son. You can't inflict any more grief on her."

"Don't try to stop me," said Grau, "I have no choice. I have committed a grievous sin against God."

"Pastor Berger was an old man. He had a weak heart."

"I know. And my action hastened his death."

Saxon took a couple of steps closer. "Why did you attack him?"

"Stay back, Kommissar. I was angry. When I saw those pictures, I thought he was the one who corrupted Stephan. But I was wrong. I killed the wrong man."

Out of the corner of his eye, Saxon saw Keller circling toward Grau.

Saxon moved to his left to distract Grau from Keller. "You made a mistake, Tristan. I'm sure God will forgive you, but not if you take your own life."

Keller lunged toward Grau, wrapping his arms around his legs.

"I have him, Boss—" And Grau vanished.

The cries of horror from the tourists in the square below coincided with the triple cockcrow signalling the end of the Glockenspiel noonday display.

#

Glasser demanded that they charge Weiss with murder.

"I have no evidence that he killed anyone," said Saxon.

"Well, charge him with something. I have to have something to report to Gestapo *Hauptamt*."

"You can tell them that Richter killed the two boys and Grau killed the pastor. Surely, two dead murderers is a fine result. It saves the Fatherland the cost of two expensive trials."

"There is that, I suppose. And we can charge Bernhard Franck with Richter's death."

"We can, but no one would blame him, given Richter's heinous crimes. And besides, Franck is unfit to stand trial. But you can add both Franck brothers to your quota of undesirables."

Glasser shook his head. "You can forget about the quota. I've decided not to put my name forward for the Schutzstaffel training school."

Saxon was relieved. Ruth and Samuel were no longer at immediate risk.

#

Bouncing Samuel on his knee that evening, Saxon tried to imagine what he would do if he discovered that his own son had been corrupted by an older man.

"Papa," said Samuel, handing his giraffe to his father.

Saxon smiled at him. "Thank you, Samuel."

Assuming he was certain who the defiler was, would he kill him? Yes, he would. Would he be prepared to hang to rid the world of a child molester?

"Giraffe," said Samuel, clear as a bell.

No question about it.

THE END – QUEEN SACRIFICE

CASE 3 – THE WHITE KNIGHT

A Kommissar Saxon Novel

First published April 2019
Copyright 2019 © JJ Toner Publishing

PROLOGUE

Munich – December, 1935

Saxon stood by the window watching a light flurry of snow descend on Piper Strasse. Orange, red and yellow Christmas lights from the windows of the houses opposite gave the scene a magical look. Ruth sat by the fire, mending a toddler's coat that she'd picked up from a street market.

"Isn't there anything we can do?" she said.

"Nothing." He looked at her. He loved her and he would have given his right arm to take away her distress. "Even German citizens have no right to question the law."

"That's ridiculous. I'm just as much a German citizen as you are. I was born here. My parents were Germans. My grandparents on both sides were German."

"I know, my darling, but these new laws have brushed all that aside. Jews are no longer citizens."

She bit a thread and turned the garment over on her knee. "What about Samuel? Surely they can't deny him his birthright."

They'd had a bruising argument over Samuel's circumcision shortly after he was born. Neither of them wanted to dredge all that up again, but he knew it was on her mind. He made no reply, but settled into his armchair by the fire.

"And what are we going to do when he reaches school age? Where can we send him?"

"There are Jewish schools..."

"The nearest one is half-way across the city. How am I supposed to get him there?"

They'd had these discussions several times since September when the first of the laws had been passed. He lit a cigarette, filled his lungs, and blew smoke into the fire.

"And what about this ban on marriages between you *Aryans* and us Jews? What will that mean to us?"

"We are legally married. Nothing can change that."

She held up the coat to show him a torn pocket. "Look at this. How on earth does a toddler tear his clothes?" The line of her jaw told him the conversation was far from over.

She arranged the coat on her knee and began working on the torn pocket. "What makes you think we'd be better off in Austria?"

"There's no Nazi Party there. It's the perfect place to go."

She dropped her hands in her lap and looked at him. "Why can't you *do* something? You're a highly regarded police Kommissar, surely you can get them to make an exception for your family."

"I've told you, Ruth, there's nothing I can do. It's hopeless."

She busied herself with her needle and thread. There was a long pause.

"Very well, have it your way. I'll write to Cousin Rudolf. Assuming he agrees to take us, we'll leave after Samuel's birthday, but only on one condition." She folded the coat on her knees. Their eyes locked through the smoke from his cigarette. "You must come with us."

PART 1

Chapter 1

Six months later: June, 1936

Kriminalkommissar Saxon lingered in his office. It was well past the end of the working day, but he was reluctant to abandon his familiar desk and his comfortable chair. He preferred the gloom of the police station to the glaring evening sunshine. A cold half-chicken was the only comfort waiting for him in his apartment.

For two years the streets of Munich had been calm, the sounds of rampaging SA squads and the screams of their victims replaced by raucous laughter from the beer cellars. He preferred the creak of familiar floorboards and the ticking of the clock on the wall to Bavarian oompah music.

He still had plenty of work to keep him busy. Arson was a continuing problem. The most serious recent case had cost the lives of four members of one family; only the father had survived, and he was being held in a cell as the primary suspect.

"Glad I caught you, Kommissar." The skeletal figure of Kriminalrat Glasser hovered in the doorway. "What are you working on?"

"The Kluge fire."

"Any progress to report?" Glasser's position was complicated. Having been promised a position with the Gestapo, he had assumed the vacant role of Kriminaldirektor as an interim measure.

"None. I'm hoping the father will confess if we hold him overnight."

Glasser smiled his rictus smile. "And if that doesn't work, you can always beat him to a pulp."

123

Saxon straightened his back. He would never tolerate strong-arm methods in his police station.

Glasser swayed toward him, waving a palm. "Joking. I was joking."

Glasser must have been at the schnapps. He never joked.

Reaching the safety of Saxon's desk, Glasser used it to prop himself up. "I've had a call from the SS."

"What do they want this time?"

Glasser responded with a shake of his head. "Not the Munich SS, Berlin headquarters."

The dreaded Gestapo office! He had never been there, but every policeman had heard the horror stories. "Are congratulations in order?"

"Sorry to disappoint you, Saxon. They want you up there for a special job."

"The SS in Berlin want me? What for?"

"They didn't say. They asked for you by name, so it must be important."

His immediate reaction was to resist. But his mind went numb. He needed time to think, to formulate a rational objection.

Glasser turned to leave. "You're to report to SS-Standartenführer Karl Ulman."

"How long will the posting last?"

Would I have to move out of my apartment? He thought.

"Ask the Standartenführer when you arrive. They want you on station by Monday 8:30 am sharp. Leave the arson file on my desk." And Glasser was gone.

He had four days! His mind was racing now. The thought of his name being bandied about at Prinz-Albrecht Strasse gave him goosebumps. And what could be so urgent that they needed him in Berlin at such short notice?

#

Piperstrasse was a playground that evening, full of laughing children enjoying the warm evening, many on bicycles. The apartment was unbearably hot. He opened both windows. Then he took the cold chicken from the larder, added two slices of yesterday's bread and sat down to his meal. A couple of bluebottles flew in through a window, heading straight for the chicken. He swore and flapped at them to keep them away. They backed off but hung around.

The food disappeared quickly. He tidied up and lit a cigarette. Then he steered the flies back outside before closing both windows.

Watching the children in the street below, it struck him that he had few ties in Munich. A trip to Berlin might be just the tonic his flagging career needed. What would it matter to Ruth and Samuel where he was stationed?

He found some paper and pen, took a photograph of Ruth and Samuel from his wallet, placed it on the table, and began to write.

Piper Strasse, June 18, 1936

Dear Ruth,

I hope you and Samuel are well and enjoying the Austrian summer. I miss you both, of course.

I have been assigned to Berlin. I won't know what the job is until I get there on Monday next, but I'm hoping I'll be able to return to Munich before too long.

I will write again as soon as I can.

Take care. Kisses for Samuel.

Your loving husband,

Roland

Chapter 2

Sunday June 21

He posted the letter on his way to the train station on Sunday evening.

The last train from Munich to Erfurt was packed with families returning home after their holidays. He found a seat by the door of a second-class carriage. From the moment the train lurched into life, he kept his nose in a book, doing his best to ignore the children running up and down the corridor, opening and closing the compartment door and tripping over his feet.

One frazzled mother apologised to him. "I do what I can to keep order, but it's impossible. I hope you understand, sir. Do you have children?"

"No, I'm not married." He lifted his hat and gave her a smile before returning to his book.

His sole intention was to discourage further discussion, but he hated the lie. He had denied Ruth and Samuel, and he hated himself for it.

The train rattled through the countryside at an alarming pace, its carriages juddering and rocking from side to side. The window provided a small measure of relief from the heat. The other passengers kept it open, despite an ingress of eye-smarting soot from the locomotive. The cattle in the fields, standing like statues under lone trees or in clusters around water troughs, looked every bit as miserable in the unrelenting heat as the occupants of the train.

They had to change trains at Erfurt. He took the opportunity to buy a newspaper and scoured it for anything that might explain the reason for his reassignment. There was nothing. The whole newspaper was peppered with news about German athletes and the upcoming Olympic Games.

The fast train from Erfurt to Berlin made the journey in good time, stopping only at Leipzig, and arriving at Anhalter Bahnhof at 11:32 pm, three minutes ahead of schedule.

He found a small hotel in Bernberg Strasse, within easy walking distance of Prinz-Albrecht-Strasse, and asked for a room for the night.

The young man at the reception desk recognised his Bavarian accent and adopted an officious tone.

"How long will you be staying?"

"I'm not sure. I'll take the room for one night and let you know if I need it for longer." He signed the registration book and handed it back.

The receptionist peered at the book. "Will you require breakfast, Herr Saxon?"

"Yes, I think so."

"That will be seven Reichsmarks, payable in advance."

Saxon paid him the money.

The man snapped his fingers. "Let me have your identity papers. We are obliged to notify the police whenever anyone takes a room."

"Of course." He handed over his identity card and flashed his Kripo badge. "What is your name?"

The man blanched. "M... Manfred Püttner."

Saxon flipped open his notepad and made a note. "You have a key for me, Herr Püttner?"

Püttner gave him a key. Saxon thanked him and set off with his suitcase to find his room.

The room was on the second floor, a faulty street lamp casting a strange, flickering light through the window. He barely had time to shed his clothes, slide his case under the single bed and climb into it before exhaustion overcame him and he fell asleep.

#

Monday June 22

It wasn't until he saw it in daylight the next morning that he realised how small the room was. There was just enough room for the bed, a kitchen chair, and a rickety card table with a jug of water and basin on top. He dressed quickly and pushed his case back under the bed. There was no time for breakfast; it was after 8 am.

The Gestapo building on Prinz-Albrecht Strasse was an impressive structure, its 20-foot high portico topped by two statues of seated figures. Inside, a broad hall sported an elaborate crystal chandelier hanging over an ornate staircase. Male and female figures in grey or black uniforms bustled about carrying files and bundles of papers.

He was surprised at the low level of security. A man at a desk was all the security he could see. Once past this desk, the whole building would be open to him. Even in his modest police station in Munich, they had a desk sergeant behind a counter to handle visitors.

"Herr Saxon?" He turned to find a middle-aged woman, with grey hair in a bun and a matching field grey uniform, smiling up at him. "Follow me, Kommissar." She strode toward the stairs.

In spite of the heat outside, the corridors were as cool as an icehouse or an undertaker's parlour. They stopped on the third floor at a door with a frosted glass panel. She pushed it open, and he stepped inside. He was in an anteroom occupied by a young adjutant, who scurried into the inner office before emerging to usher Saxon inside.

A cleanshaven man bald as a billiard ball, with heavy grey eyebrows sat at a desk. He wore the black uniform of the SS, an Iron Cross pinned to his breast pocket.

"Herr Ulman?"

"Come in, Saxon. Take a seat."

He sat facing the massive oak desk flanked by two swastika flags. The desk was covered in a chaos of papers and folders. More papers sat in piles on top of a file cabinet in a corner. A framed picture of a stern Adolf Hitler glowered down at them from over the doorframe.

"Do you have any questions before we start? You came up last night, I presume? You found somewhere to stay?"

Saxon crossed his arms. He was aware of the negative signal this conveyed, but the journey had been tiring and he hadn't had a lot of sleep on the lumpy mattress in his hotel room. "May I know why you've brought me here, sir?"

"You will be taking command of a troop of uniformed officers on a special task. Their previous kommandant has been relieved of his duty."

There were two red flags right there. First, command of a troop of uniformed officers was no job for an experienced criminal investigator, and second, what had the previous man done to lose the job?

Ulman reacted to the look of alarm on Saxon's face. "Don't look so worried, man. It's merely a temporary assignment. And there will be much to be gained from making a success of it. Reichsführer Himmler has a personal interest in the matter. He himself was responsible for removing your predecessor."

A classic double-edged sword. No one in Berlin wanted to take this on. "How many men in the troop, sir? And what is this special task?"

"Twenty men, all highly experienced. I will explain the task in due course."

"Why was I chosen for this position?"

"Kriminalrat Glasser recommended you. He tells me you're his finest officer."

So Glasser lied. He wasn't surprised. No doubt Glasser recognised it for the poisoned chalice it was and relished throwing him into the snake pit.

"May I ask who my predecessor was, and why he was dismissed?"

Ulman waved a hand to brush off the trivial query. "His name was Zimmermann. As for the reason why he had to be reassigned, that need not concern you. Let's just say he fell short in his duties."

Chapter 3

Ulman got to his feet and led him back down the stairs to the front of the building, where a black Mercedes was waiting, its engine running. The SS-man opened the back door and climbed in. Saxon circled the car and got in on the other side.

The interior of the car was uncomfortably warm. Ulman opened his window and Saxon did the same, but with little effect.

They drove west. He was unfamiliar with the city, but he recognized the Tiergarten and the entrance to the zoological gardens. Increasing numbers of signs on the lampposts told him where they were headed.

"You must have guessed where we're going by now," said the SS-man.

The car drew up on the vast concourse directly in front of the Olympic Stadium. Ulman allowed him a moment to admire the twin towers at the entrance. Saxon used the opportunity to peel his pants from his sweaty legs.

"Magnificent, isn't it? The Olympic rings will hang between the towers. They are 50 metres high. The clock tower behind the Stadium is still under construction. It will be even higher, at 77 metres. Apart from that, the building programme is nearing completion. All but a few minor details remain. Come, time is precious. I'll explain as we walk." He strode forward, his boots beating a hollow tattoo on the paving stones. Saxon picked up his pace to fall into step.

"As you can imagine, the Games represent a huge challenge to all of us. By the first day of August, Berlin will host 4,000 athletes as well as an untold number of spectators from all around the world. My job is to ensure the security of the athletes and visitors."

A feeling of dread was already invading Saxon's bones.

"Your first job will be to sanitize the city. It is most important that these visitors experience the very best that our city has to offer. They must see a clean, safe, free city, and go home with the best possible impression of us – and of the Third Reich." His chest swelled with pride. "Let me be clear: the streets must be completely cleansed of undesirables."

A poisoned chalice indeed! And as distasteful a job as he could imagine.

Saxon hung back, and the SS-man slowed. "Is there something the matter?"

"This is not something I will be any good at, sir," he said.

"Nonsense. You are an experienced policeman are you not? Your men will pick up every homeless vagabond, pickpocket, prostitute and beggar and put them under protective custody. What could be simpler? I'm sure you will do an excellent job."

"How will we identify these people? And where do we move them to?"

"No need to worry about that, the city police know how to find them. And we are planning to open a small camp in Oranienburg."

"Oranienburg?" Saxon had only a vague idea where that was.

"Yes, to the north of the city. It should be open within two or three weeks. You will need to coordinate your operations with the kommandant there. In the meantime, the cells within the city police stations will suffice to hold the prisoners."

Ulman strode onward and Saxon increased his pace once more, to keep up.

His first view of the interior of the Stadium gave the lie to Ulman's contention that the building was close to completion. The oval superstructure was in place, but half the seating was stacked in piles at various locations in the centre, and the running track had not yet been laid. Workers swarmed everywhere. He watched a tall crane lifting a massive spotlight to the highest point on the rim above the spectator area.

"The track area is 86 metres by 100. Rim to rim, it's 100 metres across by 200 metres long. There will be room for 37,000 seats. The upper tiers are for standing only." Ulman swept an arm across the view.

Saxon wrote the numbers in his notepad. "What is the total capacity of the Stadium?"

"A little over one hundred thousand."

"Where will the Führer be sitting?" He was already aware of the security problems that an open-air event with such a vast crowd could create.

Ulman pointed to his left with a podgy finger. "The preferential seating will be located in the centre on the south side. The leather upholstered seats have been specially constructed. They are stored in a secure location under the Stadium to keep them in pristine condition. They will be installed on the last days before the opening ceremony. Come! It's time I introduced you to the man in charge of the construction programme."

Saxon tripped on a low metal structure fixed to the concrete at his feet.

"That's a stand for one of the Telefunken television cameras," said the SS-man. "The Post Office will broadcast pictures to various viewing rooms in the city during the Games."

Television! Saxon had read about it. He knew they were working on it, but he'd thought it was years away. The scale of the project was making him dizzy, now.

Ulman was off again. Making their way through the labyrinth of corridors under the seating of the Stadium they came to a door guarded by an armed Wehrmacht soldier. The soldier saluted and stood aside, allowing Ulman to open the door.

The room was unfinished, the walls rough plastered, with cement dust everywhere. Two men stood at a table containing a pile of schematics. The older man was dressed in civilian clothes, the younger in the uniform of a Wehrmacht Hauptmann.

Ulman clicked his heels. "Herr March, may I introduce Kommissar Saxon."

The older of the two men gave a short Hitler salute. "Welcome to Berlin." He introduced his colleague. "Kommandant Fürstner. The kommandant is in charge of the development programme for the Olympic Village."

Fürstner offered a hand in a firm handshake. "I merely command the Wehrmacht building crew."

Herr March said, "Wolfgang is being modest. He plays a central role in everything we do here."

"You flatter me, Walter."

"Not at all, Wolfgang. Without you we would have no hope of completing the work in time."

Fürstner smiled. "Herr March is the architectural genius responsible for designing the Olympic Village. His brother designed the Stadium."

March's face registered a flicker of pride. "I'll be leaving now, Wolfgang. Until tomorrow morning." He nodded to Saxon, stepped toward the door, and Ulman followed him. Placing a hand on the architect's back, Ulman ushered him from the room. "A word in your ear, Walter..."

From Wolfgang Fürstner's bearing, Saxon identified him as a career officer, and an experienced one, judging by the grey hair at his temples.

"How is the programme coming, Kommandant?" he said.

"Well enough. We have setbacks every day, but we work our way through them. My biggest problem at the moment is a shortage of workers. We had 2,000 at one point, but we're down to less than 1,200 now, and only 200 of those are working on the Village."

"Herr Ulman seemed confident that everything will be ready in good time for the opening ceremony."

"Of course. Herr Ulman is SS." Wolfgang's gaze was direct, his eyes shining with amusement. Saxon liked the man instantly.

"May I ask whom I report to?"

"As a member of the police, you report to Herr Ulman, of course, but I am available to help you wherever I can. As well as my role of manager of the Village building programme, I have a watching brief over everything to do with catering and security for the Village."

"Herr Ulman seemed to imply that only he was responsible for security."

"Of course," said the kommandant, "he is SS."

They both laughed.

Fürstner looked at his watch. "I have fifteen minutes. Let me show you some of the Stadium."

Ulman re-entered the room. "Come, Saxon, it's time you met your men."

The kommandant said, "Of course, go ahead. Come to my house tomorrow evening at seven o'clock. We are holding a small party. I'd like you to meet my wife."

"Thank you, Kommandant. Where do you live?"

"Ask your driver. He will know where to go."

Chapter 4

They took the car back to the city. Again, Ulman and Saxon sat side by side in the back with all the windows open, sweltering in the heat.

He said, "The kommandant said something about a driver..."

"This car and driver are at your disposal for the duration of your stay in our city," said Ulman.

The driver caught Saxon's eye in the rear-view mirror.

"There's a lot more to see," said the SS-man. "The Stadium is only a small part of the sports complex. There are also various sports fields, the Olympic swimming pool, and the Olympic Village. Your driver will be your guide."

"You said my first task is to cleanse the streets of the city," said Saxon. "Is there a second task?"

"Didn't I mention that? You will be responsible for security in the Olympic Village when the athletes arrive."

Saxon tuned out while Ulman continued talking. Providing security for athletes was well outside his area of expertise. Why had they chosen him for the role?

Ulman's voice droned on. "... covers an area well over one hundred hectares."

"One hundred and thirty," said the driver. "It's the biggest sports complex in the world."

"Yes, thank you, driver," said Ulman. "Keep your eyes on the road and your mind on your job."

As they approached the city centre, Ulman placed a hand on Saxon's knee. "What did you think of the Stadium?"

Saxon shifted on the seat, and Ulman removed his hand. "It is quite magnificent. But won't it be a security nightmare when it's full of people?"

Ulman pursed his lips like a schoolmistress. "That is not your concern. Let's be clear about one thing: security for the Stadium is a matter for the SS."

They were driving along a wide boulevard between two rows of gigantic swastika flags, the Brandenburg Gate straight ahead in the distance.

"Isn't this the famous Unter den Linden?" he said.

"Yes indeed. One of the highlights of our city."

"Where are all the linden trees?"

"They have been removed in order to create this magnificent spectacle for the Festival of Peoples. The trees will be replaced when the Games are over."

He thought the trees would have made a better spectacle than the flags, but he said nothing.

The driver turned the Mercedes into an alleyway between two tall buildings and parked in a car park full of police vehicles.

As they walked toward the building, Ulman put a sweaty hand on Saxon's shoulder. "A word to the wise, my friend. Be careful whom you associate with."

They entered the rear of the building and took a service stairway to a room on the top floor.

The floorboards were bare. There were two desks, side by side in a corner, with a single black telephone on one and a typewriter on the other. A large map of Berlin covered one wall. A group of men, some dressed in Orpo blue, the others in a variety of uniforms, stood about smoking cigarettes.

"Put those out!" barked Ulman. "And stand to attention for your new officer-in-charge. Kriminalkommissar Saxon."

The men tossed their cigarettes down and stomped on them, and each man stood to attention where he was, with no attempt to form up.

"At ease," said Saxon, making a beeline for the only man in the room wearing sergeant's stripes.

The men relaxed. The sergeant saluted in the old-fashioned way. "Sergeant Willi Schmidt, sir."

"I'll leave you to it," said Ulman, heading out.

Saxon followed him through the door. He lowered his voice. "Where am I to sleep? Is there a billet?"

"What's wrong with your hotel?" Ulman gave him a look that suggested Saxon was soft in the head. "Send the hotel receipts to my adjutant, Canstatt. Monday's his day for administration." And he hurried away.

There were 16 men in total, a collection of misfits. Five were taller than Saxon. One, named Reckendorfer, was a giant, two metres tall and broad as a bus. Two Schupo men, Heller and Kleinholz, seemed joined at the hip. Heller was painfully thin, Kleinholz looked close to retirement age. As Sergeant Schmidt introduced him to the men, Saxon realised, with increasing gloom, how much of a ragtag bunch they were. He wrote their names in his notepad. Only eight were police: four Schupo municipal police, two from the water police, and one from the state rural police. Reckendorfer was Orpo. The remaining seven had been recruited from outside the police forces: there was one fireman, three coastguards, and two were from civil defence. The smallest man in the team, Clasen, was an administrator from the head office of the Hitler Youth.

Saxon laughed. "Don't we have anyone from Traffic?"

Sergeant Schmidt coughed, and Saxon looked askance at him. "Twenty years' service in the Traffic Corps in Stuttgart, sir."

Saxon shook his head in exasperation. "Tell me what you've done so far."

Schmidt took him over to the map. "The city is divided into thirty-seven police sectors, with a total of five hundred and twenty police stations. A general order has been sent out, and clearance operations are well in hand."

"So, if I conduct a random check will I find the streets completely clear of these elements?"

"Ah, perhaps not. That's not something we can guarantee, sir. The problem is that these people move around a lot. The streets require constant monitoring. We'll have to revisit each of the sectors at some point..."

"You keep records?"

"No, sir, the police stations keep their own records."

"Right, from now on, I want a record made of everyone detained."

Clasen, the HY administrator, raised a hand. "I kept records when we started, but Hauptmann Zimmermann said it wasn't necessary."

"Do we know how many have been taken into protective custody so far?"

Clasen pulled a ledger from a desk drawer and opened it. "Two weeks ago, we had one hundred and thirty-seven names."

"So that's your first job, Clasen. We need to contact the police stations to collect the details of everyone detained so far."

"They won't be happy about that," mumbled Clasen.

Ignoring that remark, Saxon addressed the sergeant. "Describe the method of operation."

"The local police conduct regular methodical sweeps. They arrest anyone who cannot account for their presence on the streets. We conduct our own street inspections to ensure that they have done a good job, and we arrest any that they missed."

"What are these people arrested for?"

"Loitering, mostly."

"What if they're simply going about their business in a normal manner?"

The sergeant lifted a shoulder and spread his hands. "In those cases, we have to be creative."

"What does that mean?"

"People are placed in protective custody if they look as though they might be doing something wrong."

He knew that the operation was on slippery legal ground, but this was worse than he'd anticipated. "Any citizen held in protective custody has to be released after twenty-one days. You know that, Sergeant."

"Normally, yes sir, but I was under the impression that the normal rules have been relaxed for the duration of the Games."

"What types have you detained so far?"

"Mostly prostitutes, but there are some beggars, drunks, pickpockets and vagabonds. Anyone suspected of a crime."

"What if they're not committing a crime?"

"They could be thinking about committing one."

"We can't arrest people for what they might be thinking."

The sergeant said nothing. Clasen piped up again, "We have to carry out our orders, Kommissar, one way or another."

Another man said, "What does it matter as long as we clear the streets? They will all be released again when the Games are over."

Saxon wasn't so sure about that. The Third Reich had a poor record when it came to releasing people from protective custody.

He pointed to Clasen's typewriter. "Type me a note for circulation to all sectors. Tell them we want names and details of all detainees held so far, and a weekly list of those newly detained by close of business each Monday.

Clasen typed up the note, Saxon signed it, and Clasen went off to find a duplicating machine.

#

After that, he went in search of his driver in the car park.

The driver's name was Nemec. When Saxon reacted to his strange accent, he explained that he was from Bohemia.

Nemec took him to sector 5 where a 3-man police unit was busy cleansing the streets of 'undesirables'. Saxon watched them at work from the privacy of the car as Nemec cruised around the streets.

All went well until midday, when the gang arrested someone for loitering. He got out of the car and signalled to the men in the unit that he wanted to speak with the detainee, a slight individual, wearing spectacles and shaking like a linden tree in a high wind. The detainee didn't look anything like a thief or a vagabond.

"I wasn't doing anything illegal, officer," said the man.

"Why were you loitering here on the street?"

"I'm a teacher. I was waiting to meet with one of my students who is in need of extra tuition."

"Couldn't you give him this extra tuition in the classroom? Why meet him on the street?"

"It's complicated," said the man, blushing, throwing furtive glances up and down the street. He seemed totally on edge.

Then the student – a buxom teenage girl carrying a school bag – rounded the corner and advanced toward them.

"You may go about your business," said Saxon. "But if you don't get off the street you are liable to be arrested again. Do you understand?"

"Yes, officer, thank you." He scurried away to rendezvous with his student.

Saxon had a word with the gang. He pointed out that the man was innocent of any wrongdoing and should never have been detained.

The police gang resumed their duties amid much eye-rolling and laughter, bordering on insubordination.

He climbed back into his car and Nemec took him across the city to his hotel.

At the hotel, he stepped out and opened the passenger door to speak to the driver. "I have an invitation to Kommandant Fürstner's home tomorrow evening. He said you'd know where that is."

"Yes, sir." Nemec tipped his cap and drove away.

Saxon went inside to a deserted reception desk. He rang the bell and waited for the receptionist to appear.

Püttner pulled the Kommissar's key from its pigeonhole.

Saxon said, "I'll be staying for a while."

"How long?"

"Until the middle of August, certainly."

The receptionist ran a hand through his hair. "The hotel is fully booked for the Games, from the last week of July until mid-August. I hope you understand."

"Are you saying I can't keep the room after the third week of July?"

The man blanched visibly. "No, of course not, Kommissar. You may keep the room as long as you wish. However, I will require payment for a week in advance."

Saxon paid for seven days and asked for a receipt.

As Saxon was heading for the staircase, Püttner said, "You should be aware that the rate for the room will double from July fifteenth, Kommissar."

Chapter 5

Tuesday June 23

At Saxon's request, his driver took him on a tour of the Olympic sports complex the following morning. Nemec's knowledge of the facilities was impressive. Standing at the side of the huge, empty pool, he said, "The water will be pumped from the river to the north. The pool is lower than the river, to allow gravity to assist in the process. The pool will hold 2 million litres. The experts say it will take several days to fill."

They visited the *Maifeld*, a large green area behind the Stadium for equestrian and general sports. They went on to the sports forum, an indoor venue, and the outdoor venues for boxing, football, cycling, shooting, etc. There were spectator stands at each venue. He tried to keep track, but lost count.

Finally, Nemec drove 26 Kilometres south to the river Spree at Grünau, where more spectator stands and a pontoon bridge were being erected in preparation for the watersports, rowing and canoeing.

"Sailing will be at Kiel," said Nemec.

Saxon's heart was in his boots. Ulman had said that the SS would take care of security. But would they? He couldn't shake the feeling that he would be involved, to some extent at least. Providing effective security for the athletes at all of these locations was going to be difficult. With only 16 men he could do very little. He could only hope that he wouldn't be asked to much.

"Is that everything?" he said.

"We haven't visited the Olympic Village, yet, sir."

"We'll do that another day," Saxon said. "Take me to the hotel."

Before leaving the car at the hotel, he said, "I have to present myself at Kommandant Fürstner's house this evening. You said you know where that is."

"Yes, sir," said Nemec.

"Good. Give me an hour and a half."

He rang the bell on the desk several times before the receptionist appeared and handed him his key.

"I'd like to take a bath."

"Of course, sir. The bathroom on the second floor is at the end of the corridor."

The water was lukewarm, but he found the bath relaxing nonetheless. His first two days in Berlin had been depressing. Tiring and depressing. He could understand the need to clear the streets before exposing the city to a host of young people from outside Germany. The Third Reich had a lot to hide from the world. It was a disagreeable procedure, and not one he would have volunteered for, but he would play his part. He would sanitize the streets of Berlin, but his men would never be accused of using excess force. And he would do his best to ensure that all of those detained were returned to their homes after the Games.

He ducked under the water, blowing angry bubbles.

He surfaced and shook the water from his hair. Providing effective security for 4,000 athletes was going to be a major challenge, but would it fall to him? He resolved to demand clarification on the matter from Wolfgang Fürstner as soon as the chance presented itself.

He could hear Ruth's admonishments in his head. How had he got himself into such a mess? Glasser would answer for putting him in this unpleasant situation.

\#

Kommandant Fürstner's home in the Olympic Village was a beacon of light in a darkened, tree-lined street. A neat and tidy 2-storey dwelling, it was small by Munich standards, but compared to the low dwellings built to house the athletes, it was a mansion.

The guests strolled about in evening wear and military uniforms, carrying wine glasses and beer glasses. Saxon felt underdressed in his best blue suit and Bavarian Police Academy tie, but Fürstner hadn't said it was a formal occasion.

His host introduced him to his wife, tall and elegant in a full-length, low-cut dress, made of a shiny blue material that he couldn't identify. She was in conversation with a dumpy woman with long hair.

"This is Lotte, Frau Ulman," said the kommandant.

Saxon shook the hands of both women.

Frau Fürstner peered at him over her glass. "Lotte was telling me about her two boys. Do you have a family, Herr Saxon?"

"My wife and I are blessed with a 3-year old son." He opened his wallet and showed her the photograph of Ruth and Samuel.

"This posting must be difficult for you, so. I'm sorry."

"My family has moved to Austria for the time being." He returned the picture to his wallet.

"Oh, that is unusual." Lotte Ulman tilted her head, like a vulture with its eye on a juicy morsel of carrion. "An extended vacation, perhaps?"

Before he could reply, Fürstner took his elbow and steered him around the room, introducing him to various dignitaries.

"There's something I need to discuss with you," said Saxon.

"Later." Fürstner steered Saxon across the room. "There's someone else you must meet."

He approached a middle-aged man in a general's uniform, complete with Iron Cross at his throat. The general was in conversation with a woman half his age. When they paused to sip their wine, Fürstner stepped in.

"Herr General, allow me to present to you, Kriminalkommissar Saxon, newly arrived from Munich to help with security at the Games. Saxon, meet Generalleutnant von Reichenau, Germany's representative on the International Olympic Committee."

The general adjusted the monocle in his right eye before scrutinizing Saxon's face. "From Munich, you say? I served there for a time."

Saxon remembered him. The general was head of the army in Munich during the time of the Night of the Long Knives purge in 1934.

Saxon clicked his heels. "Honoured, sir."

"Heil Hitler," said the general, and he resumed his conversation with the woman.

Chapter 6

Fürstner led Saxon to another reception room, which was less crowded. "The general likes to be informed when anyone senior joins the team. He keeps a watching brief over everything we do."

"Am I that senior?"

"Of course. Once the Games start, you will have overall responsibility for security."

A wave of dizziness struck him. He put his hand to his head.

"Are you all right?"

"Yes, I was surprised by what you said."

"Didn't Ulman make it clear that you will be responsible for security?"

"No, Kommandant, he did not. In fact, he told me that, with the exception of the Village, security was none of my concern. He said the SS would look after all that." He suddenly felt the need to sit, but there were no free chairs available.

Fürstner grabbed two fresh bottles of beer from a table and led him into the rear garden, where there were fewer people to overhear them.

"I'm sure the SS do an excellent job of guarding the Führer, and they have a lot of experience with policing large Nazi rallies, but the Games present a whole new set of challenges. I'll have a word with him in the morning." He handed a bottle to Saxon, and they topped up their glasses.

"I have seen the Stadium and the other venues, Kommandant. There are many other venues. If I am to provide security for a stadium of 100,000 spectators and all of those other venues, I will need a lot more men."

"How many?"

"I don't know, yet. I'll have to think about it."

"If Karl Ulman takes on those tasks it won't be an issue, but it won't do any harm to give me your best estimate. And please call me Wolfgang. What's your given name?"

"Everyone calls me Saxon."

"Saxon it is, then." Fürstner looked amused. He raised his glass to his lips. "I wanted to hear your views about security for the Olympic Village. You know that the Sports Council have objected to the American negroes?"

Saxon nodded. "I suspected as much. I read in the newspapers that Avery Brundage threatened to withdraw the entire American team from the Games."

"That's right. The official position is that everybody and anybody can participate, but the Americans have been warned that the reaction of the German people cannot be predicted if the negroes win."

Saxon said, "I believe the Americans have several world-class black runners."

"Jesse Owens and sixteen others. I have a list of the names. They will all need special protection."

"I will need to see that list."

"Of course. It's in my office. Drop in anytime and I'll let you have a copy."

While Saxon sipped his beer, Wolfgang Fürstner cast his gaze around the garden. He had something more on his mind. Then the kommandant lowered his voice. "Did Ulman say anything about me?"

"Nothing that I can recall..." He searched his memory. "He did say I should be careful who I associate with – or something like that."

"Ah! Did he mention my name?"

"No, I don't think so. Why?"

"It's nothing." He shook his head, in a gesture that suggested otherwise.

"Can you tell me why I was recruited to the security team?"

"You are a replacement for Hauptmann Zimmermann."

"Yes, but why me? Couldn't they find a Berlin policeman for the job? Why bring in an outsider?"

"That would be the White Knight business. As I understand it, there was a suggestion of a conspiracy within the police force. They needed to appoint someone beyond suspicion."

"The White Knight? What sort of conspiracy?"

"Some threat to the Games. I didn't see the document myself."

"What document?"

"The White Knight letter. Hasn't Ulman told you any of this?"

"No, he hasn't." He paused to give Wolfgang time to elaborate, but the kommandant said nothing more on the subject.

"I did ask Ulman what happened to Zimmermann."

"What did he say?"

"He was evasive. He said the Hauptmann failed in his duties. The men were unproductive under his command – something like that."

Wolfgang laughed quietly. "I expect that's what's recorded on his file, but it's far from the truth. Ulman engineered his downfall."

"Ulman said that the Reichsführer himself fired him."

Wolfgang' eyebrows rose. "An obvious distortion of the facts."

"So why was he fired?"

"I suspect that Ulman took a dislike to him. Probably because he wasn't a Party member. He used the letter as an excuse to have him removed."

Saxon took a mouthful of beer. It was not as good as Bavarian Helle, but passably good. "What was he like?"

"Who, Zimmermann? Young, a career Wehrmacht officer, like me. I have a photograph of him somewhere. I'll send it to you if I can find it."

"Where is he now?"

"No one knows."

Saxon knew exactly what that meant.

#

Hotel Südberg, Bernberg Strasse 27, Berlin
   June 23, 1936
   Dearest Ruth,
   I'm writing to you from a small hotel in Berlin. I have been asked to oversee security for the Olympic Village!
   It's a big job, and I feel honoured to have been asked to take it on.
   The good news is that I should be back in Munich when the Games end in the middle of August.
   Look after yourself and young Samuel.
   All my love
   Roland

As he got into bed, he considered his position. He had no intention of ever joining the Nazi Party. Would the SS-man take a dislike to him and have him removed? That would be one way to escape the unpleasant task he'd been set, but it would surely end his career, and he had no desire to see the inside of a Gestapo cell. The thought of spending his last years of service in a blue Orpo uniform or directing traffic, sent shivers through his body.

What had Zimmermann done to end up in the hands of the Gestapo? Was there really a police conspiracy to disrupt the Games? And what was in that 'White Knight' letter? Wolfgang said that Ulman had taken a dislike to the man. Was that enough to have him removed?

He needed clarity on his role. He would be in charge of security for the Olympic Village, that much was clear, but what about the athletics venues and the Stadium? He resolved to contact Ulman in the morning.

Switching off the bedside light, he consoled himself with the thought that, whatever happened, the job would be over by mid-August. He could survive two months.

Chapter 7

Saxon rang the Gestapo building in the morning to arrange a further meeting with Ulman but when Canstatt, the SS-man's adjutant, said he was unavailable, he asked his driver to take him to the Olympic Village.

Covering an extensive forested area 14 kilometres to the west of the Stadium, the Olympic Village consisted of a small number of 2-storey communal buildings and over 140 single-storey houses to be used as living accommodation by the athletes. Construction was at an advanced stage, under the direction of Kommandant Fürstner and Walter March. Saxon came across March in the central administration building in what was to become a canteen: a wide room with seating space for 300 and a kitchen, partially installed, at one end.

They shook hands. The expression on March's face was one of barely-suppressed panic.

"This is the dining hall for the athletes?" said Saxon.

March shook his head, and specks of plaster fell from his hair onto his shoulders. "It's one of forty-one."

"Forty-one dining halls? How many kitchens? How many kitchen staff?" He was starting to appreciate the size of the task facing him.

"Each dining hall has its own kitchen. Each kitchen has a cook and two helpers. There are additional staff for dishwashing, cleaning and so on."

March pulled a fob watch from a pocket and looked at it pointedly.

"I'd like to take a closer look at the Village, but if it's not convenient, I could come back another time, or perhaps one of your staff could show me around?"

March grunted. "I can spare a half-hour. What is your interest, exactly?"

"I need to take a look around to see what security measures will be required to keep the athletes safe."

"Safe from what? There are no hidden dangers in the Village. Unless you think the athletes might be a danger to one another."

"We mustn't be complacent, Herr March," he said. "Imagine what a catastrophe would face us all if one of the athletes was injured here."

"Injured how?"

"By the actions of a criminal or somebody motivated by jealousy or racial hatred, perhaps."

March paused to consider this. "I take your point. Where would you like to start?"

The guided tour of the Village took less than an hour. Saxon recognised the kommandant's 2-storey house when they passed it.

At the end of the tour they came to a sauna on the bank of a small lake. "It's fed by a natural source of pure spring water. The sauna has two separate cubicles."

"For segregation?"

"Precisely."

They entered a 2-storey building called the Hindenburg House. It contained a cinema and a large empty hall. Sitting in a circle in a far corner of the hall, was a group of people in conference. Saxon assumed they were part of March's construction team.

"This is the sports hall and gymnasium," said March. "It's a recreational area where the athletes can relax. You'll have to imagine the hall filled with mats, gymnastic equipment, exercise machines, weights, and so on. Over there, a boxing ring."

"Baths?"

"Upstairs. And showers, the latest thing from America."

"Segregated, I assume?"

March nodded solemnly. "Of course. Now tell me what conclusions you have reached about security."

Saxon said, "The area is too large and has too many buildings for any sort of conventional security operation."

The vestige of a smile passed over March's face. "So, we won't need any of your blue uniforms in the Village?"

A young woman detached herself from the group in the corner and approached.

"I'll have to think about the best way to handle it, Herr March. Whatever we decide, you can be sure security for the Village will be of the highest quality."

The woman touched March on the arm. "Walter, aren't you going to introduce us?"

"This is Kommissar Saxon of the Munich police," said March. "Kommissar Saxon, meet Fräulein Riefenstahl. The Fräulein will be filming the Games."

Saxon shook the young woman's hand. He was surprised by her height and noble bearing. He knew who she was.

"Call me Leni." She gifted him a lukewarm smile.

His own smile was more generous. "Everyone calls me Saxon."

March checked his watch again. "I must get back to work. You'll be able to find your way back to your car, I think?"

"Yes, thank you," he said. And Walter March hurried away.

"He's a busy man," Leni said. She fixed him with her gaze. "You're the replacement for Zimmermann, right?"

"That's right." He hesitated. "I've long admired your work, Fräulein."

Her eyes narrowed. "You've seen my films? Which ones?"

"The Blue Light."

He had also seen her other two films, *The Victory of Faith* and *Triumph of the Will*, but he had no time for Nazi propaganda.

"Ah! *The Blue Light*? You enjoyed it?"

"Very much. You are an excellent actress. Why did you switch to directing your own films?"

She shrugged. "Working closely with a film aficionado, I suppose some of his enthusiasm rubbed off on me. But tell me about yourself. I hear you're a famous detective."

"A simple country policeman, nothing more."

"Don't be modest, Kommissar, your reputation precedes you."

He found that idea disturbing. "Tell me about your plans for filming the Games."

"What would you like to know?"

"I assume you will have camera crews at all the venues?"

"Only the main ones. We couldn't hope to cover everything, and the film will be no more than two hours long. We hope to film the finals of all the main events, but even that will be a nightmare to organise."

He offered her a cigarette and she accepted. He took one himself and lit both before continuing, "How many cameras do you have?"

"Twelve. Four will be mounted in static positions in the Stadium, the remainder will follow the action. Oh, and we will have an extra one in the zeppelin. I'm hoping for some spectacular shots from high above the Stadium."

Her smile froze. "I trust your men won't disturb my camera crews in their work."

"My only concern is the security of the athletes, Fräulein. My men will carry out their duties, nothing more."

"Are you anticipating trouble?"

"Nothing in particular, but we must remain vigilant."

"Shouldn't you expect trouble when the black Americans start sweeping up the medals, perhaps?"

"As I said, we must be vigilant."

She opened her handbag, extracted a long cigarette holder and inserted her cigarette. "My only concern for the moment is the torch relay. The last thing I want is hordes of police uniforms cluttering up my film."

"The torch relay?" Saxon's stomach muscles tightened. He had no idea what that was, but it sounded like something that would complicate his job.

She drew on her cigarette and blew smoke through her nose. "Haven't they told you? A relay of runners will transport the Olympic flame from Olympia in Greece to the Stadium, to arrive during the opening ceremony. But, as I've said, there will be no need for any special security for the relay."

A definite complication, full of security problems. Why had no one mentioned this?

He did his best to keep the concern from his voice. "I was aware of the Olympic flame at the Amsterdam Games, but no one said anything about a relay. How far is the journey? And when will it start?" He opened his notepad.

She shook her head. "You don't need to concern yourself with it."

"Please answer my questions, Fräulein."

"Am I being interrogated, Kommissar?"

Before he could respond to that, her companions approached to call her away. She puffed on her cigarette and blew smoke in his face. "Olympia to Berlin is 3,200 kilometres. It will take 12 days and nights for the runners to carry the flame to the Stadium in Berlin, starting at Olympia on July 20."

He wrote the numbers down, aware that his mouth was open in astonishment. "That must have taken some careful planning. How many runners will be involved?"

"The plan is for each runner to carry the torch for one kilometre, taking an average 5 minutes."

"So, there will be 3,200 runners?"

"Roughly, yes. But as I said, you needn't concern yourself with it." And she strode away with her companions.

Chapter 8

The next morning, Saxon went looking for Wolfgang. The kommandant was not in his office at the Stadium and none of his staff knew where he might be found. Nemec suggested driving back to the kommandant's house, but Saxon decided instead to talk to the SS-man.

The car drew up at the entrance to the Gestapo building, under an overcast sky. A summer storm was gathering from the west.

Clutching his hat, he ran from the car to the portico, just as the skies opened. The reception desk was deserted and he climbed the stairs to the third floor, unchallenged. The adjutant made him wait for Ulman's invitation to enter.

Ulman was standing behind his desk in his shirtsleeves, a pair of red braces straining over a paunch that Saxon hadn't noticed before. He wondered fleetingly if the SS-man had been wearing a corset when they first met.

"What do you want, Saxon? I'm busy, can't you see?" His massive desk was covered in a new layer of scattered papers.

"I won't keep you long," said Saxon. "I have some questions."

Ulman waved a hand at a chair. Saxon took the chair and the SS-man resumed his seat behind the desk.

"I visited the Olympic Village yesterday."

"Walter March showed you around?"

"He did. The Village could present us with several challenges. It is absolutely enormous. It's going to be most difficult to police. It's difficult to see how we can ensure the security of so many athletes spread out over such an extensive area."

Ulman leaned forward, his chair creaking under his weight. "But you have a plan, I take it?"

"I suggest we provide the athletes with servants or tour guides – carefully selected men, of course."

"Selected by whom?" The SS-man's brow furrowed, his eyebrows forming a solid grey line across the top of his nose.

Saxon pressed on. "I thought your men could do it. They could ensure that the athletes visit only the best parts of the city, and their narrative could stress the more positive aspects of life in Germany..."

Ulman shook his head. "A similar idea was proposed at a recent high-level meeting. It was rejected. The feeling around the table was that the best approach was to trouble visitors as little as possible with propaganda. The athletes and the other visitors from overseas will be free to travel around the city wherever they wish."

"Of course." He wondered briefly about that 'high-level meeting', but he gathered himself and moved on. "I spoke with Leni Riefenstahl at the Village."

Ulman met Saxon's eyes. His lips parted in a salacious smile. "Ah, the lady film director. A delightful young lady, don't you agree?"

"Yes, indeed. She told me about the planned torch relay from Olympia in Greece."

"An idea thought up by our Olympic Committee. A splendid innovation, don't you think?"

"I think someone might have mentioned it to me before now. The security implications are serious."

Ulman glared at him. "The torch relay is none of your concern. Please be clear, as I keep telling you, your sole tasks are to sanitize the streets of the city and provide security for the Olympic Village."

Saxon took a breath. "Kommandant Fürstner has indicated otherwise."

"You have spoken with the kommandant about this?" Ulman pursed his lips.

"I couldn't locate him this morning. Do you know where I might find him?"

Ulman picked up a pen, unscrewed the lid, examined the nib, and replaced the lid. Without looking up, he said, "Can the badger live with the fox?"

Saxon had no idea what that meant, but he had the distinct feeling of quicksand beneath his feet. He waited.

Staring into space above Saxon's head, Ulman allowed a few seconds to pass before he said, "Perhaps we should rely on the goodwill of the people during the torch relay, eh, Kommissar?"

"Isn't that a risky policy?"

"As I've said, you may leave me to worry about that. Now, I must get back to work."

Saxon crossed his arms. He was going nowhere. "Tell me about this White Knight letter."

"Who have you been speaking to?" His eyes narrowed.

"I'd like to see it."

"It is with the scientists in the laboratory, undergoing tests."

"Is it true that you're investigating a conspiracy within the police force?"

Ulman's eyes opened wide. He looked like a startled rabbit. "You've been talking to Wolfgang Fürstner about this, haven't you?"

"Tell me about the conspiracy."

"That is no concern of yours. For the moment, your job is to sanitize the streets before the athletes and overseas visitors arrive. Is that clear?"

"Why have you found it necessary to keep me in the dark? Surely I should know if I'm working among possible conspirators."

"As I have said repeatedly, Kommissar, these are matters you need not concern yourself with. Now, tell me what progress you've made with sanitizing the streets of the city."

"You are refusing to brief me on the White Knight letter?" He got to his feet. "Very well, thank you for your time." Ulman outranked him by a long way, but he was not prepared to be bullied by the man.

He had reached the door by the time a spluttering Ulman found his voice. "Answer my question, Kommissar. How many have you taken off the streets...?"

Saxon closed the door and walked away past a gaping adjutant to the sound of the SS-man shouting after him, "Kommissar, answer me!"

He was halfway down the staircase to the first floor before Ulman emerged from his office and called after him, "Come back here, Kommissar."

Outside, Prinz-Albrecht-Strasse was gripped in a violent summer storm. A brisk wind blew the teeming rain in through the porch, where a small group of passing pedestrians had taken shelter. He put a hand on his hat, launched himself from the building, and ran to his car.

#

Nemec drove Saxon to Kommandant Fürstner's house in the Olympic Village. Saxon got out and knocked on the door. The man who opened it had the dress and bearing of a butler. Saxon asked to speak with the kommandant.

"The kommandant is not here today."

He left his name and a message to say he'd return in the morning.

They hit heavy traffic on the journey back to the city centre. During one of their frequent stops, the rain started again. It seemed they would be in the car for hours.

He asked Nemec about the team.

"The sergeant is as reliable as they come," said Nemec. "He was a great help to Hauptmann Zimmermann. You could trust him with your life. Clasen is as clever as fox, but he'd be no use in a fight, obviously."

"Obviously. What about the giant?"

"That's Dieter Reckendorfer. He used to be in the Gestapo. A leutnant, I believe. They kicked him out after the killing. You've heard that story?" He looked in the rear-view mirror for a reaction from Saxon.

Saxon shook his head.

"It happened a couple of years ago. He had an affair with the wife of a lowly Schupo Wachtmeister. The Wachtmeister confronted him, pulled a gun and pointed it at the big man. Reckendorfer threw his axe at him. Split his skull like a melon."

Saxon's voice went up an octave. "His axe?"

"A ceremonial axe. They say he carried it everywhere with him."

"Wasn't he tried for murder?"

"The Kripo said it was self-defence. He got off, but he was expelled from the Gestapo and transferred to the Orpo as a lowly Oberwachtmeister. He's not allowed to carry the axe anymore."

Chapter 9

Friday June 26

The storm raged all night. Thunder rumbled like a grumbling giant, and sheet lightning flashed across the western horizon.

Saxon slept in fits and starts, his thoughts revolving around the White Knight letter, the axe-wielding giant, the torch relay, and Ulman's enigmatic question: Can the fox live with the badger?

The morning dawned with clear blue skies and a beaming sun, innocent as a newborn. Only the water-soaked streets and overflowing storm-drains stood witness to the havoc of the night before.

Nemec drove Saxon back to the Olympic Village. He knocked on Kommandant Fürstner's door.

The butler opened it. "Good morning, sir."

"Is the kommandant at home? I'd like to speak with him."

"I'm sorry Kommissar, the kommandant is unavailable."

"I won't detain him for long."

"I'm sorry, sir. As I said, the kommandant is unavailable."

"It's quite urgent," said Saxon. "I just need a few moments of his time. Please tell him I'm here."

The butler closed the door. Saxon waited. There was a chance that he might yet get to speak with the kommandant.

After two minutes, the door opened again. The butler's face reappeared.

"I'm sorry, sir, the kommandant is not to be disturbed. He suggests you speak with Standartenführer Ulman. And he said to give you this." He handed Saxon an envelope and closed the door.

The envelope contained a handwritten note list of the black American athletes from Wolfgang as well as a photograph of

Wolfgang with a group of men. The note read: "That list of athletes, as promised. The picture shows the team before you joined."

He showed the photograph to his driver. Sergeant Schmidt and officers Reckendorfer and little Clasen of the Hitler Youth were easily identifiable. "Which one is Zimmermann?"

Nemec pointed to a square-chinned Wehrmacht officer in the front row. "That's Hauptmann Heinrich Zimmermann."

What on earth was the matter with the kommandant? He was obviously in the house, but totally incommunicado. He must be seriously ill. Considering the rapid approach of the Games, nothing less would keep the man from his duties.

Saxon returned to Orpo headquarters on Unter den Linden to review Clasen's progress. On reaching the office, he found only three men in attendance, two Schupo officers and Clasen, the recordkeeper, bent over his ledger, pen in hand.

"Where's everyone else?" said Saxon.

"They're out doing their job," said one of the Schupo men.

"Checking the streets of the city," said the other.

Saxon said, "Did I give orders to resume those duties?"

Clasen shrugged. "We have to get on with it, Kommissar. And you never gave instructions one way or the other."

Saxon glanced at the calendar on the wall. The opening ceremony was five weeks away. "Give me something to write with." He took the pen Clasen handed him, tore a blank page from the back of the ledger and wrote in large letters:

OPERATIONS ARE SUSPENDED UNTIL FURTHER NOTICE.

ALL MEMBERS ASSEMBLE HERE 0900 MONDAY MORNING.

He signed it and pinned it to the map on the wall. "Now let me see your records."

Clasen closed his ledger and handed it over.

"Is it up-to-date?"

"Nearly, sir. I have received the lists of prisoners from all but one of the sectors. I expect I will have a complete set of records when the returns come in on Monday."

"They're not prisoners, they are detainees." He tucked the ledger under his arm. "I want you to remain here, Clasen. Spread the word to the other men. Tell them not to conduct any more checks until I say otherwise. Am I clear?"

Clasen's face was unreadable. "Yes, sir."

One of the Schupo men shuffled his feet nervously. "What about us, what do you want us to do?"

"You are dismissed. Just make sure you're here first thing on Monday morning." He started for the door.

Clasen said, "Shouldn't you be at the security briefing, sir?"

Saxon whirled on his heel. "What security briefing?"

"In the kommandant's office at the Stadium. The Hauptmann used to attend them every Friday."

Saxon suppressed a curse, and called for his driver. It took them nearly an hour to make it through the morning traffic, and he arrived to find the kommandant's office empty. The smoky atmosphere and full ashtrays scattered about the room were testament to the security briefing which he'd obviously missed. This is getting to be a habit, he thought. Empty offices and colleagues unavailable everywhere I go.

#

He took Clasen's ledger back to his hotel and went through it. The records were remarkably clear and detailed, each line showing the name and sex of the detainee, where and when they were picked up, the name of the station where they were held. There was a column for nationality; the vast majority were German. A code classified each detainee: A for workshy, P for prostitute, T for pickpocket, S for tramp, B for beggar. Some of the entries showed several, like P/A or S/T. Others showed no classification.

A total of 342 people had been arrested and detained. Of those, 218 were classified as doxies, 17 were suspected pickpockets. There was one pimp. The rest were beggars or vagabonds. Many of the girls were non-Germans.

He drew some lines on a blank piece of paper and began to compile a list of names...

#

On Sunday morning, Herr Püttner knocked on his door and told him there was a telephone call for him. He followed Püttner to the lobby. The hotel man pointed to a coin-operated telephone in a wooden booth. Saxon picked up the receiver.

"Saxon? This is Rudolf."

It took a moment to remember who this was: Rudolf Marcus, Ruth's cousin in Austria.

"Rudolf, what can I do for you? Is Ruth there?"

"Ruth and Samuel went out for a walk. I thought I'd take the opportunity to talk with you. How's the job going in Berlin?"

"It's going well, thank you. How have you been getting on with Ruth and Samuel?"

"That's why I'm calling," said Rudolf. "This apartment is rather too small for two adults and a small child. I wondered how long Ruth and Samuel will need to remain here."

Saxon felt the blood drain from his face. "We have no definite plans," he replied. "You must know how difficult it is for Ruth and Samuel in Germany at present. I was hoping that they could stay with you as long as necessary."

Rudolf's voice hardened. "What does that mean?"

Saxon had no answer to that. "Have you spoken to Ruth about this?"

"We have had some conversations, yes, but her answers are always vague. Don't get me wrong, I am happy to accommodate them for a while, but I was hoping for an indication as to how long things will continue as they are."

A bead of sweat formed on Saxon's forehead. "Would it help if Ruth paid a small rent?"

Rudolf's voice rose. "It's not a question of money, man. Ruth pays for her groceries. Haven't you been listening?"

"I understand, Rudolf."

Rudolf moderated his voice again. "I am a bachelor, Saxon. I'm used to my solitude. I'm sure you understand. And I was happy to come to Ruth's aid when she needed me. But it's been six months now, and there's no end in sight. I'm not sure if you are aware how small my apartment is."

The call ended shortly after that. Saxon swore quietly as he replaced the receiver with a greasy hand. Rudolf would have obtained the hotel's telephone number from the Berlin directory. He wondered whether Ruth had given him the name of the hotel or whether Rudolf had stolen a look at Saxon's letter to her.

Chapter 10

His team of misfits assembled at the office in Unter den Linden on Monday morning. He handed the ledger back to Clasen, and, taking great care with his penmanship, Clasen added in the names of the weekend's new detainees.

While he waited, Saxon ran his eyes over the men. They shared cigarettes and humorous tales of their weekend. As usual, Kleinholz and Heller were together in a corner. Reckendorfer roamed around the room, clearing a path like a killer whale through a shoal of mackerel, his rumbling laugh rolling over all their heads. They all seemed wary of him. Even Sergeant Schmidt gave him a wide berth. Saxon wondered whether this was because of his bulk and obvious strength, or his history as a Gestapo axe murderer.

When Clasen was ready, Saxon signalled to Sergeant Schmidt and the sergeant raised a hand. "Come to order men for Kommissar Saxon."

Saxon stood at his desk with his hand on the ledger.

"First, I want to congratulate you all, men. You have done an excellent job. There are now..." He paused and looked to Clasen.

"Three hundred and fifty," said Clasen.

"...There are now three hundred and fifty names in the ledger – men and women tucked away out of sight."

The men smiled, nodded, slapped one another on the back.

Sergeant Schmidt stuck his chest out with pride. "We have now checked the three sectors in the north of the city, sir. We plan to complete at least two more sectors by the end of this week."

Saxon nodded. "As I said, a job well done, Sergeant."

A congratulatory hubbub greeted his words. He held up his hand for quiet. The noise continued.

"Quiet!" shouted the sergeant, and the noise abated.

"You have all followed your orders to the letter. But has anyone considered if any of these detentions are legal?"

The men exchanged confused glances. No one ventured a reply.

"I have checked the list of names, and none of these people should have been arrested."

"Why not?" came a voice.

"Quiet in the ranks," said the sergeant.

"There are limits to the amount of time we can legally hold people in police cells. And there are costs involved."

"We need to move them to the labour camp as soon as possible," said the sergeant.

Saxon ignored that comment. "Most of these people have no criminal intent. They should never have been detained."

There was shocked silence.

"I want these detainees released immediately."

"How many of them?" said a white-faced Clasen.

"All of them."

This was greeted with uproar. Sergeant Schmidt had to hammer on the table to restore order. "Let the Kommissar speak."

"Thank you, Sergeant." Saxon lifted the ledger and brandished it. "The work you have done already will not be wasted. We can pick up these people again, if we need to, when the time comes. We have their details in these records."

"Sir, the police stations will react badly if we ask them to release that number of prisoners," protested the sergeant.

"That can't be helped, Sergeant. Tell them they can pick the detainees up again closer to the start of the Games if necessary."

"That may not be possible, sir! Manpower resources in the police stations is limited," said the sergeant.

"Then I will request more men from the commandant." He handed the ledger to Sergeant Schmidt. "See that all these people are released today."

Clasen went through the ledger, painstakingly filling out release forms for each detainee. Saxon signed each one. When all 350 were complete, the sergeant sorted them by police sector. Then he organised his men into pairs and despatched them to carry out the Kommissar's instructions, one pair to each police sector.

After the men had gone, Saxon and the sergeant sat by the telephone. Within 30 minutes, the calls started to come in. Most were from desk sergeants or duty officers who required verbal confirmation of the release instructions. In stations where they knew Sergeant Schmidt, his word was enough. For others, Saxon had to take the calls, and a few of these proved troublesome. No one had heard of the Kommissar.

"I have two of your officers here, Kleinholz and Heller," said one especially pedantic official – one Oberleutnant Schultz from the station at Reinickendorf. "They tell me that you have replaced Hauptmann Zimmermann. Is that correct?"

"Yes."

"Where is Zimmermann? Let me speak with him."

"I'm in charge now. My name is Kommissar Saxon. Talk to me."

The Oberleutnant took a moment to gather his wits. "Heller has requested that I release thirteen prisoners in our cells."

"That is correct. Is there a problem?" Saxon spoke in a crisp, impatient tone.

"I will require your signature on one of our station release forms for each prisoner."

"Tell me, what crimes are these detainees accused of?" said Saxon.

"None, but they are held under Gestapo protective custody. I cannot release them on the basis of a telephone call from someone I don't know."

"Have my men not provided release forms for these detainees?"

"Yes, Kommissar, but these general release forms are insufficient. I can only release them on foot of our own station release forms. Good day." The Oberleutnant terminated the call.

Schultz's police station at Berliner Strasse, Reinickendorf was a blocky, 7-storey structure, and Oberleutnant Schultz proved to be an Orpo officer built from a similar blueprint. Carrying over 150 kilograms in weight, he waddled to the front desk to attend to Saxon.

Looking a little sheepish, Saxon's officers kept out of the line of fire in the public waiting area.

Schultz examined Saxon's credentials and asked a few probing questions. Where was he from? When had he taken over from Zimmermann? Whom did he report to at SS headquarters?

"SS-Standartenführer Ulman," snapped Saxon.

Schultz lifted a telephone and called Ulman at Prinz-Albrecht-Strasse. He introduced himself by name and rank. "I'm calling from the station at Reinickendorf. I have one Kriminalkommissar Saxon here with me. He claims to know you... He has signed release forms for thirteen detainees... Yes, I've checked them... I don't know, sir... He didn't say..." He handed the receiver to Saxon. "The Standartenführer wants to talk with you."

"Saxon? What are you doing? Why are you releasing prisoners?"

"I'm doing my job, sir."

"But why are you releasing prisoners?"

"They're detainees, and you gave me this task. You really must trust me to do it in whatever way I choose."

After a short pause, Ulman said, "Give the telephone back to the Oberleutnant."

Saxon handed back the receiver. Ulman and Schultz completed the call, and Schultz hung up. He handed thirteen blank forms to Saxon. "Fill these out, please, and give them to the desk sergeant." And Schultz waddled off.

#

Back at base in Unter den Linden, Saxon found a disgruntled-looking Sergeant Schmidt.

"What's the matter, Sergeant?" he said.

"It's nothing, sir."

"Go ahead, man, speak your mind."

"I understand your reasoning," said the sergeant. "We probably should have released some of the prisoners..."

"But?"

The sergeant stared at Saxon, unblinking. "But not all of them. I'm not sure the men understand."

Saxon shook himself free of the sergeant's piercing stare. "I expect the men to follow their orders. And that includes you."

Schmidt set his jaw. "Yes, sir."

"Now, we have work to do. It's time we thought about the next phase of the operation."

Together, they considered the question of how many extra men they would need to complete their work in the accelerated manner proposed by Saxon, starting on July 25, one week before the Games.

Covering the 37 sectors over a period of 7 days, working 3 shifts per day, and assuming they could get one local man from each sector to work with them, they calculated that the team would need a total of 75 men.

Saxon wrote a note addressed to the kommandant and handed it to Sergeant Schmidt. "See that Kommandant Fürstner gets this."

Chapter 11

Tuesday June 30

On Tuesday morning, he handed his hotel receipt to Ulman's adjutant.

"I'll sort it out as soon as I can," said Canstatt. "But Monday is my day for this sort of work."

Saxon thanked him and asked where he might get some information about the holding camp where the detainees were to be held.

"Try the kommandant. His office is on the ground floor," said the adjutant.

His enquiries led him to a plain unmarked office. He knocked and entered and was surprised to see a face he knew. Michael Lippert was one of the men who arrested Ernst Röhm, the leader of the SA, in Munich on the Night of the Long Knives. Lippert was known as a fanatical Nazi, and the man rumoured to have fired the shot that killed Röhm.

He introduced himself to Lippert. "You are in charge of building this new camp at Oranienburg?"

"I am the camp kommandant, yes. What is your interest?"

"My men have been tasked with cleansing the streets in preparation for the Games. We are using the police stations for the moment, but we will have need of your camp. When will it be open to receive detainees?"

"That's hard to say, Kommissar. The officials in the Reichskommissar's office are causing problems, and I have had difficulties finding enough workers for the construction work."

"Your best estimate?"

Lippert averted his eyes in a classic defensive manner. "I hope the work on the site will start next week. If I can find enough workers with the necessary skills, construction shouldn't take long."

Saxon waited for a date.

Lippert checked the calendar on his wall. "July 31 should be attainable."

"But the Games start the day after that!"

Lippert offered him a thin smile. "I'm sorry, but that's the best we can hope for."

#

Saxon sat in the front passenger seat on the way back to Unter den Linden. Nemec's white-knuckle grip on the wheel told him how uncomfortable the driver felt about the seating arrangement.

"Relax, man," he said. "I wanted to ask you what the men are saying about my appointment."

"I have heard nothing." Nemec's eyes slid in a sideways glance at Saxon.

"They must be saying something."

"Very little, Kommissar. They know you come from Munich. You have a strong record of good police work."

Either this man is the soul of discretion or he's heard a scandalous rumour.

"Anything else?"

"Nothing."

It must have been something really bad.

"What of my predecessor, Zimmermann, did the men like him?"

"I couldn't say, sir. I was his driver, nothing more."

"Why was he fired?"

Nemec glanced at Saxon, his eyes wide in alarm. "Fired? He was called away on a private matter. We assumed a death in the family, or some other personal tragedy."

"Is that what Ulman told you?"

A sour smell of nervous sweat filled the car. "The Standartenführer told us nothing, sir. Hauptmann Zimmermann was there one day and gone the next."

"What does the grapevine say? There must have been rumours."

Nemec fixed his gaze on the road ahead. "There were stories, but I didn't believe any of them."

He pushed the driver for more details, but Nemec refused to say another word.

It seemed that Zimmermann really had disappeared.

Chapter 12

Standing by the window overlooking the rear of the Orpo offices, he watched an early morning summer mist pass like a shroud across the cars and motorbikes in the car park. "How did the kommandant react when he read my note?"

Sergeant Schmidt grunted. "He didn't."

"What? He didn't read my note, or he read it and said nothing?"

"I couldn't deliver it to the kommandant, sir."

"He was ill when I called to speak with him on Friday," said Saxon. "He's still not back on his feet?"

"He's gone, Kommissar."

"Gone? Gone where?"

The sergeant inhaled deeply. "I don't know. The kommandant is no longer working on the Olympic Village project. That's all I know."

For a moment he thought the sergeant was playing a practical joke on him. The expression on the man's face and his pallor told him otherwise.

"Do we know why?"

"The word on the grapevine is that he failed in his duties somehow."

That phrase rang a bell of recognition in Saxon's head. Wasn't that what Ulman had said about Zimmermann? And Wolfgang had said Ulman took a dislike to Zimmermann because he wasn't a member of the Party. Saxon ran a finger under his collar. "Do we know whether the kommandant was a Party member?"

The sergeant didn't know.

Saxon lifted the telephone and spoke to Walter March. "My sergeant tells me that Kommandant Fürstner is no longer in charge of the Olympic Village. Is that correct?"

"Yes. As of midnight last night the Village project is under the supervision of Oberstleutnant Werner von Gilsa, kommandant of the Berlin Guard Troop."

Saxon searched his memory. "That's a ceremonial regiment, isn't it?" His stomach was churning, his heart racing. He forced his body to calm down. "Do we know when the new man is due to arrive?"

"I believe he will take up residence in the next few days."

"Do you know why Wolfgang has been... removed?"

"No, Kommissar. There has been no official word yet."

"Thank you, Herr March." Saxon terminated the call. He brought the sergeant up to date with the news.

"That's a marching regiment," said the sergeant. "I've taken my children to see them. Very well drilled marchers. They march from the Brandenburg Gate to the War Memorial every day."

The sergeant's hangdog look told Saxon how he felt about the new appointment. "What did you do with my note?" he said.

"I delivered it to the kommandant's house in the Olympic Village."

Saxon put his head in his hands.

#

When the men arrived for work, Sergeant Schmidt called them to order and Saxon announced the new appointment. The men reacted in silence much as they had to his controversial order at their last meeting.

"Any questions?" said Saxon.

"What do we know about the Oberstleutnant, sir?" said one man.

At a signal from Saxon, Sergeant Schmidt answered the question. "He is kommandant of the Berlin Guard Troop."

This was greeted with a shocked silence.

"That's a ceremonial regiment," said the same man. "Don't they have a band?"

"What does he know about setting up an Olympic Village?" boomed Reckendorfer.

This was greeted with a loud murmur.

The sergeant held up a hand to restore order. "Remember that Kommandant Fürstner knew nothing about how to build an Olympic Village before he took over."

Saxon said, "We must accept the command decisions of our superiors and complete the tasks we are set to the best of our ability."

"But there's only one month to go," said Clasen. "Do we know why the kommandant was replaced?"

Saxon gave a rebuking cough.

"That's not for us to question," said Schmidt.

"Have you worked out how many extra men we will need to cleanse the streets?" said one of the men.

"Sergeant Schmidt and I have worked that out." Saxon paced up and down, his heels clicking against the floorboards. "I have put in a request for the extra men we will need. I'm sure the new kommandant will give it due consideration when he arrives."

"You mean he hasn't arrived yet?" said someone.

"No need to concern yourselves," said the sergeant. "We still have plenty of time."

Saxon sneaked a glance at the calendar on the wall. They had 30 days before the start of the Games. A worm of self-doubt stirred in his chest. Perhaps he shouldn't have released all those detainees.

Sergeant Schmidt added, "We have no reason to suppose that the Oberstleutnant won't do a first-class job."

From the looks on their faces, the men clearly had their doubts, and Saxon would have found it hard to disagree with them. He dismissed the men. Then he wrote a short note addressed to

Oberstleutnant von Gilsa, requesting an urgent meeting. He handed it to Sergeant Schmidt to deliver.

"Where will you be if I get a response?" said the sergeant.

"I'm going back to the hotel. There's nothing more to be done here today."

The telephone rang as the two men were leaving the room.

The sergeant answered it. "Good morning, Standartenführer." He signalled to Saxon with his eyebrows. When Saxon indicated that he didn't want to take the call, the sergeant said, "The kommissar is not here, sir. Would you like to leave a message?"

"What did he want?" said Saxon when the call had ended.

"You're to contact him as soon as you get back to the office. He sounded angry about something."

"I wonder why that could be," said Saxon.

Nemec dropped him off at the hotel, and Saxon dismissed his driver for the rest of the day.

PART 2
Chapter 13

The hotel receptionist handed him his key and a letter. A glance at the envelope told him it was from Ruth.

Sunday June 28, 1936

Dear Roland,

I received your letter. I'm happy that you have been chosen for such an important job. I'm sure you will do it well, as you do everything you set your mind to. Samuel and I both miss you terribly. We cannot wait for the day when we can be reunited as a family again.

Cousin Rudolf's apartment is small, and not designed for a lively 3-year-old. His glass-fronted cabinets are stocked with porcelain and other fragile objects. I'm sorry to have to tell you that Samuel has broken two of his most treasured figurines. Cousin Rudolf is most unhappy about these losses, and I fear there may be more to come. There are so very few places where we can hide these shiny items away from an inquisitive child.

Cousin Rudolf has some irritating habits that I find infuriating. First, he smokes a large Meerschaum pipe that fills the apartment with choking smoke, which I'm sure cannot be good for the lungs of a growing child. Second, he drinks to excess. Honestly, some nights I'm afraid to sleep in case he loses his natural restraint and comes into our room. Third, he plays his gramophone records endlessly. I enjoy Wagner as much as the next person, but it grates when he plays the same pieces over and over and over again.

Worst of all, he treats me like a servant. Apparently, I must undertake all his domestic chores in boundless gratitude for the enormous favour he is bestowing on Samuel and me by allowing us to share his miserable apartment. Can you imagine how it feels to have to wash the undergarments of a stranger!

The past 5 months and 8 days have been torture. I'm not sure I can survive much longer here without losing my mind.

All my love,

Ruth and Samuel

After reading it a second time, he was sweating. He lit a cigarette with a shaking hand. How could he reply to a letter like that? It was imperative that Ruth and Samuel remain in Austria. Since the enactment of the Nuremburg Laws, Germany was no place for Jews. Perhaps he could write to Cousin Rudolf and demand that he change his ways. But how could he demand anything of a man he hardly knew? He'd only met him once, and Rudolf had been kind enough to take Ruth and Samuel in when they needed his help.

He sat on the edge of his bed and began to compose a reply.

Hotel Südberg, Bernberg Strasse 27, Berlin

July 2, 1936

Dear Ruth,

He sat there, discarding opening lines one after the other in his head. Finally, he settled on one.

It was good to hear from you.

He paused for thought and then continued:

You should talk to your cousin. Tell him how you feel about his smoking, his drinking and his music. Demand that he change his ways,

He stopped, read back what he'd written. Then he bundled the page into a ball and threw it against the wall. He started again.

Hotel Südberg, Bernberg Strasse 27, Berlin

July 2, 1936

Dear Ruth,

It was good to hear from you. I miss you both.

I'm sorry that Rudolf is causing you distress. Talk to him. If he has any spark of humanity and any feelings for you, I'm sure he can be persuaded to modify his behaviour. If not, maybe you could look for other lodgings where you are, or somewhere else in Austria. You really need to settle in Austria. It's best for you and it's best for Samuel.

We will be reunited one day soon, I promise. Please be patient, my darling.

With all my love,
Roland

It was a bit weak, but he couldn't think of anything else he could say. He had to rely on Ruth's good sense. He was hopeful that Cousin Rudolf would modify his behaviour if she spoke to him about it. And surely he would remind her how unsafe it would be for her to return to Germany.

#

Feeling unsettled, but lacking a driver, he took a U-Bahn train to the Olympic Stadium. Once again, the sheer scale of the place took his breath away. He tried to imagine what it would be like filled with athletes and 100,000 noisy spectators. The VIP seats were still not in place, but the spectator seats were – all 37,000 of them.

Three Transport Corps motorbikes were racing each other up and down the concourse, weaving around the troop trucks and other vehicles that littered the scene. He assumed it was a training exercise, although the riders seemed to be getting too much fun out of it for that.

Using his Kripo badge to gain access through the turnstiles, he began by walking all the way around the structure, seeking any places where an assassin could hide. There was nowhere. Every inch of the place, right up to the rim on all sides, was wide open to public view.

He checked the entrances and exits. There were turnstiles at the front concourse where tickets would be checked, and many exits for rapid mass egress. The architect had done an amazing job.

The exit corridors under and behind the seating could provide hiding places, however, and he resolved to have these patrolled during the Games.

Satisfied with his survey, he took the U-Bahn back to the hotel.

Chapter 14

Kommissar Saxon attended his first security briefing in the kommandant's office in the Stadium first thing on Friday morning, July 3. Ulman introduced him to a bewildering number of people: Gestapo and SA leaders; a representative from the NSKK – the Transport Corps; officials from the Ministry of Propaganda, and a man from the office of the Reichskommissar of Berlin. The Berlin police was represented by a tall, thin individual called Major Bruno Büchner. Kommandant Fürstner was absent, of course, and there was no sign of von Gilsa, his replacement.

The meeting was called to order by the chairman, Hauptmann Titel. "As I'm sure you all know by now, Kommandant Fürstner has been relieved of his duties. His position will be taken soon by Oberstleutnant Werner von Gilsa. In the meantime, we must soldier on without him."

He waved a hand in Saxon's direction. "I think you've all met our newest member, Kriminalkommissar Saxon. The Kommissar comes to us from Munich with an enviable police record. Perhaps we should start by asking the Kommissar to give us an update on his progress at cleansing the city streets."

Saxon got to his feet and drew a deep breath. "Thank you, Herr Hauptmann. My men have been active preparing for the cleansing operations, which will start one week before the opening ceremony. The detainees will be held in the city's police cells awaiting the commissioning of the camp at Oranienburg. Of these detainees, I estimate that close to fifty per cent will be women of the night, twenty per cent will be beggars or vagabonds. The remainder will be thieves, for the most part. We have devised a detailed plan to sweep all sectors of the city in time for the start of the Games. I should add that our plan will require the assistance of the standing force in each sector."

"You will forward a copy of your plan to me?" said Bruno Büchner.

Saxon nodded his agreement.

A red-faced Ulman asked a question when Saxon had resumed his seat. "I seem to recall Hauptmann Zimmermann had already arrested over three hundred prisoners."

Saxon made no response, and the chairman moved on to the next item on the agenda: new uniforms for the municipal and traffic police.

#

After the meeting, Nemec drove Saxon from the Stadium to the kommandant's house in the Olympic Village to speak with the new man, Werner von Gilsa. The immaculately-dressed butler who answered his knock on the door was the same one who had served under Kommandant Fürstner.

"I'd like to speak with the kommandant," said Saxon.

"I'm sorry, sir, the kommandant no longer lives here."

"You have a new kommandant in residence?"

"Oberstleutnant von Gilsa is not here yet, sir. He is due to take up residence at the weekend."

"I am Kriminalkommissar Saxon, in charge of security for the Village..."

"I know who you are, sir." That sounded impudent to Saxon, but the butler's steady stare gave nothing away.

"My sergeant delivered two notes, the first addressed to Kommandant Fürstner, the second to Oberstleutnant von Gilsa. Do you have them?"

"I have many notes and letters here for the attention of the Oberstleutnant. He will receive them when he arrives." The butler began to close the door. "Good day, Kommissar."

Saxon put a hand on the door to hold it open. "Can you tell me where I might contact Kommandant Fürstner? Did he leave a forwarding address?"

The butler hesitated before answering. "I expect he has returned to his own home."

"Where is that? Do you have an address?"

"I'm sorry, sir." The door closed.

Saxon turned away from the door to find his driver standing close behind him. "I have a rough idea where the kommandant lives, sir."

"How rough?"

"I know he lives somewhere in Neukölln."

"That's in the north of the city, I think. Is it far?"

"I could get you there in an hour. But we'd have to search for him there, sir. That could take a while."

"I need to take another look around the Village," Saxon said. "Why don't you take the car to Neukölln, see if you can find Kommandant Fürstner's home."

Nemec saluted and headed off to find the car.

Saxon set off on foot, plunging into the maze of buildings standing silent and idle in preparation for the arrival of the athletes. He tried the doors of several bungalows, but they were all locked. Then he saw a woman moving between the houses in the distance. He moved to intercept her, but by the time he'd reached the point where he'd seen her, she was gone.

He tried three more doors. The third one opened and he stepped inside.

A woman appeared in his path. "Can I help you, Kommissar?"

She was dressed in a blue linen coat, her hair tied back and contained in a scarf. She carried a dust-cloth and a bucket.

Surprised, Saxon said, "You know who I am?"

"Yes, of course. Is there something I can help you with?"

"What is your name?" he said.

"Marja Karol." A man wearing an identical coat, and wielding a hand-brush, emerged from one of the rooms. "This is Stefan, my husband. Our job is the keep the Village clean for the athletes."

Saxon had heard the family name before somewhere. "You are Slavs?"

"Yes, Kommissar," said Stefan. "We're from Belgrade."

"Are there more like you?"

"Slavs?"

"Cleaners."

"There are six of us in the Village. The others are somewhere..." He waved his brush.

"You have keys to all the houses?"

Marja lifted a bunch of keys from her belt. "Yes, Kommissar."

Marja took Saxon on a tour. His second visit to the Village was more revealing than his first. There were 142 single-storey houses for the athletes who would be accommodated 16 to 24 in each house, two to each bedroom.

He asked to see the area reserved for the athletes from the United States and immediately noticed that the accommodation had been divided into two distinct parts.

"Why the two parts?" he asked. "I assume this is to segregate the sexes."

"Not at all, Kommissar," said the cleaner. "This area is for the white male athletes. The other area is for the negroes."

"Won't they take exception to this arrangement?"

"The Americans insisted on it," said the Slav.

Saxon blinked. He asked where the women athletes would be housed.

"In the Friesenhaus, in the Sports Forum."

"And are the American accommodations there also segregated by race?"

"Yes."

He wondered how they would accommodate married couples, and what about interracial married couples? He didn't ask.

#

Nemec returned within two hours with the news that he'd had no luck finding Kommandant Fürstner's home.

"You're sure it was in Neukölln?"

"I think that's what he said. It's a vast area. I covered less than half of it. I could try again on another day if you wish, Kommissar."

"Do you know where Hauptmann Zimmermann lives?"

"Yes, sir, he lives in Tirpitz House, Pankow."

Saxon handed the driver his notepad and pen. "Write down his address."

#

Back in the office, he used Clasen's typewriter to type an outline of their plan for street sanitizing operations. When it was complete, he put it in an envelope, and brought it to Major Bruno Büchner's office.

The Major waved him in, dismissing the man he was talking to. "I'm receiving reports that you have released large numbers of prisoners from the police cells. Is this true?" He looked down his long nose at Saxon.

"Yes, Major. They were detained too early. We would have had to release them again before the end of the Games."

"I see. How many have you released?"

"All of them. Over three hundred."

Bruno made no further comment on the matter. Saxon handed him the plan, and the police chief ran his eyes over it.

"You need one member of my force in each sector for each of three shifts? Over what period?"

"Seven days starting from July 25 should do it."

Bruno picked up his telephone. After a couple of telephone calls, he said, "I'm sorry, Kommissar, all sectors are under pressure. I simply cannot promise you any men, but you may get some help from the local police at the time."

"Thank you, sir," said Saxon. "I expect we'll manage."

Chapter 15

He was preparing for bed when he was startled by a sharp knock on the door.

"There's another telephone call for you, Kommissar."

He returned to the telephone kiosk in reception and picked up the telephone receiver.

"Roland? Are you there?"

"Ruth? I'm here. Are you all right?"

"How are you? I miss you. Samuel misses you. He asks me where you are, every day."

"I'm well. How are you?"

"Samuel's not well. I've asked Rudolf to drive us back to Munich to see the doctor."

He nearly dropped the telephone receiver switching it from one ear to the other. "That's not a good idea, Ruth. You must stay where you are. Are there no doctors in Austria?"

"I want Doctor Benjamin to see him."

"Listen to me, Ruth, you must stay in Austria. Ask Rudolf to recommend a doctor. Driving a sick child all the way back to Munich is not a good idea."

There was silence on the line.

"Ruth? Are you still there?"

"Yes." She paused. "I want to come home. I don't like it here."

"Why? Is it Rudolf? I got your letter."

"It's not that. Rudolf is a gentleman, really..." He had difficulty reconciling this statement with her last letter and his telephone conversation with cousin Rudolf. Was Rudolf within earshot?

"...It's the country. They don't speak German like we do."

"They speak German."

"Yes, it's German, but they have their own words for things. They say..."

He spoke across her. "Ruth, my love, they are bound to have their own dialect. I'm sure you'll get used to it in time."

She hadn't heard him. "...And their accent grates on my ears."

She paused for breath.

"Try to see the big picture, Ruth." He thought: To hell with the Gestapo if they are listening. "Germany is not a safe place for you or Samuel. I want you to promise you won't try to come back to Munich."

"I miss you, Roland." She sounded on the verge of tears. "Samuel needs his father. When will we see you again?"

"When I'm finished this assignment, I'll take some time off and visit you there."

"You swear?"

"I swear. I want you to promise me you'll take Samuel to a local doctor. What's the matter with him?"

"He has a sore throat and a fever. He's not eating, and he cries all the time."

"Take him to Rudolf's doctor. Promise me."

She hesitated again before answering, "I promise."

#

The hotel receptionist was waiting for Saxon as he left the telephone booth. The straight line of his lips conveyed his disapproval. "This telephone is not for receiving calls, Kommissar."

"Not even for emergencies?" Saxon took the first few steps up the stairs.

Püttner moved to the foot of the stairs. "Was it an emergency?"

Saxon turned to face him and delivered his final word on the subject. "It was a police call."

Chapter 16

Oberwachtmeister Reckendorfer hung around the Litfass column at Wilhelmstrasse U-Bahn station. Although he was off duty, he wore his uniform. The street was unbelievably crowded. The Litfass column and Reckendorfer together made a formidable obstacle for the people to manoeuvre around. Not for the first time he thought the city authorities should institute traffic flow regulations for pedestrians. How much more ordered it would be if the people on the right moved one way and those on the left moved the other way, just like the cars.

He checked his watch. She was a few minutes late. Andrea Abel, the sweetest girl in all of Germany, had agreed to meet him after work and he planned to take her on a tour of the Olympic Stadium. In truth, it was all he could afford. Since the 'accident' when he'd been demoted to the ranks, his wages had been slashed.

When he looked up again, there she was, grinning at him from behind the column, like a cheeky imp. They came together in the throng. She held his arms and he bent down to allow her to kiss his cheek.

"Where are we going?" she said.

He gave her an anxious smile. "I thought you'd like to see the Olympic Stadium. It's closed to the public, but I can get us in."

Her face lit up in pleasure. "I'd love that, Dieter."

They joined a stream of humanity pouring into the station. He bought two tickets and they boarded a crowded U-Bahn heading west for Spandau. They stood together clinging to a pole until the carriage became less crowded and there were seats available. Then they sat side by side for the rest of the journey with Andrea crammed into the small space between his bulk and the window.

During the walk from the station to the Stadium, he tried a little conversation. "How's your mother?" He couldn't recall any details, but she'd mentioned that her mother was ill on their first meeting.

"She's a little better, thank you. The doctor has given her something to take."

He couldn't think of anything else to say and Andrea said nothing. They walked in silence.

He shared her frisson of excitement at her first sight of the twin towers. "Wait until you get inside," he said. "You'll be amazed."

His police uniform and badge got them through the turnstiles.

She gasped when she saw the interior of the Stadium. A gang of workmen were laying the running track while others were installing the seats.

"You'll have to imagine what it will look like during the opening ceremony, when it's full of people and the Führer is present up there." He pointed to the VIP area.

"I'd love to see that," she said. "But all the tickets have been sold."

"I could probably get you a ticket," he said, without thinking.

"Oh, could you, Dieter? And one for my mother as well?"

Chapter 17

Saturday July 4

Saxon awoke with a bellyache, skipped breakfast and left the hotel. Armed with Zimmermann's address that Nemec had written in his notepad, he took a tram to Berliner Strasse and found Tirpitz House, a monstrous grey 5-storey apartment building. He knocked on the door of Zimmermann's apartment on the fourth floor. An old man opened the door a crack and peered out.

"I'd like to speak with Hauptmann Zimmermann," he said.

"Who are you?"

Saxon flashed his Kripo badge. "Police."

The old man opened the door. "Zimmermann doesn't live here anymore. What's he done?"

"What is your name?"

"Schwartz, Karl-Heinz Schwartz."

"How long have you lived here?"

"Five weeks."

"Did Zimmermann leave a forwarding address?"

"I don't know. You'll have to ask the Hausmeister about that."

He went back down to the ground floor and knocked on the Hausmeister's door. The woman who opened the door wore a filthy apron over baggy pants and boots that looked three sizes too big for her. She was every bit as old as Schwartz. He showed his police badge again.

"I need to ask you a few questions about Hauptmann Zimmermann."

"Wait here." The woman disappeared into her apartment and came back with an envelope in her hand. "This came in the post." She handed him the envelope.

A glance told him it was addressed to Zimmermann and re-addressed to Herr Ulman at Prinz-Albrecht-Strasse 8. "When did this arrive?"

"Yesterday or the day before. I was going to send it on, but my husband has been ill. I couldn't leave the house."

"Herr Zimmermann left no forwarding address?"

"As I told your Gestapo friend, I have no forwarding address. Why do you play these games?"

He could only guess what she meant by this. He thanked her and left.

#

He waited until he was back in his hotel room before looking at the envelope. It was postmarked Berlin – Marzahn, July 1. He opened it carefully.

The letter inside was written in an elaborate loopy hand on a single sheet of paper.

Bayern House, Marzahn

June 30, 1936

Heinrich,

I know you've been busy, but your behaviour during the past few weeks has been cruel and heartless. I thought you had feelings for me. Obviously, I was wrong about that. Please consider our affair at an end. I wish you every happiness in the future, although I don't hold out much hope for you. You really can't treat people like objects to be used or discarded when you feel like it.

I've put your stuff in a bag. You can collect it whenever you like. But don't expect any more favours from me. I have moved on.

Helga

Saxon smiled. He had a partial address and the prospect of a bag of Zimmermann's belongings. This was a trail he could follow!

#

By the time he stepped off the bus at Marzahn, it was early Sunday evening. Bayern House was hard to miss. Another gargantuan multi-storey apartment block overlooking a rundown street. This one had a concrete staircase on its eastern flank. He started by knocking on the Hausmeister's door. He got no answer.

Looking around for someone to ask, he selected a young man in a Hitler Youth uniform coming down the staircase.

He showed the youth his police badge. "I'm looking for Helga."

The youth squinted up at him, shielding his eyes from the sun. "There's quite a few Helgas here."

"This one would be a young Fräulein."

"How old?"

"Twenties or thirties."

"That would be Helga Töplitz on the second floor or Helga Thorman on the seventh."

He thanked the boy and gave him 5 pfennig. Then he checked the names on the postboxes in the foyer and took the stairs to the second floor.

His knock on the door of the Töplitz's apartment produced a shout from inside. "Leave them at the door, Hermann."

He knocked again, waited, and the door opened, releasing a smell of boiled cabbage. A middle-aged woman appeared.

"Frau Töplitz?" He lifted his hat.

"Where's Hermann?" said the woman.

"I'm looking for Helga. Is she at home?"

The woman's eyes narrowed. "Who're you?"

"I'm a friend of Heinrich's."

"Who's Heinrich? Is this another one of Hermann's practical jokes?"

"No, no, I'm a friend of Heinrich Zimmermann's. I'd like a quick word with Helga."

A young woman appeared behind Frau Töplitz. "Who are you?" she said.

"Fräulein Töplitz, my name is Saxon. I'm trying to find Heinrich Zimmermann. Do you know where I can find him?"

"Who's Heinrich Zimmermann? I never heard of him."

Cursing his luck, he climbed the stairs to the seventh floor and took a moment to gather his breath before knocking on the Thorman apartment door.

A young woman opened the door straight away. "Where's Hermann?" she said.

"Are you Helga?"

"Yes, but where's Hermann? Do you have my tickets?"

"I'm trying to find Heinrich Zimmermann."

"That makes two of us." She hesitated, and then said, "You'd better come inside."

She led him to the living room but didn't offer him a seat.

"Tell me how you know Heinrich," she said. "Do you know where he is?"

"When did you last see him?"

She frowned. "Thursday June fifth. We had a dinner date for that Sunday, but he never appeared. I waited for over an hour..." Her voice trailed off.

"And you haven't seen him since then?"

She shook her head.

"Did you try his apartment?"

"I knocked on his door, but no one answered. The Hausmeister was no help. He just said that Heinrich was gone."

"Gone where?"

"He didn't say. He told me to stay away – for my own safety."

"You wrote him a letter?"

"Yes, do you know if he got it?"

"He never received it. I have it."

Her eyes opened in shock or surprise. "You opened it? You read it?"

"That was how I found you."

She sat down, her hand over her mouth. He gave her a moment.

"Who are you? Why are you looking for him?"

He showed her his Kripo badge.

"You're police. You must know where he is."

"I'm with the Kripo. I'm as much in the dark as you, Fräulein."

"He's gone, isn't he? The Gestapo..."

"That seems likely, I'm afraid."

"But he's Wehrmacht. A Hauptmann! They can't arrest Wehrmacht officers, can they?"

Saxon's silence was all it took to confirm her worst fears. She cried. Silently. Big tears rolled down her cheeks. She hurried to the bedroom and returned with her face in a handkerchief. After a few minutes she regained her composure.

"I hate the police. I hate the Orpo, and the Schupo." She sobbed. "But most of all I hate the Gestapo." She got to her feet and glared at him. "And I hate the Kripo. Get out of my apartment."

"Fräulein, you said in your letter you had a bag of Heinrich's belongings."

"You shouldn't have read my letter. That was private. Now get out!"

"I'm trying to help you. Let me have a look at the bag. There might be something in there to explain what happened to him."

"We know what happened to him. He was arrested by the Gestapo. I'll never see him again." Teetering on the brink of tears again, her eyes ablaze, she screamed at him, "GET OUT!"

Chapter 18

He had a bad night and woke late on Monday morning. His stomach ache was still there. He skipped breakfast. His driver took him first to the Gestapo building, where he dropped his weekly hotel receipt into Ulman's adjutant's office, and then on to the Orpo office in Unter den Linden.

There was a note waiting for him at the reception desk on the ground floor. He tore it open.

Greetings, Kommissar Saxon.

An appointment has been made for you at 0930 hours Monday, July 6, at the office of the Chief of Development of the Olympic Project, the Olympic Village, Spandau, Berlin.

Signed: Werner Freiherr von und zu Gilsa, Oberstleutnant, Reichsheer

Saxon checked his watch. It was 09:10. He ran to the carpark, but there was no sign of his driver.

"Where's Nemec?" he demanded of a passing mechanic.

"Try the canteen, sir," said the mechanic.

He found his driver in the canteen approaching a table with a cup of coffee, a Danish pastry, and a newspaper.

"Sorry, Nemec," he said. "I need to get to the Olympic Village in the next 15 minutes."

Nemec abandoned his coffee and pastry, and both men dashed to the car.

They arrived at the kommandant's – now the Oberstleutnant's – house in the Olympic Village 30 minutes late. He was shown into the study where Gilsa and Ulman were already in conference at a table.

Saxon apologised as he shook Gilsa's hand. "I came as soon as I got your note, Herr Oberstleutnant. The traffic was impossible."

Gilsa waved him to a chair. "No time for formalities here, Kommissar. Call me Kommandant. Karl you know. What should we call you?"

"Everyone calls me Saxon."

The kommandant blinked. "Karl has told me about your work. How is it progressing?" He paused expectantly.

"Well, Kommandant. I have drawn up a plan and a rota, and I am satisfied that my men will complete the task in good time." Saxon felt like a puppy dropping a ball at his master's feet.

"You have a plan?" said Ulman, sharply.

"I wrote you a note about my manpower requirements, Kommandant."

"Yes, I have your note here. You have sixteen men, but you say you will require an additional sixty by July 25. Is that correct?"

"Yes, that is correct. If we are to sanitize the streets effectively during that week and maintain the situation for the duration of the Games, as well as providing security for the athletes in the Village, I will require seventy-five men in total. The same men will provide security for the Stadium, if required."

Karl spoke through clenched teeth. "We have discussed this, Saxon. Security for the Stadium will be provided by the Waffen-SS."

"How many men can the SS provide for security duties?" said Gilsa.

"Sufficient to cover the Stadium, I assure you, Kommandant," said the SS-man.

"And what about the other venues?"

"The Schutzstaffel will cover the Führer wherever he goes," said Ulman.

"And will your men cover the other venues when the Führer and his entourage are not present?"

"No."

The kommandant turned to Saxon. "They will be your responsibility, so. How many sporting venues are we talking about, Kommissar?"

"Twenty, sir. We may need as many as one hundred men to cover them all, as well as the Village."

Gilsa said to the SS-man. "Are you still happy to look after security for the Stadium, Karl, in addition to the Führer and his party?"

"Yes, of course," said Ulman. "I have a Waffen-SS troop at my disposal."

Saxon took a deep breath of relief. Ulman had claimed the lion's share of the glory by taking on security for the Stadium. He was welcome to it – and to the lion's share of the nightmare if anything went wrong!

Gilsa sat back in his seat. "That's settled then, Saxon will take care of the Olympic Village and the external venues." He nodded to Ulman. "Karl's SS troop will secure the Stadium for the duration of the Games as well as for the Führer and his party wherever they go. I will speak with Bruno Büchner in the morning to arrange the extra manpower for you, Kommissar. Now, is there anything else?"

"We need to consider the torch relay, sir," said Saxon. "I understand that it will depart from Olympia on July 20 and will arrive at the Stadium in time for the opening ceremony."

"As I've told you, my SS men will cover that," snapped Ulman. "It is all in hand."

"That's settled, then." Gilsa escorted them to the door. "One more thing, gentlemen, I don't wish to see any firearms at any venues during the Games."

"That is not possible," said Ulman. "The Waffen-SS is a military unit and the Führer's guard always carries sidearms."

Gilsa hesitated. "I'll have a word with Reichsführer Himmler about that," he said. "And I'd like all officers on security detail to wear civilian clothes. Strictly no uniforms. Is that clear?"

"Perfectly," said Saxon.

Ulman grunted.

Saxon dragged his feet, hoping for a moment alone with the Oberstleutnant, but Ulman could see what he was doing and hung back.

"I had some unfinished business with your predecessor, Wolfgang Fürstner," said Saxon. "Can you tell me where I might be able to contact him?"

"I'm sorry, I can't help you with that," said Gilsa. "Dismissed."

Ulman took Gilsa's elbow. "A moment of your time in private, please, Kommandant."

Saxon made a quick exit at that point. He had no doubt that Ulman was about to blacken his name in the kommandant's ear.

Chapter 19

Tuesday July 7

He barely had time to get in through the door of his office the next morning before Ulman began his tirade, standing before him with fists clenched. "I am getting reports that you released all the prisoners!"

Saxon took his time to settle into his chair. "You are questioning my method, Herr Standartenführer?"

"I'm questioning your actions. Are you mad? You were given one simple job. All you had to do was cleanse the streets of Berlin, and what have you done? Your first action was to wipe out all the good work done by your predecessor. Explain to me how your *method* is going to accomplish your goal."

"I realise you outrank me, sir, but I am under no obligation to explain myself to you. The job will be done. That's all you need to know."

"You will address me by rank."

Saxon took a file from his in-tray and opened it.

Ulman's voice rose to a falsetto. "Who do you think put you in your position? I was the one who sent for you to replace Heinrich Zimmermann."

"And it was you who had Hauptmann Zimmermann removed?" Saxon closed the file and dropped it in the in-tray.

"That's none of your business, Kommissar."

"And the way I do my job is none of yours, Standartenführer."

Ulman's colour deepened. "Have you any idea how important it is that the visitors to our city see the best Berlin possible? The Reichskommissar of Berlin has given the highest priority to the task of cleansing the streets before the athletes and spectators arrive. The Minster for Propaganda and Public Enlightenment has a personal interest in this work. Indeed, the Führer himself has placed the seal of his office on the order."

"You don't need to tell me how important the work is." Saxon spoke slowly, deliberately, to quell a tremor in his voice. "I know what I'm doing. Under the law, a detainee under protective custody may be held for no more than twenty-one days."

"Normally, yes, but the Reichsführer has issued a directive permitting six weeks' detention under Special Protective Custody for the duration of the Games."

"Why wasn't I informed of that directive? Where is it to be seen?"

Ulman ignored those questions. "Your actions are reckless in the extreme. Be warned, Kommissar." He waved a finger in Saxon's face. "Failure will fall on your head, and yours alone. I will not be held responsible if anything goes wrong. Is that clear?"

Saxon cleared his throat. "Perfectly."

"Now tell me what possessed you to interfere in the torch relay."

Saxon rose and placed his hands flat on his desk. "You are confident you can provide security for three thousand athletes over that long journey through five foreign countries? You are prepared to shoulder the risks?"

"None of that is your concern. Just keep your mind on the Stadium and the external venues."

Alarm bells rang in Saxon's head. That didn't sound like what was agreed at the meeting with Kommandant Gilsa the previous day.

Before he could frame a response, the door opened, and Sergeant Schmidt came in carrying some papers. Ulman snapped at him, "Leave us, Sergeant."

The sergeant turned on his heel and left the room.

Saxon said. "We agreed yesterday that your Waffen-SS men would handle security for the Olympic Stadium."

"That is not what was agreed. Let us be clear. The SS will take care of security in the Stadium, as well as the external venues, as long as the dignitaries are present."

"What are you saying? You want my men to take responsibility for the Stadium..."

"Yes, and all the external venues, except when the Führer is present."

"That is absolutely not what was agreed yesterday."

"I assure you it is."

Ulman was rewriting the rules. Saxon could only suppose that the SS-man no longer had the use of the Waffen-SS troop.

"I may have to revise my manpower estimates. Major Büchner will have to be informed."

"You must do as you see fit." Ulman turned toward the door.

"Before you go..." said Saxon. "If I am to be held accountable for security at the Village and all the Olympic venues, don't you think it's time you briefed me on the White Knight letter?"

"I've told you, that is none of your concern. Our best minds have come to the conclusion that the threat is not to be taken seriously. The letter is probably the work of a harmless madman."

"And what if it isn't?"

Ulman strode to the door. "The Gestapo has launched a full-scale investigation. No need to concern yourself. The matter is in good hands."

Saxon called out after the departing SS-man, "I'd like that in writing."

He got no response.

Sergeant Schmidt came in a moment later. "What was that all about?"

Saxon waved a dismissive arm. "The Standartenführer was letting off steam. I have secured a promise of more men from

Kommandant Gilsa for the Village. But, as of today, we have responsibility for security for the Stadium."

"In addition to all the external venues?"

"Yes."

"*Scheisse!* Excuse my language, sir, but will we have enough men?"

"I think so, but I'll ask the police chief for more, if necessary."

He told Schmidt about the Special Protective Custody directive.

The sergeant blushed. "I thought you would have known about that, sir."

"No one bothered to tell me," said Saxon. "Anyway, it means we can start operations any time we're ready. I'll ask if I can get the extra men sooner."

"What about the torch relay?"

"The SS will look after that."

The sergeant groaned. "A pity. A trip to Greece is just what I needed. But I'm not surprised. Leni and Ulman..."

"What about Leni and Ulman?"

He rubbed his two index fingers together in the universal symbol for sexual activity. "You know, sir. They're the best of friends."

Saxon took a moment to chew over that morsel. He remembered how close they seemed at the reception, but he couldn't picture Ulman and Leni actually in bed together. He remembered meeting the dumpy Frau Lotte Ulman in Wolfgang's home. Didn't she mention that she had two boys?

"What about the Stadium, sir?" said Sergeant Schmidt.

"Ulman will look after security for the Führer and his party wherever they go, but otherwise the job is ours. I hope you have a good suit, Sergeant."

"Yes, sir, why?"

"The new kommandant wants all the men dressed in civilian clothes for the duration of the Games. And they are to carry no guns."

The sergeant grimaced. "The men won't be happy about that."

He handed Saxon a police notice and a sealed envelope. The notice was from the office of the president of the Berlin police, Count von Helldorff, announcing that new uniforms had been issued. All front line police officers were to collect their new uniforms from the central supply depot.

Saxon handed the notice back. "Have you seen these new uniforms?"

"Yes, sir. They're green." The expression on the sergeant's face showed what he thought of the colour. "White for traffic control."

The sealed envelope was addressed to 'the Kommissar'. He opened it.

"A runner left that for you while you were in conference," said Sergeant Schmidt.

It was an invitation from Kommandant Gilsa to a celebration reception to be held in the Olympic Village the following night.

#

Later, he called Kommandant Gilsa on the telephone. The kommandant snapped at him "What is it, Kommissar?"

"I've had a visit from Karl Ulman, Kommandant. He has asked me to handle security in the Stadium."

"I thought his Waffen-SS was going to look after that. You were to look after the external venues."

"Yes, I thought that's what we agreed, but it seems the plan has changed."

The kommandant paused. "I can only suppose that his Waffen-SS troop is not available after all."

"I'm going to need more men, sir."

"How many?"

"A total of one hundred should be enough, but I'll need as many field radios as you can get me."

"I could have a word with Karl, I suppose, but he's more senior than either of us... I'll speak with Bruno and see if I can get you more men. One hundred, you say? That's eighty-four additional men?"

"Yes, sir, and those field radios. And by the way, sir, Ulman has informed me of a special executive order, issued by the Reichsführer, that allows for an extended period of detention under protective custody during the Games."

The line crackled. "And the significance of that order?"

"It means we can start the street cleansing operation earlier than planned. In fact, we could start today, if we had the manpower."

"Will you need more men for that?"

"No, sir, not if you can get my complement up to one hundred."

"Leave it with me, Saxon," said the kommandant. "I'll see if I can get you the men you need by the end of this week."

#

Ruth called again on the public telephone that evening. He ran down the stairs of the little hotel to take the call.

"How is Samuel? Did you find a doctor for him?" he said.

"He's a little better. I took him to Rudolf's doctor. He's a good doctor. Perfect." Code for *he's Jewish*. "Samuel has tonsillitis, but the doctor says it's not serious. He's given me a prescription."

"That's good. And how are you? How's Rudolf been?"

"Rudolf is Rudolf. I explained in my letter."

"I know. I wondered if he'd changed."

"Not really, Roland. And there's not much I can say. It *is* his apartment, after all. How much longer will you be in Berlin? I thought you might take some time off when the job is finished, come and visit us here."

Saxon said doubtfully, "Is there room there for another guest?"

She paused before answering, "We could take a hotel room for a few nights. When will you be posted back to Munich?"

"After the Games, I expect. The Games start on August the first and go on for sixteen days. So some time after the sixteenth."

"We'll see you after that? You promise?"

"I promise. If I can get away."

After the call, the receptionist, Püttner frowned at Saxon, but he said nothing.

Saxon's bellyache eased. By the morning it was gone.

Chapter 20

Wednesday July 8

Gilsa's grand reception was held in the sports hall in the Hindenburg House of the Olympic Village. Once again, surrounded by military men in dress uniforms and women in elaborate evening gowns, Saxon felt under-dressed in his best blue suit and Bavarian Police Academy tie.

He seized a glass of schnapps from a passing waiter's tray, slipped to the back of the room, and did his best to stay out of sight. He recognized General von Reichenau, with the monocle, and Heinrich Himmler's chief of staff, Gruppenführer Karl Wolff, in a huddle with Kommandant Gilsa, who was dressed in a dazzling ceremonial uniform to rival any of Field Marshal Göring's.

Karl Ulman had corralled Leni Riefenstahl into a corner and they were chatting like the best of friends. While Saxon watched, a tall, tanned man approached the pair.

"She looked in need of rescue," said a voice.

He found Wolfgang Fürstner standing by his shoulder, dressed in full Wehrmacht dress uniform, complete with his Iron Cross.

"Wolfgang! It's good to see you. I've been trying to find you."

"That's Charles Lindbergh, the American aviator with Ulman and Leni. Have you met him?"

"No."

"Talk to him. He's a fascinating man."

Another group caught Saxon's eye.

"Who's that big man?"

"That's Max Schmeling, the heavyweight boxer, with Bill Dodd, the American Ambassador, and that's his daughter, Martha, over there with the sprint relay team."

Laughing loudly, Martha Dodd appeared enraptured by the attention of her four companions.

"I'm happy to see you, Wolfgang," he said. "I thought we'd lost you."

"We must speak privately," Wolfgang replied softly. "But not here. Later, at my house."

"Where do you live?"

A young officer in Kriegsmarine dress uniform approached. "A word in your ear, Kommandant Fürstner..."

"I'll see that your driver gets my address," Wolfgang said in Saxon's ear, and he moved to intercept the navy man.

The army band played a strange mixture of folk and martial music. People danced to it. Newspaper cameramen mingled with the guests like wolves amongst a flock of sheep.

Ulman stuck close to Leni Riefenstahl all evening, and Saxon avoided them both. Everyone drank a lot of wine. The hubbub of conversation and laughter grew louder.

At 15 minutes before midnight, the band played a short fanfare. General von Reichenau climbed onto the stage and tapped his glass. The hubbub died.

"Ladies and gentlemen, thank you for coming here tonight to honour our colleague, Werner von und zu Gilsa." This was greeted by a ripple of applause. Gilsa clicked his heels and bowed, the people around him raising their glasses to him. "The Oberstleutnant has agreed to take our Olympic Project through its final stages to fruition."

Reichenau's voice rose. "I am confident that his experience during the War and more recently with the Berlin Guard Troop has prepared him for this onerous task. I have known Werner for at least ten years. He and I fought together during the War at several battlefronts. I'm sure he won't object if I remind him of a few notable moments from those times..."

He droned on for a few minutes. When he paused, everyone applauded. Cameras flashed. "The eleventh Olympiad of the modern Games will be a great success, I am sure, and will show the world what wonders can be achieved in a strong, progressive country like Germany under the Third Reich."

They all clapped again.

"Raise your glasses. The toast is the health of our Führer."

"The Führer!" echoed the assembled guests.

Kommandant Gilsa made a short speech in reply. When he'd finished and the applause had died, the general called for quiet again. "And now, it gives me great pleasure to acknowledge the fine work done by the Oberstleutnant's predecessor, Kommandant Wolfgang Fürstner. On the instructions of the Führer, the kommandant is hereby awarded the Olympic Medal, first class, for his contribution to the Reich's 1936 Olympic enterprise."

Once again, everyone applauded. Wolfgang stepped onto the stage, and the general pinned a medal on his chest. They exchanged Hitler salutes while the cameras flashed again. Then the general signalled to the band and they struck up a lively folk tune.

Not long after that, the gong sounded and the entire company moved from the sports hall to one of the athletes' dining halls, where a table, decorated with flowers and candles, had been prepared for the banquet.

Saxon's placename was near the end of the table farthest from the dignitaries. He took his seat and found a woman and her husband sitting opposite, another woman with a shock of blond hair sitting on his right, wearing a crumpled khaki dress.

The woman in khaki offered a hand and he shook it. "Kommissar Saxon? I'm June Leybourne, *Sydney Morning Herald*. I'm here to cover the Games." She spoke in nervous German, but when he replied in broken English she smiled in relief and switched to English.

During the first two courses, Saxon discussed trivial matters with the journalist and the woman and her husband opposite. When the main course was served, everyone concentrated on the food for a while, as the duck à l'orange was on the cool side of lukewarm.

When that was taken care of, Leybourne dabbed her mouth with her serviette and said, "I understand you have taken over from Heinrich Zimmermann. I lost contact with Heinrich. Do you know where he went, or how I can contact him?"

Saxon put down his knife and fork and turned to look into Leybourne's face. "No, I'm sorry. When did you last see him?"

She hesitated. "It was about a month ago. He told me about a strange letter that he'd received. He promised to show it to me, but I never saw him again after that."

Saxon's heart leapt and began to pound in his chest. "Did he say what was in the letter?"

"It was a threat to the United States athletes. That's all I know."

"What's your interest in security," he asked. "Aren't you here for the Games?"

The journalist raised her blond eyebrows and smiled. "I'll be covering the Games, of course, but my editor is relying on me to give our readers in-depth coverage of the entire event."

"By which you mean...?"

They paused to allow a waiter to remove their plates.

"Everything. Australian readers are interested in everything to do with the Third Reich. Your Führer is a fascinating character, don't you agree? If I could print the colour of his drawers, I'm sure they would lap it up back home."

"The colour of his drawers?"

"You know, his undies."

The woman opposite giggled.

"I'm sorry, Miss Leybourne, but I have no knowledge of such matters. And press relations are not part of my responsibilities."

Saxon turned his attention to the woman opposite. When the meal was over, he rose from his seat, took his leave of the woman and her husband, bowed farewell to Leybourne, and headed for the door. Leybourne matched him, stride for stride. Once they were outside, she put a hand on his arm. "We really can help one another, Kommissar. You have extensive knowledge of policing and security in Germany. My readers would love to know all about such matters. And I can supply valuable information in return."

He locked eyes with her. "What kind of information?"

"Well, for starters did you know there's a battle royal going on between the German and American Olympic committees? Your committee demanded that the US remove all the black athletes from their team."

"And you think that's going to happen?"

The Australian gave an unladylike snort of derision. "The president of the US committee, Avery Brundage, pointed out that more than half of their team are blackies, and many of those are world record holders. The team would be decimated without them. Do you know what one German committee member said in closed session?"

Saxon raised his eyebrows. The last thing he wanted was to hear common tittle-tattle from this stranger, but it seemed there would be no way of avoiding it.

"A member of your committee is reported to have said, 'We might as well allow gazelles to compete on the track, or dolphins in the pool.'"

"Did you print that?"

"I submitted it, but without a name it couldn't be printed."

He stepped toward his car.

The Australian said, "Do you know how your Olympic Committee is keeping Jews off the German team?"

He turned back. "That's a malicious lie. Any athlete that attains the required standard will be allowed to compete."

Leybourne's lip curled. "Any *Aryan* athlete. When the competitions start, there won't be a single Jew competing, male or female, on any team."

"I don't believe that. The Americans have at least two Jewish athletes that I know of – Glickman and Stoller."

"I'll bet you 100 Reichsmarks. In fact, I'll bet 200 marks that there won't be a single Jew from any country competing in any event in these Olympics."

It occurred to him that maybe Leybourne knew about Ruth and Samuel and was trying to provoke him into providing a sensational quote. He changed the subject. "What information do you think I can give you?"

"I'd like to get my hands on that threatening letter, of course, but I'm interested in anything to do with your police force. I understand there are several branches, like the Schupo, the SA, and the Secret Police. I'd welcome an insider's view of how these different branches work together, and where the Wehrmacht fits in."

"I wouldn't be able to help you there, I'm afraid, I lack the wide perspective needed to express an opinion on such matters."

"Oh, come on, man, you're obviously an experienced, senior police officer. Who better to express an opinion?"

Saxon reached the door of the car and opened it, before delivering his parting shot. "I'm just a simple country policeman. I have no knowledge or opinions about internal police rivalries."

"Who said anything about internal rivalries?" Leybourne called after him.

He climbed into his car and slammed the door. What had induced him to mention police rivalries? Could the journalist build a story out of that? Past experience had taught him how difficult and dangerous it was talking with journalists from the German newspapers. Dealing with foreign newsmen was well out of his league. But he couldn't help liking the woman.

Chapter 21

The next day, he asked Nemec to take him to Wolfgang Fürstner's home in Neukölln. Wolfgang invited him in. Soon, they stood face to face by a bookcase in the kommandant's study, glasses of iced tea in hand.

"What did they tell you?" said Wolfgang.

"Nothing. We were simply told that Oberstleutnant von Gilsa was taking over in your place."

"Hah! No surprises there. I've been sacked."

"So close to the opening? You must be devastated."

"I confess I was a little upset at first. But this government is so rotten, nothing they do surprises me. I'll get over it."

"What reason did they give?"

Wolfgang handed Saxon a folded piece of paper. He was reluctant to read it.

"Go ahead, read it."

Saxon put his glass on the mantelpiece and unfolded the paper. It was a letter from the office of Dr Karl Ritter von Halt, Joint Chairman of the Olympic Organising Committee, dated June 24. It informed the kommandant that he was relieved of his position, effective immediately. The reason: he had permitted sightseers to rampage through the Olympic Village, causing much damage.

Saxon refolded it and handed it back.

"Was there much damage to the Village?"

"We had one or two minor breakages, nothing that couldn't be repaired. That's not why I was sacked." Wolfgang took a book from the bookcase, opened it and pulled out an old, sepia picture of a man and a woman on their wedding day. The man was wearing a yarmulke. "Those are my grandparents," he said. "They converted to

Christianity nearly thirty years before I was born, but apparently there's no erasing the blemish of my birth."

An image of 3-year-old Samuel sprang into Saxon's mind and icy fingers stepped up his spine. "You have the Iron Cross, first class. The Wehrmacht must recognise your true worth."

"Perhaps, but there's nothing any of my superiors can do as long as the chicken farmer is in control of the security services."

"You blame Himmler?"

"Of course. Who else?"

"Karl Ulman, perhaps?"

Wolfgang replaced the picture in the book and returned the book to its place in the bookcase. "Ulman played his part, I'm sure, but Himmler signed the order, the bastard. I would happily slit his throat from ear to ear if I could get close enough."

Saxon sipped his tea. Wolfgang Fürstner stood tall and proud, a strong military man of integrity and courage. Not the first good man that he had seen brought down by Hitler's SS. "What will you do? You should leave the country. I suggest Austria. As long as the Nazis continue to be outlawed there, the political situation will remain stable. My wife and son are living there with her cousin."

"How long have they been away?"

"Nearly six months."

"I'm sorry," said Wolfgang. "You must miss them."

"They are safe, and I'm quite used to living alone again." A white lie.

The kommandant said, "I have a smallholding near Cologne. My wife and I will spend our last years in peace there. I'll be happy to retire after the Games."

He tried to guess Wolfgang's age. Late thirties perhaps, certainly too young for retirement.

The kommandant peered into his glass. "My army career is over. That much is certain. I fear for my future. They may send me to one of the labour camps... or worse."

Saxon said, "You must get out while you can. Forget about Cologne."

Wolfgang grabbed Saxon's forearm and stared into his eyes. "I am Catholic. If something should happen to me, Saxon, you may be certain it was not by my own hand. Suicide is against God's law. The worst of all sins."

Poor, paranoid Wolfgang, Saxon thought as he left.

#

The first batch of reinforcements arrived that afternoon. The place was teeming with souls dressed in all sorts of strange uniforms.

Sergeant Schmidt recorded their details in an anteroom before steering them into the office to meet Saxon.

He asked each man a series of open-ended questions to assess his suitability for the operation. The first set of questions were designed to set the candidate at his ease:

Name?

Age?

Married or single?

Number and ages of children?

From what service?

Any interest in athletics?

The answers to this question were lively, if unconvincing. The candidates obviously believed it a necessary qualification for the task at hand.

Not many had an inkling of what was expected of them.

He explained that the first task would be sanitizing the streets of the city, arresting pickpockets, prostitutes, beggars and vagabonds.

"How do you feel about that?"

None of the candidates had any objection.

"How do you feel about the black American athletes?"

The answers to this question varied. Some were sceptical that black men could beat our own Aryan runners in a fair race; others said they had no feelings one way or the other. Three of the candidates thought negroes were subhuman and expressed their disgust that they would be allowed to compete. Those three were rejected and packed off back to their units.

At the end of the vetting process, Saxon and Schmidt conferred.

"How many do we have now, Sergeant?" he said.

"Ninety-one. Ninety-three counting me and you."

"That'll have to do. We'll start the process tomorrow. But first, we need to draw up a detailed plan."

Chapter 22

The chairman of the Security Committee welcomed Kommandant Gilsa to the Friday morning briefing at the Stadium, and Gilsa made a short speech in reply. Neither made any mention of Kommandant Fürstner.

At the invitation of the chairman, Saxon explained his approach and outlined his plan to cleanse the city. The reactions around the table were strangely muted. It seemed they had all been briefed privately by Ulman before the meeting about the release of the detainees and no one wanted to say anything. There was no time to raise objections; cleansing operations would start the following day.

Karl Ulman used a map to show the planned route and timing of the torch relay, which he and his team would accompany. Leni Riefenstahl's cameras would be present every step of the way, creating additional security problems for the SS.

#

By mid-morning, Saxon was in his office in Unter den Linden where the team had assembled. The room was bursting at the seams, but at least they looked like a cohesive force now that they were all dressed in the new, nauseating green Orpo uniform.

Sergeant Schmidt split them up into six teams with carefully chosen team leaders. Then each team was sub-divided into three 5-man workgroups, or gangs. Problems began to emerge immediately, and some juggling of the names was necessary, but by lunchtime, all of the gangs had been agreed. Each gang had a leader reporting to one of the six team leaders. The men were given detailed instructions and dismissed.

Saxon used the telephone to contact the police headquarters in the first four sectors to arrange for local support, one man per sector per shift. The results were discouraging; not many police stations could commit men to shift work, and especially not on Saturdays and Sundays, and they were reluctant to commit men and resources to a job that they felt they'd already done.

"We'll have to rely on our own resources," said Saxon.

Sergeant Schmidt said, "I have seen a vagabond family hanging around the Olympic Stadium in the past week. I saw them again yesterday. Could we send a couple of men to pick them up?"

"Not yet, Sergeant," said Saxon. "Hold your nerve and wait. We will start operations tomorrow, as per the plan."

#

Ulman strode into the office at 2 pm. "Excuse us, Sergeant," he said, flexing his swagger stick.

Sergeant Schmidt looked to Saxon for confirmation, and Saxon said, "Take a half-hour, Sergeant."

The door closed behind the sergeant and Ulman took a seat facing Saxon's desk. "I assume your men have started their work?"

"They start in the morning," said Saxon.

"That's good. I only hope you've left enough time to complete the exercise before the athletes and spectators start to arrive."

Saxon resisted an urge to cross his arms on his chest. "That has all been taken care of."

"Let's hope so. But tell me why you found it necessary to take on so many extra men. Zimmermann's approach was to use the local police to clean up each sector. I'm curious, tell me why you found it necessary to flood each sector with your own men?"

Saxon barely restrained himself. Several sharp responses sprang to mind, but he settled for the simple, "I prefer my approach."

The SS-man crossed his legs and brushed something from his knee. He smiled. He looked like a self-satisfied spider after a juicy morsel had fallen into his web. "I'm told you have a family."

Saxon tensed. "What of it?"

"Your wife's name is Ruth, is that right?"

"What concern is that of yours?"

"Every detail of the lives of German citizens is of interest to the SS. You also have a son, I believe"

"What is this? What possible interest could you have in my family?" Saxon knew the answer, of course, but he had to ask the question.

"His name is Samuel, unless I'm mistaken. How old is young Samuel?"

"He's three." Saxon straightened his back.

Ulman's smile had melted. He placed both hands on his knee. Now he looked like a people's judge about to deliver his verdict. "I'm told your family has moved to Austria."

Saxon watched him in silence.

"That would seem to be a wise move."

Again, Saxon made no response. He felt like a man on a raft drifting toward the rapids without a paddle.

"On the other hand, it suggests some sort of cover-up on your part. Are you attempting to deny their existence?"

Saxon exploded. He hammered the top of his desk with a palm. "You're crazy! Why on earth would I do such a thing?"

Ulman raised an eyebrow. "For the sake of your career. I have known many similar cases."

Saxon spoke through clenched teeth. "I would never do such a thing."

"You are still a relatively young man. You have a solid reputation for good work. You could go far in the Kripo. You might even be accepted into the SS. But you will need to regularize your domestic affairs."

"Meaning what?"

Ulman dropped his eyes to the floor before raising them again and fixing his gaze on Saxon.

"It seems to me you have two options. You could resign from the force and join your wife in Linz. I expect you could take up some other career there."

Saxon was speechless. He shook his head.

"Or you could apply for a divorce."

#

He couldn't remember how the conversation ended. He was in shock. Clearly, Ulman and his SS team had been rummaging in his personal affairs, and they were making capital of his marriage. He had no doubt that an application for a divorce would be expedited by the people's courts.

The threat to his career was real. Ulman had made no mention of his third option, which was to continue as he was for another ten years until he reached the age of retirement. Perhaps that was no longer an option.

Ulman's mention of Linz was worrying. Where had he picked up that detail? Had he or Ruth mentioned the name of the city during their telephone calls? He didn't think so, but he couldn't be sure. He checked Ruth's letter. Linz showed clearly on the postmark. That explained it. Püttner must have passed the information to the SS or the Gestapo.

That evening, he wrote another letter to Ruth, more as a way of calming his own nerves than anything else.

Hotel Südberg, Bernberg Strasse 27, Berlin
Friday July 10, 1936
Dearest Ruth,

It was good to hear your voice again, and the good news about Samuel. I'm happy that you found a good doctor for him, and I hope his health continues to improve.

My work continues apace. I have a good squad of men under my command. The work starts in earnest tomorrow morning, and I am confident that we will reach our goals in good time for the Games.

Please write again when you have a chance. Send me some photographs of Samuel and yourself if you have them. I'm sure Rudolf must have a camera.

I miss you both.
All my love to you and Samuel,
Roland

Chapter 23

Saturday July 11

Second Lieutenant Harvey Johnson of the United States Marine Corps had had a bad week. New York to Hamburg aboard the *Bremen* had been a rough 6-day crossing. The German beer was pleasant enough, but he hated the Kraut food. Travelling tourist class meant living cheek by jowl with riff raff, and as he disembarked, he couldn't shake the feeling that he'd picked up a flea from his fellow passengers.

The train to Berlin had forced him into even closer proximity to the unwashed. Finding a seat had been a triumph, but even that was short-lived when he had to surrender it to a woman with a baby.

His only consolation was that his assignment would be a short one. He should be back in Pittsburgh in plenty of time for the start of the NFL season and the Pirates' first game against the Boston Redskins.

Sitting in a high-ceilinged office in Prinz-Albrecht-Strasse, facing an empty desk, did nothing to improve his mood. This Ulman individual was trying his patience, he should have been here to meet him ten minutes ago.

The door opened and a bald guy in a black uniform came in and hurried around to sit behind the desk. "Sorry to leave you waiting. Can I order anything for you? A cup of coffee, perhaps?"

His English was okay, but his accent was woeful.

"I'm okay. I'd like to get to my hotel and freshen up as soon as I can."

"Yes, of course. This won't take long. What may I call you?"

"Lieutenant Johnson. Harvey. Call me Harvey."

"My name's Karl." He checked a piece of paper in front of him. "This briefing document from your Legation says that security for the American athletes will be provided by a unit from the United States Marine Corps. Is that correct?"

Johnson nodded. "Yes."

"When will the rest of your unit be arriving?"

"They won't. I mean, it's a one-man unit, and I'm it."

Ulman's face creased into a broad smile. "I see. Well, it's gratifying to know that the United States government is content to leave the security of its athletes in the hands of the German police."

"Who've you put in charge of security at the Olympic Village? I'll need to speak with him."

"His name is Saxon. He's an experienced police Kommissar, equivalent to a leutnant in your country."

"Where can I find this Kommissar?"

"Talk to my adjutant on your way out. He'll give you everything you need."

The Marine stood up and swung his kitbag onto his shoulder. "I have to find my hotel and check in."

"Of course, Harvey. Welcome to Germany."

#

At 7 am on Saturday morning, Saxon and Sergeant Schmidt met in the office. Sanitizing operations would start that morning. The men were due to arrive in an hour.

They spent a half-hour double-checking the shifts they'd planned and the teams and units that would carry them out. Saxon was concerned about one of the combinations. Reckendorfer, the ex-Gestapo giant had been paired with Clasen, the smallest man on the team. "You don't think they'll look ridiculous?"

"No, it's the logical combination. Clasen has little hope of exercising any real authority out there, but no one's going to argue with the giant. They'll get on famously. You do know why Reckendorfer was thrown out of the Gestapo?"

"He killed a fellow officer with an axe. Yes. my driver told me the story."

With 30 minutes remaining, he offered Schmidt a cigarette. "Tell me about Zimmermann."

"What would you like to know?"

They lit up together.

"What was he like? Was he a good leader? Did he enjoy the work?"

Sergeant Schmidt peered at the lighted end of his cigarette as if he might find the answers to the question there. "He wasn't as thoughtful about the work as you, sir, but I think you could say he did a good job as leader. What was he like? He was like any young member of the Wehrmacht – a little paranoid, perhaps, anxious to please his superiors."

"How old is he?"

"Late twenties, early thirties maybe."

Saxon looked at his cigarette and asked casually, "Do you know what happened to him?"

"Not really. There were rumours, of course, but they told us nothing. We had him for a few weeks, then he disappeared, and you arrived."

"How did he feel about the black athletes?"

"I don't know. He didn't say one way or the other. He was fairly quiet, kept his own council."

"Do you know where he lives? Does he have family in Berlin?"

The sergeant shrugged. "No idea, sir, sorry. Ask your driver. He will know where he lived." He thought for a moment. "I think he might have had a girlfriend."

"What gave you that impression?"

"I'm not sure. His uniform was always neatly laundered and pressed, his hair washed, and he had good teeth."

"Maybe he's married."

"Maybe he was."

All of the sergeant's responses about Zimmermann were in the past tense. That alone revealed something of Sergeant Schmidt's thoughts on Zimmermann's fate.

Chapter 24

Saturday July 11

By 8 am the men had arrived, and sanitizing operations started anew. Saxon suppressed a laugh when he saw the variety of clothes that his men wore. The term 'plain clothes' was totally inadequate to describe some of the outfits.

Clasen wore a green tunic and buckskin boots, Heller and Kleinholz wore almost identical corduroy trousers and Bavarian hats. Reckendorfer's outfit was a faux Gestapo uniform – light grey with epaulettes on the shoulders. Sergeant Schmidt wore a pinstripe suit that made him look like a financial advisor or a snake-oil salesman.

The sergeant had arranged to have six Orpo cars ready, and these were used to deploy the first gangs from the six teams across the streets of six sectors.

That shift ended at 4:00 pm when the second set of gangs took over. And they handed over to the third shift at midnight.

On Sunday, the teams moved to the next sectors and the gangs rotated.

As the sanitizing operation progressed, Sergeant Schmidt reported regularly to Saxon. His job was to ensure that operational guidelines were followed and that no undue force was used by the gangs in the execution of their duties. Clasen recorded precise details of each detainee in his ledger. Saxon reviewed every case, ordering the release of three detainees.

The telephone was in constant use, with police stations ringing in for clarification of individual cases and angry or distraught citizens demanding explanations. Saxon marvelled at the calm professionalism of his sergeant in deflecting these callers, reassuring them that the detentions were for the general good.

Saxon took over whenever the calls reached crisis point. "I assure you madam, it is only a temporary detention... The men are carrying out their orders... Our records clearly show that your daughter... That is correct... I'm sorry, madam, but she has a long criminal record... I have it here in front of me... Yes, that is true, madam, and I can only suggest that she obtain employment in one of those establishments when she is released... After the Games, in the middle of August. Yes, madam..."

#

By Tuesday morning, 18 sectors had been cleared. The police stations were host to 459 new guests.

On Tuesday afternoon Saxon had a surprise visitor. Lieutenant Harvey Johnson of the United States Marine Corps presented his credentials. He spoke in English. "I've had a word with your Karl Ulman. He tells me you are in charge of security for the Olympic Village."

The lieutenant and the sergeant shook hands. "Welcome to Berlin, Lieutenant," said the sergeant.

The American smiled. "Call me Harvey."

"I'm Willi," said the sergeant.

"What should I call you, Kommissar?" said the American.

"My name is Saxon. Tell me, have you visited the Olympic Village yet?"

"I sure have. It looks swell. I'm sure our team will be comfortable there. But what security measures are you planning to put in place?"

"We are not anticipating any problems, Harvey, but we must be vigilant at all times."

"Yes indeed. Complacency leads to mistakes. How many men do you have?"

"We will have about thirty men when the time comes."

Lieutenant Johnson raised an eyebrow. "You reckon that's enough to cover the whole Village? It's a huge area."

"I think so. How many men are there in your unit?"

"You're looking at it."

"Just you?" The sergeant feigned shocked surprise.

"Afraid so. I assume you have been briefed about our negroes?"

Sergeant Schmidt glanced at Saxon. Saxon said, "We have been fully briefed."

"Okay, good. Can I take it your men will meet the boat when it docks in Hamburg?"

"Of course."

"The latest word I have is that it will arrive on Saturday morning."

"My men will be there," said Saxon.

After the American had left, Sergeant Schmidt said, "I thought the ship was docking on Sunday."

"So did I," said Saxon.

Chapter 25

Friday July 17

At the Friday security briefing, Saxon reported that the sanitizing operations were nearing completion. Nearly 900 people were being held in special protective custody. The police cells in every city sector were full.

Saxon asked Ulman if he had received word from Kommandant Lippert. Was the camp ready to receive the detainees yet?

"I have heard nothing," said Ulman. "I suggest you contact him yourself by telephone."

The representative from the Ministry of Propaganda asked if Saxon could guarantee that no athlete or foreign visitor would meet a pickpocket, a beggar, or a prostitute anywhere in the streets of Berlin.

"The Berlin police and my men have done a first-rate job," said Saxon. "But no one could give a guarantee like that. These are people we are dealing with, and people are unpredictable. They move around. However, my men will continue to keep a close eye on the streets for the duration of the Games."

A lively discussion followed, at the end of which it was agreed that large parts of the city would have to be cordoned off. That job would fall to Bruno Büchner, the Berlin police chief.

The chairman asked Bruno how many men he would need for the job, and how much it would cost.

Bruno's facial expression showed the level of his concern. "It could take every man we have. I'll have to get back to you on that, Herr Hauptmann. The cost will be high. The overtime alone could be significant."

The SA representative offered to help with manpower, if needed.

Moving on to the next item on the agenda, the chairman invited Karl Ulman to say a few words to the committee.

"Thank you, Herr Hauptmann. As you all know, the United States has sent over a specialist to oversee our security arrangements. His name is Lieutenant Harvey Johnson of the United States Marine Corps. I've spoken to him about the arrangements and I believe he has also spoken with the Kommissar here."

"Kommissar?" said Hauptmann Titel.

"I spoke with him on Tuesday last," said Saxon. "He expressed himself satisfied with our security measures. The American team is due to arrive in Hamburg tomorrow aboard the *SS Manhattan*."

"The *Manhattan* docked in Hamburg early this morning," said the Transport Corps man. "We have provided a fleet of buses to take the American team and their supporters to the city centre."

Saxon flushed at this news. None of his men was in place to protect the American team; they were scattered all over the city, checking the streets. "When are they due in Berlin?" he said.

"They should arrive early this afternoon, all being well," said the Transport man.

Saxon made his excuses and left the meeting early.

#

There were close to 500 people in the American contingent, 300 participants and their coaches. In addition, the athletes were accompanied by about 200 friends and family members, easily filling the fleet of 10 buses that carried them to City Hall in Spandauer Strasse.

A large crowd had gathered to welcome them. They cheered as the doors of the leading bus swung open and Harvey Johnson, the US Marine, stepped out.

Saxon, his sergeant, and two of his men were there to keep order. They were not needed. To a man, the Berlin crowd was delighted to welcome the team to Germany, godlike creatures, all of them. Waving miniature swastika flags and American and Olympic flags, the crowd cheered. The loudest roar was reserved for Jesse Owens, the most famous of the American athletes. It seemed the colour of his skin didn't matter one whit to the people of Berlin.

By the time the American supporters had dispersed to find their hotels and the buses had delivered the athletes and their coaches to the Olympic Village, Saxon had a 5-man contingent on watch close to the American section.

He breathed a sigh of relief. What had all the fuss been about? There was no immediate threat to any of the American athletic team.

It was two weeks before the opening of the Games, and two days before the start of the torch relay that would carry the Olympic Flame from Olympia in Greece to the Stadium in Berlin.

Chapter 26

Monday July 20

First thing on Monday morning, Ulman and several of his men boarded an airplane to Athens from Berlin's Tempelhof Airport. Saxon was relieved. Ulman's absence would give him an opportunity to concentrate on the tricky business of providing security for the Olympic Village, now more pressing than ever since the early arrival of the American team.

In Ulman's absence, his adjutant telephoned Saxon. "I have your receipt for the week, Kommissar. Last week your hotel bill was 49 Reichsmarks. This week it's 84. Can you tell me why it's so high?"

"The hotel is charging double from July 15," said Saxon. "Does that present a problem?"

"No, but I will have to clear it with the Standartenführer when he returns."

On Wednesday morning, he was deep in discussions with Sergeant Schmidt when the telephone on his desk rang.

"This is the front desk, Kommissar. You have a visitor."

"Who is it?"

"An Australian lady journalist."

"Send her up."

"I'm sorry, sir. We can't have civilians wandering around the building unaccompanied. You'll have to send someone down to escort her."

Saxon went down to the ground floor to meet June Leybourne. He shook her hand. "This is an unexpected surprise. I trust you're not here to get an update on the colour of my underwear." He grinned.

Without a flicker of humour, she handed him a piece of paper. "This was waiting for me on my desk in the press office this morning. I thought you should see it."

He thanked her and tucked the paper into his pocket. "Shouldn't you be in Greece covering the torch relay?" He placed a hand on her back, propelling her toward the door.

Leybourne planted her feet on the marble floor. "You should read it, Kommissar."

"I'll read it later. I'm very busy just at the moment."

She glared at him. "Read the letter."

He pulled the paper from his pocket and unfolded it. It was a short, typewritten note.

The negro Jesse Owens must die
For the Fatherland
Heil Hitler
The White Knight

It took a moment to register. "How was it delivered?"

"By a child, early this morning. A messenger boy, I suppose."

"Was it in an envelope?"

"I threw it away."

"Who was it addressed to? Did you look at the postmark?"

"It was addressed to the newspaper. There was no stamp and no postmark."

"So, it was delivered by hand?"

"I suppose so, yes." A notebook and pen appeared in her hands. "Would you like to respond to the contents? For the newspaper."

A knot in his stomach told him he was on quicksand. He took the journalist by the elbow and steered her to a quiet corner of the vestibule. "You can't print this. Think of the panic it would cause, the disruption to the Games."

"I'm a journalist, Mr Saxon. And this is an exclusive scoop. I wouldn't be doing my job if I failed to report it to my editor."

Saxon tried to keep his voice down. "But would it be wise to alarm the public? This is obviously a hollow threat from some sort of lunatic looking for publicity. It's nothing but a clumsy attempt to disrupt the Olympic Games."

"Maybe so, if it was the only one. But you know as well as I do this is the second one." Her pen hovered over the notebook. "Tell me what security measures will be put in place to combat the threat to Jesse Owens."

"I'm grateful to you, Miss Leybourne – the German people are grateful to you – for bringing this to our attention, but I cannot stress enough the importance of keeping this story secret until after the Games."

She wrote something in her notebook. "Is that all you have to say?"

He placed a hand on the notebook and pushed it down. "I'm serious. You can't print this story. What must I do to persuade you?"

She hesitated. Then she chewed the end of her pencil. "I'd settle for exclusive interviews with some of the athletes. If you arrange those for me, I'll hold the White Knight story until after the Games."

"Write me a list of the names."

She tore a page from the back of her notebook and handed it to him. "I look forward to hearing from you. I have a room at the Excelsior Hotel. You can reach me there."

#

Saying nothing to Sergeant Schmidt about the letter in his pocket, Saxon showed him the list of names. The American runners, Jesse Owens and Ralph Metcalfe were the first two names on the list. He recognised the names of two of Germany's competitors, Erich Borchmeyer the sprinter and Max Schmeling, the heavyweight boxer.

"Who's this?" He pointed to the last name on the list. "Helene Mayer."

"She's a champion fencer. She's German, but she's also a Jew."

He remembered the journalist's bet. Would she compete for Germany? If she did, it would earn him 200 RM.

PART 3

Chapter 27

Thursday July 23
    Orpo headquarters Unter den Linden 74

Saxon was shown in to Major Bruno Büchner's office on the seventh floor of the Orpo building. This was obviously a temporary office, stripped of all but the essentials: a desk, a picture of the Führer on the wall and a mahogany table equipped with four chairs and a tray of coffee and Danish pastries.

Bruno poured two cups. The aroma of fresh coffee brought a smile to his lips.

"How are you settling in?" said major.

"Well, thank you, Major," said Saxon.

"I'm not one for formality," said the major. "Call me sir. What should I call you?"

"Everyone calls me Saxon." He placed the White Knight letter on the table. "This came into my possession yesterday, sir."

Bruno took one look at the letter and his smile evaporated like a mudhole in the Sahara. "Have you alerted the SS or the Gestapo?"

"No, sir, I thought we should have a private talk about it first."

"I'm listening," said Bruno.

"My understanding is that my predecessor, Heinrich Zimmermann was the primary suspect for the first of these letters..." He paused for a reaction from Bruno.

The police chief remained silent, lifting his cup to his lips.

"Zimmermann can't be responsible for this one, which means we must look elsewhere."

"Indeed, and I'm sure the Gestapo and Ulman's SS team will work on that."

"Ulman is covering the torch relay, sir. He must be somewhere in Bulgaria by now. And I wonder if we can be confident that the Gestapo inquiry is making any progress. They seem to have put all their eggs in one basket."

"What are you suggesting?"

"I would like to conduct my own investigation into the letters."

"Don't you have enough on your plate looking after the athletes in the Olympic Village?"

Saxon said, "You're absolutely right. I'm going to have to assign a special unit to watch over Jesse Owens, day and night. I'll need fresh men. We can't trust any of my existing team."

Bruno nodded. "How many will you need?"

"Two plainclothes officers on three shifts with a couple extra for cover should be enough."

"Right. I'll pick out eight suitable men for you and send them around. In the meantime, keep a close eye on your men. Watch for tell-tale signs of racial hatred. If any of them shows any intention to harm Owens or any of the black athletes, he must be removed immediately. Now tell me why you wish to start your own investigation."

"My expertise is in criminal investigation. And as an outsider, who could be better placed to pursue this matter?"

Bruno brought his coffee to his lips but replaced the cup on the saucer without drinking any. "What you are suggesting would cut across every police protocol, every long-established principle of territorial control."

"Yes, sir, I realize that."

"You are asking me to appoint an officer from a jurisdiction entirely outside the precincts of the city to investigate a suspected subversive operating within the Berlin police force."

"Within one or other of the various police and security forces operating in the city – yes, sir."

Bruno lifted his cup again and drank some of his coffee. Saxon did the same.

"What would you need from me?" said Bruno.

"To start with, I would need to meet and question the Gestapo team involved in the case."

"You want to interrogate the Gestapo?" A thin smile passed over the police chief's lips.

"Yes, sir. And I will need to see the first threatening letter."

Bruno hesitated. He hadn't dismissed the idea out of hand. "I am inclined to turn this down. You do realize you are asking me to kick over a hornets' nest?"

"Yes, sir."

"On the other hand, you are the only man in Berlin above suspicion, and I am aware of your reputation as an investigator."

The police chief seemed to reach a decision. He put his cup down, lifted the telephone and dialled a single digit. "This is Bruno Büchner, do you have a moment to talk?"

Saxon could hear the tinny response from the other end of the line. Clearly, Bruno's boss had something on his mind.

Bruno responded, "Yes, sir, of course... Next Wednesday, yes sir... They have been ordered... They should be... How *is* the Countess...? Yes sir... The western end of the Stadium, I will see to that, sir..."

Finally, Bruno managed to get to the reason for the call. "I have Kommissar Saxon with me... From Munich, yes, sir... A second White Knight letter has come into his possession... Yes, sir... They look similar... No sir."

He paused to receive a stream of invective from the other end of the line.

"My thoughts exactly, sir... But Karl Ulman is with the torch relay... Yes, sir. Kommissar Saxon has requested permission to proceed with the investigation on his own... Yes, sir... Yes, sir, somewhere in Hungary, I imagine... He will be back in time for the opening ceremony... I do, sir, yes. He has a first-rate record of criminal investigations back in Munich... No, I realize that, sir, but Ulman is not here, and I think we should act without delay... The negro athletes are already in the country... Yes, sir... I think we should take the opportunity that presents itself. The SS and the Gestapo have made little progress... As you say, sir... Very well. Good morning."

He put the telephone down.

"You may proceed with caution, for a few days, until Ulman returns. If you find anything or make any progress, report it to me. Do you understand?"

"Yes, sir."

"Now, you said you want to start with the Gestapo. You'll need to speak with Obersturmführer Otto Engel." He picked up the telephone again.

Chapter 28

Thursday July 23
Prinz-Albrecht-Strasse 8

Otto Engel's office was on the second floor, more or less directly below Ulman's office. Both offices had anterooms. While Ulman's was manned by Canstatt, the adjutant, Engel's was graced by a striking young female clerk. She sat cross-legged at her desk, her shapely legs adorned with sheer grey stockings. She wore the standard dull grey uniform, but there was nothing standard or dull about the way she wore it. Her ample bosom strained her tunic, her behind overflowed the edges of her chair. Her bright red lips and the disinterested look on her face suggested that she was destined for greater things – Hollywood, starring alongside Marlene Dietrich, probably.

Her hips swayed as she crossed the room and ushered Saxon into the inner office. The decor of Engel's inner office was identical to Ulman's. The oak desk, the file cabinet in the corner, the two swastikas behind the desk and the picture of Adolf Hitler glowering on the wall over the doorframe. Where Ulman's office was a chaotic jumble of papers and files, though, Engel's was completely clear. No files or papers were to be seen anywhere and there was nothing on his desk apart from a telephone, his intercom, and a framed photograph.

Saxon remembered Engel from the security meetings. He was closely shaven, with a strong head of hair, neatly barbered and parted in the middle. His uniform was immaculately laundered and ironed. His hat hung on a hat-stand behind the door.

Engel held out a hand. "Major Büchner tells me you have received a second letter signed by the White Knight."

Saxon handed it across. "Do you have the first one? I'd like to examine it."

Engel put on his glasses and peered at the letter. "It's with the laboratory. The scientists are looking at it. I will send this letter to them. They should be able to confirm that they are from the same source."

"Isn't that obvious?"

"Yes, but they may come up with something else of value to our investigation."

Saxon took a seat, while Engel pulled a large envelope from a desk drawer. He ran his eyes over the letter again before placing it inside. "You have the envelope?"

"No, unfortunately there was no envelope." Saxon waited for Engel to look up. "I understand you are holding Heinrich Zimmermann on suspicion."

"Who told you that?" Engel sealed the envelope and placed it on his desk.

"I think you'll agree this letter proves that Zimmermann is not the man you're looking for. May I take it that you will release him soon?"

Engel moved his glasses to the end of his nose and placed his chin between his thumb and forefinger. He looked like a young, learned professor. "He could still be a member of a subversive group."

"So you do have him under interrogation."

"I didn't say that, Kommissar. You have no authority to ask that sort of question."

"Major Büchner has approved my investigation of these matters."

Engel shifted on his seat. "Yes, and as long as the security of the state is not under threat, I will be happy to help."

"I'd like to speak with Zimmermann."

"That won't be possible."

"Why not?"

He got no answer – just a vacant stare.

"What did Zimmermann tell you under interrogation? Do you have a transcript I could read?"

Engel looked at his watch. "You're going to have to excuse me, Kommissar. I have work to do, and I need to get this letter to the laboratory as quickly as possible." He removed his glasses, tucked them into his breast pocket, and stood up. He walked to the door and opened it.

Saxon was fuming inside, but he accompanied Engel out of the office with a pleasant smile plastered on his face. Once in the corridor, Engel locked his office door and headed for the staircase. Saxon waited until he was out of sight, then he went back into the anteroom and spoke with the young clerk.

"My name is Kommissar Saxon..." he began.

"Yes, sir, I know who you are."

"I have been asked to do some work on the Zimmermann case."

She gave him a look like a goose on Christmas Eve.

"Engel said you have his file. I'd like to see it."

Her eyes flashed to the in-tray on her desk and back again. "I'm sorry, Kommissar, I cannot release a file without the Obersturmführer's direct instruction."

Saxon strode across to the desk. Before he could reach it, she grabbed a file from the in-tray and leapt to her feet, clutching it to her breast. A pink sticker attached to the front of the file held three characters in black ink: 'F17'.

"Stay back!" she shouted. She looked terrified.

He held up both palms. "I mean you no harm, Fräulein. I will ask Herr Engel for the file the next time I return."

He turned on his heel and left.

Chapter 29

The Friday morning security briefing of the police command was well under way by the time Saxon arrived. Otto Engel was on his feet, glasses perched on the end of his nose, informing the committee members about the White Knight letter.

"It was handed to the Kommissar by a newspaper reporter," said Engel.

"Who knows about this?" said the chairman, Hauptmann Titel.

"Only the members of this committee and the journalist," said Engel.

Saxon answered the obvious alarm that this statement had generated. "I have secured a promise from the reporter not to publish anything about the letter in exchange for some interviews with the athletes."

"And you're satisfied that this reporter will keep his word?"

"I am, Herr Hauptmann."

"Very well," said the chairman. "Every precaution must be taken to ensure that the information is contained. It could cause panic among the athletes and would damage the public image of the city that we have taken such pains to preserve."

Major Bruno Büchner, the Berlin police chief, stood up. He looked at the faces around the table. "This is not the first such threat we have received."

"Explain that statement," said the man from the Propaganda Ministry.

Engel took over the narrative. "We have received a number of threats and subversive communications since the beginning of the year. We have a file full of them at headquarters. They are all from crackpots."

"How can you be sure of that?" said von Gilsa.

"Put that down to experience," said the Gestapo man. "Karl Ulman and I have been working closely on these incidents, and there's nothing to worry about."

"Until now," said Saxon. "This is the second direct threat to Jesse Owens from this source. This one we must take seriously."

This statement was greeted by a murmur of voices around the table.

"May we see these letters?" said the SA representative.

"They are undergoing tests in our laboratory," said Engel.

The man from the Propaganda Ministry rose from his seat, cleared his throat and made a speech. "We must ensure that nothing untoward befalls these athletes. No resource should be spared in this effort. I cannot stress enough the seriousness of this task. For the duration of the Games, the Third Reich will be under the watchful gaze of the world. Imagine what a disaster would befall us and the Reich if anything happened to Jesse Owens, or any of the athletes from the United States."

Saxon thought how disastrous it would be for the athletes.

The chairman waved the Propaganda man back to his seat. "I'm sure that Ulman and his team have the matter in hand. We should inform the United States security representative. What was his name again?"

"With due respect," said Engel, "I would advise against that. We must proceed on the assumption that the threat will evaporate, as they all do."

"And what if it doesn't 'evaporate', as you put it?" said Saxon.

"If it is real, we will thwart it, Kommissar. Why worry the Americans when it may mean nothing? It would be best to keep it amongst ourselves."

Nobody raised a word of objection.

"Very well," said the chairman. "The information will be limited to those in this room for the time being."

"And the laboratory scientists," said Saxon.

The chairman nodded. "Yes, and the scientists. Please treat it as strictly confidential."

At the end of the meeting, Bruno called Saxon aside and handed him a bundle of personnel files. "I have picked these eight men myself. They are all utterly trustworthy and loyal to the Reich. You may safely put them to work watching over the United States athletes. I've told them to dress as civilians."

"Thank you, sir." Saxon took possession of the files.

As they parted, Bruno said, "I've had word from Kommandant Lippert. His camp is open for business. You may start to move your prisoners as soon as you like."

"They're not prisoners, they're detainees," said Saxon.

\#

When he told Sergeant Schmidt that they could start moving the detainees into the camp, the sergeant said, "The police stations will be pleased. Their cells are full to overflowing. We'll need to find some trucks. I'll speak with the Transport Corps. How many will we need?"

"How many detainees do we have?"

"Nine hundred and twenty-seven, sir."

He did a quick calculation. "Five trucks should be enough to get the job done in a few days."

He lifted the telephone and spoke with the kommandant to arrange an inspection visit for the following day.

By evening, the sergeant had acquired a promise of three old troop transport trucks for Wednesday. There were no more available.

Chapter 30

The camp was located 35 kilometres to the north of the city. Nemec parked the car outside the entrance. He showed his and Saxon's papers to the guard and explained the purpose of Saxon's visit.

The guard lifted a telephone.

"I'll wait here," said Nemec, searching his pockets for his cigarettes.

Saxon checked his watch. "Give me an hour."

While he waited to be admitted, he read the slogan *Arbeit Macht Frei*[1] - Work Makes You Free – in solid steel letters, mounted on the massive steel gates, painted black. The words reminded him of one of his father's favourite sayings: 'Hard work never hurt anybody'. This slogan looked out of place for a detention centre.

The kommandant welcomed him with a grim smile. "Welcome home, Kommissar."

"Home?"

"Didn't Karl Ulman tell you, the camp now has a name. It's called Sachsenhausen."

The houses of Saxon!

He groaned inwardly. "Very droll, Kommandant. Herr Büchner tells me you are ready to accept the people we have detained for the duration of the Games."

"Indeed. I look forward to welcoming them. Let me show you what we have to offer. So far, we have only the basic facilities, but you will see how it will be a model camp when it's finished. Everything is carefully planned, the layout, the rostering, the discipline. Our camp will set the standard for others. Nothing is left to chance." He beamed and Saxon caught a glimpse of a gold tooth. "I am hopeful

---

1.   *https://en.wikipedia.org/wiki/Arbeit_macht_frei*

that Sachsenhausen will become a training centre for SS officers who will serve in other camps. Now, if you'd care to follow me..."

They left the administration block and set out into the camp.

"First, let me assure you that the camp is already perfectly secure. You will observe the guard towers in the main gate and the others around the perimeter. Each is equipped with a powerful searchlight and an 8mm Maxim machine gun. These are manned 24 hours a day. The outer perimeter wall is not complete yet, but it will be three metres high. The inner wire fence that you see will be charged with high-voltage electricity, and inside that we will have a gravel path. That area will be absolutely forbidden to the prisoners. In addition, the area between the wall and the fence will be patrolled by guards with attack dogs. So you see there will be no possibility of escape."

Saxon shook his head. "The people we will be sending you are detainees. They are innocent of any crime. They will be released as soon as the Games end."

"Of course. And they will be allocated the lightest labour."

So it is a labour camp, he thought.

"What happens if a detainee enters the gravel path?"

"They will be shot immediately. Every prisoner will be made aware of this as soon as he arrives."

They approached the western boundary.

"The perimeter is an equilateral triangle. The original designers intended that the whole area would be overseen by just three guard towers at the points of the triangle, but this proved impractical for such a large site. We added an extra tower on each side, offset in relation to one another. This one is two-thirds of the way along the boundary. The corresponding tower on the eastern boundary will be one-third along. That way, their combined field of vision will cover the entire camp."

They strolled back to the centre of the front concourse.

"In this semi-circular area the prisoners will appear for morning and evening roll call. Those are the barrack huts you can see in the area to the rear. We have six so far and you can see another 12 under construction. The standard barrack will have central washing and latrine areas."

It was difficult to avoid the stark contrast between these barracks and the living conditions for the athletes in the Olympic Village.

"Will the detainees be segregated?" Saxon asked.

"For sleeping, yes, but not otherwise."

Lippert pointed out several low buildings under construction inside the perimeter. The infirmary, the camp prison, the food hall and kitchen, and the camp laundry.

They returned to the administration block. Saxon had to sit down. He was feeling nauseous and lightheaded. "Are you all right, Kommissar? You look a little green."

He waved a hand. "It's just a little dizziness. I'll be fine in a minute." He lowered his head close to his knees.

Kommandant Lippert sent a man to fetch a glass of water. When Saxon had refreshed himself with the water, he said, "Much of the camp is not yet built. Are you confident that you can receive and accommodate our detainees at this time?"

"Yes, as I've shown you, the camp is totally secure. No prisoner will escape from Sachsenhausen."

"But can you assure me that you have the facilities you need to cater for the daily needs of these detainees?"

"Yes, Kommissar. Send them to me and my camp will fulfil everything it was designed for. Can you give me an estimate of numbers?"

"I don't have an exact figure, but it will be over 900."

"We have just a few female inmates so far. We can easily accommodate that number."

Saxon took several deep breaths to clear his head, before getting to his feet. He checked his watch. "I must get back to the office."

As he was leaving the camp, his parting words were, "My men are keeping detailed records. I expect everyone that we send here to be returned to their homes after the Games. Is that clear?"

"Clear as crystal," said the commandant, with a gleam of his gold tooth. "Heil Hitler."

#

"You were wise to wait outside," Saxon said as he emerged from the camp. "Camp Sachsenhausen is not a pleasant place."

Nemec threw away his cigarette. "Is that what they're calling it?" The corners of his mouth lifted in the hint of a smile.

"You find that amusing?"

"No, not at all, Kommissar. Forgive me."

"No matter. I don't find it amusing to carry the name of a labour camp."

Chapter 31

Saturday July 25

He had to queue for the telephone booth in the hotel, surrounded on all sides by prattling tourists and overactive children. When his turn came, he slipped into the booth and closed the door. He had a pocket full of change but had to use almost all of it to get connected to Rudolf's number in Austria.

"Oh hello, Saxon. How are you? How's the preparations for the Olympics going?"

"Fine, is Ruth there?"

"The newspapers are predicting that the United States will capture a lot of the track and field medals. They have a strong team. Their negro runners seem to be world-beaters."

"Yes, I'm sure that's right. Put Ruth on. Is she there?"

Finally, Rudolf handed the telephone to Ruth.

"Roland, is that you?"

"Yes, Ruth, how are you? How's Samuel?"

"It's good to hear your voice. We're both missing you terribly. Samuel is well. How's the job going?"

"Fine. The job's going fine. The Games will begin next Saturday. They'll be over two weeks after that. I thought I might ask for some leave, come and visit you there."

"Oh, that would be wonderful. There's a very nice hotel near here. We could take a room for a week, maybe."

"A week? I was thinking maybe three days."

"Three days! Is that the best you can do?"

"Four days, maybe, but a week is probably out of the question."

"Why do you always find problems where there aren't any? You'll surely be entitled to a decent holiday after all the work you've done for the Olympic Games."

"You know what Glasser is like. My desk in Munich is probably buried in new cases by now."

"Are you the only policeman in Munich that can solve crimes?"

He laughed. "Sometimes it seems that way."

Ruth was silent for a moment.

"Hello, Ruth, are you still there?"

"I'm here, Roland. Where else would I be?"

She put Samuel on. He was bursting to tell his papa something. He launched into a long, rambling monologue involving some animal with a big tail. Saxon couldn't get the sense of it. When Ruth came on again, she explained, "He made friends with a squirrel in the park."

"How are you getting on with cousin Rudolf?"

"Fine."

He waited for more, but she said nothing for a couple of moments.

"He's in the room with you, isn't he?"

"Yes."

"I'd better go. It won't be long until we see each other again."

"Hello, caller," said the operator. "Please enter some more money if you wish to extend this call."

"Three weeks."

"About three weeks, certainly less than four. Tell Rudolf I sent my best wishes."

"Goodbye, Roland. I love you."

The call was disconnected before he could reply.

Afterwards, he ran through the conversation in his mind. Constrained by Rudolf's presence, Ruth had been limited in what she could say, but he sensed tension in her voice. Samuel sounded more grown-up than ever.

#

On their second date, Reckendorfer took Andrea to the cinema. The movie was a horror called *Fährmann Maria*. He had seen it before, but he had fun watching her reactions as the story unfolded on the screen.

At the point when the main character, Maria, realises her lover must die, Andrea reached for Dieter and he gave her a tender hug, careful not to squeeze her too tightly in case he might break her.

After the show he pulled two tickets from his breast pocket and handed them over. "You wanted to take your mother to the opening ceremony..."

"Oh Dieter, you're an angel!" He bent down to receive her kiss and she threw her arms around his neck.

He dropped her outside her apartment and walked home. It was an hour's journey, but he'd had to buy the Olympic tickets on the black market, leaving him seriously short of money.

Chapter 32

Sunday July 26

He was dozing in his hotel room on Sunday when a loud knock on the door jolted him awake. He glanced at his watch. Mid-afternoon. The cursed heat had robbed him of half the day.

"Who is it?" It could only be the receptionist. Another telephone call from Ruth, so soon?

"Open up, Saxon." That wasn't Püttner.

He opened the door, and Bruno Büchner pushed past him.

The police chief's lip curled in disgust. "There's no space in here. Where can we talk?"

Every room in the hotel was now taken. Püttner, the hotel receptionist, was not happy; he was run off his feet.

Saxon checked the residents' lounge, but it was full of visitors, the noise deafening. They headed outside into streets packed with people and shimmering in the heat. They walked south, away from the city centre and eventually found a cool, quiet corner in a tavern where they could talk without being overheard.

Bruno ordered a couple of glasses of beer. "I need to talk to you about this White Knight business. That letter your journalist friend received is a serious matter."

Saxon took a breath. "What did the first letter say? I haven't seen it." This was his first chance to get some solid information about the affair.

"Pretty much the same thing as the second one. Somebody intends harm toward Jesse Owens." Bruno sipped his beer. "I've seen a report from the laboratory."

"They've come up with something?" said Saxon.

Bruno sat back with a satisfied grin. "In the first place, we know the letters originate from inside the police force."

"The Berlin police?"

"All we know is that this White Knight is to be found somewhere among the various police forces operating in Berlin. The watermark in the paper tells us that." He swallowed a mouthful of beer.

"Does that mean you have located this typewriter?"

"We have."

Saxon lifted his glass. Get on with it man, he thought.

"Both letters originate from the typewriter in your office."

Saxon's hand shook. He spilled some of his beer on the leg of his trousers. "*Scheisse!* What are you saying? You suspect one of my men?"

"Yes, of course. Zimmermann was our prime suspect."

"Is that why Ulman sent for me?"

"Not you, specifically, but we needed someone from outside Berlin, someone that we could be sure was above suspicion."

"Why did you suspect Zimmermann? Had he shown a hatred of black athletes?"

"We believed so, yes. But this letter proves it wasn't him. It must be someone else in your team."

"Where is Zimmermann now?"

"You'd have to ask the Gestapo. They interrogated him. The question is who has access to the typewriter in your briefing room?"

"Any of the men."

"Anyone in particular?"

Saxon shook his head. "Anyone can use it."

Bruno chewed his lip. "Is the room locked at night?"

"No. There's no reason to lock it. There's nothing in there."

"Apart from the typewriter," said Bruno.

And the ledger, thought Saxon.

They finished their beers and left the cool of the tavern for the inferno outside.

Chapter 33

Monday July 27
Five days before the opening ceremony

On Monday morning, telling his driver that he wouldn't be needed for a couple of hours, he left the hotel and made his way on foot to Prinz-Albrecht-Strasse. Even at that early hour the heat rose from the pavements. The streets were packed with pedestrians. He caught snatches of languages from all around the world. Low in the sky to the east, the rays of the sun reflected off the shop windows, casting long shadows, the glare blinding him.

He dropped his weekly hotel receipt into an empty adjutant's office. He was happy to have avoided the man, as his bill for the week had risen to 98 Reichsmarks, and he was sure Canstatt would have raised some objection.

At the reception desk, he asked the young officer for directions to the laboratory. He checked his credentials before directing him to a corridor on the ground floor.

Most of the offices along this corridor were clearly identified by signs hanging over their doors. Administration, Finance, Racial Affairs, Personnel, and so on. He reached a set of double doors marked 'Laboratory', with an extra sign underneath that read, 'Entry Forbidden. Knock and Wait'.

He knocked and waited a minute, before knocking again.

The door was opened by a scientist in a white coat. Saxon introduced himself and said, "I'm working on the White Knight letters."

"On whose authority?" The scientist looked at him as if he were a specimen in a Petri dish.

"Major Bruno Büchner."

The scientist stood aside to allow him into the laboratory. "What can I do for you, Kommissar?"

"I'd like to see the letters."

The scientist led him to a table where the two letters lay side by side under a sheet of plain glass.

Saxon examined them. They looked very similar. The first letter read:

For Germany
The negro Jesse Owens will die
Heil Hitler
The White Knight

The second letter was almost identical:

The negro Jesse Owens must die
For the Fatherland
Heil Hitler
The White Knight

It was obvious that the two letters had originated from the same typewriter. The letter 'e' was smudged, and the left vertical line in the 'H' was worn.

"As you can see, the same typewriter was used to produce both letters."

"And you have identified the typewriter?"

"That is correct. The one in your office, Kommissar."

The scientist knows exactly who I am, thought Saxon.

"The words used in the two letters are not the same," he said. "Does that tell us anything?"

"I don't think so, but a detailed examination of the letters has proved one other important fact..." The scientist paused for effect. "We now know, to a reasonable level of certainty, that both letters were typed by the same person."

"How is that possible?"

"By calculating the finger pressure applied to each letter, we can be seventy-five per cent certain that one person typed both letters."

On his way back to the hotel, he thought about what the scientist had said. Even if the same person had typed both letters, Zimmermann was still not in the clear. The two letters could have been typed at the same time and delivered later, at different times.

#

Bruno's eight handpicked men presented themselves in the Orpo office for duty mid-morning. They were unarmed and wore civilian clothes. Bruno had briefed them about their duties guarding Jesse Owens and the other American athletes. Their leader was a corporal called Paul.

They looked just right, Saxon thought approvingly, looking them over: not too smart, but not too scruffy either. He gave Paul Wolfgang's list of black athlete names; Sergeant Schmidt organised the three shifts and sent them on their way to the Olympic Village.

When they'd gone, Saxon handed the journalist Leybourne's list of five athletes to the sergeant and gave him the special task of arranging the interviews for the Australian reporter.

The sergeant's brow furrowed. "I'm extremely busy, Kommissar. Since when is arranging interviews for foreign journalists part of my duties?"

"This is important work, Sergeant. I promised her these interviews as my part of a bargain."

The sergeant raised a questioning eyebrow.

"Don't ask," said Saxon.

The sergeant sighed. "How will I get in touch with this June Leybourne?"

"You'll find her in the Excelsior Hotel."

#

A few of the work units continued clean-up operations on Monday and Tuesday, while they waited for the trucks to arrive.

The office telephone rang early on Tuesday morning. Sergeant Schmidt took the call and passed it to Saxon. "It's the Standartenführer."

"Good morning, Karl, where are you?" said Saxon.

The SS-man hesitated before answering, "I'm calling from somewhere in Hungary. We will be in Vienna this evening."

"How is the torch relay going?"

"Everything is going according to plan. I called to say that you may concentrate your efforts on the Village and the external venues. The Waffen-SS will look after the Stadium as originally agreed in the kommandant's office."

Saxon took a moment to absorb this news.

"You did say that my men should take responsibility for the Stadium when the Führer is not present..."

"Yes, I did, but that was because I couldn't depend on the availability of the Waffen-SS. I received confirmation yesterday that the troop will be available for those duties."

"So, this troop will look after the Stadium for the duration of the Games?"

"Haven't I made that clear?"

After the call, the sergeant said, "That will make life easier for us."

Saxon tapped a tooth with a fingernail, thinking. "Yes, but I don't trust him. We will still put a few of our own men in the Stadium."

"Very good, sir."

He showed the sergeant the group photograph he'd received from Wolfgang Fürstner.

The sergeant grinned. "What a bunch of reprobates! I look positively shifty. Heller and Kleinholz look as though they're holding hands."

Saxon told him that he'd made enquiries about Zimmermann in Gestapo headquarters, but had failed to find him. "But they do have a file on him."

"You saw his Gestapo file?"

"I saw the file, but I wasn't allowed to open it. It was marked with a code. Do you have any idea what the code F17 means?"

Schmidt shook his head. "You need to ask the giant. He's ex-Gestapo, he might know."

Later, when Saxon asked him, Reckendorfer scratched his head. "I'm not sure, Kommissar. It's definitely a release code. F stands for *Freilassung* – release. I know the first few, are codes for execution, hanging, pistol shot, guillotine and so on. The middle ones, F10 to F14, are for criminal trials, I think..."

"Do they have a code for sending someone home?" said the sergeant with a snort.

"F8 is release without further action," said the giant. "F9 is release under continuing surveillance."

"What about F17?" snapped Saxon.

"I think the higher ones are used for releases to civilian prisons and hospitals."

#

Nemec drove Saxon around on a tour of the city's civilian prisons in the hope of finding Zimmermann. Drawing a blank with the prisons, they returned to the office, took a quick lunch in the canteen and started on the hospitals.

At each stop, Saxon enquired about recent admissions, pointing to the figure of Zimmermann in the photograph.

"Is he a relative of yours?" said one matron.

"A cousin, yes. I'm from Munich. I came to Berlin to visit him, but he has disappeared."

She looked up sharply. "Have you tried Prinz-Albrecht-Strasse 8?"

"Yes, Matron, he's not there."

"Well, he's not here."

The sun was low in the sky by the time they reached the end of their list of hospitals. Leaning on the car, Saxon tapped out a cigarette for himself and offered the packet to Nemec. They both lit up.

"Are you sure that sticker on his file said F17?" said Nemec. "Perhaps it was one of the execution codes, F7, maybe?"

"No, I'm pretty sure it said F17. Either he's in one of the prisons under a different name or we missed a hospital."

Nemec took a long drag on his cigarette. "We haven't missed any hospitals, but..."

"But what?"

"We could try the lunatic asylums."

Chapter 34

First thing on Wednesday morning, with three days to go before the opening ceremony, the trucks began to roll. The team began the process of visiting the city's 520 police stations to pick up the detainees and move them to the Sachsenhausen detention camp at Oranienburg.

After he'd given the order, Saxon asked Nemec to take him to the city's five mental asylums. They started with the biggest one, St Hedwig's Psychiatric Clinic in Grosse Hamburger Strasse.

A pair of iron gates opened to a wide driveway through landscaped grounds, where patients and nurses wandered about or sat on benches in the bright sunlight.

His Kripo badge got him through the front door and into the office of the Director of the clinic.

"How may I help you, Herr...?" said the Director, scrutinising Saxon's badge.

"Kommissar Saxon. I'm searching for a man who may have been admitted in the past few days. His name is Heinrich Zimmermann."

He showed the Director the photograph and pointed out Zimmermann's, face. The man's eyes showed a flicker of recognition that lifted Saxon's spirits. Zimmermann was here!

"What is your interest in this man?"

"I would like to interview him. I believe he may have vital information in connection with a case I'm investigating."

"We are a long way from Munich. Is this man also from Bavaria?"

"Not that I know of. I am working for the Berlin police on this investigation. Hauptmann Zimmermann was a suspect for a while. Do you have this man in your hospital?"

The Director opened a box on his desk and pulled out a Russian cigarette. Then he leant back in his chair. Saxon detected a minor tremor in his hand as he struck a match.

"I'm sorry, Kommissar, everything we do here is covered by doctor-patient confidentiality. I'm sure you understand. We cannot discuss our patients with anyone, or expose them to outside contact beyond visits from close family members..."

Saxon said nothing. There was more to come.

"You will be aware that Herr Zimmermann was thoroughly interrogated by your colleagues in the Gestapo before being sent to us?"

"Yes, I assumed so." He let the word 'colleagues' go.

"And yet you believe there is more information that you can extract from him?"

"Some fresh evidence has come to light that proves the Hauptmann's innocence..."

"His innocence?" The Director looked disgusted. "Have you any idea what they did to him?"

"No, we've never met."

"His physical injuries will heal in time, but the damage to his mind may never heal."

"I'm sorry, Herr Doktor. That all happened before I arrived in Berlin. It is my hope that my investigation will confirm his innocence."

The Director pounded his cigarette half-finished into a glass ashtray. He stood up. "I'm sorry, Kommissar, I'm afraid you have had a wasted journey. I have no wish to impede an active police investigation, but I cannot permit you to add to the harm that my patient has already suffered."

He ushered Saxon toward the door. As soon as Saxon was in the car and Nemec had set off toward the gate, the Director turned and re-entered the hospital.

Nemec pointed to one of the benches, nestling under a large chestnut tree. "I found him, sir. He's over there."

"Stop the car."

Saxon got out of the car and approached the bench where Zimmermann sat, casting a long shadow.

"Heinrich," said Saxon. "It's good to see you." He sat on the bench beside the Hauptmann.

There was no reaction from Zimmermann. He stared vacantly at nothing.

"I'm investigating the White Knight case. I was hoping you could help me."

Still no reaction.

"Can you tell me how the letter was received? Was it delivered by hand?"

Zimmermann stirred. He passed a hand across his brow. "It makes no sense."

"A second letter had been received," said Saxon. "A second White Knight letter. It proves that you couldn't have written the first one." He peered into Zimmermann's eyes, but the man had returned to his unresponsive state. "It proves your innocence."

He placed a hand on Zimmermann's shoulder. "I have spoken to Helga, your girlfriend. Would you like me to tell her where you are?"

Zimmermann stirred again. He peered at Saxon without seeing him. "It makes no sense."

Nemec appeared in front of Saxon, illuminated by the low sunlight. "They're coming, sir."

A glance at the hospital building confirmed it. Two burly orderlies in white coats were hurrying across the grass toward them.

Saxon stood. "Get well, Heinrich."

Shepherded by the two orderlies, Nemec and Saxon strode to the car and drove out of the hospital grounds.

#

The office was deserted. That seemed reasonable. All the men were busy watching over the athletes in the Olympic Village or moving the detainees from the prison cells to the labour camp. And yet, he found the silence disturbing. Something was not right, he could feel it in his gut.

The telephone rang. He picked it up.

"Kommissar?" It was Clasen.

"What is it, Clasen?"

"Our truck broke down on Esplanade in southern Pankow."

"What's the matter with it?"

"I don't know, sir. It won't move and there's a horrible sound from the engine."

Sounds like a gearbox failure, thought Saxon. He swore silently.

"You need to call the Transport Corps."

"Yes, sir. We've done that. They are sending help."

"That's good, but it sounds bad. I'll call them and ask for a replacement truck."

"Yes, sir, thank you. But we have another problem."

He switched the receiver to his other ear. "What problem?"

"One of the prisoners has escaped."

"How did that happen? Never mind. Do you know his name?"

"Yes, sir. His name is Peska."

Saxon terminated the call and immediately rang the Transport Corps to order a replacement truck. By the time he'd succeeded, he had made five telephone calls, including one to Bruno Büchner for support.

He found his driver in the canteen and they drove to Pankow to coordinate the search for the missing detainee.

Clasen's explanation was rambling, but Saxon gathered that Reckendorfer had been watching the detainees. A strange noise from the truck's engine diverted his attention for a moment, and the detainee escaped.

"What do we know about him?" he said.

"Dominik Peska. He's a Slav from Serbia with known links to a notorious criminal family," said Clasen. "The Berlin police have a thick file on him. They suspect his involvement in several murders going back a number of years."

"Shootings?"

"Yes, sir. They say he's an excellent marksman."

Saxon swore. This was the last thing he wanted to hear with just three days to go before the opening ceremony. A marksman on the loose in a stadium filled with 100,000 people, and a known threat to a foreign athlete.

The detainee was long gone, swallowed up in the huge crowds that filled the streets. Their only hope was that the Berlin police would find him and arrest him again.

Chapter 35

Thursday July 30

Mid-morning the following day, Karl Ulman stormed into the office. Saxon's shock must have shown on his face, because the SS-man said, "Take that look of surprise off your face, Kommissar. The torch relay is running smoothly. I have more pressing business here, in Berlin. Now tell me how you lost one of your prisoners."

"One of our trucks broke down. A detainee took advantage of the situation and escaped into the crowds."

"Wasn't that careless? I hope you have disciplined the man responsible."

"I have taken care of it," Saxon said.

The smirk on Ulman's face showed how much he was enjoying the situation. "I hear the man who escaped is a Czech and a crack shot."

"Is there something you want? I'm extremely busy."

"That tone is close to insubordination," said Ulman. "You would do well to address me in the appropriate manner."

"Is there something I can do for you, *sir*," Saxon said.

"I have had a call from Harvey Johnson, the United States Marine. He is naturally disturbed by this latest turn of events. I've arranged to meet him at his hotel this afternoon and I'd like you to attend."

Saxon sighed. "How much does he know?"

"He's aware that you have released a sharpshooting criminal into the streets, but he knows nothing about the White Knight letters."

"What are we going to tell him?"

"As little as possible. He will need reassurance, nothing more."

They agreed to use Saxon's car, and the SS-man left.

Saxon's immediate reaction was one of extreme irritation. He lit a cigarette and paced the room. Ulman's early return would make it difficult to continue his investigation of the White Knight letters. But really, was there much more he could do?

A few minutes later the telephone rang. It was Major Bruno Büchner.

"I hear we have a sniper on the loose."

"Yes, sir, a mechanical failure of one of our trucks gave him his opportunity and he seized it."

"You have men looking for him?"

"The streets are so crowded we would have no chance of finding him. I'm hoping your men will catch him. He's a well-known criminal, apparently, name of Peska."

Bruno coughed. "I know him. Where did this happen?"

"South of Pankow."

After a long pause Bruno said, "Better increase your security presence at the Stadium. I know Ulman says he has it covered, but I'd feel happier if you had some men on guard duty there during the Games."

"Very well, sir."

#

Saxon and Ulman met the US Marine in the foyer of the Adlon Hotel. The vast high-domed foyer was awash with people, but Johnson had picked out a quiet corner for their meeting. He waved them over. He had chosen to sit with his back to a wall, giving him a clear, uninterrupted view of the entire area. The bulge in his jacket told Saxon that the American was armed.

"Give me some good news," said the American as they sat down.

Ulman gave him his best sugary smile. "There is no need for concern, Harvey, my men will have every corner of the Stadium covered, and Saxon's team are looking after the Olympic Village."

Johnson was tight-lipped. "What do we know about this sniper?"

"We have no reason to suppose that he could be a threat to the athletes."

"A sharpshooter and a criminal?"

Ulman shrugged expansively. "Yes, but he was picked up as part of a general sweep of the streets for pickpockets and prostitutes. He would have nothing to gain by attacking the athletes." He launched into a homily designed to reassure the Marine. Johnson chewed his lip while he listened. Saxon tuned out.

"... I think you'll find that Third Reich security is second to none..."

Johnson interrupted Ulman in mid-flow. He pointed at Saxon. "Why are you not carrying a gun, Kommissar? Shouldn't you be armed?"

Saxon shook his head.

Ulman said, "The Berlin police chief has decreed that all civilian police will be unarmed during the Games. And many will be dressed in plain clothes. But rest assured that my men of the Waffen-SS will be armed at all times."

"With a sniper on the loose, I'd feel happier if the Kommissar here was carrying a sidearm."

They were talking about him as if he were a child and not in the room. "I prefer not to carry a weapon," he said.

"You can leave us, now, Saxon," said Ulman. "Take the car. Harvey and I have matters to discuss, and I'm sure you have work to do."

Saxon shook hands with the Marine and left. In the car on the way back to Unter den Linden, he went over his meeting with Zimmermann in the mental asylum. The words of the Director rattled around in his head. 'His physical injuries will heal, but the mental damage will be much longer lasting.' The Gestapo had tortured an innocent man. The second letter proved that. But no one would ever be held to account for what was done to Heinrich Zimmermann.

Zimmermann was right when he said it made no sense. If the system allowed innocent people to suffer like that, then the system was flawed. It made no sense. The law allowed the Gestapo to use their abhorrent methods with impunity, acting as judge, jury, torturer and executioner without any vestige of external oversight.

It was a reality that he'd tried to deny for three years, but Germany had finally turned into a 'police state', and he was an important part of it. A shudder of revulsion ran through his body.

Chapter 36

Friday July 31

The weekly security briefing, the last one on the eve of the opening ceremony, was in turmoil. Hauptmann Titel hammered the table to restore order.

Bruno Büchner, as police chief, stood up to address the meeting. "There is no need for concern, gentlemen. I am confident that we will recapture the fugitive soon. Even if we fail to find him, the Olympic Games will be secured. The measures we have in place will prevent any major catastrophe. Karl Ulman and his SS team will ensure security for the Führer and his entourage and for the Stadium, while Kommissar Saxon's men will look after the athletes within the Olympic Village and all the external venues. Also, a special squad has been assigned to protect the United States team."

Ulman looked white as a ghost, but he took the floor next. "My Waffen-SS troop has been briefed and meticulous preparations are in hand. The NSKK will provide the necessary transport. The Stadium will be blanketed with security forces at all times – discreetly, of course. Nothing has been left to chance. The athletes, the spectators, and the VIPs will have nothing to fear for the duration of the Games."

The chairman thanked the SS-man and invited Saxon to take the floor.

Saxon was brief. "As Herr Büchner has said, my men have secured the Olympic Village, and we will attend to the external venues when they are in use. In addition, we have arrested over nine hundred pickpockets, petty thieves, prostitutes and so on. All of these detainees have now been moved from the police cells and placed in the labour camp at Oranienburg, where they will be held until the end of the Games."

He resumed his seat.

"May we take it that the sanitizing operations are now complete to your satisfaction?" said the Propaganda Ministry man.

Saxon stood up again. "Yes, sir. However, Herr Major Büchner has undertaken to continue this work while the Games are in progress."

Major Büchner chipped in, "With the invaluable help of our friends in the SA, we now have over sixty thousand men providing a cordon that restricts access to the less attractive parts of the outer reaches of the city, and I have instructed our men to maintain vigilance within the inner circle."

As the meeting broke up, Ulman grabbed Saxon by the arm. "I have requisitioned a pistol for your use for the duration of the Games."

"I told you, I don't want a pistol," said Saxon.

"Nevertheless, you will wear one. That is an order." And Ulman walked away without waiting for a response.

#

The rest of the day was spent in the office, tidying up loose ends. Clasen spent his time double-checking that his detainee records were complete. A small part of the team completed the transfer of the last of the detainees to Sachsenhausen camp; the remainder were on duty at the Olympic Village.

Sixteen field radios borrowed from the Wehrmacht were delivered that afternoon. Saxon and Schmidt set the frequencies and tested each one before reviewing the planned programme for the Parade of Nations and the opening ceremony.

Sergeant Schmidt pulled a swastika armband from a cardboard box and offered it to Saxon.

"Thank you, Sergeant, but I won't be wearing that."

"As you wish, sir. What about the men? I have enough here for everyone."

Saxon wrinkled his nose in disgust. "I won't have my men wearing those."

"But the men are supposed to be incognito, mingling with the crowd. Won't they attract attention if they are not wearing the armband?"

The sergeant had a point, but Saxon pointed out that many in the Stadium would be foreigners who wouldn't be wearing the armband.

"That may be so, Kommissar, but if our men speak, they will be identified as Germans, Germans without armbands."

"All right," says Saxon. "Tell the men to wear their best civilian clothes and let each man decide for himself whether to wear the armband or not."

#

By early evening, he was in his hotel room facing a sleepless night, his mind imagining all the things that might go wrong during the opening ceremony. There was only one thing for it – he needed to get drunk. He found a small restaurant, ordered a meal and a bottle of wine.

At 10:30 pm he returned to the hotel, half-drunk, hoping to get some sleep.

He was dressed for bed when there was a knock on his door.

"Telephone call," said Püttner.

Slightly unsteady on his feet, Saxon stumbled down the stairs and lifted the telephone receiver in the kiosk. "This is Saxon. Who's calling?"

"It's Rudolf Marcus. How are you, Saxon?"

"I'm fine, Rudolf. What do you want? I was just about to go the bed."

"I'd like to talk to Ruth. She's left some of her belongings here—"

"What are you talking about, man?"

"Ruth left some of her clothing behind and I wondered—"

"What do you mean? You're making no sense."

"Isn't she with you?"

Saxon was suddenly aware what Rudolf was implying. He sobered up instantly, his evening meal churning in his stomach.

"Tell me she's still in Linz."

There was prolonged silence on the line.

"Rudolf? Are you still there?"

"I put Ruth and Samuel on a train to Berlin yesterday morning. Isn't she with you yet?"

Chapter 37

Saxon felt a sharp pain behind his eyes. He pinched his nose. "For God's sake, what were you thinking? You know as well as I do how bad things are here at the moment. You have put Ruth and Samuel's lives in serious danger."

"It was Ruth's decision. I couldn't prevent her from leaving."

"Did you try? Did you tell her how dangerous it is in Germany?" He lowered his voice and added, "for Jews..." Püttner raised his head sharply and stared across at him.

Rudolf was almost whispering as if their conversation could be overhead. "I tried. Honestly, I did talk to her, but you know Ruth better than anyone. When she makes up her mind about something, no amount of discussion will change her mind."

"You shouldn't have let her get on a train!"

"What are you suggesting? Should I have tied her to a bedpost? Locked her in the apartment?"

Saxon ground his teeth. He thought he might throw up at any moment. "You could have called me on the telephone to give me a chance to talk her out of it."

"I did!" said Rudolf indignantly. "I did! I called yesterday morning, but you weren't there. I left a message."

Saxon slammed the telephone down and hurried back to his room to splash cold water on his face. He made it to the bathroom at the end of the corridor in time to throw up.

Staring at his image in the mirror, his head pounding, he roared, "I married a crazy woman!"

Then he got dressed and went in search of the hotel receptionist. Püttner was busy with other guests.

Saxon interrupted him. "I've been told my wife and son left Austria yesterday morning on a train. They should have been here twelve hours ago. Have you seen them?"

"No, sorry, Kommissar."

"Did you take a telephone message for me yesterday morning?"

Püttner checked his pigeonholes and handed a piece of paper across to Saxon.

"Why didn't you give me this earlier?"

Püttner shrugged. "I'm sorry, sir. I've been busy. I can't be expected to remember everything."

Saxon headed out into the city with no idea where he was going.

There seemed to be no reduction in the size of the crowds in the streets. Everyone was in good form, the bars and beer cellars doing good business, music blaring in the streets.

He wandered through the crowd looking for Ruth, jostled and elbowed by people more inebriated than himself.

"Hey, watch where you're going!" snarled a big fellow as Saxon shouldered him aside.

Saxon ignored him. He continued south until he arrived at the Anhalter railway station. The place was almost deserted, winding down for the night. The last train was due in from Erfurt in a few minutes.

He showed his photograph of Ruth and Samuel to a ticket inspector. "Have you seen these two? They would have arrived on an earlier train."

The ticket inspector shook his head. "The trains have all been packed with people arriving for the Olympic Games. I couldn't be expected to remember one face in so many. There's a train due in any minute now. Perhaps they'll be on that."

When the train arrived, he stood beside the ticket inspector and checked the faces of the passengers. Ruth and Samuel were not among them.

He turned away, made his way back to the hotel. He was going to need help to find Ruth and Samuel. And the opening ceremony was due to start in 15 hours. He had to get some sleep.

Chapter 38

Saturday August 1
The opening of the Olympic Games

He leapt awake at dawn, his head still throbbing. By 6:00 am, he was dressed and ready to resume the search, although there was nothing he could do until Nemec picked him up in the car. He forced himself to eat a light breakfast and scoured the newspapers for anything that might hint at what had befallen Ruth and Samuel. There was nothing.

By the time the car arrived at 7:00, he had smoked half a packet of cigarettes, his stomach was churning again, he had a foul taste in his mouth, and a bellyache to match his headache.

Nemec was dressed in shorts and a brightly-coloured shirt. "Where to this morning, Boss? The Stadium?"

"Unter den Linden as fast as you can."

The traffic was as badly snarled up as he'd ever seen it. It took them the best part of an hour to get to the end of Hermann Göring Strasse. From the Brandenburg Gate, all along Unter den Linden, everything was at a complete standstill. Despite the best efforts of two traffic policemen in gleaming white uniforms, they made little progress. He abandoned the car and pushed his way through the crowds on foot.

As he entered the Orpo building, the crowds were all looking up to the sky to watch the zeppelin sailing past, trailing a huge Olympic flag.

He was gratified to see that, in spite of the traffic chaos outside, 33 of the 35 men he'd selected to patrol the Stadium were assembled in the office. Clasen and Kleinholz were the two absentees. All the men were wearing their civilian clothes.

Sergeant Schmidt handed him a Luger and a shoulder holster. "This arrived for you from Prinz-Albrecht-Strasse."

He accepted it reluctantly and put it on. No matter how hot it got during the day, he would have to keep his jacket on to hide the weapon.

It took 15 minutes to brief the men on the planned sequence of events for the opening ceremony and send them on their way in pairs, with 15 of the 16 radios. When the men had left, he told the sergeant about Ruth and Samuel.

"Do you know whether they made it as far as the city?" said the sergeant.

"I don't know, but I have to assume so."

"Right," said the sergeant. "We're going to need help to find them." He searched the desk drawers for the list of police stations and their telephone numbers, tore the list in two, and handed one half to Saxon.

Sergeant Schmidt went in search of a free telephone. Saxon sat down behind the desk and dialled the first number on his list...

Clasen arrived at the office at 10:00 am. Saxon explained quickly what was happening, tore his list in two and handed one half to Clasen.

Clasen went off to find another telephone, and Saxon carried on making calls. By 1:00 pm, working without a break, he had spoken to 72 of the 130 stations on his quarter of the list, and Kleinholz had arrived, sheepish and full of apologies.

It was time to leave for the Stadium. The opening ceremony and Parade of Nations were due to start at 2:00 pm. He instructed Clasen to carry on with the search. "I'll get back as soon as I can. When you get to the end of the list of telephone numbers, join us at the Stadium."

Schmidt strapped the spare radio to his back. He handed his list to Clasen, and he and Kleinholz ran with Saxon to the canteen where they found Saxon's driver. The four of them set off for the Stadium. The streets, so crowded just a few days earlier, were almost deserted now.

#

The giant Oberwachtmeister Reckendorfer hovered around the Stadium entrance waiting for his girlfriend Andrea and her mother. He'd told her to get there early so that he could get on with his work. She was late. He checked his watch. He could wait another five minutes and then he would have to go to his station.

Ten minutes later he was still waiting. And then he saw her hurrying across the concourse toward him. She didn't look happy – and she was alone.

He bent down to kiss her cheek. "Where's your mother?"

"She's been arrested."

This was not the reply he expected. "Where? When? Why?"

She stifled a sob. "Yesterday in Lustgarten. I don't know why, and I don't know where they've taken her. Can you find her? Can you get her released?"

"I'll try," said Reckendorfer.

#

Nemec made good time in light traffic and they arrived at the Stadium to the sound of the peals of the great Olympic Bell. The concourse was full of military trucks and vehicles of the NSKK motor corps. A Waffen-SS unit stood in readiness at the main entrance.

Kleinholz went in search of Heller. Saxon and Schmidt climbed to the highest point on the south side, directly above the VIP seats where a television camera and three powerful searchlights had been installed.

"I'd like you to join Reckendorfer at the entrance," he said to the sergeant, "but do a radio check first."

Schmidt switched on the field radio and called in to the units scattered around the Stadium. They all responded with nothing to report. Heller confirmed that Kleinholz had reached his intended position near the marathon entrance.

Reckendorfer said, "Where's Clasen?" His voice sounded strangely thin on the radio.

"He won't be coming. The Kommissar has given him something else to do," Schmidt replied. "I'll join you in a while."

Saxon ran his eyes over the scene. The Stadium was full to capacity, buzzing with excitement, the last of the late arrivals taking their seats. Somewhere, a full orchestra was playing martial music that blared across the crowd from loudspeakers positioned around the rim. The zeppelin hovered overhead. Over the main entrance, the huge scoreboard displayed Modern Olympic founder Pierre de Coubertin's declaration: 'The most important thing in the Olympic Games is not to win, but to take part, the objective is not to conquer but to have fought well.'

Saxon nodded to Schmidt and the sergeant headed off to join Reckendorfer.

A fanfare announced the arrival of the Führer and his entourage of VIPs as they strode down the steps at the marathon entrance. Accompanied by more fanfares and music, Hitler and the dignitaries made their way across the running track to the VIP seating area, while 100,000 spectators rose to give the Hitler salute and raised a great cheer that rolled on and on, resounding around the Stadium.

Hitler paused to allow a child in a white dress to present him with a bouquet of flowers. This was truly Hitler's Olympics, his finest hour, his opportunity to show the world what the thousand-year Reich was made of.

The spectacle, together with the knowledge of his own contribution to it, turned Saxon's stomach.

Another fanfare signalled the raising of the flags of the 51 participant countries all around the rim of the Stadium. Then the president of the Olympic Organising Committee, Theodor Lewald, made a short speech about peace. And the Parade of Nations started. Following tradition, Greece was first country to enter the Stadium. Saxon scanned the crowd.

The athletes of each nation wore their own unique costumes. Some athletes gave the Nazi salute as they passed Hitler, others gave the similar Olympic salute.

For a few moments, the spectacle took Saxon's mind off Ruth and Samuel. It resembled a ghastly religious rite, the crowd swaying, saluting, and screaming for their Führer.

When the United States team entered the Stadium, they marched to their allocated position without saluting. Instead, they held their hats over their hearts. Saxon picked out some of the black athletes and his heart rate increased. Schmidt checked in with all units. No one had anything to report.

Once the German team had marched in – to ear-splitting screams of joy – and taken their place, Adolf Hitler advanced to his microphone, removed his hat and announced: "I proclaim the Olympic Games of Berlin, celebrating the Eleventh Olympiad of the modern era, open." That was greeted with a great cheer and another mass demonstration of the Hitler Salute.

As dusk began to fall, the television camera crew switched on the three massive searchlights. Next, a fanfare accompanied the raising of the huge Olympic flag. After that, a cannon sounded, and 25,000 pigeons were released into the air. As they rose above the crowds, the cannons fired again.

Saxon caught a telltale flash from over the entrance and picked out the crack of a rifle hidden amongst the cannon fire. Tearing the nearest spotlight from its operator's grasp, he spun it around so that it shone directly on the point where he'd seen the flash. He grabbed the radio handset.

"All units closest to the entrance, I have a gunshot from inside the noticeboard. Move to intercept."

He kept the spotlight trained on the same spot.

PART 4

Chapter 39

The television camera crew turned a second searchlight on to the noticeboard. He gave them instructions to keep both searchlights trained on the scoreboard and ran to the entrance.

The giant, Reckendorfer, stood on his own behind the scoreboard, the radio on his back looking like a toy.

"Where's Sergeant Schmidt?" said Saxon.

The giant pointed at the back of the scoreboard where a small door stood open. "He's gone inside."

"Stay here. Arrest anyone that comes out that you don't recognise."

He drew his pistol and followed Schmidt in through the door, acutely aware that his sergeant was unarmed. Inside, it was dark. A deserted desk and keyboard. A quick search revealed the scoreboard operator lying tied up and unconscious in a dark corner. Sergeant Schmidt was working on the ropes that bound him. Saxon checked the man's neck and found a strong pulse. Schmidt untied the man's ropes and Saxon shook him awake.

"What happened?" He grimaced and put a hand to his head.

"Someone hit you and tied you up. How do you feel?"

He mumbled, "Dizzy."

"What's your name?"

"Jakob, Egbert Jakob." He tried to stand.

"Don't try to get up by yourself, Herr Jakob. Help me with him, Sergeant."

They got him to his feet and took him outside. Saxon left him in Schmidt's care, saying, "Get him an ambulance."

Saxon went back inside. It didn't take him long to find the rifle, lying beside the open panel. He looked out through the panel and was immediately blinded by the searchlights – all three of them now – concentrating their beams on the spot.

Heller and Kleinholz arrived at the same time as four Waffen-SS men in full uniform, armed with carbines. Saxon gave orders to search the crowd. "Ask if anyone saw anything suspicious, someone emerging from this door, or someone joining the spectators from this direction."

He knew it was hopeless, but he had to follow standard police procedure.

He returned to his position above the standing area, gestured to the searchlight operators to direct their beams to the arena, and trained his eyes on the athletes. In the Stadium, the pageantry was continuing. No one had noticed anything of the sniper and there was no sign that anyone had been injured.

A lone runner appeared in the main entrance, holding the flaming Olympic torch. He stopped near the bottom of the steps, as if unsure where to go next. The music stopped, 100,000 spectators roared and gave the Hitler salute, as if pointing the way, and the runner ran on around the Stadium to the marathon entrance. There, he ran up the steps, took his position beside the giant cauldron and held the torch high in the gathering gloom. This was greeted by massed screams of joy.

The runner paused before using the torch to light the cauldron, accompanied by the sounds of the Olympic bell tolling and the bells of the city ringing in the distance. A great cheer echoed around the Stadium, and the music started again.

After that, a choir dressed in white sang a special Olympic hymn, composed and conducted by Richard Strauss. As dusk fell, the crowd sang *Deutschland Über Alles* and *Die Fahne hoch* – the Horst Wessel song.

Raise the flag! The ranks tightly closed!
The SA marches with calm, steady step.

"I hope they don't," Saxon muttered under his breath. The strange ecstasy of the multitude was making his hair stand up on the back of his neck.

A hazy sun dipped toward the horizon behind the Olympic cauldron.

Whoever he was, the White Knight had failed in his objective, leaving his rifle behind. It seemed unlikely that he would try again.

Saxon ran to the concourse and found Nemec by the car, dressed in his loud, colourful shirt and shorts. "Get me to the office as fast as you can," he told the driver.

Chapter 40

Saturday August 1

They made it back to the office in good time. Clasen was working his way through the last few numbers on the list of police stations. His ears were red from the effort, but he'd picked up no trace of Ruth and Samuel.

Saxon thanked him for his dedication. Then he opened Clasen's ledger. "Have you looked in here?"

"Yes, sir. I'm sorry, Kommissar, they're not in there."

Ten minutes of painstaking work, searching through the late entries in Clasen's ledger, and he found them. It was only when he saw the record that he remembered Ruth's identity card still carried her maiden name. Ruth Marcus had been picked up in Fehrbelliner Strasse in the north of the city and transported directly to Sachsenhausen. There was no mention of Samuel.

Saxon sat down hard. Cold sweat broke out on his brow while a mixture of apprehension and relief flooded his mind. He prayed that she hadn't lost contact with Samuel and that they were together in the camp. They had been locked up in the camp for two nights. The place was a death-trap for a child, he thought. He had visions of Samuel running about, stumbling into the electric fence or onto that gravel path where the guards would shoot on sight. But surely not a child?

He picked up the telephone, called the camp and demanded to speak with Kommandant Lippert. "My wife has been picked up in error by the police. She had our 3-year-old son with her. I understand they are in your camp."

"In error, you say?" Lippert's voice held an astonished sneer. "Their names?"

"Ruth and Samuel Marcus."

He held the line while Lippert checked his records.

"Yes, we have them here. They were admitted on Thursday."

He had found them. Both of them. The relief made him weak at the knees.

"I'll be there in an hour to pick them up," he said.

"Very well, Kommissar, but bring the appropriate release forms with you."

Saxon paused to absorb this idea.

"You will require release forms? These are my family."

"I understand, but I cannot release anyone from the camp without the correct authorization. For Jews there are two forms. I will require both."

"Where can I obtain them?"

"Only SS-Standartenführer Ulman has the authority to sign those forms."

Saxon terminated the call and rang Karl Ulman's office.

"The Standartenführer is in conference," said Canstatt.

"Interrupt him. It's urgent."

"I'm sorry, Kommissar, he has left strict instructions not to be disturbed."

He ran down to the canteen and dragged Nemec from his peaceful meal. Nemec drove him to Prinz-Albrecht-Strasse. It was heavy going this time, with the crowds pouring out of the Stadium and heading home. The traffic was snarled up almost as much as it had been before the start of the Games, and drunken pedestrians presented an additional obstacle, reeling across the streets in bands with arms around each other's shoulders, singing and shouting.

He told Nemec what was happening. "I'm hoping I'll find someone who can help me at Prinz-Albrecht-Strasse."

Nemec said nothing, but Saxon caught his quizzical look in the rear-view mirror.

It was 9:30 pm by the time they arrived at Gestapo headquarters. He jumped from the car before it was completely at rest and ran into the building. The signs were not good. Apart from a night watchman on duty at the reception desk, the building looked deserted. The lights in the corridors and offices had all been switched off. He threw the name Ulman at the night watchman and ran up the stairs to the third floor before the man could reply.

Ulman's office was in darkness. He tried the handle of the anteroom. It was locked.

A stream of obscenities flowed from his lips. Ruth and Samuel would have to spend a third night in the camp.

He arranged for his driver to pick him up again at 10 o'clock the following morning and sent him home. Then he stopped at a tavern and drank two glasses of beer before walking back to the hotel to take refuge in his room.

He undressed, dropping the heavy pistol on the bed. He took it from its holster and removed the bullets. They could order him to carry the damn thing, but they hadn't said anything about ammunition.

Consoling himself with the thought that at least he now knew where Ruth and Samuel were, he got into bed and closed his eyes. He hadn't eaten since lunch time, but he wasn't hungry. His mind awash with apprehension, fuelled by adrenaline, sleep eluded him. Leaving Ruth and Samuel in the hands of Michael Lippert for another night sent ripples of anxiety up and down his spine.

Finally, he took the photograph from his wallet and propped it up on the table. He would see them in a few hours... He fell asleep gazing at the picture of his family illuminated by the flickering lights from the window.

#

In the Sachsenhausen camp at Oranienburg, Ruth lay in her bunk with Samuel nestled against her chest. She was facing her third sleepless night in a row but was afraid to close her eyes. The wooden cabin was unbearably hot, even in the dead of night. Everything about it – the smell of pine from the walls and traces of sawdust in the corners, the glaring newness – told her that it was newly built, but already it was home to all manner of unwelcome creatures. She shared the cabin with thirty strange and wild women, all of whom seemed to hate or despise her, for some reason. Perhaps it was because of her Bavarian accent.

She had no understanding of why they'd been arrested and taken to this dreadful place, or how long they would be held here. Escape was impossible; any attempt would get them both killed. Her only hope was that Roland would find them soon and get them out.

Her eyelids were closing... Something dark scurried across the central aisle, and she was wide awake again. Lying as still as she could so as not to disturb Samuel, every muscle in her body tensed. She said a silent prayer.

Chapter 41

Sunday August 2
Day 1 of the Games

The door to Ulman's anteroom was open. Saxon strode past the adjutant and barged into Ulman's office. The SS-man was sitting at his desk, tunic off, red braces draped over his bulging belly, a glass of something amber in his hand. He swivelled his chair to face Saxon.

It was not yet midday. A bit early for strong liquor, thought Saxon.

Canstatt had followed Saxon into Ulman's office. "I'm sorry, sir—"

Ulman waved him back to his station. "What is the meaning of this intrusion, Saxon?"

"I tried to reach you at eight-thirty last evening, but your adjutant refused to put me through."

"I was in conference. What could be so urgent that you needed me at that hour?"

Saxon's blood was boiling, but he needed to stay calm. He took a deep breath and spoke deliberately and slowly. "My wife and son have been arrested and placed in Sachsenhausen. I called Kommandant Lippert, but he refused to release them without the official forms signed by you."

"I see. Well, the kommandant's response was quite correct. All prisoner releases from the camp are my responsibility. Do we know why they were arrested?" Ulman swivelled away on his seat.

"There can have been no reason. They arrived in the city on a train. I can only suppose they were confused by the crowds."

"So you say. You have an arrest record?"

"No. All I know is that they were taken to the camp. Do you have the forms?"

The SS-man waved a hand at the jumble of papers on his desk. "I expect they're here somewhere. Leave it with me. I will let you know when I have completed your forms. Dismissed."

Saxon stood his ground, holding his hands flat against his thighs, to keep them from closing into fists.

The SS-man got to his feet. "Is there anything else, Kommissar?"

"I need those forms now. My wife and son have been in the camp too long already."

The SS-man gave a heavy sigh and pressed a button on his intercom. Canstatt came bustling in "I need two prisoner release forms. And see if you can find two J12s."

The adjutant looked puzzled.

"The J12 is a form for the release of a Jew. If you don't have it, Racial Affairs will have it."

Canstatt saluted and hurried away on his errand.

Ulman gestured to Saxon to take a seat. "We might as well be comfortable while we wait. How long have they been in the camp?"

Saxon sank into the seat. "Three nights."

"I'm sure they're perfectly safe in the kommandant's care."

Saxon's temper flared. "Have you seen Sachsenhausen? They have attack dogs and lethal electric fences!"

Ulman threw him a steely look. "You know how much anti-Jewish sentiment there is in the city now. That camp is probably the safest place for them."

"What are you talking about? They have machine guns in guard towers and orders to shoot to kill." He was shouting. He checked himself and lowered his tone. "This is my family."

"I'm sure the camp was designed with the prisoners' safety in mind."

Saxon made no further response. He was having difficulty catching his breath. He was sure Ulman was trying to goad him into another discussion about his poor choice of spouse and its effect on his future career.

It took Canstatt ten minutes to return with the two forms.

"The names of the prisoners?" said Ulman.

"Ruth and Samuel Marcus."

Ulman filled in the forms, stamped them, and handed them across his desk to Saxon.

He grunted his thanks and left, his stomach churning.

Chapter 42

Sunday August 2
Day 1 of the Games

An SS officer entered the food hall at Sachsenhausen, and the whispered conversations of the prisoners died. He rapped a table top with his cane. "Which one of you is Ruth Marcus?"

Ruth stood.

"Come with me," he said. "Bring the child."

He took them to their cabin. "Collect your things."

Where were they sending her? If they were moved away from Berlin they could be swallowed up in the system and lost to Roland forever.

She gathered her belongings and swept them into her suitcase. "Where are you taking us?"

"Your husband has come to set you free."

Her heart leapt in her chest. "Where is he?"

"Follow me. I'll take you to him."

He led them to the kommandant's office where Saxon stood with open arms and she fell into them, sobbing. "I thought you'd never find us. This place is—"

Samuel clung to his mother's leg.

"We can talk about it later," Saxon said. "I have a car waiting outside. Let's get you and Samuel to my hotel."

Saxon lifted the child and hugged him. Samuel clutched a small swastika flag in his fist. He gave his father a broad smile.

"Where did he get the flag?" he said.

"They were handing them out free of charge on the train and at every railway station." She shrugged wearily.

No one stopped them as they walked out through the gate of the camp and got into the back of the car.

"I can't believe how much Samuel has grown," he said. "How are you?"

"Exhausted. Sleep was pretty much impossible in there."

"What about Samuel?"

She gave him a wan smile. "God bless him, he can sleep anywhere."

#

Manfred Püttner stared open-mouthed at Ruth and Samuel. The look on his face was so comical, Saxon had to suppress a smile.

"This is my wife and son. They'll be staying with me for a few days."

"Kommissar—"

"We'll need a bigger room."

Püttner shook his head. "We have no rooms free. I'm sorry, Kommissar, you know how busy we are."

Ruth picked Samuel up. "We'll go somewhere else."

"We can't," said Saxon. "All the hotels are full."

"He's right, Frau Saxon," said Püttner. "There isn't a free room in the whole of Berlin."

Saxon snapped his fingers. "Hand me my key."

"That room is far too small," said the hotel man. "It's only intended for single occupancy."

Ruth narrowed her eyes. "Give us the key. If you don't, we'll bed down right here behind your desk."

Püttner handed over the key, and they trudged upstairs.

When she saw the room, Ruth dropped Samuel on the bed and turned on Saxon. "This is ridiculous. We can't sleep here."

"We're going to have to manage," he said.

She put her fists on her hips. "Tell me how!"

He looked around the room. "You and Samuel can take the bed. I'll sleep in the chair."

She shook her head. "I'm not sharing a bed with a 3-year-old again, and you'll never be able to sleep in that chair."

Samuel began to cry, reaching for his mother. She picked him up.

Saxon said, "I could sleep on the floor. I'll ask for a spare mattress."

"Leave this to me." She thrust the child into his arms and stormed out of the room.

Samuel howled. "Mama! Mama!" over and over. Saxon did his best to calm his distressed son, but it was a difficult task. A dart of guilt struck him in the chest; the 6-month separation had loosened the bond between father and son.

On her return, Ruth was accompanied by the sheepish receptionist carrying a folded cot. She took Samuel in her arms and spoke gently to him. His tears dried up immediately.

"Take the chair and the table away and put the cot there," she said to Püttner. "I'll need a mattress, sheets and a blanket for the cot and some food suitable for a small child. You do have food suitable for a 3-year-old?"

"Yes of course, madam, I'll have a word with the kitchen staff."

#

"That was impressive," he said, when the receptionist had left. "I think Herr Püttner finally met his match."

She sat on the bed with Samuel on her knee. "Tell me why we had to spend three days and nights in that horrible place."

"I didn't know you were coming until Rudolf rang me on Friday. Why didn't you warn me?"

"I wanted to surprise you, and anyway I knew you'd try to stop me. Why did it take you two more days to get us out?"

"I didn't know where you were. And after I found you, I had to get various official forms signed. It was difficult. As I keep telling you, Ruth..." He dropped his voice. "...the Kripo are not as strong as we used to be. There are more powerful forces in charge nowadays. Perhaps now you'll believe me when I tell you how dangerous it is in Germany these days."

She gave him a look that said she thought he was just making excuses for his own failings. And perhaps he was. A second twinge of guilt passed through his heart. This episode proved what a spectacular failure he had been at the job of protecting his family.

"Aren't you glad to see us?"

"Of course I am. I missed you both so much." He hugged her.

When they separated, they both had tears in their eyes.

"Why are you carrying a gun?" she said.

"My boss has insisted on it. It's not loaded. Can I leave you for a few hours? I have to get back to the Games. I have work to do."

She gave him a weak smile and wiped her eyes. "Yes, of course. We're both starving. I'll feed Samuel and get something for myself. Then we'll get some sleep."

He kissed them both. "Stay indoors. I'll get back as quick as I can."

"Take your time. We'll be fine," said Ruth. "I could eat a horse, and then I'll sleep for a week."

Chapter 43

Sunday August 2

His head was still full of the emotion of his reunion with Ruth and Samuel. Yes, he thought, he was happy to see them, in spite of all the trouble they had caused.

"The Stadium, sir?" said Nemec.

"Not yet. Take me to Gestapo headquarters first."

He found Ulman's adjutant, Canstatt, at his desk, sweltering in the heat in full uniform. Ulman was not in his office.

"You've recovered your wife and child, I trust?" said the adjutant with a thin smile.

"Yes, thank you for your help."

Saxon took a seat and asked to be brought up to date.

"We have checked with all the athletes. No one was killed or injured during the incident."

"That is a relief."

"Indeed. We recovered a single spent bullet cartridge behind the scoreboard, which seems to confirm your story that a single shot was fired."

"You doubted it? I saw the flash and I heard the shot."

The adjutant remained tight-lipped. "The cartridge and the gun have been sent to the laboratory."

"I hope you have secured the door to the scoreboard control area."

"Yes, the door has been locked, and a guard was placed on it overnight. The troop conducted a careful fingertip search of the grass around where the American team had been positioned, but they failed to find the bullet."

"In the dark?"

"Under the Stadium searchlights. A search of the scoreboard in daylight revealed a canvas bag that must be where the gun was stored. It was well hidden, and could have been placed there days, or even weeks, earlier."

"Do we have any further clues about the sniper or the White Knight?"

"Not as far as I know." Canstatt smiled. "But let's see what the scientists come up with."

The US Marine Corps man, Harvey Johnson, came bustling in, demanding to see Karl Ulman. When Canstatt told him that the SS-man was unavailable, he turned on Kommissar Saxon. "Tell me you've recaptured the shooter."

"Not yet, but we have the rifle."

"I knew something like this would happen the moment I heard that you'd allowed a sharpshooter to escape. What was his name again, Petra, was it?"

"Dominik Peska," said Saxon, calmly. "But I don't believe it was him."

The American turned on the adjutant. "Where the hell is your boss?"

"I'm not sure, sir. I expect he's reporting to his superiors."

"He's carrying the can for what happened?" said the US Marine to Saxon.

Saxon said, "His men are in charge of security in the Stadium, so yes, I can't see how he could avoid it."

"His men are SS men, right?"

"Waffen-SS, yes."

"Well I hope they're kicking his bony ass all the way to hell and back. What's your part in all this?"

Saxon stood. "My men are in charge of the Olympic Village and the external venues."

"But you're part of Ulman's team, right?"

"No, I'm not SS, I'm a Kommissar with the criminal police, the Kripo."

"Okay, so I guess you report to Bruno?"

Saxon explained patiently, "No, I'm from the Kripo in Munich. Kommandant von Gilsa looks after the Olympic Village, so I report to him. But Karl Ulman has overall responsibility for security, so I report to him, too."

Johnson blew through his teeth. "Gilsa's Wehrmacht, that's Army, right?"

"That's right."

"Jeez! What a mess! Why do you Germans have to make everything so complicated?"

Canstatt said, "The Olympic Village was built on Wehrmacht barracks land."

"Sounds like a recipe for disaster to me. How could you let the sniper have a clear shot at our team? I'll be facing a major shitstorm back home over this."

Saxon said, "It wasn't your fault, Leutnant, and no one was killed, or even wounded."

"Thank God." Johnson looked at his watch. "I need to get to the Stadium. Jesse Owens was in action this morning."

"I'm going there now," said Saxon. "I have a car. You can travel with me, if you like."

"Thanks, but I have a cab waiting outside."

\#

By the time Saxon arrived at the Stadium, the officials on the track were preparing for the quarter-finals of the 100-metres for men. The heats had been completed in the morning without incident. As expected, Jesse Owens won his heat and quarter-final easily, setting a new Olympic record time of 10.3 seconds, to massive acclaim from the spectators.

Sergeant Schmidt reported that Jakob, the scoreboard operator, had been admitted to hospital with a suspected case of mild concussion, but no serious injuries. The ambulance crews had been kept busy with spectators suffering from heat stroke. Apart from that, all was quiet following the sniper incident.

Saxon took another look at the sniper's perch. The missing scoreboard panel had been well chosen. It provided a perfect view of the entire Stadium, while the scoreboard superstructure was a perfect location for a gunman. It was the only place in the Stadium where the sniper could possibly have concealed himself and used a weapon.

The quarter-finals of the 100 metres yielded another Olympic and world record of 10.2 seconds by Jesse Owens, to the tumultuous adulation of the crowds. This was later discounted – to collective groans – due to an assisting wind reading.

Chapter 44

Monday August 3
Day 2 of the Games

He woke up with a crick in his neck after an uncomfortable night, sharing a single bed with Ruth. She complained about the lumpy mattress, but her eyes told him she was as happy as at any time since their first night together.

As she was dressing Samuel, he asked her why she came to Berlin. "I thought we agreed you would stay in Austria."

"It was difficult, living in that small space with Rudolf. I told you in my letter."

There must be more, he thought, but when he pressed her, she said, "I never felt comfortable there, and Rudolf hated the disruption to his orderly life."

"How did you manage to get arrested?"

Ruth paled at the memory. "I'm not sure what happened. We took a taxi from Anhalter station. The driver drove us to a hotel somewhere in the north of the city. We got lost. And a police squad picked us up."

"Did you mention my name?"

"Yes, of course I said I was married to you. They didn't believe me. They laughed. Then they took us to that horrible place."

They made their way down to the dining room. Saxon ate a quick breakfast. Then he got up from the table. "I have to go to work. Can I trust you to stay off the streets?"

She shuddered. "Don't worry. I'm not going to risk being taken back to that camp again."

"I could get tickets to the Games for you and Samuel, if you like."

She embraced him, and laid her cheek against his. "I don't think so. Samuel would find the Games boring. I'll find something to amuse him. What time will we see you again?"

"I'm not sure. I'll get back as soon as I can." He leant down and hugged Samuel. "Be a good boy for your mother."

#

There was no sign of Sergeant Schmidt at his perch above the Stadium. Clasen had taken charge. Saxon asked where the sergeant was. Clasen had no answer.

The 100 metre semi-finals went as everyone predicted. The three Americans, Owens, Metcalfe and Wykoff made it through to the final, along with Germany's best hope for a medal, Erich Borchmeyer.

Jesse Owens won the final in 10.3 seconds with his teammate, Ralph Metcalfe in the silver medal position and a Dutch sprinter, Tinus Osendarp, in third. Erich Borchmeyer finished a disappointing fifth. Even so, the crowd went wild cheering and applauding the United States athletes. Chants of "O-vens! O-vens!" echoed around the Stadium.

A glance at the VIP area showed Hitler sitting stiffly, surrounded by uniformed members of the Reich, his mouth a trap-like line under his moustache.

#

Leaving Clasen in charge, Saxon took his car to the hospital. He had arranged to meet the Gestapo man, Otto Engel, there to interview the scoreboard operator.

Egbert Jakob was a student from the University of Berlin. The found him sitting up in bed, his head bound in a bandage, flowers from is mother in a vase on the window sill. Jakob was from a military family, but his only direct involvement with the police or the security services had been a year spent as a reservist with the civil defence. Saxon doubted that the man had ever fired a weapon of any kind.

It was soon clear that he had nothing worthwhile to tell them. He'd heard a noise behind him during the athletes' parade when the French team was marching around the track, but before he could turn to investigate, he was knocked out cold. Jakob was a poet studying German literature, Engel became suspicious when he heard that, and wanted to interrogate him further, but Saxon persuaded him that it would be a waste of time.

As they parted at the hospital entrance, Engel suggested that Saxon might check with the television people to see if they had anything on film that might identify the sniper.

When he arrived back at the Stadium Saxon was astonished that there was still no sign of Sergeant Schmidt. Where was he? The sergeant was the most reliable man on his team. It was very unusual to find him absent without leave.

He sent Clasen to look for Schmidt, and himself went in search of the television studio, which he found in an office inside the bowels of the Stadium. He asked a senior producer if they had any film on record that might show the sniper entering or leaving his hiding place. The producer replied that their television cameras focused exclusively on the athletes. And besides, the television pictures were broadcast in 'real time'. They recorded nothing.

"You should ask Leni Riefenstahl," said the producer.

Leni wasn't difficult to track down. He found her in the body of the Stadium, directing two cameras trained on the athletes. He had to wait a few minutes before he could interrupt her to ask her the same question.

She shook her head. "There was nothing of significance happening on or near the scoreboard during the opening ceremony. I'm sorry, Kommissar, but I'm certain we have nothing for you."

He returned to his station where Clasen was waiting for him. There was still no sign of Sergeant Schmidt, and no word from him.

Where the hell is he?

Then a thought struck him. Could Schmidt be the sniper? He couldn't recall whether he had ever asked the sergeant how he felt about the black athletes. He made a mental note to check the sergeant's file as soon as he could.

#

Ruth and Saxon shared the single bed while Samuel was asleep in his cot. She whispered, holding him close. "I thought you'd never find us."

He kissed her.

"It was horrible," she said. "We slept in a wooden cabin with thirty other women." She swallowed. "The cabin was badly built. There were holes in the floor. There were cockroaches and rats, even though the place was brand new."

"What were the other women like?"

"Some were okay. They had to work ten or twelve hours every day. I was excused work because of Samuel, and some of them resented that. There were a lot of criminals, thieves and women of easy virtue. I never felt safe. I couldn't sleep. We had to use communal wash-houses and latrines. There was no privacy."

He asked her about the food.

"It was revolting. We were given two meals a day. Watery potato soup with something gritty in it. There was nothing for Samuel. I had to share my rations with him."

"I saw the camp shortly after it was built," he said. "The security arrangements were like something for a prisoner-of-war camp, the dogs, the electrified fence..."

"Yes, it was terrifying! I had to keep Samuel close to me at all times. I kept imagining him touching that fence."

"I worried about that, too."

"And there was a gravel path between the outer wall and the fence. We were warned not to go there. The guards had orders to shoot anyone who went in there."

"Thank God I found you and got you out of there." He tightened his arms around her.

She held on to him like a piece of driftwood in an ocean. "I understand now why you sent us to Austria. I love this country, but if innocent people can be arrested for no reason and thrown into horrible camps, Germany is not a safe place to live anymore."

Chapter 45

Tuesday August 4
Day 3 of the Games

On the third day of the Games, the 200 metres heats for men were held on the track. Security was ratcheted up as the threat to the black American athletes continued to be taken seriously.

In his heat, Jesse Owens equalled the Olympic record of 21.1 seconds. The crowd went wild.

#

The following day, Saxon went in search of Sergeant Schmidt's file in the Orpo Administration office. The diminutive filing clerk behind the counter was eager to serve. He trotted off to his shelves to fetch the requested file.

The transformation from professional pride to confusion and abject misery was a sight to behold. "It's missing! I can't understand it. The file's not where it should be. I'm sorry, Kommissar."

"I assume you make a record of every file that's removed or returned?" said Saxon.

"Yes, sir. Everything is recorded on here." The clerk pointed to a ledger on the counter.

Saxon opened the ledger and checked the last week's entries. He found nothing of interest. "So the sergeant's file has been removed from your files by...?"

"By someone acting without authorisation."

"Perhaps it's on the shelves somewhere, misfiled?"

He drew himself up to his full 1.6 metres. "I certainly don't think so, sir. We are most careful. Nothing is misfiled here."

#

Karl Ulman called Saxon and Otto Engel to a meeting in his office at midday. Ulman looked at his watch when Saxon arrived. "What kept you?"

"Traffic. I came as soon as I got your message."

The SS-man was in full uniform. He looked uncomfortable in the heat, but trim around the belly again. "I've summoned you here to review progress in your hunt for the White Knight. Who wants to start? Otto?"

Otto Engel made an enigmatic statement. "We have several suspects in custody and under interrogation. I have nothing definite to report yet, but we may count on a breakthrough in the next few days."

"What about you, Kommissar?" said Ulman.

"That's not how we work in the Kripo. I prefer to investigate, to follow the clues until I can be sure I have the guilty party."

Engel smirked. "So, tell us how your investigation is progressing."

Saxon answered with a question. "Who are these suspects that you have under interrogation?"

"I'm not at liberty to say."

Ulman wiped his brow and mopped the sweat from the top of his head. "Let's get this over as quickly as possible. Perhaps you could tell us something about the suspects you have under interrogation, Otto. We don't need their names. Just tell us how many you have and if any of them are likely to be the White Knight."

Engel replied, "We have three, and I wouldn't have arrested them if I didn't think they were likely candidates."

"What about you, Saxon, can you name any likely suspects?" said Ulman.

Saxon straightened his back. Ignoring Ulman, he glared at the Gestapo man. "You have my sergeant, haven't you?"

"His name?" said Engel.

A momentary look on Engel's face convinced Saxon that the Gestapo had Sergeant Schmidt under interrogation. He leapt to his feet. "You have no right to seize and interrogate my men."

Engel stood to face Saxon. "I have every right to arrest and interrogate whomsoever I choose."

Saxon thumped the table. "I demand that you release Sergeant Schmidt immediately. His file is missing from the Orpo Administration office. You have removed his file, and you have been torturing him, haven't you?"

"Calm down, Kommissar. I don't have your sergeant."

"Sit down, both of you," said Ulman.

Saxon and Engel resumed their seats, still glaring at each other.

"Arresting the Kommissar's man would be a step too far, even for the Gestapo," said Ulman. "Give me your word that you're not holding him."

"You have my word, Herr Standartenführer," said Engel.

Saxon wasn't convinced. "I haven't seen him since Sunday."

"That's an end of it, Kommissar," said Ulman. "Whatever has happened to your sergeant, I'd like to hear your report about the events of the day."

"Haven't you had an update from your troop?" said Saxon.

"The Waffen-SS captain has given me his report. Now I'd like yours. First tell me why you had men stationed in the Stadium despite my express orders to the contrary."

"It's just as well that I did. The sniper would have fired more shots and one of the athletes might have been wounded or killed if we hadn't been there to stop him."

"Nevertheless, you disobeyed a direct order."

Engel smirked at this but said nothing.

"Herr Büchner asked me to put some men in the Stadium," said Saxon. "Take it up with him."

Ulman waved a dismissive hand. "So, tell me exactly what happened during the opening ceremony."

"The sniper fired one shot from inside the scoreboard. He hit no one. I managed to blind him with one of the television searchlights before he could fire again."

"But he escaped," said Engel.

Saxon said nothing.

"We must assume this was the work of the White Knight. Which of your men were closest to the scoreboard?" Ulman stared into Saxon's face.

"You still believe the White Knight is one of my men? Have you considered the possibility that the sniper might have been a member of your Waffen-SS troop? They were all armed with rifles. None of my men carried firearms of any kind."

The Gestapo man reacted to that. "What are you suggesting? That a member of the Waffen-SS troop used the typewriter in your room in the Orpo building? That's ridiculous." He snorted.

"No more ridiculous than accusing my men."

"I hate to pour cold water on your theories, Kommissar," said Ulman, "but, as you know, the Waffen-SS carry the Carabine 98k. The scientists in the laboratory have identified the rifle used by the sniper. It's a Mauser 1924."

"Is that significant?" said Saxon.

"It's a Serbian gun. It demonstrates clearly that we may be dealing with a militant Slav, probably a Serb or a Croat."

"Does it?"

"I think so. It's a reasonable assumption."

"Is the gun accurate?"

"In the right hands, yes, a sniper's rifle."

Chapter 46

Over the next few days, Jesse Owens won his semi-final in the 200 metres. He won the gold medal in the final, breaking 21 seconds. In the long jump, he kept his best jump to last, clearing 8.06 metres to win that event as well.

The crowds all knew they were watching an exceptional athlete at the peak of his powers. They loved him. They cheered and clapped and screamed. He was interviewed on television, and Leni's film cameras followed him everywhere he went.

Sergeant Schmidt's absence dragged on. It seemed he'd dropped out of the world as if he never existed. Saxon had to take personal charge of his teams overseeing security in the Olympic Village, the Olympic pool, and the other external venues.

The weekly security briefings had ceased, but Major Bruno Büchner summoned Saxon to his office on the top floor of the Berlin Police Praesidium on Friday morning, day 6 of the Games.

Saxon had been in the major's temporary office in the Orpo building. This was something entirely different. Spacious and populated with matching oak furniture, Saxon thought it the height of luxury and good taste. The obligatory picture of Adolph Hitler was hanging on one of the walls, but there were no swastika flags behind the desk.

They sat side by side at a conference table with eight luxury chairs. Bruno poured two cups of coffee. "How's your investigation progressing, Kommissar?"

"I've been too busy to make much progress, sir. My sergeant has been missing since the opening ceremony, and I've had to take personal charge of security."

"You think Engel might have him?"

"He denies it, but it seems likely. The sergeant's file has been removed from the shelves in the administration office."

"I'll look into it for you. What's his name?" Bruno wrote the name down. "Tell me what you have on the shooting."

"It seems the White Knight has made his move. He fired one shot during the opening ceremony, but no one was injured."

"You think that's the end of the affair?"

Saxon tapped the table for luck. "I hope so. We have his rifle."

"Ulman tells me it's a Serbian Mauser," said the police chief. "He points the finger of blame at your team. He's convinced that your escaped prisoner, Dominik Peska, must be the White Knight."

"I doubt that, sir. Why would it be him?"

"He is a known sharpshooter, and he's a Serb."

"Hmm," said Saxon doubtfully, "But what would he gain by killing a black athlete? The White Knight is political. Peska is a criminal."

"Perhaps you're right. We should know one way or the other in a day or two."

Saxon cast a questioning look at the major.

"Oh, haven't you heard? We picked him up near the cathedral last night. Engel has him in his cells." He sat back, smiling. "Do you have anything else to report?"

Saxon said, "I found Hauptmann Zimmermann in St Hedwig's psychiatric clinic. His mind is gone. I think Engel and his men tortured him pretty badly."

"Did you get anything from him?"

He was tempted to tell Bruno about Zimmermann's girlfriend, but he knew that to do so would put Helga in peril. The fewer people who knew about her the better. "Nothing. He is lost to this world."

"Nothing. You're sure?" Bruno had picked up on his momentary hesitation.

"I'm certain."

"I believe you've done an excellent job of cleansing our streets. My sector managers tell me Berlin is like a ghost town at night."

"That I don't believe."

Bruno grinned. "Something of an exaggeration, I admit, but the people of Berlin will be grateful for what you've done."

"It was not work that I enjoyed, Herr Major. A most unpleasant task."

"So why did you accept it? You could have refused."

"I didn't think I had a choice. I was ordered to report to Berlin with no foreknowledge of what would be required of me."

"That is unfortunate. Well, your distaste does you credit, Kommissar. You have all the instincts of a fine policeman. I hear your wife and child were caught up in the operation."

Saxon nodded. "They spent three nights in Sachsenhausen."

Bruno gulped down the dregs of his coffee and looked at his watch. "I have another meeting in five minutes. I just wanted you to know that I was impressed by the way you handled a difficult and challenging situation. I knew you must have found it distasteful. I found it so. It goes against the grain and runs contrary to everything they taught us in the academy."

"Yes, sir."

"Your approach was morally, ethically, and legally sound, and you stood your ground in the face of the SS. You can be proud of what you did. It was a fine example of good policing in trying circumstances."

"Thank you, sir."

"We badly need men of integrity like you in the Berlin police force. Come to me when the Games are over. I can offer you a senior position in the Berlin Kripo. I hope you'll consider it."

Saxon had to take a moment to recover from the shock of that statement. "To tell you the truth, I've been thinking about early retirement. The police force is not what it used to be when I first signed up."

"What do you mean by that?" Bruno was on his feet, putting on his tunic. He paused.

"Since the SS took over, we are forced to be much harder with the public than we used to be. Everything is black-and-white nowadays. In years gone by a police officer could exercise discretion. The demands of justice could be tempered by human compassion."

Bruno spread his hands. "But don't you see, that's exactly why you're needed. People like you and me need to hold the line against the SS. Together we can make a difference."

"What did you have in mind, Major?"

"Our head of Internal Affairs will be retiring shortly. I'd like you to take his place."

Saxon shook his head.

"You don't have to decide right now. Just tell me you'll think about it."

#

His thoughts were in turmoil after that meeting. The prospect of a promotion to a senior position was tempting. He had been treading water in his career for a number of years. A significant promotion could catapult him to the very top of the police hierarchy, not just in Berlin, but maybe even in the whole of Germany. Bruno seemed sincere. But then an annoying inner voice asked him if he thought two men could stem the irresistible tide of the SS. And did he really want to be elevated to the heights if he was going to be tangled up in a brutal 'police state'. He might be forced to join the SS, and then he might have to carry out horrific tasks against German citizens, including Jews like his own wife and son. He quelled his inner voice with the thought that Bruno had selected him for his high morals.

Bruno wouldn't force him to do anything against his own nature and good judgement. The dream of a better future career was still alive.

Chapter 47

Friday August 7
Day 6 of the Games

Oberwachtmeister Reckendorfer was wrestling with a dilemma. Andrea's mother had been arrested and transported to the Sachsenhausen labour camp. He'd checked the records in Clasen's ledger. Christa Abel was classified as a prostitute.

He'd taken Andrea out on three dates already, but she was still holding out on him. The arrest of her mother could be the lucky break he was waiting for. All he had to do was get her out of the labour camp, and Andrea would fall into his arms. He licked his lips.

But how on earth was he going to get Frau Abel out of Sachsenhausen? In his glory days as a leutnant in the Gestapo it would have been simple enough. A word in the right ear, accompanied by a small bribe and the right paperwork, and she would have been free in the wink of an eye. But he was no longer a leutnant in the Gestapo, he was a lowly Oberwachtmeister in the Orpo – an ordinary policeman. He cursed his luck. Everything had changed after the 'accident'.

He tossed the puzzle around in his head for a full day before coming up with the perfect solution. When you boiled it down to its essentials, every SS system relied on precise records and perfectly completed forms. The only real stumbling block was the paperwork. Andrea's mother was in the system because the paperwork said so. As long as there was a record that said she was a prisoner, that's what she would be. All he had to do was remove the right record and she would be a prisoner no longer. It was so simple, it was laughable.

Saturday was the ideal day for what he had in mind. He waited until well after nightfall before slipping inside the Orpo building, unseen, and climbing the stairs to the top floor. The team room was empty, and in darkness. He slipped inside, found Clasen's ledger in the desk and took it to the window where the moonlight would allow him to read it. He soon identified Christa Abel's record.

Then he was presented with a new puzzle. How could he remove one line from the ledger without disturbing any of the others? It took him a few minutes of feverish mental activity to realise that it couldn't be done. There was only one way he could be sure that Frau Abel's record would be removed. He tore the page from the ledger, dropped it into the fireplace, and set fire to it. Satisfied with his night's work, and already anticipating Andrea's grateful reaction, he left the building and made his way home.

#

In the hotel in Bernberg Strasse, Saxon was lying in bed with Ruth's head on his shoulder, listening to Samuel's regular breathing in his cot.

Ruth had taken a huge risk in leaving the safety of Austria. She understood that now – finally. Hadn't he been trying to explain that to her for at least nine months?

She must have been desperate to flee from Austria, to escape from Rudolf's apartment. Living with a 3-year-old in a cramped apartment with a single man must have been difficult. She would have had nothing to distract her from the misery of her situation, and nothing but Samuel to keep her from going stir-crazy. What sort of company could Rudolf have been? He clearly resented her presence as much as she hated his personal habits. It must have seemed like a prison sentence.

He rubbed her back.

She stirred. "Not now, Roland." Her voice was thick with sleep.

He smiled. He resolved to make it up to her. He would take the promotion on offer and set up a new home for her in Austria, far away from Linz, far away from cousin Rudolf. He would stay in the job for a couple of years. Hopefully the situation in Germany would have improved by then. If not, he would resign on the higher salary and walk away with a good pension. It was a perfect plan. He couldn't wait to tell her.

He dozed for a while until his mind turned to his meeting with Zimmermann. What had the Hauptmann meant when he said, 'It makes no sense'? Torturing him for information that he clearly didn't have made no sense, but Saxon was certain that the Hauptmann's words had a deeper meaning. Zimmermann had something on his mind that he wanted to communicate with the world. But what was it?

'It makes no sense.' What makes no sense? Allowing black runners compete against the master race, perhaps? Or holding the Olympic Games in the heart of the Third Reich when the Nazis were clearly gearing up for war?

And then it hit him. Of course! The Hauptmann was questioning the reasoning behind the first White Knight letter. What was to be gained by writing it? Why write either of the letters? If someone was planning to kill one of the athletes, why would they give the police advance notice?

Following that line of thought to its conclusion, he realised that the athletes were never the target of the sniper. The letters were designed to direct security toward the Olympic Village and the athletes, in order to distract attention from the real targets – the VIPs.

But which VIP? Who would want to shoot one of the VIPs? His mind settled on Wolfgang Fürstner. The kommandant blamed Heinrich Himmler for removing him from the Olympic project and having him demoted. He had a profound hatred for the Reichsführer. Hadn't he said he would slit his throat from ear to ear if he had the chance?

Chapter 48

Sunday August 9
Day 8 of the Games

Three heats of the 4 x 100 metre relay were followed by the final. The United States team – including Jesse Owens and Ralph Metcalfe as last-minute replacements for two Jewish runners – won the race in a World Record time of 39.8 seconds. The Italians won the silver medal, the Germans took the bronze.

June Leybourne, the Australian journalist, came looking for Saxon while the excited roars of the crowd were still resonating around the Stadium.

"You owe me 200 Reichsmarks," she said. "The American sprinters, Stoller and Glickman, were the only two Jewish athletes on any team in Berlin, and they were replaced in the relay by two black runners. I told you no Jewish athlete from any country would compete in these Olympic Games. Those two were your only chance of winning the wager."

"I don't carry that sort of money. I'll have to pay it to you later," he said. "How long will you be staying in Berlin?"

"I'll be here for a week after the Games. You know where I'm staying. The Excelsior Hotel." She left with a triumphant toss of her hair and a broad grin on her face.

#

At the end of the day's events, he asked Nemec to drive him to Wolfgang Fürstner's home in Neukölln. They drove through the streets of a vibrant city. A brisk evening breeze kept the streets cool, and there were good-natured revellers everywhere. The scenes of the jubilant crowds contrasted sharply with his mood. Could Wolfgang be the White Knight? Could he have tried to assassinate Heinrich Himmler, his archenemy? It was hardly believable. Wolfgang was such a pleasant individual. But then, if his experience of tackling crimes in Munich had taught Saxon anything, it was that you couldn't judge a man by how he looked or what he said.

#

The door was opened by Wolfgang's wife, clutching a handkerchief to her face, her eyes red-rimmed. He asked to speak with the kommandant, and she burst into tears.

He stepped inside and closed the door. Taking her by the arm, he guided her into the study and sat her on the couch.

He sat beside her. "What's happened?"

She took a moment to collect herself. "Wolfgang is missing. He went out to buy some cigarettes and never returned."

"When was this?"

"Six days ago. Monday. I've spoken to Bruno Büchner. He said he'd make some enquiries and call me back."

"But he hasn't?"

"No." She scrubbed her eyes with the sodden handkerchief. "I rang Gestapo headquarters, but they would tell me nothing." She blew her nose on her handkerchief. "I'm very much afraid that's where he is."

"What did they say to you?"

"I spoke to someone's secretary. I asked if she knew where I could find Kommandant Fürstner. She said, 'He's not a kommandant anymore' and hung up on me."

"This is not good," Saxon said. Then, realising he'd spoken out loud, "It'll be all right, Frau Fürstner. Don't worry."

"They must suspect him of a crime. They're holding him in the basement dungeons of that horrible place, interrogating him, I know it."

He patted her hand just the way he would have if she had been recently widowed. "I'll make some enquiries next week and see if I can find him."

He let himself out, leaving here there, staring hopelessly into space.

#

Samuel was asleep and Ruth was sitting on the bed engrossed in a book when Saxon let himself in.

"I have something to say to you," she said as she kissed him.

"Right," he said. "And I have something to tell you as well."

She put down her book. "You go first."

"No, no, say what you wanted to say first."

She took a deep breath. She'd rehearsed what she wanted to say. "You know how unhappy Samuel and I were in Rudolf's apartment."

"It was too small, and Rudolf was difficult to live with."

"It wasn't just that. I hated living away from you. I missed you every day. Samuel missed his father." She reached out a hand and he grasped it. "We've been so happy here with you."

"You know why we've had to live apart, Ruth, Germany is not safe for you."

How many times have I heard that! she thought.

"We are a family, Saxon. We need to live together. We can't let the political situation drive us apart. Samuel needs you. I need you." She struggled to hold her composure.

"We've had this conversation a hundred times," he said. "What you call the 'political situation' has not improved. If anything, it's worse now than it was six months ago. The government is determined to make life impossible for your people. They want all Jews to leave Germany, and they don't care how, or where they go."

That's crazy talk, she thought. She said, "Everybody knows that Hitler has been demonising the Jewish people in order to gain power.

His attitude will change once he has consolidated his position as Chancellor."

Saxon was silent for a moment. Then he shook his head. "That's wishful thinking, my darling. He's been in power for three years already, and there's been no sign of a change in attitude."

Her heart dropped. "Are you saying that we will never be able to live together as a family?"

"No, that's not what I'm saying. We just need to be patient and wait until the Nazis lose power."

"How long will that take?"

He gave her no answer that question. She went across to the cot. Samuel was sleeping peacefully. He had rolled away from his giraffe. She put it close to his arms again. Then she returned and sat on the arm of Saxon's chair. "What was it you wanted to tell me?"

"Never mind," he said. "It was nothing."

"It can't be nothing. Tell me."

He touched her hand. "Now's not the best time."

She removed her hand and stood up. Whatever it was, she wanted to hear it. "Tell me."

He got up from the chair and stood facing her, running a hand through his hair. "I've had an offer of a job from the chief of police."

"Here, in Berlin?"

"Yes. His name is Bruno Büchner. He has promised me a senior position with a significant promotion. I will need to make up my mind in the next few days."

"You haven't turned it down?"

"No, but I haven't accepted it yet, either."

She felt her world turning upside down.

"How can you take a job in Berlin? How would we stay together?"

"We couldn't. I've told you, there is no safe place for us as a family anywhere in Germany. It doesn't matter whether I'm working here or in Munich, you and Samuel can't stay in the country."

Her eyes filled with tears, but her anger kept them from flowing. Her voice cracked. "So, you're saying we can never be together as a family?"

"Not as long as the Nazis are in power. You need to go back to Austria."

She took a moment to catch her breath. "I'm not going back to live with Rudolf."

"You won't have to. This promotion will give me a big increase in wage. We'll be able to rent a place in Austria."

"Somewhere in Linz?"

"Anywhere you like in Austria."

Oh God! He's already decided to take this new job.

Chapter 49

Monday August 10
Day 9 of the Games

"What is the meaning of this?" said Canstatt when Saxon handed him a hotel bill for 140 Reichsmarks.

"They are charging me for a double room for the week."

"This is because your wife has joined you? You should have checked with the Standartenführer before you moved to a larger room."

"I haven't moved to a larger room. There are none available."

The adjutant made a clicking sound with his tongue. "These charges are a disgrace. The Reich will no longer tolerate shysters and crooks."

"I did ask to speak with the hotel manager," said Saxon. "He wasn't available. The receptionist said he'd leave a note for him to contact me."

"I don't have the authority to sign this without discussing it with the Standartenführer. The receptionist's name is Herr Püttner, I think?"

"Manfred Püttner. Do you know him?"

"Yes, I know him." Canstatt sneered. "Herr Püttner has played you for a fool. He is the manager of the hotel."

#

Determined to find his sergeant and feeling aggrieved after his ego-bruising encounter with Ulman's adjutant, Saxon hurried down to the second floor and barged into Engel's outer office.

The Gestapo man's clerk was filing her nails, her elegant legs up on her desk, crossed at the ankles. The effect was much the same as the last time he'd seen her, although he could see a lot more of her thighs and she was wearing an even brighter shade of lipstick than before.

He rifled through the files on her desk. "Where's Sergeant Schmidt's file? It's not here."

"Who?" She dropped her feet to the floor and placed her nail file on her desk.

"Sergeant Willi Schmidt. Engel is holding him. Where's his file?"

She shook her head, lining up the nail file with the edge of her blotting pad, as if to prove she was calm, and in control of the situation.

He slammed the files back onto the desk, making her jump. Then he strode across to the door to the inner office.

"He's not in his office, Kommissar." She peered at her fingernails. "And before you ask, he doesn't always tell me where he's going."

"He's interrogating some poor soul, isn't he? Where are the cells?"

"You can't go crashing into Gestapo business. Why don't you leave a message?" She picked up the nail file again and waved it at him. "I'll see that he contacts you as soon as he reappears."

He stormed into the corridor and took the stairs to the basement. An officer barred his way at the foot of the stairs.

He showed the guard his Kripo badge. "I'm looking for Obersturmführer Engel."

The guard peered at the badge. "He's not down here, Kommissar. His office is on the second floor."

"He's not there. I've checked."

"In that case you'll find him in the interrogation area."

"Is that not here, in the basement?"

"No, sir. Interrogations are conducted on the top two floors."

Saxon didn't believe him. "If that's the case, what are you guarding down here?"

"These are the prisoner cells, sir. They're too small for interrogations."

He took the stairs to the fourth floor where he found two Waffen-SS guards on duty, armed with Schmeisser MP 18s. He flashed his badge again and demanded access. The bigger of the two guards, a blocky individual with a heavy stubble on his square chin, raised his gun across his chest in a clear signal of intent. "No one is allowed past this point without the correct paperwork."

"I need to speak with Obersturmführer Engel, urgently. Tell him Kommissar Saxon is here to speak to him."

The other guard left to deliver the message, and Saxon knew he'd come to the right floor. The big guard stood his ground, with a finger hovering close to the trigger guard on his machine pistol.

Engel appeared within a couple of minutes, dressed in his shirt sleeves. "What do you want, Saxon?"

"I demand that you release Sergeant Schmidt. He has important work to do, and you have no business holding him any longer."

The Gestapo man snorted. "You would be wise not to pursue that line with me. Interfering with my work could have serious consequences."

"Is that a threat?"

"A warning. I will not have a country policeman throwing demands at me."

"You have been holding my sergeant for seven days. If you are not going to charge him with a crime, the law says you must release him."

"Cases of threats to national security are exempt from that stipulation, as you well know."

"The law must be respected. Any derogation from common law is an abomination."

"I could arrest you for what you just said, Kommissar. That sort of talk is subversive. But I will pretend I never heard it."

"You suspect Sergeant Schmidt of involvement in a threat to national security?"

"Not any longer. Your sergeant has been released. Now, I must return to my work." Engel turned to go.

"Wait," said Saxon. "What about Kommandant Fürstner? Are you holding him?"

Engel turned back. "Wolfgang Fürstner is no longer a kommandant. He has been disgraced and dismissed."

Saxon's voice rose. "And you suspect him?"

Engel's glasses slid to the end of his nose. He adopted his 'learned professor' pose, stroking his chin. "Has it not occurred to you that the White Knight letters may have been intended as a distraction? While we are scurrying about protecting the negro athletes, the sniper could have some other target in mind?"

"Yes, that thought had occurred to me," said Saxon. "But the real target could have been anyone. Why suspect the kommandant?"

"He had motive. He may have been trying to shoot Standartenführer Ulman, who fired him."

"That's ridiculous. Why would he choose the Olympic Stadium? And why would he use a Serbian gun?"

"To throw us off the scent, perhaps. Use your imagination, Kommissar." He turned on his heel and marched back to work.

Chapter 50

Wednesday August 12
Day 11 of the Games

"Have you any idea how dull my life is?" said Ruth. "All I get to do every day and all day is look after Samuel. Isn't there somewhere we could go?"

"I did offer to get you tickets for the Games."

"Yes, and I told you that wouldn't interest Samuel. Can't you suggest something else?"

"There's the zoological gardens. Samuel enjoyed the Munich Zoo when we went there."

"Good idea. When can we go?"

"How about just after the closing ceremony? As long as the Games are continuing I'll be too busy. Let's say this day next week."

#

Schmidt finally made an appearance at the Gymnasia building during the final of the gymnastics events. He looked unharmed.

"You look well after your vacation," said Saxon.

The sergeant laughed. "That was some vacation! I got very little sleep for the entire week. The Gestapo kept the pressure on the whole time."

"They tried to get you to admit to the shooting?"

"Yes, and apparently I was suspected of writing some threatening letters under the name 'The White Bishop'. I laughed at that. How could anyone imagine me as a bishop of any colour?"

The substitution of one chess piece for another was bizarre. Perhaps the interrogator threw that in, hoping that the sergeant would incriminate himself by correcting the error at some point.

"They didn't use physical torture?"

"No, just a lot of repetitive questioning and sleep deprivation. It took a supreme effort, but I managed to hold them off."

"You did well, Sergeant. Are you fit to go back to work?"

"Never fitter, Kommissar."

Saxon marvelled at the man's strength of will. Most men would have crumbled under a week's interrogation. He had known men who would have betrayed their own wives and children under Gestapo interrogation.

After briefing the sergeant, Saxon left him in charge and called for his car. Nemec drove him to Sachsenhausen camp at Oranienburg.

He presented his credentials at the gate and was admitted to the kommandant's office. Lippert invited him to sit. A junior SS officer stood by the door.

"What can I do for you, Kommissar?" said Lippert.

"In four days' time, the Games will come to an end. At that time, all the detainees that my team have sent here must be released."

"Yes of course, Kommissar, but as I've said before, SS-Standartenführer Ulman will have to sign release notes for each of them."

"All nine hundred-and-twenty-seven?"

"Each and every one of them. The camp was set up under his direct authority. Only he can decide who should be released and when. Herr Ulman may prefer to retain some of your 'detainees' for one reason or another. We shall see."

They drove back to Prinz-Albrecht-Strasse where he made his way to Ulman's office with a heavy feeling of foreboding. The SS-man had the power of life and death over the detainees; Saxon couldn't imagine him releasing them all without a fight.

Setting his jaw and straightening his spine, he entered the anteroom.

The adjutant, Canstatt, looked up from his work. "Ah, Kommissar, I have your expenses here." He pulled an envelope from a tray on his desk and handed it over.

Saxon opened it and found a money order for 98 Reichsmarks.

"Your expenses for a single room have been endorsed. The extra costs incurred by your wife's presence have been discounted."

Saxon tucked the money order into his pocket without comment. "I'd like to speak with Herr Ulman."

"The matter has been decided. Your money order has been written. He won't change his mind."

"I wish to discuss another matter with him."

Canstatt knocked on Ulman's door and ushered Saxon inside.

The SS-man was fully dressed, his desk even more untidy than usual. He waved Saxon to a seat. "What can I do for you, Kommissar?"

"The Games will be over in four days. We need to arrange for the release of the detainees."

"You've spoken with Kommandant Lippert?"

He could tell from the inflexion in the SS-man's voice that Lippert and Ulman had discussed his visit on the telephone.

"I have. He advised me to talk to you in order to get things started."

"I see. Well it's a straightforward process. Let me have a complete list and I'll go through them."

"I trust you will release all of these people."

Ulman raised an eyebrow. "As I've said, forward a list and I will go through them."

"These people were detained for the duration of the Games. There can be no justification in holding them any longer."

"That is not your decision."

"May I suggest that my team completes individual release forms for the detainees to reduce the administration burden on your staff?"

"Good idea, Kommissar. Now, if there is nothing else, I have work to do, as I'm sure you have."

#

He dismissed Nemec and strolled toward the hotel. He needed the fresh air and the exercise. And he needed to think. The temperature had dropped to a tolerable level, the crowds had thinned. He turned to his left, taking a longer route back to the hotel.

Filling Sachsenhausen with innocent citizens of Berlin had been a repulsive task. It was something he would never have volunteered to do. But having taken it on, he was determined that every one of the detainees would be returned to their homes as quickly as possible after the closing ceremony. He had no choice. It was a matter of personal honour.

His goal was clear, but he had no idea how he was going to achieve it. If he did nothing, the chances of all the detainees regaining their freedom were slim. And any that were lucky enough to be released would have to wait. Ulman would see to that. Ulman was a bastard, plain and simple; he was relishing the prospect of exercising his position to make their lives as miserable as possible, not for any valid policing reason, but just because he could. The man was intoxicated with his own power.

PART 5

Chapter 51

Thursday August 13
    Day 12 of the Games

Oberwachtmeister Reckendorfer hung around the office on Thursday morning, hoping to ensure that Frau Abel was released from the camp. He spent most of the time perched on a stool that rocked unsteadily under his weight.

Kommissar Saxon arrived with a bundle of release forms that he handed to Clasen. He ordered Clasen to fill them in, one for each detainee in his ledger.

Clasen started immediately on this task, and Reckendorfer began to have doubts about what he'd done. Frau Abel and the others on the page he'd torn out of the ledger would not have release forms filled in for them. Would they remain in the camp?

He sidled over to Clasen's desk and offered to help.

"I can handle it," said Clasen.

Reckendorfer watched as Clasen transferred the details of each detainee from his ledger to a release form. "What happens if a detainee is not in your ledger?"

"That's not possible," said Clasen. "I have recorded every detainee."

"Yes, but what would happen if you missed one?"

"You mean if someone was sent to Sachsenhausen and I had failed to record the details in here?"

"Yes."

"Then I wouldn't have their details and I couldn't complete a release form for them, could I?"

"What would happen to them?"

"I suppose they wouldn't be released."

Reckendorfer cleared a blockage in his throat. "You mean they would remain in Sachsenhausen?"

"Yes."

"For how long?"

Clasen shrugged. "Forever, I suppose."

Reckendorfer went back to work in the Olympic Stadium, consumed by his black mood. What had he been thinking when he tore that page from the ledger? His beloved angel Andrea would never see her mother again, and his chances of capturing her heart had flown out the window.

#

By early evening, Clasen had completed about 500 release forms.

Saxon congratulated him. "You should have the job completed by tomorrow, so."

"I'm afraid not, Kommissar," said Clasen. "There's a page missing from my ledger."

"What do you mean?"

"Someone has torn a complete page out of the ledger." He showed Saxon the jagged edge of the missing page.

"Is there nothing we can do?"

"I'm going to have to match the original arrest sheets to the release forms. When I've completed that process the arrest sheets that remain will be from the missing page."

"That could take hours. Isn't there any faster way of finding the missing records?"

"It's the only way I can think of. It's lucky I kept the arrest sheets."

Saxon sat down to help. "Hand me a bundle of arrest sheets and release forms and find some paperclips."

#

By 10:00 pm they had completed all 927 release forms, parcelled them up, and marked the parcel for Ulman's attention. Saxon took a taxi to Gestapo headquarters and left the parcel at the reception desk.

It was 10:30 pm by the time he arrived at the hotel.

"Where were you until this hour?" said Ruth. "We've had our evening meal, and Samuel's been asleep for three hours."

"I had to work late. There was a problem in the office."

"I was worried. I thought we'd lost you. You could have telephoned."

"Yes, I'm sorry. I didn't think."

"What was the problem? Was it something to do with security? Something about the athletes?"

"Nothing like that." He reached out and tucked a stray strand of hair behind her ear. "We had a problem with the paperwork. It took several hours to sort it out."

"Have you eaten?"

"No." His stomach was growling.

"The kitchen is closed. I kept a few things back in case you were peckish." She handed him a few slices of cheese, a hunk of bread, and an apple. "It was all I could smuggle out of the dining room."

She sat beside him on the bed while he ate. He devoured the food, washing it down with tap water.

"The city is starting to empty. The crowds are going home," he said. "I'll talk to Herr Püttner tomorrow and ask him to transfer us to a double room."

She snorted. "I have a better idea. Why don't I see if I can find a better hotel?"

Chapter 52

Friday August 14
Day 13 of the Games

Saxon took a bus back to Helga Thorman's apartment in the high-rise building in Marzahn.

Helga's mother answered his knock on the door. She gave him a dark, hostile look. "Who are you?"

"Kommissar Saxon. I've spoken to Helga previously."

"About what?"

"About her boyfriend, Heinrich Zimmermann."

Helga appeared in the doorway behind her mother. "What about Heinrich?"

"I found him. I thought you might like to know where he is."

"Let him in, Mutter."

Reluctantly, Mutter admitted him to the apartment. The three of them sat around a table in the kitchen.

"I hope you're not going to upset Helga again," said Frau Thorman. "You policemen are all the same in my book, harassing innocent people, locking them up for no reason."

"Make tea, Mutter," said Helga. "Say what you've come to say, Kommissar."

Frau Thorman went to the sink and filled a kettle.

He took out his notebook and opened it. "I found Heinrich. He's in a hospital..."

Helga put her hand across her mouth. "Is he injured? What did they do to him?"

"He's not physically injured. He's in St Hedwig's clinic. I have the address here."

Frau Thorman stopped, holding the kettle in mid-air between the sink and the stove. "That's a mental hospital," she said.

Saxon lowered his gaze. "Yes, I'm afraid he has mental problems."

"What do you mean, *mental problems*?" Helga looked horrified.

"I'm not sure, but the doctors are treating him. He's in good hands."

"Should I visit him?" said the young woman. "Can he receive visitors?" her voice was trembling.

"I think you should," said Saxon. "It could help to speed his recovery."

"Thank you, Kommissar," said Helga.

Frau Thorman was waiting for the kettle to boil. "Does anyone really want tea?"

"No thank you," said Saxon.

She removed the kettle from the heat with a thump. "I didn't think so."

Helga got up from the table. "I need to go to him right away."

"I'll go with you," said her mother.

"No, Mother, I'll go on my own. If he's fit to receive visitors, you can come with me the next time."

"Before you go," said Saxon, "you said in your letter you had a bag of his belongings. Do you still have it? May I take a look?"

Helga left the room and returned with a leather satchel. She placed it on the table and Saxon picked it up. "I'll hold onto this, if you don't mind."

"What do you want it for?" said Helga's mother.

"Keep it," said Helga.

#

Back at the office he tipped the contents of the satchel onto his desk and discovered an empty envelope addressed by hand to 'The Police'. He was certain this was the envelope that contained the first White Knight letter. Why else would Zimmermann have kept it?

He examined the handwriting on the envelope. It looked familiar. Could it be Wolfgang's? He needed a sample of Wolfgang's handwriting for comparison. Then he remembered that Wolfgang had written out the names of the black athletes. He needed to get his hands on that list!

He found Nemec grimacing over a mug of staffroom coffee, and the driver took him to the Olympic Village where Saxon went in search of the special team of eight that Bruno had supplied to guard the American athletes.

"Remember when you started this assignment I gave you a list of the names the black athletes?" he said.

"Not me," said one of the guards.

The second man shook his head. "Nor me. Paul would have it. He's on the next shift, starting in an hour."

Saxon waited for the hour. When the shift changed, he asked Paul if he had the list, and Paul found it in his jacket pocket. It was crumpled and dogeared, but Saxon was able to compare the handwriting. There was no match. Whoever had written the White Knight envelope, it wasn't Wolfgang Fürstner.

#

That evening Saxon paid his final bill at the Hotel Südberg and he, Ruth and Samuel moved to the Excelsior – the luxury hotel where he had met the Australian reporter, June Leybourne.

The nightly rate for a double room at the new hotel was 85 Reichsmarks – about a week's wages for Saxon. He made no complaint. It would eat into the family savings, but it was worth it. The hotel provided a cot for Samuel and everyone had a great night's sleep.

Chapter 53

Sunday August 16
The last day of the Games

By the time the closing ceremony came around, many of the athletes had left the city and the streets were no longer crowded. The Olympic Stadium too, was less than half full as the trumpets sounded their final fanfares. All around the rim of the Stadium, the searchlights shone straight up into the sky, gradually moving inward until all the beams converged in a light display first performed at the 1934 Nuremburg rally. Then the flags of the nations were lowered and the Olympic flame died in its cauldron.

#

Saxon paid another visit to Ulman's office. Ulman was in the Olympic Stadium. Saxon had to be content with talking to his adjutant.

"You have received all the release forms?"

Canstatt said he had. "Over a hundred prisoners have been released already. The rest of them are under active consideration."

"What does that mean?" said Saxon.

"It means what it says. Standartenführer Ulman will give the matter due consideration when he has the time. You must understand that he is a busy man. He will consider each form on its merits in due course."

"All he needs to do is to stamp the forms and dispatch them to kommandant Lippert at Sachsenhausen. You could do that. There is nothing to consider. These people were detained for the duration of the Olympic Games. They are innocent of any crime. Now that the Games are over, they must be released at once."

Canstatt smirked smoothly. "As I've said, I'm sure the matter will be attended to as soon as time permits."

"May I ask where are they?"

"I beg your pardon?"

"Where are the release forms?"

"They're safe and secure under lock and key."

"Where?"

Canstatt pointed to a walnut cabinet. "In there."

"Don't you think you should place them in plain sight on Ulman's desk?"

"Have you seen his desk?" said the adjutant.

He had a point.

Saxon's expenses for the week, including two meals in the restaurant, amounted to 385 Reichsmarks. He knew he'd only be reimbursed 98 Reichsmarks, but he submitted it anyway.

#

After a sumptuous evening meal in the hotel restaurant, followed by a hot bath, Ruth was feeling optimistic about the future. Six months living in cramped conditions in Rudolf's apartment had been difficult, and their three nights in Sachsenhausen were like a visit to Hell. Now that they were finally together living as a family again, she had something solid to cling to.

They would soon have to leave the luxury of the Excelsior Hotel, but she was determined that they would never be separated again. Whatever happened and wherever they went, she would keep the family together.

Saxon seemed content – if a little sleepy – after his glass of brandy.

They returned to their room and she got Samuel ready for bed. By the time she'd settled him in his cot, clutching his toy giraffe, Saxon had dozed off in an armchair.

She tidied herself up, put on a touch of lipstick, and sat on his lap.

He opened his eyes and yawned. "What time is it?"

"Close to nine o'clock. It's too early for bed."

He tickled her ribs. "It's never too early for that, Frau Saxon."

She laughed. "We need to talk, Roland."

"About what?"

"About our future. Have you made up your mind about that job offer?"

"I have. I've worked out a perfect plan."

She looked up sharply. "Perfect for who?"

"Perfect for all of us. I've decided to take the promotion."

She opened her mouth but couldn't put her thoughts into words. He said, "Let me finish."

"Go on." She slid off his knees and stood facing him with her arms crossed.

"I'll find you a new place to live in Austria, far away from Linz. I'll take this job and keep it just long enough to get a decent pension. Then I'll join you and Samuel in Austria."

"How long?"

"Two years at most if the political situation doesn't improve."

"What if the situation improves?"

"If the Nazis lose power, you mean?"

"Yes."

"In that case you'll be able to come back to Germany and we'll all be together gain."

"And if the Nazis stay in power?"

"Then I'll retire after two years and move to Austria."

"So we won't see you for two years?"

He took a few infuriating moments to fish a cigarette out of his pocket and light it. "I'll take frequent trips to Austria to visit you. The time will fly past. You'll see."

"That's your master plan, is it?"

"Yes. It's perfect, don't you see?"

She rolled her eyes. "Why not retire now?"

"I'm too young, and my salary's too low."

She sat on the bed. "You're old enough. Didn't you say you could retire after fifteen years?"

"That's true. I have nearly fifteen years' service, but if I want a full pension, I'll need at least thirty."

"You could do something else, start a new career."

"What could I do? Police work is all I know."

Her blood pressure rose. "Think about it, Roland. You could do anything you liked. You could paint and decorate people's houses. You could teach, maybe. Or we could run a small hotel."

"Ruth..."

"Think about it. That's all I ask."

"This job offer is a wonderful opportunity." He made a face. "Can you see me up a ladder with a can of paint and a brush?"

"Don't dismiss the idea out of hand. Maybe you could be a youth leader, take youngsters on camping trips," she said. "You'd be good at that."

"I don't think so."

"Well, think about what you'd like to be."

"I'd like to be a senior police officer."

#

Samuel's sleep was disturbed by a dream. While Ruth tended to him, Saxon took out the White Knight envelope and placed it under a strong light on the dressing table. Why was the handwriting familiar? Whose handwriting had he seen, apart from Wolfgang's? Then he remembered that Nemec had written Zimmermann's address in his notepad. It took a few moments to locate it in the pocket of his trousers, hanging in the wardrobe.

He found the page with the address, placed it beside the envelope and compared the handwriting. They matched. There was no question about it, Nemec was the White Knight. But had he fired the shot?

Chapter 54

Monday August 17

He said nothing to Nemec about his discovery, not yet. He needed to confront him with something more solid than matched handwriting.

As soon as he reached the office there was a message with a telephone number asking him to call Frau Fürstner. He dialled the number.

"Thanks for ringing, Kommissar. I just wanted to let you know that Wolfgang has been released. He's here with me again."

What a relief! "Can I speak to him?"

"He's resting. I'd prefer not to disturb him. He said to tell you he was aware of your efforts to have him released, and to thank you."

"I'll visit as soon as I can." He left the hotel telephone number. "Tell Wolfgang to expect me in a day or two if I don't hear from him."

#

He thanked his team for a job well done and disbanded them. Their final task, to escort the American athletes on their buses to the port at Hamburg, had been successfully completed.

The giant, Reckendorfer, asked if and when the remaining detainees would be released. Saxon replied that the SS were responsible for that. Ulman was continuing to drag his heels with the release of the detainees.

#

Ulman, Engel, Bruno Büchner, and Saxon held a final meeting in Bruno's office in the Praesidium to wrap up the White Knight affair.

"We still have no idea who it was," said Bruno.

"I suspect the Communists," said Ulman. "They would be happy to stir up trouble between Germany and the United States."

Engel shook his head. "I disagree. This was the act of a German or a Slav."

Close enough, thought Saxon. Nemec is from Czechoslovakia.

"What do you think. Saxon?" said Bruno.

"I think we'll never know. And perhaps we'll never know who the sniper was firing at."

"We have very little proof that anyone fired a shot," said Ulman. "We only have Saxon's word for it. Saxon is the only one who saw the flash of the rifle."

"I heard it, too," said Saxon.

"So you say, but the cannons were firing at the time. Perhaps you were mistaken."

"Perhaps I was."

"That's ridiculous. We have the rifle," said Bruno.

"And the spent cartridge," said Engel.

"It could have been a blank bullet," said Ulman. "My men conducted a fingertip search of the grass and found no sign of a bullet."

"What do you think, Saxon?" said Bruno, again.

Saxon said, "What I'd like to know is how many good men were interrogated to breaking point by your men, Engel."

The look Engel gave Saxon in response was almost strong enough to kill.

As the meeting was breaking up, Bruno took Saxon to one side. "My office has received a message for you from Leni Riefenstahl. She'd like you to call her as soon as you can." He handed Saxon a card containing Leni's telephone number. "Have you thought about what we discussed the last time we met?"

"I've given it a lot of thought, sir. I'm very grateful for the offer..."

"You will accept?"

"Yes, sir, I'd be delighted to take the job."

A broad smile broke over Bruno's face. He grasped Saxon's hand and shook it vigorously. "How soon can you start?"

"As soon as I clear my desk in Munich. A month perhaps."

"Very good. You'll have that other matter resolved by then, I expect."

"What other matter, sir?"

"Your divorce. Karl Ulman said he spoke to you about that. He said you had set those wheels in motion."

Saxon grabbed the edge of the door for support as his knees buckled under him. He shook his head. "No, sir, I haven't set those wheels in motion."

"Get back to me when you have."

#

He rang Leni as soon as he found a free telephone.

"Kommissar Saxon, is that you?"

"Yes, Fräulein, what can I do for you?"

"You asked if we had any film coverage of the entrance and noticeboard during the opening ceremony, and I said we hadn't. But it occurred to me that you might check the coverage taken from the zeppelin..."

His heart skipped a couple of beats.

"We have a film studio in Wedding where the footage is edited. Do you have a pen? I'll give you the address."

He took a taxi to the film studio. It was expensive – but this was one occasion when he needed to travel without Nemec. The police driver would be sure to deduce what was going on.

Once he mentioned Leni Riefenstahl's name, the studio staff were eager to help. They had extensive film coverage taken from the camera in the zeppelin. He was able to narrow it down. He needed to see whatever film they had of the opening ceremony, and he was only interested in the main entrance. It took no more than 35 minutes to find what he was looking for. The film was in black and white, but even so, Nemec was easy to spot in his colourful clothing, emerging from behind the noticeboard and slipping into the crowd.

He had him!

He asked the technicians to let him have that section of film. They cut it from the reel and placed it in a tin can for him.

Chapter 55

Wednesday August 19

First thing on Wednesday morning, he received a telephone call in the hotel room from Frau Fürstner. She was in some distress. "Come quickly," she sobbed. "Wolfgang is dead."

He abandoned Ruth as she was getting dressed.

"I have to go. I'll see you later."

"What about our trip to the zoo? Samuel has been looking forward to it all week."

"I'm sorry, Ruth, this is important."

"Aren't you going to have breakfast with us?"

"There's no time."

"When will we see you again?"

"I don't know. I'll get back as soon as I can. Maybe we can still go to the zoo later."

"Your driver could take us. You could meet us there whenever you can."

"No, Ruth, we won't ask Nemec. I'll get back as quickly as I can." He wasn't going to leave his family in the hands of a gunman!

He took a taxi to Wolfgang's home in Neukölln.

Frau Fürstner let him in. Her nose was running, her eyes red.

"Have you called the police?"

She shook her head, with a look of dread, and led him to the back of the house. "He's in the garden, at the back." She stood and waited for him to go on alone.

He found Wolfgang lying on the grass. His eyes were open. Saxon closed them. There was nothing more anyone could do for him. He had been shot in the temple, and a gulf of a wound leaked brain matter on the opposite side of his head. A gun lay on the grass beside the body.

His first reaction was that he was looking at a suicide. Then he remembered that Wolfgang was Catholic. And what had he said about suicide? It was the worst of all sins. *If you find me dead, know that I would never have taken my own life.*

Could it be murder? If it was, it was an official act, an extrajudicial killing, like the purge of the Night of the Long Knives.

Saxon spent some time attempting to console Fürstner's inconsolable wife. He persuaded her to take a glass of schnapps. Then he made her coffee. He suggested that she call the family doctor or any family members.

She shook her head. They had no children, only a distant cousin in Stuttgart. When she had recovered some of her composure, he asked her if he was alone when it happened.

"I don't know. I was shopping."

He called the local police station and waited with her until they arrived and had taken control of the scene before leaving.

His heart was heavy with grief, but he put a brave face on it and returned to the hotel to take Ruth and Samuel to the zoo.

The room was empty. Suppressing a feeling of panic, he asked the hotel reception desk if they knew where Ruth and Samuel had gone.

"They left with your driver," said the receptionist. "I think the boy said they were going to the zoo."

#

Nemec took Ruth and Samuel around the lake, populated by geese, ducks and water hens. The birds delighted the child, so much so that Ruth couldn't persuade him to move on.

Nemec hunkered down to Samuel's level. "Wouldn't you like to see the bears?" Samuel shook his head. "How about the elephant?"

"You'll like the elephant," said Ruth.

Samuel agreed that he'd like to see the elephant. Nemec picked him up, and they moved on.

Ruth and Nemec chatted. Nemec mentioned that he used to live in Munich where his father was a policeman, many years earlier. "My father died in 1923 and when my mother died soon after, I was sent to Bohemia to live with relatives."

Ruth thought it best not to pursue that line of discussion.

Samuel marvelled at the elephant, but when the animal turned and took a step toward them, he became frightened. Nemec picked him up to comfort him and then handed him over to his mother. Samuel put his head on her shoulder and promptly fell asleep.

They found a bench and sat down.

She said, "How long have you been in the Wehrmacht?"

"Five years."

"Many young men have joined up since Hitler came to power."

"I never wanted to enlist. I trained as a baker," said Nemec. "I have no love for the Nazis."

"So why did you?"

"I worked for a Jewish baker, a good man." He cast his gaze down. "Let's just say he ran out of options and I lost my job."

When Samuel woke up he was fully refreshed and they took him to the petting zoo. That was where Saxon caught up with them.

Samuel had a great day. He took to Nemec like a new uncle and by the end of the day they were firm friends. Ruth enjoyed it too, although something of Saxon's gloom rubbed off on her.

"What is it, my love?" she said after she'd put Samuel down for the night. "You've been like a bear all day."

He gave her a short reply. "I lost a friend."

#

Later, in bed, she spoke enthusiastically about Nemec. "Samuel really enjoys his company. I think he's made a friend for life." Saxon said nothing. "What's the matter, Roland? You're not jealous, are you?" She laughed.

"You need to distance yourself – and Samuel – from Nemec," he said. "I'm going to have to arrest him in the morning."

She sat up in the bed. "What? What are you talking about?"

"Nemec. He's guilty of a crime. He'll spend the rest of his short life in prison."

"You cannot be serious. If you'd seen him in the zoo with Samuel, you'd know he doesn't have a criminal bone in his body. What could he possibly have done?"

"I can't tell you that, but it's a serious crime."

She leapt to her feet and turned on a bedside light. Samuel stirred in his cot. "I don't believe that. You must be mistaken."

He climbed out of the bed and poured himself a glass of water. "There's no mistake, Ruth. I'm sorry."

"This crime must be really terrible if you have to throw him to the Nazis!"

"I'm a policeman. I swore an oath to enforce the law—"

Her voice rose. "Since when did you bother about the letter of the law?" Samuel stirred again, and she dropped her voice to a whisper. "Justice needs to be tempered with a little common humanity. Who else knows about this?"

"No one."

"So it's in your power to let him go?" Her hands were bunched on her hips, now.

He climbed back into the bed.

"How many times have you said that Germany is turning into a police state. If people like you do their dirty work, we have only ourselves to blame."

Saxon said nothing.

She turned out the light and got into bed beside him. "I don't care what he's done, Roland. Nemec is a good man."

Chapter 56

Thursday August 20

The following morning, Saxon asked Nemec to take all three of them to one of Berlin's famous lakes.

Saxon sat up front with Nemec. They exchanged a few words about the death of Wolfgang Fürstner, and after that they drove in silence. Saxon was too preoccupied to engage in idle chit-chat, and Nemec was silent. Ruth kept Samuel amused in the back seat.

"This is Wannsee," said Nemec as the car drew to a halt at the edge of a wide expanse of shimmering water. The scene was bathed in bright sunlight and there were sailing boats running before a light breeze on the lake.

Ruth and Samuel joined a crowded sandy beach where Samuel could play. Nemec and Saxon lit cigarettes and strolled along the edge of the lake together.

"It's a beautiful spot," said Saxon.

Nemec puffed on his cigarette. "Yes, it reminds me of home."

"Where's home?"

"Karlsbad in Eger. We have lakes there. It was once a beautiful spot."

"But not anymore?"

"Not since the Nazis came."

Saxon drew on his cigarette. "Is that why you did it?"

"What?"

"Is that why you hid a rifle in the Stadium and fired a shot during the opening ceremony?"

Nemec reacted with wide-eyed shock. "I don't know what you mean, sir."

"I know you are the White Knight. I know you wrote those letters, and I know it was you who fired that shot. What I don't know is what you were hoping to achieve or who you were firing at."

"You have proof?"

"I can identify your handwriting on the first envelope, and you were caught on film emerging from behind the noticeboard."

"How is that possible?"

"The zeppelin."

"Ah!"

A brief moment of peril passed quickly. Saxon had the comfort of his pistol under his jacket. Nemec was unarmed.

Nemec looked down and kicked a pebble, avoiding eye contact. "So what happens now?"

"That depends on your answers to my questions. Tell me who you were shooting at."

"I was hoping to kill Adolph Hitler, of course, but it was an impossible shot. It would have been impossible even without all those birds, but the torrent of bird-shit from those goddamned pigeons spoiled my aim completely." He took a moment to gather himself. Then he said, "My father was a policeman. In 1923, Hitler and two thousand of his supporters marched into Munich. They were stopped by a small force of police..."

"The *Hitlerputsch*. I remember that. I was there." It had been a nerve-jangling episode for a young policeman. "What was your father's name?"

"David Nemensch. He was shot. He died on the street. Hitler was arrested. They put him on trial for treason. I was eight years old at the time..."

Saxon had clear memories of the incident. On that dark, icy evening, he had been a young police officer fresh out of the academy. Nemensch and the others had protected the younger members of the force. "I remember your father. He was a fine police officer."

Nemec covered his face with his hands. "My mother was destroyed by the loss. She died within two years. My sister and I were sent to live with an uncle in Bohemia."

Saxon said, "Hitler was tried for treason. He got a light sentence."

"They gave him five years. But he was released after just nine months."

At last, Saxon had an explanation for the rifle shot. "And what was the purpose of the White Knight letters?"

"I knew the Stadium would be swamped with security. I needed a distraction."

Saxon nodded. It was as he'd suspected. "And Zimmermann..."

Nemec's face fell. "That was terrible. I couldn't have predicted that they would suspect him, that they would treat him the way they did!" His voice shook. "That will be on my conscience for as long as I live."

"And the second White Knight letter...?"

Nemec spread his hands. "It was to show them they had the wrong man. It was too late. I should have written it much sooner, but I had to wait to get access to the typewriter."

They walked on, bathed in the soft glow of the evening sunshine. The lake view was stunning, an expanse of blue, decorated with the colourful sails of a dozen yachts.

"If you had succeeded, what good would it have done?"

Nemec stopped walking abruptly. "What do you mean? The man is an abomination. He has destroyed this country and he will surely lead Europe to war."

Saxon looked at Nemec with new eyes. This was no simple police driver with a personal score to settle, but a man with deep political convictions. Subversive convictions, but a man of action with the courage of those convictions, nevertheless. "I can't disagree with your assessment of our leader, but don't you see that killing him would make matters worse?"

Nemec said nothing.

"The Nazi movement is much more than just one man. Without him they would simply elect a new leader – someone like Hermann Göring or Himmler or Heydrich, perhaps – and things would continue along the same path."

"But Hitler is their inspiration. They would be weakened without his leadership."

They strode on, coming to rest on a low wall. "No, my friend, a dead leader would be a great symbol, a martyr to the Nazi cause. Don't you see? A dead Hitler would be a thousand times worse than a living Hitler. Now, tell me how many people are in your group."

"None. I acted alone."

Could he be telling the truth? Saxon waited, watching his eyes for the tell-tale signs that Nemec was lying. There were none. But could he really believe him?

Nemec drew one last time on his cigarette and threw it toward the water. It fell short. "Am I under arrest?"

"Why? Nobody has been shot or injured. No crime has been committed."

Nemec said nothing for 30 seconds. Then, "What about the letters?"

Saxon shrugged. "They will be filed away with all the other subversive letters received by the police. There have been many of them."

"Are you saying I am free to go?"

"Maybe not entirely free. There are ongoing Gestapo and SS investigations that may reach the same conclusion as me. Do you have family here?"

"Not in Germany, no. I have a sister in Zurich."

"Then you should leave the country. Get out as soon as you can."

They watched the boats skimming across the surface of the water for a few minutes in silence, two friends enjoying a smoke and a conversation together on a warm summer's day.

Chapter 57

Thursday night August 20

They lay side by side on the bed. It was late. Samuel was sleeping in his cot, mumbling occasional words in his sleep. Ruth was trying to concentrate on her book. There was so much on her mind.

"I've had a rethink about the future," he said. "I've decided to turn down the job that Bruno offered me."

She snapped the book shut. "You've decided? Are you sure?"

"I was never more certain of anything in my life."

"You're going back to Munich?"

"I think I'll leave the police."

Her heartrate increased. "You'll move to Austria with us? What made you change your mind?"

"You were right when you said we need to live together as a family." He kissed her with a passion, and she responded.

She drew back and looked into his eyes. "We'll manage perfectly well on your half pension."

He rolled off the bed and began to dress. "I thought I might leave the force right away. To get half my pension I'd have to stay on until March of next year."

"Won't you lose it all if you leave now?"

"Yes, Ruth, but it's time we left Germany." His voice dropped to a whisper. "I hate what the country has become under the Nazis."

Her heart was really thumping in her chest now, like a rabbit in a snare. "I don't understand. Why the change of mind? And why do you have to leave immediately? Wouldn't it be better to complete your fifteen years and take the half pension? It's just a few more months."

"It's complicated, Ruth. I'll explain everything, but not right now."

"What will we live on?"

"I'll find something. Perhaps I could buy a paintbrush and set up in business as a housepainter, as you suggested."

She laughed nervously. "I wasn't being serious, but I'm sure there are lots of things you could do."

"The Austrian police could probably use an experienced investigator like me." He put on his shoes. "Better start packing. We'll leave tomorrow."

"Why so soon? And where are you going?"

He replaced the bullets in the luger and slid the gun into its holster before putting on his jacket. She was frightened now. What was he not telling her?

"I have to go out for a couple of hours. There's something I must do before we leave. Don't wait up for me."

#

Reckendorfer sat in a dark corner of the empty Stadium. He'd had a bad day. His beloved Andrea had berated him, calling him every name under the sun. He had broken his promise and failed them. Her mother was still being held in Sachsenhausen with no word of when she would be released – if ever. In her tirade, Andrea returned again and again to their loss of income. As long as Frau Abel was under lock and key, how could she earn a living? And the inflow of athletes and spectators for the Olympic Games represented the opportunity of a lifetime for someone in her line of business.

He had tried to appease her with soft words and flowers, but it turned out his sweetheart had no interest in him at all. Not as a potential lover, anyway, only as a way of getting her mother out of the labour camp.

His mind drifted back to 'the accident', that fateful day when he'd split open the skull of his lover's husband with his axe, and he'd been thrown out of the Gestapo. How he wished he could go back in time and set things to rights.

He dozed off.

He woke with a start, and realised he'd heard a gunshot. The echoes of the sound still rang in his ears. He ran his eyes around the Stadium and saw a figure in the VIP stand, holstering his pistol and moving toward the entrance.

He watched the figure leave. There was something familiar about the man's gait... And what had he been firing at? There was no one else in the entire Stadium.

Chapter 58

Friday August 21

Saxon was outraged when he read the newspaper reports of the death of Kommandant Fürstner. The official press report said that he had been struck down by a car.

Nemec drove him to Prinz-Albrecht-Strasse, and he took the stairs to the third floor, clutching his newspaper.

Ulman was in conference with his adjutant in his office. Saxon barged in.

The SS-man sprang to his feet. "How dare you interrupt us? Leave my office this instant."

Canstatt too had leapt up. Saxon held the door open for him. "Leave us."

"Stay where you are," Ulman shouted.

"Get out!" roared Saxon.

The adjutant scurried from the room. Saxon slammed the door and approached Ulman's desk. He leant in, thrusting his face toward the SS-man.

Ulman's colour deepened. "What is the meaning of this outrage?"

"I need a few moments of your time," said Saxon, his voice low, menacing.

"If it's about your blessed prisoners, I would advise you to let the matter rest. They will be released if and when I am satisfied that is the correct thing to do."

"That's not why I'm here. I'm here about this." He threw his newspaper on top of the pile of papers on Ulman's desk. "How could you have allowed this lie to be published?"

Ulman glanced at the newspaper headline. "It was considered expedient. We couldn't release the real story, it would besmirch the Games and reflect badly on the Reich."

"And what was the real story?"

"Fürstner was a coward." Ulman picked up the newspaper and threw it into a bulging wastepaper basket. "He took his own life."

"Did he? Or was he shot?"

"What are you suggesting?"

"I'm suggesting that you shot him, or you had him shot. You made it look like suicide."

"That's preposterous!"

"The kommandant was Catholic. He would never have taken his own life. He said as much to me."

Ulman hesitated. "What difference does it make? He was washed out and finished, anyway."

Saxon stood back. That was as close as he was going to get to a confession from the man. Whatever the truth of the kommandant's death, no one would ever be held responsible.

"Is that everything?" said Ulman.

Saxon opened the door. "Come with me. I have something to show you."

#

They travelled together to the Olympic Stadium in the back of the car with Nemec driving, as they had when Saxon first arrived in Berlin. It was later in the day, but not nearly as hot. They opened both windows. No words were exchanged until they arrived at the Stadium concourse.

"Those White Knight letters were a distraction," said Saxon as they walked across the concourse.

"What do you mean?"

"There was never any threat to the black athletes. The sniper had another target in mind."

Saxon led the way through the entrance and up the stands to the VIP seating area.

"Why are we here? What is this foolishness?" said Ulman.

Saxon pointed to the seat at the centre. "Whose seat is this?"

"The Führer's. What of it?"

"Take a close look."

Ulman moved closer. "What am I looking for?"

"Take a look at the seat. What do you see?"

"I see nothing. What are you playing at, man?"

"Run your fingers along the leather on the side of the seat." Ulman did so, his eyes fixed on Saxon. "What do you feel?"

Ulman's hand stopped. "There's a hole... Oh God, that's a bullet hole!" He turned and sat in the Führer's seat. All the blood left his face. "The sniper intended to assassinate the Führer?"

"Exactly. And he nearly succeeded. Fifteen centimetres to the right and the Führer would have been killed."

Ulman shook his head. He was speechless.

"And who had responsibility for security in the Stadium and for the Führer's safety?"

Ulman bowed his head, waving his hand in a submissive gesture. "You've made your point, Kommissar. If this gets out, I will be ruined. What do you want?"

Chapter 59

Within 24 hours all the detainees were released and Saxon's expenses were reimbursed in full.

He called June Leybourne at the Excelsior Hotel. "Could we meet? We have some unfinished business."

They met in the lounge.

He handed her 200 Reichsmarks. "I owe you this."

"No you don't," she said. "I lost the bet. Germany's Jewish fencing champion, Helene Mayer, won the silver medal in the women's foil." She opened her purse, pulled out a pile of notes, and offered them to him.

He waved the money away. "You owe me nothing. It was a foolish wager. Let's just be content that one Jewish athlete competed at the Games and won a medal."

She put the money back into her purse. "Tell me about the White Knight letter. May I assume it was a hoax?"

"Yes, there was no threat to the athletes. How did you get on with your interviews?"

"Fine. Fantastic. I have six great articles to submit to my editor when I get back home."

"I can give you another one, an exclusive scoop," Saxon said.

#

Within a couple of hours, they were on a train heading south. Samuel was cranky and out of sorts. He sat in Nemec's arms, and soon the motion of the train lulled them both to sleep.

Saxon asked Ruth about her life in Rudolf's apartment. She went over all that she'd spoken about in her letter – his pipe, his drinking, the loud music, and how he expected her to be his housekeeper.

"Was that why you left?"

She looked at him sharply. "It was after he tried to force himself on me. He came home drunk one night and barged into our room."

Saxon looked shocked. "You never told me that!"

"He was too drunk to do anything, really, but I gave him a bloody nose." She smiled. "Didn't he mention that when he spoke to you on the telephone?"

"I'll kill him when I see him," said Saxon, quietly.

"It was nothing. Really, Roland, just forget about it."

Later, Saxon told Ruth the rest of his story. He told her how he solved the White Knight mystery and how he had tricked Ulman into releasing all of the detainees.

She was shocked when she heard what Nemec had done. She looked at Samuel sleeping in Nemec's arms.

Saxon touched her arm. "Samuel is perfectly safe."

"If you're sure..."

"I'm certain. Nemec is no killer. His motives were personal and political. I've given him a chance to get away, but I don't think my bluff will hold for more than a few days. As soon as they dig that bullet out of the Führer's seat, they will discover that it is not a rifle bullet at all, but a pistol bullet."

"What did you do with the film footage from the zeppelin?"

"I burnt it."

"You won't be returning to your office in Munich? Don't you need to resign from your job?"

"There won't be time."

"What about your clothes and stuff in the apartment?"

He shrugged. "There's nothing there that I need."

She said, "You will regret not taking that job."

He shook his head. "It was never really an option. You were right all along. I just wasn't listening. We need to be together as a family.

We need to be together as a couple. And I want to see Samuel grow up."

She hugged him.

"I couldn't have taken the job anyway."

"Why not?"

"Bruno asked me to make a sacrifice that I could never make."

"What sacrifice?"

He paused. He knew the answer would scare her. "He insisted that I get a divorce."

#

Engel and Ulman met in Ulman's office.

"Who's this?" Ulman turned a jaundiced eye toward the third man in the room, an ugly giant in a crumpled, ill-fitting, light grey suit.

"This is Oberwachtmeister Reckendorfer," said Engel. "He was a member of Saxon's team and he has a story to tell."

"Speak," said the SS-man.

Reckendorfer opened his mouth, but nothing came out. He closed it again.

Engel poked him in the ribs. "Go ahead man, tell the Standartenführer what you told me."

"I was in the Stadium. I saw someone fire a gun..."

"Tell us when," said Engel.

"It was last night, late. It was very dark."

"And you saw someone fire a gun?" said Ulman. "Who was he shooting at?"

"I couldn't see anyone else, sir."

"Where was he, this gunman?"

"He was in the VIP seating area, close to the Führer's seat."

Ulman sat bolt upright. "Did you see who it was?"

"It was too dark to see his face, sir, but I'm sure I know who it was."

"Who was it?"

"The Kriminalkommissar from Munich, Kommissar Saxon."

Ulman lifted the telephone with a trembling hand...

Chapter 60

With an exhausted release of steam, the train drew to a halt in Munich Central Station at 6:05 pm. As they disembarked, Saxon let his eyes roam over the people hanging around the station. A soldier cradled his rifle behind the ticket inspector at the exit barrier. A third man in plain clothes was checking the identity papers of every male passenger.

Ushering Ruth and Samuel ahead of him, he said, "If they stop me, go ahead without me. Wait for me in Innsbruck station. I'll catch up in a few hours."

Nemec went through the checkpoint first, without a problem. Ruth and Samuel went through next. When Saxon presented his identity papers, he was immediately arrested.

Ruth moved on through the crowd without looking back.

They bundled Saxon into a Kubelwagen and drobe him to the central police station. A greeting from a startled Kriminalrat Glasser was cut short, as Saxon was propelled into the building and placed in an airless interview room. They left him there for an hour in the unrelenting heat.

Standard operating procedure, he thought.

When the Gestapo man appeared, he took a seat at the table and demanded to see Saxon's identity papers once more. "Kriminalkommissar Saxon. I should perhaps welcome you home, but my colleagues in Berlin have issued a general warrant for your arrest."

"On what charge?" said Saxon.

"I believe there are a number of serious charges, treason, fraud, perverting the course of justice. My orders are to detain you and return you to Berlin under armed guard where the charges will be put to you formally." The Gestapo man tossed the identity papers onto the table and got to his feet. "Do you have anything to say?"

"Whose orders are you following?"

"The arrest instruction came from the Gestapo in Berlin."

"That would be Obersturmführer Otto Engel?"

The only reaction to this was a blank stare that he took as affirmation.

"This is a misunderstanding. A call to my superior SS-Standartenführer Karl Ulman in Berlin will clear the matter up immediately."

The Gestapo man left the room.

As the time ticked by, Saxon sweated more and more in the heat. His anxiety levels rose. Had Ruth and Samuel made it safely out of Germany? Would he be able to get out of here and join them? What if they held him overnight? Would he find them again in Innsbruck? Or perhaps his race was run.

Finally, after 30 minutes, they took him to a telephone and made the call.

Adjutant Canstatt answered and put the call through to his boss. "Saxon, you bastard. Are you there?" said Ulman. "You will rot in prison for what you did to me."

"Good evening, sir," said Saxon. "There has been some mistake. The Gestapo in Munich have detained me. I'm not sure why."

"You know very well why. I have exposed your trick with the bullet. It had me fooled for a while, but we have a witness who saw what you did. Just wait until I get my hands on you. You will hang for high treason."

Saxon gave Ulman a moment to recover his senses. "Tell me, sir, how is your wife? Lotte, isn't that her name?"

"What? What are you taking about?"

"Your charming wife, sir, and your two boys. How old are they now?"

After a short pause the SS-man said, "How do you know my wife and sons?"

"I haven't met your sons, but I was introduced to your wife by a mutual friend – the charismatic Leni Riefenstahl. You know Fräulein Riefenstahl quite well, I believe. You must have got to know her even better during the torch relay."

After a longer pause, Ulman lowered his voice, "Are you attempting to blackmail me again?"

A couple of moments passed in silence as the line crackled. Then Ulman spoke again. "Put the Untersturmführer back on the line."

Saxon handed the telephone to the Gestapo man who listened for a moment and then replied, "I understand, Herr Standartenführer, but I have my orders..."

Ten minutes later, the Gestapo man was talking with Otto Engel, and within 30 more minutes, Saxon was standing on a platform in Munich Bahnhof waiting for a train to Innsbruck.

Chapter 61

Ruth was waiting for him at Innsbruck Bahnhof, Samuel sleeping in her arms.

He told her how he had been arrested by the Gestapo and taken to the Munich police station.

"I bet Glasser was surprised," she said.

"We didn't have a chance to talk."

"What was the charge and why did they let you go?"

"It was nothing but a minor misunderstanding. A telephone call to a friend in Berlin sorted it out. I assume Nemec got away?"

"Yes, he caught a train to Zurich."

Samuel woke up, rubbed his eyes and nose and reached out to his father. Saxon took him in his arms.

Fleetingly, he thought about the future.

As God is my witness, he thought, we will never be separated again. We are free, and we are a family again. I will find work and we will set up a new home. Ruth and Samuel have nothing to fear here; there are no Nazis in Austria.

EPILOGUE

On September 1, 1936, the *Sydney Morning Herald* carried an article by June Leybourne, an overseas reporter. The article was a follow-up to her series on the Berlin Olympic Games.

DEATH AT THE BERLIN OLYMPICS

The XI Olympiad, held in Berlin, Germany, has been overshadowed by a tragic death. The man responsible for the building of the Olympic Village, Kommandant Wolfgang Fürstner, was found dead at his home in Berlin.

A member of the German Army, the body of the kommandant was discovered in the garden of his home on August 19, three days after the closing ceremony. He was killed by a single bullet to the head. His own pistol was lying beside the body.

No reason has been put forward for the death of the charismatic and popular kommandant. Early reports that he died as a result of a traffic accident have now been discounted as inaccurate.

The Olympic Village, is a compact, well-designed village providing high-class accommodation for over 4,000 athletes from all around the world, including our own. "The digs were beaut and the tucker was bonzer," said Gerald Backhouse, our 800-metre runner.

The Olympiad was a triumph for Adolph Hitler and his Nazi regime. It produced some spectacular new world records and proved that athletes of all colours, races, creeds and nationalities are world-beaters. Jack Metcalfe was the only Australian athlete to win a medal, but by taking part we proved that we can compete to the highest international standard in sport.

No doubt our athletes are already preparing for the next Olympic Games, which will take place in Tokyo, Japan, in September 1940.

Sincere sympathy and condolences go out from the team at this newspaper to Kommandant Fürstner's wife and family on their tragic loss.

THE END – THE WHITE KNIGHT

Thanks for reading these stories. If you liked them, tell your friends. If you want to encourage the author to write more like this, please write a review.

Reviews really help.

ABOUT THE AUTHOR

JJ Toner writes short stories and thrillers. He lives in Ireland. Watch out for his Black Orchestra series of WW2 spy stories. https://www.jjtoner.com/

www.ingramcontent.com/pod-product-compliance
Lightning Source LLC
Chambersburg PA
CBHW030355030726
47497CB00002B/345